The C
They Came to Conquer and Endure . . .

THE YEARS OF POVERTY AND PASSION

A woman of indomitable power and beauty, Ruth Cutter took her courage from the very soil. Torn between loyalty to the husband who abandoned her and passion for the powerful Don Alonzo, she would sacrifice everything for the future—even her own heart.

THE YEARS OF PAIN AND POWER

Ruth established Casa Grande. Her daughter, Anna, would expand it until it stood for the wealth and power of Southwest Texas. But Anna, too, would give her very heart to the land, aching for a secret love, bound to Will Channing and his cruelly shattered dream.

THE YEARS OF PRIDE

The Cutters—they had carved an empire from the dust of the land. But brilliant Sandro would willingly sacrifice everything to conquer Europe with his musical talent . . . and exquisitely defiant Mina, craving danger and sensual adventure, longed to flee far from the . . .

HEART OF THE LAND

Books by Dennis Sanders

Nonfiction

THE FIRST OF EVERYTHING
THE AGATHA CHRISTIE COMPANION: The Complete Guide to
  Agatha Christie's Life and Work (with Len Lovallo)

Fiction

HEART OF THE LAND

HEART

OF THE

LAND

Dennis Sanders

A DELL BOOK

Published by
Dell Publishing Co., Inc.
1 Dag Hammarskjold Plaza
New York, New York 10017

Copyright © 1986 by Dennis Sanders

All rights reserved. No part of this book may be reproduced or
transmitted in any form or by any means, electronic or mechanical,
including photocopying, recording or by any information storage
and retrieval system, without the written permission of the Pub-
lisher, except where permitted by law.

Dell ® TM 681510, Dell Publishing Co., Inc.

ISBN: 0-440-13708-X

Printed in the United States of America
February 1986

10 9 8 7 6 5 4 3 2 1

For Sharon,
who always said I would write a novel

Cast a cold eye on Life, on Death,
Horseman, pass by!

—W. B. Yeats

Prologue:
1909

IT WAS LATE ON A COLD JANUARY AFTERNOON. OUTSIDE the windows of Wilkins's Mercantile and Supply the main street of Myrtlesburg had already fallen under the shadow of approaching night.

Inside the store, under the glow of the gaslights, Jonah Cutter was closing early. He fidgeted about his work, straightening merchandise on the crowded shelves, tightening lids on the several scores of candy and spice jars that lined the counter, tamping down covers on barrels of flour and sugar and pickles, throwing crisp white cloths across tables piled high with ready-made clothing, yard goods, and household supplies.

Had there been customers in the store—there were none—they would have noticed that the short, wiry clerk, more boyish-looking than his actual years, was even more preoccupied than usual. Jonah's eyes seemed to be focused on some invisible spot closer or farther than the counters and shelves, and his lips occasionally moved soundlessly, as if carrying on some secret, inner conversation.

Wilkins won't mind, Jonah said to himself as he went about the familiar closing routine. No folks buy this late on a Friday, anyway. No harm done, no money lost, me closing up early today. No real use me standing idle by the stove for half an hour when I can be home talking things over with Ruth.

He stopped to warm his hands at the wood stove before tossing a slow-burning oak limb on the coals to keep the shop from freezing overnight. Then he took out the stepladder and set it up under the first lamp in the first row of ceiling lamps. As he climbed up and reached for the valve to shut down the gas, he felt the reassuring bulge of the newspaper in his pocket. He couldn't help slipping his fingers down, touching the coarse paper.

With the two rows of ceiling lamps darkened, Jonah folded the ladder and put it back in place. On most days he would have quickly turned out the single wall lamp behind the counter and made his way through the darkened store to the front door. Instead, by the faint yellow light, Jonah pulled the folded newspaper from his pocket and, with a childlike, almost conspiratorial look on his face, unfolded it on the counter. He turned the pages quickly. Past news of presidents and Kaisers, Rockefellers and railroad magnates, past doings in Lexington and Louisville, past accounts of ladies' organizations and local funerals. Finally he stopped and focused on a small but boldly decorated advertisement box in the lower corner of a back page. In the margin next to the box were some penciled figures he had made that morning. The advertisement itself began forthrightly in large black letters:

UNLIMITED LAND OPPORTUNITIES

He read through the ad again, though he had read it many times already. His lips moved as he read, and carefully studied about every optimistic word in the ornate box. Then, satisfied for the moment, he folded the paper and replaced it in his pocket. The last gas valve was shut, and he hurried through the dark aisle to the door. The familiar, tedious clink of the suspended bell announced his departure, and he was outside in the cold air, fumbling to fit the brass key in the lock.

Jonah smiled to himself. Even if Wilkins did get mad at him for closing early—businessmen could be funny about those things at times—there wasn't much he could do to a former clerk who was two thousand miles away. After Jonah was gone Wilkins could hire a clerk who didn't mind a bit working from eight to five, no exceptions.

Pulling his coat close around him, Jonah hurried past the single block of stores that made up the shopping street of Myrtlesburg and into the quiet residential streets, streets lined with neat, modest frame houses, tucked away beneath leafless trees. As he neared the side street that led to his own home, he paused for a moment and looked up the deserted main street to where it ended at a steep hillside. On the hill, with a manorial view of the town and valley below, stood a great, sprawling pile of brick mansion with stately granite-columned porticoes and blazing electric lights that proclaimed for all below to see that here lived the wealthiest family for miles around.

Jonah looked long and hard at the grand house, his eyes alight with a mixture of appreciation and envy. He had looked at the house often in his years in Myrtlesburg. Every morning, to and from work, he never failed to look up the hill to savor the presence, the meaning of the place. It meant wealth, luxury, comfort. The owners of that house didn't stop at the mercantile; they had servants who did that. They didn't harness mules to a plow or hack coal out of a seam with a pickax; they had laborers and foremen to work their farms and coal mines. They didn't have to walk to work; they owned an automobile, the only automobile in town. The wife and daughters didn't have to make do with made-over hand-me-down dresses; they went to Louisville and even New York to buy the latest Parisian fashions. They didn't try to have a bit of fun on a Sunday picnic up at the lake in Harmon's Holler; they sailed to Europe, first class, on ships with names like *Mauritania* and *Carpathia*.

More than anything else, Jonah knew they had the respect, the awe, the envy, of other folks. He could always sense it, in folks' tone of voice when they talked about that house and its inhabitants. A sense that here was a family apart, separate from everyone else, above everyone else. They were special.

The fragrance of someone's supper wafted through the chill evening air, jostling Jonah Cutter out of his reverie with a reminder that his supper was on the stove as well. He turned down the dark, narrow lane toward the distant, welcoming yellow lights of his home. When he got there, he knew that, as usual, his Ruth would be standing in front of the hot, dark wood stove, tending to her pots and kettles as she tried to manage the wisp of dark hair that always strayed from the confines of her pinned-up hair as she perspired over her pots and kettles. Anna, almost as grown-up and serious as her mother, would be setting table, while his sons would be making the kind of noisy mischief that only hungry little boys can make.

Jonah felt a little shiver of anticipation as he hurried through the shadows toward home. He always looked forward to supper happily, and a quiet evening with his family after the restless boredom of a day at the store. Tonight was different, though, because in his pocket he carried a piece of paper that was going to change his life. He could hardly wait to tell Ruth of his plan, even though he knew her well enough to know what her first reaction would be. She'd heard his big ideas before, many times. But this time was different. It was really going to happen. They would soon be out of Myrtlesburg, out of the quiet run-of-the-mill life they had known all their married life. Jonah pictured Ruth in her solemn beauty, not in front of the stove as he had known her for fifteen years but in the house on the hill, living the life she deserved. It would be theirs, all of it.

And they would be happy at last.

Part I
THE YEARS
OF POVERTY
1910–1912

Chapter One

SAND.

Ruth Cutter pulled her shawl closer around her face in a futile attempt to keep the stinging blast of the sandstorm out of her eyes, her nose, her mouth. Still, the stinging particles driven by the hellish fury of the hot desert wind cut against her face. Blinded her. Choked her. She tried to pull her body farther down among the trunks in the back of the wagon, but they offered only a little protection against the brutal abrasion of the sandstorm that swirled all around her. Next to her, encircled in a motherly, protective arm, were her sons, curled down among the folds of a quilt like frightened kittens. Through the roar of the wind and the layers of the quilt, Ruth could hear the muffled sounds of their crying. They were only boys, she thought. Only six and ten years old. Too young to understand—to understand that this sandstorm wouldn't last forever, to understand that somewhere out there in the blasting fury was their new home.

Jonah sat behind them, up on the plank seat of the mule-drawn wagon, next to the withered, brown-skinned old Mexican who had come to fetch them in Casilla when they had gotten off the train in the midst of the furious sandstorm. The town had been only a ghostly collection of vague shapes; the old man, clad in loose-fitting white cotton pants and shirt, had appeared like a specter out of the storm. He had driven his mule wagon toward them, his straw hat pulled low over his face as he called their name in a shrill, plaintive voice.

"Cutter! Cutter! *Vámanos!*"

With no explanation, only a few gestures between him and Jonah, the old Mexican had loaded their trunks and parcels onto the wagon bed, then helped his passengers up. A few minutes later they were joined by two others, an old, foreign-looking couple who had gotten off the train with the Cutters. There

had been hardly a sound exchanged between any of the people
in the wagon. They had mutely followed the old man's gestured
directions with the solemn resignation of condemned prisoners
being carted to the gallows.

Ruth wanted to reach back and take her husband's hand for
reassurance, as she had so many times during their four-day
train journey from Kentucky, but she knew Jonah was facing
away from her, huddled up against the stinging sandstorm. Everything had been so confused, so nightmarish since the train
had creaked to a halt, after more than a day of traversing the
bleakest kind of desolate land imaginable, and left them in
Casilla, the town that was to be their new home. The sandstorm, the kind of storm that Ruth knew plagued the deserts of
the earth, had enveloped the train an hour before, as quick and
furious as the summer thunderstorms back home. Ruth had
expected to arrive in Casilla with a sunlit vista of distant fields
and trees in the Rio Grande Valley. Instead there was only this
brutal, yellowish cloud of sand.

"Always get these sand blows out here come February and
March," the conductor had told them as the storm had hit the
train. "Scrapes the skin right off a man's face, it does. Hard to
believe, but in hardly an hour or more it'll be clear as heck out
there."

Ruth opened her eyes into careful slits. It was hard to imagine an end to the fury, the vigor of the storm. Through the sand
she saw Anna, huddled against a heap of carpetbags, a scarf tied
across her nose and mouth. Anna had been so good through all
this, more like a grown woman than a girl of twelve, and Ruth
was grateful for that. Most girls Anna's age would have cried
and sulked at being pulled up by the roots, taken far away from
her friends, her home, her school, the happy world of childhood. But from the first Anna seemed to share her mother's
understanding of Jonah's need to move "out West" to start a
farm, that it was something the Cutter family had to do. Whatever fears, regrets, hurts that Anna felt, she had, like her
mother, kept them hidden inside as she went about the business
of helping her mother and father dismantle a lifetime. Anna had
cried only once, that day when they had left the house in Myrtlesburg.

Now that it was behind them Ruth was especially grateful for

Anna's acceptance of their new life: it made Ruth feel that she and Jonah were less alone, less vulnerable.

With her eyes shut Ruth Cutter pictured the white frame house back in Myrtlesburg, with its green shutters and deep porches and bright flower beds, all shaded by the leafy canopy of chestnuts and elms. It was gone now, that lovely little home, with its musty rooms full of the treasures and memories dear to a woman's heart; with its damp cellar chock-full of preserves and stores and dark places where the children could play hide-and-seek; with its quiet parlor with the lace curtains, the ticking mantel clock, the ruby glass lamp, and the burgundy mohair settee festooned in antimacassars. Only a week ago and the house had been just as she had always known it, the home of her childhood, her youth, her married years. Now it was all gone—the furniture sold, the house sold. Everything that was left of the Cutter family's possessions was packed in the half a dozen trunks and carpetbags that were loaded in the back of the open wagon that had picked them up in the middle of the sand-storm.

You must be brave, Ruth Cutter. Be strong.

As if to test her, the sandstorm unleashed a gust of special fury. The air roared, and her skin stung as if she had been struck with sandpaper. The wagon lurched as one wheel slipped into a deep rut in the dirt road, and the trunks and cartons bumped and slipped in the wagon bed. There was a small short cry of alarm from the old woman who huddled next to her husband in the opposite corner of the wagon. Ruth wondered what twists and turns of life had brought this old couple apparently all the way from the Old World, all the way to the strange desolation of Casilla.

Casilla. It had sounded so romantic, so exotic when she had first heard the name that night last year when Jonah had come home from the store, full of excitement about his plan to sell everything in Myrtlesburg and buy a farm in Texas. It had just seemed like another of Jonah's daydreams at the time. His description, of course, had been glowing and enthusiastic. A farm, a real cotton farm, just a stone's throw from the Rio Grande River, within sight of Mexico. Rich land, good land. Land with a future, with potential for growth. And all of this in West Texas, the land of *señoritas* and *caballeros,* of cowboys and

painted ladies, just like in the dime novels. *Texas!* How romantic, indeed, it had all sounded then. The land where men rode
horses and carried guns and wore those funny hats and pointed
boots. The land of desert and blue skies, longhorn cattle, and
rattlesnakes. The land, the glorious land that would make the
Cutters rich.

How different it all was from the land Jonah had described.
She remembered the shock, the stunned surprise that morning
on the train when she had awakened and looked out through
the curtains of the window by her berth to get her first glimpse
of the desert. She wasn't sure what she expected—something
colorful and dramatic with yellow hills and purple skies perhaps, like the covers of the dime novels. But not this—not this
scorched, barren earth, stretching from horizon to horizon. Not
these brown, parched mountains, spotted with dry, half-dead
brush. It was horrible, a dead part of the earth. Brutal and ugly,
like the strip mines gouged out of the green hills of Kentucky.
She imagined that this was what hell looked like. The blasted
plain.

Be brave, Ruth. Again she thought the words. She kept her
eyes closed but tried to shut out the picture she had in her mind
of the shady lawn back home. Best to forget all that now. It was
gone forever.

Ruth felt the touch of her husband's hand from above. The
touch was tentative, asking more for reassurance than giving it.

Jonah leaned down and whispered in his wife's ear. "The
storm's letting up a bit. And we're almost there. I can make out
the line of trees by the river. Won't be long now—it's almost
over."

Ruth opened her eyes cautiously, afraid of another tearful
blast of sand. Jonah was right. The wind that had swept across
the desert that March afternoon with its cloud of sand had
suddenly died down to fitful gusts, and a watery, yellow sun was
burning through a dusty sky that was gradually shading back to
blue. From her seat in the back of the wagon Ruth could now
see, beyond the jumble of trunks and cases, the narrow dirt road
along which the wagon had come. It was a barren landscape, a
white strip of road, surrounded on either side by a flat expanse
of dry, brush-dotted land. No sign of farms, not a speck of
green.

The old couple sitting opposite Ruth smiled at her. They seemed as relieved as she that the storm had died down.

Ruth could now see the town of Casilla behind them on the road, about a mile distant. When the train had stopped to let off the Cutters and the couple who shared the wagon, the sandstorm had obscured the town, even though the train had left them in the middle of it. As they had loaded their belongings onto the wagon in the midst of the storm's fury, the town had been only the shadows of buildings lurking in the storm.

Casilla stood out clearly now: a collection of low, squat, brown-and-white buildings. There seemed to be a church tower, too, and along the horizon, the faint, dark line of the railroad-track bed.

The sandstorm had fully abated now, and the sky, almost if by magic, had turned a clear, bright blue. Ahead, about a quarter of a mile, was a line of trees—tall, broad-branching trees with thick, pale trunks and leaves of pale yellowish green. It was the first sign of growth and green she had seen in the desert. Ruth knew the trees must stand on the banks of the Rio Grande, the only source of water in the desert. That's where their farm would be.

They were all curious now that their destination was in sight. Hank and J. J., their fear of the storm vanished, were up now, too, clinging to their sister's skirts and vying for a view ahead.

The wagon slowed almost to a halt as the driver yelled something to the mules in Spanish and whacked them solidly with a stick. The wagon lurched to the right, off the road, and onto a rough dirt track. They were turning toward the farm. Ruth felt a welling up of fear. She reached up to wipe away the coarse film of grit that coated her face.

Sand. Dust.

Brave, Ruth, she told herself. *You must be brave.*

The wagon lurched along the rough, dry gully that passed for a road. The land on either side was not much different than what they had seen from the train before the storm hit. Flat, dry land of monotonous gray-brown, land barren of the flowers and grasses one might expect in springtime. The sun, now hot and yellow above them, beamed down on an earth dotted only with brown, twisted scrub, a land of thorn and gnarled branch.

The living things here survived not by turning leaves and flowers to welcome the elements but by turning branch and root
away from the elements. Only a line of trees along the Rio
Grande with its lifegiving water, still a half of a mile south, held
in their topmost branches a hint of spring, of green leaves, of
life.

The flat land spread out like a dry sea around them, to distant shores of hazy blue mountains with sharp, ragged tops that
cut into the now-turquoise sky like islands in the ocean. About
a thousand feet ahead the Cutters saw two lofty cottonwood
trees standing alone in the waste. They were once-proud trees,
now gaunt and broken by age and disease and crowned by only
a few branches that clawed at the sky with broken fingers. A
building came into view beneath the trees. At first it looked like
only a mound of earth, but as the wagon neared, a man-made
shape emerged, a squat, flat-roofed box of a building punctuated by the dark holes of a door with two small windows on
either side, like empty eye sockets and a gaping mouth. When
the wagon reached the forlorn hovel, the driver pulled his mules
to a halt and, without a word, scrambled down from the seat
and went to the back of the wagon.

"What is it, Jonah?" Ruth tried to hide the tension in her
voice.

"I don't know, Mama. I wish this fellow spoke English."

Jonah gave his wife a reassuring pat on the shoulder, but as
he looked back toward the driver, there was uncertainty in his
eyes. There was a dull scrape and a thud as the Mexican
dragged a trunk off the wagon bed and let it fall to the ground.
Ruth's tension slipped over into fear. She instinctively pulled
her sons toward her. This driver was a stranger—perhaps he
was a ruffian who preyed on unsuspecting strangers, who took
them to desolate places to rob them or worse. She could easily
imagine a dark, gleaming pistol being held on them if they protested.

"*Vámanos, gringos! Vámanos pronto! Estamos a su casa.*"

The old man's voice was impatient but hardly sinister. He
seemed more bored than anything. Then a few half remembered
words from lesson books.

A su casa. At your house.

This was their farm, their home. Ruth turned back to Jonah, blurted out the old man's meaning.

"I guess this must be the place, then," Jonah said flatly as he climbed down from the seat. Ruth looked in her husband's face for some reassurance that it wasn't true, but she didn't find it there. Only a look in his eyes that she couldn't fathom, unless it was shame. He hurried away from her gaze and went to the back to help the driver unload their things.

This must be the place. The words echoed in her unbelieving mind. This hovel was their new home. This piece of hell was their farm. Ruth faced her children, forced herself to put on a calm, composed face for them. The three of them looked at her silently, their faces full of childish questioning. Behind them, the old couple looked on, confused, as the drama of the strange family was played out before them.

"Where are we, Mama?" Anna finally asked.

Ruth managed a smile, though she knew it must have looked as hollow, even to her children, as it felt to her.

"We're home."

Fifteen minutes later the Cutters stood next to the heap of their belongings that had been half stacked and half dumped on the hard-packed earth that surrounded the adobe shack. The wagon, bearing the old couple to whatever awaited them in this desolate land, crept into the distance toward the river, with a last wave of their hands in farewell to their traveling companions. The sun had lowered in the sky, turning the vast overarching canopy from turquoise to a pale peach-gold. In the dry desert air the lengthening shadows of the house and its companion trees were sharp and purple against the pale brown earth. The horizon to the west and south was marked by the purple ridges of the mountains, while from the course of the river, the sounds of evening birds broke the vast desert silence with their enigmatic calls.

Ruth and Jonah busied themselves in stacking and straightening the disorderly, dusty pile of their belongings. They were both silent and kept their backs to the house. The children, with their expected curiosity, made the first forays toward the house. First Hank, with the fearlessness of a five-year-old, then J. J., and finally Anna, who was torn between the childish curiosity of her brothers and a young-womanly need to be decorous and ladylike. From the corner of her eye Ruth saw the young ones warily approach the house. Jonah wasn't going to say anything. He was stubbornly focused on moving the largest trunk.

"Hank! J. J.! Not yet! I mean, don't go in there until your Papa's looked things over a bit!"

Her warning was too late, and Hank disappeared into the darkness of the doorway. Ruth clenched her fists, not in anger at her son but to steel herself to facing that horrible place that was supposed to be a home. She had wanted to put off stepping inside as long as she could. But she couldn't leave Hank in there.

As she ran to the house a giggle of delight came from inside. There was a pause, then Hank emerged, preceded by several noisily distraught chickens.

"Lookie, Mama!" He cried with delight. "We're going to live with the chickens."

J. J., with the cynicism of a ten-year-old, chimed in, "It sure looks and smells like a henhouse."

Ruth shushed her boys and sent them off to help their father. As she turned back to face the house Anna came up next to her. At twelve Anna was almost as tall as her mother, with her mother's dark brown hair, pale ivory skin, and cool gray eyes. Though Anna's features were finer, more conventionally pretty than her mother's were, there was a similarity in their dark, serious good looks that left little question about their being mother and daughter, or perhaps sisters. More than once it had been remarked that Anna Cutter had not only gotten Ruth's handsomeness but her quiet strength as well.

"It's pretty awful here, isn't it, Mama?" Anna fixed her mother with her gray eyes. That look of understanding passed between them. Ruth nodded in agreement.

From behind them Jonah called out with a false cheeriness, "You be careful in there now. Watch out for nails in boards and holes in the floor."

Ruth wished that Jonah had come over, taken her hand, and gone inside with her. It would have made it so much easier. But she knew her husband too well. It always took him a while to face anything difficult. He was like a little boy who dawdled and meandered on the way to school. He didn't want to set foot in the house, nor did she, but he would putter over the trunks and bags as long as he could, to put it off. That wasn't Ruth's way, though. She had to do it now, get it over with.

She extended her hand to Anna.

"Shall we go in?"

Anna took her mother's hand, and they slipped through the gaping doorway together. Inside it was worse than Ruth had imagined it—dark and ripe-smelling from what the inhabitants, human or otherwise, had left behind during their occupancy. The small square windows, covered only by torn screening, let in paltry shafts of light riddled with dust motes. There was an iron bedstead in one corner and a wooden table with several mismatched chairs, either tumbled over or broken. The table, in the dim light, showed signs of long use as a chicken roost. Ruth ran the tip of her boot through bits of debris that littered the floor, hoping to scrape away an accumulated layer of dirt to get to the planking. The debris, once moved, revealed only a hard-packed layer of earth. The house had dirt floors.

The image of the house in Myrtlesburg flashed into her mind, clean and cozy and secure. A real house, with porches and windows, with floors and doors and rooms, with lawns and hedges and big shady elm trees. Not just a house but a home. Ruth knew that for the first time in many years she was going to cry. As she walked through the dark, foul-smelling room, holding her daughter's hand, she saw Jonah through the doorway, still fidgeting with the pile outside. His golden hair was brilliant in the afternoon sun; the fine, handsome features of his face were intent on their task. It had been too long since she had cried in Jonah's arms. The last time had been years ago when they had lost their first child. Now they had lost their home, their past. It was time to cry again.

"I-I'd better go help your father," she stammered as she pulled away from Anna's grasp and half ran through the door toward him. When she got to him, she saw in his face what could not be seen from inside the house. The shame, the hurt, the tears. It was Jonah who was crying, not her. She embraced him, not minding that the children saw. His tears flowed freely now; he sobbed against her.

"I'm so sorry, Ruthie. So sorry," he said, gasping. "I never knew it was going to be like this!"

"Shhh!" She reassured him, like a mother to a frightened child. "It will all be all right. Somehow."

"How can it? This place is nothing. Just a hellhole."

Ruth held him close, melting into the troubled warmth of his body. Her own tears were forgotten now; Jonah's pain was her only concern. For now, she realized, she was going to have to be the strong one.

"We'll manage, Jonah," she reassured quietly. "We'll be all right, God willing."

Chapter Two

ANNA AWOKE FIRST. THE DAWN AIR WAS CHILLED AND dewy, sharp in her nostrils. She turned and pulled the covers up over her head without opening her eyes. She wanted to slip back into the curious dream she had been having, that she and her family were asleep under the stars in the middle of the desert. Then her half conscious mind realized that it was no dream. Anna opened her eyes. The horizon to the east was already shaded from faint pink to gold, and a thin, gray haze hung over the trees by the river. She stretched slowly, then sat upright and pulled the quilts close around her.

It was a bizarre sight—no wonder it had crept into her dreams. The little adobe hut was rosy in the morning light, as was the pale bark of the cottonwoods. In front of the house three bedsteads were lined up neatly in the open air. Two beds were the rusty ones dragged hastily from the house as night fell. The third was a magnificent brass one her mother had insisted on bringing from Kentucky, along with the best goose-down mattress. Her parents were in the brass bed, still sound asleep in the soft folds of down. Anna noted with amusement that their bodies were intertwined beneath the quilts, like two young lovers. She knew her mother and father would most likely have been upset if they knew that their children had seen them sleeping that way. Their bedroom at home always had been kept closed at night, and Anna guessed they always slept close like that.

Anna looked to the other bed where her brothers slept on an improvised mattress of blankets folded over the rusty, bare bedsprings from the house. She sat up and dangled her stiff legs over the edge of the bed. She was still in her traveling clothes, and her long, dark wool skirt and starched linen blouse were a riot of wrinkles. She stretched to sort out some of the stiffness in her back and arms; the thin layer of blankets between her and the bedsprings had not made for the best night's sleep, in spite of her travel weariness. Anna's worn boots sat rather oddly beside the bed next to a clump of grass. She picked them up and instinctively shook them upside down to chase out any creatures that might have crawled in during the night. There were none, and she quickly put the boots on and began lacing them up. Anna was debating whether or not to wake her parents—it was in her nature to be considerate of grown-ups, and they had been so weary, so strained last night after the family's light supper of pickles and smoked ham from the hamper—but she really wanted to let them sleep in for a bit. It was then that she noticed a movement in the distance, apparently on the road that led from Casilla to the river.

She made out that it was a wagon with four people in it. To her surprise the wagon turned into the gully-road that led to their house. She would have to wake her parents now. Someone was coming to see them.

"My mama may not speak much English," Max Mirkovsky said with a grin, "but she understands a good bit. She knew your names and that you were coming from back East to settle on a farm here. When she told me last night about riding out here with you folks, I knew right off that you must be the ones that bought this place. That's why we came over this morning, to give you a hand."

Vassily and Lina Mirkovsky, the couple from the wagon, were looking very pleased with themselves as they helped their son and daughter-in-law lay out a hot breakfast on the back end of the wagon. Aside from several hampers of food, the wagon

was loaded with rakes and brooms and shovels and various
cartons of supplies. The Mirkovskys' son was a complete contrast to his parents—a beefy, young giant of a man, six foot four
if an inch, with a bright-eyed, sunburned face that was quick to
laughter. His voice boomed with the shrillest Texas twang;
there was not a hint of his Serbian birth in him, and J. J. and
Hank had been favorably impressed by his Western hat and
dusty riding boots. Max's wife Kate was a homely, freckled
sprite of a woman, as good-natured and high-spirited as her
husband. She spoke with a sharp nasal Texas accent as well, and
swearing came as easily to her as it did to most men. Ruth and
Jonah had been embarrassed when a family of total strangers
had arrived to give them help on their first day on their land—
the poverty and brutishness of the place was shameful. But Max
and Kate had quickly put them at ease with the naturalness
with which they took the Cutters' plight in their stride. There
was a direct, simple charm in their neighbors, as suited to the
harsh desert as the Mirkovskys' trousers, wide-brimmed hats,
and boots. The Cutters sensed that Max and Kate could become loyal and helpful friends, and the sense of that made
Casilla seem less lonely and less hopeless.

"We knew this place was a godawful mess." Kate's voice
twanged as she poured Jonah a second cup of coffee from the
set of enameled pots on the portable kerosene stove they had
brought. "We'd been here many times when we was thinking
about buying this parcel of land for ourselves. Hell, we knew
the tramps and chickens had been using this place to roost in,
and that it wasn't fit for good Christians to live in. Soon's Max's
folks told us about you being here, we figured you'd need every
bit of help you could lay hands on."

Max and Kate were natural organizers, and soon after the
breakfast was finished, they had the day's work under way: the
men took on the heavy hauling and digging, the women scrubbing and sweeping. Even the boys were given tasks to keep them
occupied, and there was so much to be done, even their hands
were needed. Most of the day Kate and Max kept up a steady
stream of conversation about Casilla and the El Paso Valley and
about life on a new cotton farm. Ruth was especially interested
in which of life's circumstances had brought the Mirkovskys to
the valley, since she had done a great deal of reflecting on the

course of events that had uprooted her own family and taken them there.

Max had left his native Croatia as a boy of twelve and sailed to America to make his way in the world along with an uncle who had already migrated. Max had wound up in Arizona, working twelve-hour days in the copper mines. He'd met Kate at her father's saloon in Douglas, and they had, after the briefest of courtships, decided to "get hitched," as they put it, and to find a more rewarding life than that of the mines and saloons of Arizona. They had scraped up enough money to buy a hundred and eighty acres in the land in the Rio Grande Valley below El Paso that was being opened up for farm development. The Mirkovskys' plight, when they had first arrived at their land in Casilla, had been no different from that of the Cutters or any other of the new landowners in the newly developing farm community. They had been faced with the same unpromising landscape; they had been forced to stay and make the best of it, since they had given up everything to buy the land in the first place.

For two years Max and Kate had hacked and burned the tough tornillo and mesquite scrub brush; they had dug irrigation ditches a quarter of a mile long to bring water from the river to their fields; they had used pickax and shovel for hour after grueling hour to dig out pockets of hard, calcified mineral deposits, called caliche, which marred the thick, claylike river-bottom land that was slowly emerging as their cotton farm. In one respect, as Kate quickly pointed out to Ruth Cutter as the two women were scrubbing down a urine-soaked corner of the house, the Mirkovskys had been worse off than the Cutters: there had been no building of any sort on their land. She and Max had lived their first year in Casilla in a *jacaral,* a Mexican-style twig lean-to made from bent and tied branches.

"A mite breezy," Kate added. "And no place you'd want to be during one of these springtime sand blows."

Ruth had paused to wipe the sandy grime from her face as Kate spoke. Outside, the midafternoon storm was blowing furiously, as it had the day before, and the desert's fury poured through the paneless window openings. She told Kate she didn't know how they had done it for those two years. What she was really saying was that she didn't know how she and Jonah were going to manage it. Kate's only reply had been, "It's amazing what a body can do when it has to."

Twelve hours and many pails of strong lye-soap water after the cleanup began, the adobe house was at least tolerable for some sort of human habitation. The chickens, to their noisy dismay, had been banished; the door was restored to its hinges, and the torn window screens patched. Kate had been right when she had told Ruth that dirt floors really weren't so bad. After several sweepings with a stiff broom, the loose dirt had been dislodged and swept into a dustpan, leaving a hard-packed, almost concretelike surface. Max had even produced a five-gallon tin of whitewash from the back of his wagon, and a fast coat on the walls of the two rooms of the house helped give a semblance of livability to the place. The table and chairs, though stained with chicken droppings, were, after a thorough scrubbing by Lina, in reasonably good condition, wanting only a fresh coat of paint. One end of the main room contained a cast-iron cook stove. It had gone unnoticed the first time Ruth had entered because it was so littered with debris, but it was now gleaming blackly after a good working-over with a wire brush and pot black.

Max and Jonah even had time to dig a new pit for the out-house; the rickety wood privy was moved to the new and more sanitary location and the old pit, with its antique stench, filled. Ruth was also pleased to see that the outhouse at least had a door that closed tight on its hinges, even if the house itself didn't.

By six in the evening Ruth, with the help of Anna, Kate, and Lina, was able to begin unpacking the trunks and valises that had stood patiently on the ground outside during all of the long day's commotions. One of the first items removed was a hand-some kerosene pedestal lamp of finely cut ruby glass that had belonged to Ruth's great-grandmother. The lamp was Ruth's most prized possession, and it had been the last item packed before they left Myrtlesburg, for no other reason than Ruth's reluctance to subject the fragile, faceted treasure to the dangers of a journey across the continent. Ruth would sooner have stayed in Kentucky alone and sent her family on to Texas than to leave the lamp behind, yet when the moment had come to wrap and crate the lamp, she had gone cold with fear that it would arrive in Casilla as shattered as her illusions. In the end Jonah had calmed her as he demonstrated the care with which he was wrapping the lamp, even though he was both amused and irritated by her uncharacteristic fretting. It was so unlike his quiet, solid Ruth to allow herself these womanish worries. Now she showed the same concern as he pried open the orange-wood box and removed the lamp from its protective nest of shavings.

"It's made it, all right, hasn't it, Jonah? It's not broken or chipped now, is it?"

Jonah held the lamp triumphantly aloft, letting the waning sunset play on its etched and carved surface.

"You see, Ruthie, it's all right. It really is all right."

There was a certain self-conscious pride mixed with the relief in his voice. He took the lamp into the house and filled the fuel bowl with a pint of kerosene robbed from Max's cook stove, then lit the wick. The freshly whitewashed walls of the bare room were instantly turned a warm, golden color from the lamp, and the smell of the whitewash and the lye soap mingled pungently with the acrid odor of burning kerosene. Jonah stood back from the table and surveyed the lamp, incongruously elegant in the rough, bare room. He put his arm around Ruth as she stood by the table to adjust the wick of the lamp and pulled her close to him. It was an enormous relief to him that the lamp was undamaged, for, given what had awaited them in Casilla, the destruction of Ruth's greatest treasure in the move would have humiliated him beyond what he could bear. As it was, he barely could look Ruth in the eye, so sure was he that he would find nothing but disappointment and disapproval there.

"It makes it a little better, doesn't it? A little more like being home."

Ruth heard the tentativeness in his voice, like a child asking for approval from a parent. She wanted more than anything to say that seeing her lamp here in this place made it worse, made what they had left seem even farther away, even more irredeemably lost. But she couldn't say that to Jonah; she couldn't hurt him like that.

The image of the house in Myrtlesburg came into her mind, as it had many times in the last hours. Against that image of the home she had known all her life, she surveyed her new home. A mere two rooms, one slightly larger than the other. Small-windowed, dirt-floored. Empty except for the iron stove and the table and chairs in one room and for the brass bedstead in the other. The doorless opening between the two rooms was now screened by a length of oilcloth that Anna and Lina had tacked up to give a bit of privacy. As Jonah held her, as much asking for reassurance as giving it, Ruth knew that she could make this place a home for her husband and children. After all, a home was not about material luxury or even about the physical beauty of a place. It was about love and caring, about the security that comes from inner things, not worldly possessions. Kate's words came back to her. *It's amazing what a body can do when it has to.* She knew she could do it. She had to.

Suddenly the lamp looked as beautiful in its new surroundings as it ever had in the front room in Myrtlesburg. She told Jonah so, and she meant it.

That evening the Cutters went to Max and Kate's farm for supper. They rode in the back of the wagon amid the rakes and mops and pails, as Max took them along the River Road, a narrow, well-rutted dirt lane that paralleled the Rio Grande and its sentry rows of cottonwoods. The fragrance of the river's dark waters, and of the spring grasses that were already greening along the banks, perfumed the cool night air. Ahead of them, in the west, the sun threw out its last burnished rays from behind the ragged purple crest of mountains at the head of the valley above El Paso as a vast cape of deepest blue was thrown across the shoulders of oncoming night. The harshness of the desert day had vanished in the glory of sunset and nightfall, and the miracle of the transformation had its effect on the Cutters. As weary and discouraged as they were, as they lurched across the valley to their neighbors' farm, something of the hard, demanding poetry of the desert began to capture them. They saw, for the first time, the severe, yet captivating, beauty of the place. Just as something might be made of the little adobe house, something might be made of this empty land. Perhaps.

The Mirkovsky house was what Ruth had hoped for on their farm, a solid, modest structure of tin-roofed brick with deep, shade-providing porches and cluttered, comfortably furnished

rooms. Max and Kate proudly showed the house to their guests
—the roomy kitchen and front room, a small farm office, a
bedroom for Max and Kate, one for Vassily and Lina, and one
empty one for the children to come; in the meantime the short,
stout Lina expended more of what seemed to be an inexhaust-
ible supply of energy, even for a woman half her age, in preparing a massive evening meal for her family and guests. Afterward
Jonah and Max relaxed in the front room with "man-talk" and
cigars while Vassily and Lina entertained Anna and the boys
like substitute grandparents. As Ruth and Kate washed up the
dishes in the wood sink next to the hand pump in the kitchen,
Kate fell into a casual, but perceptive, questioning of Ruth. All
through the long day's toils Kate had been struck by how inexperienced the Cutters seemed to be, how unprepared for life on
a farm, especially a farm that had to be carved almost literally
by hand out of the desert. She and Max had had nothing to
start with, nothing to lose when they had upped stakes and
bought the farm in Casilla. Not so with the Cutters; she could
sense that. They were folks of more substance, more means than
she and Max. Kate had not given up anything more than the
life of a saloon brat to make a life with Max. But Ruth struck
her as a different kind of woman altogether. She'd given up a lot
to come here with Jonah.

Though Ruth was by nature a quiet, withdrawn woman, not
quick to share her feelings, Kate found her more than willing to
open up to her; understandable, given her new isolation and
separation from her past and her friends. Kate already knew
that Ruth had been a schoolteacher in her younger years, that
she had married late, that she was a few years older than Jonah.
As the evening wore on Ruth opened up more and more to her,
filling in the details of a life that Kate, in many cases, had
already guessed.

"A pretty town, Myrtlesburg," Ruth said in a quiet voice,
which hinted that she was talking almost as much to herself as
to Kate. "Up in the hills, as green as emeralds. Quiet, out of the
way, all closed in and protected by the hills. I was born there,
and my folks, too, all the way back to the days just after the
Revolution, in the days when the hills were full of bears and
Indians. My parents died young. Mama a few days after I was
born. I don't remember her, of course. Papa I barely remember.

He died when I was four, of tuberculosis. My mother's mother, my Grammy Stratton, brought me up in her little house in Myrtlesburg, the same house Jonah and I lived in until we came here. She took in sewing to help get me through school, so I could have a chance at something better than she had. She was a poor woman, at least poor in worldly things, but rich in some things that you can't put your fingers on or hold or cash in at the bank. A good woman, a God-fearing Christian, as they used to say. We lived together until she died."

"And Jonah?"

Ruth's mind went back to that November morning, years before. She remembered the freezing, wind-driven rain that had poured down on her as she had hurried from the front porch of Grammy Stratton's house out to the wagon that waited every morning to take her up the valley to the log schoolhouse at the mining camp where she attempted to teach a room full of unruly miners' children. The figure that had hunched down under a wide-brimmed hat and slicker against the sharp November weather had not been Silas, the toothless old wagoner who usually took her up to the school. This driver was a stranger. As he reached down to give his pretty young passenger a hand, she had seen his face for the first time.

Young, handsome, fair. He smiled.

He told her his name was Jonah. Jonah Cutter.

And so Myrtlesburg's young schoolteacher had fallen in love.

"He drove me up to the school every day, since Silas was crippled with a stroke," Ruth continued with a noticeable warmth creeping into her voice at the memory of that time. "By springtime he was sitting with me on the porch and staying on to supper. When we got married, there was a bit of talk. A lot of folks back home didn't exactly think Jonah was, well, a good enough match for a Stratton girl, and a schoolmarm at that. We Strattons were poor but considered good family. The Cutters were a bit rough. Hill folks. Jonah's ma was a drunkard, to be truthful, and his father just took off when he was a boy. Jonah got by as best as he could—his ma died when he was young. From the liquor, I suppose. I had to teach him to read and write after we were married. He still can't write much. But we've had a good life together. I inherited Grammy's house and a little bit of property downtown that had gained in value since my parents died. And I had a bit of my own money put by—Grammy always told me to watch my pennies. Jonah got a decent job clerking at the mercantile, and after the children were born, I went back to teaching a bit. It was a good life, all right."

Kate noticed that Ruth spoke as if the good years were all in the past. Perhaps they were. But there was still something missing in Ruth's story, the something that had gotten the Cutter family uprooted and moved to Casilla. Kate wanted to know. She fished with a crooked pole.

"It wasn't enough, was it?"

Ruth took the bait.

"We wanted more."

She put just the slightest emphasis on the word *we*—enough to make Kate realize what Ruth meant was *he*.

"So you pulled up and moved here?"

Ruth blurted out even more than Kate expected. It was more a cry of despair than a statement of fact.

"We sold everything to buy that land over there."

Kate thought it best to move on to other, less sensitive subjects. Jonah Cutter was a dreamer, all right; Kate and Max had seen that right off. It was clear that he had been the one who wanted to move out West, to look for something new, something big. It was equally clear that Ruth Cutter would have sold her house a thousand times over to help her dreamer of a husband make one of his dreams come true. That was the way love was. It did strange things to a sensible woman like Ruth, even to the point of shucking off everything on an outside chance. She'd done that with Max, and it had worked out just fine. Sometimes it didn't work out, either, but women, especially women like Ruth, who were sensible in every way except in love, would always take the chance, anyway. She didn't have a choice. A woman who felt about a man the way Ruth felt about Jonah never did have a choice about such things.

That night, later than they would have liked, given the long day ahead of them, the Cutters rode back to their place in Max's wagon. The children slept most of the way and did not even awaken when they were carried into their beds. As Max and his wagon lumbered into the darkness, Ruth and Jonah tucked the children in, then turned out the lamp and went into

the smaller room that had as its only furnishing the brass bed.
They undressed silently and changed into their nightclothes,
then got into bed. Their bodies touched under the warmth of
the quilts. In the darkness, as he always did, Jonah snuggled up
against Ruth, one arm around her protectively. He pulled the
covers close up around their necks to ward off the chill, desert
night air that streamed in through the unglazed windows. It
was the first time they had been alone since they had left Kentucky. On the train there had been the berths, and the night
before, the beds in the open air. Their day had been so occupied
with work, and the children and the Mirkovskys, that Ruth and
Jonah had scarcely said ten sentences to one another, and those
had for the most part been about matters of cleaning and scrubbing and putting things in order. Perhaps it was better that way,
Ruth thought, remembering those painful moments when the
driver had first left them at the house, and when they had taken
the lamp in at the end of the day. Ruth knew that Jonah had
not found it easy to look her in the eye. He had been so
ashamed of himself—a man didn't get over that kind of shame
in a day.

She pulled herself closer to him. His breath was warm on her
neck.

"It's not so bad here, Jonah. Not so bad at all."

When he answered, his voice had a childlike incredulity.

"Really not so bad?"

"No, especially after seeing what Max and Kate have done."

"So you're not sorry I brought you here?"

"No."

In the darkness Jonah's hand touched her breast, then slid
down along the curve of her waist to her thigh. She turned and
pressed herself fully against his body. It was as lean and hard as
it had been the first time, so many years before. She suddenly
felt an enormous need for him.

"It's been so long," she whispered.

He didn't answer. In the chill, dark room, quietly so the
children wouldn't hear, they made love.

Chapter Three

WORK ON CLEARING LAND BEGAN THE DAY AFTER THE
Cutters' supper at the Mirkovsky farm, when once again Max
and Kate arrived just after dawn to offer their help. With them
were two Mexican laborers that Max had suggested Jonah hire
to help with the brush cutting and stump pulling; he insisted
that the dollar Jonah would have to pay each of the men for a
day's work would be well worth the extra arms and backs
needed to clear the land. As the sun inched up the bluing sky
Jonah, with Max's help, paced off the eastern edge of their first
field and staked the line. The laborers, after a few words from
Max in Spanish, walked across the line and began hacking at a
large, gnarled clump of mesquite. Ruth and the children
watched with silent curiosity as the work began. The men
swung their machetes in sweeping arcs; metal glinted in the
morning sun, and the still air was broken by the *thwack* of
metal against wood. Two gnarled, severed branches tumbled to
the ground. Another swing and two more branches fell. The
mesquite, though it trembled under the onslaught, hardly
showed the loss—it stood as thick and as twisted as before. At
this rate, Ruth realized, a single mesquite clump might take an
hour, two hours, or more. And there were eighty acres of land
to clear, with hundreds, thousands of bushes to be hacked and
hauled away. She fought back a wave of despair. No time for
that now; there was too much to be done.

As Max stayed on to work with the laborers, Kate took Jonah and Ruth in to Casilla to purchase major supplies. It was
their first real look at the town they were now to call home,
though it was hardly more than a collection of buildings scattered along the Southern Pacific rail line and the dirt road that
led through the valley toward El Paso. The main street fronted

along the rails, lined on one side by half a dozen buildings. Among them was a squat stucco of one story, fronted by a bare concrete slab, with the words WASSERMAN MERCANTILE stenciled over the door. To the left and next to the mercantile was a motley collection of wood shacks, one housing a ramshackle blacksmith shop. Opposite Wasserman's, across a narrow dirt lane, was Casilla's second most important business after the mercantile: the Red Star Café, housed in a porched, false-front building. The Red Star, so Kate told them, rivaled Wasserman's as the social center of Casilla, presided over by its owner, Ola, a thin, leathery-skinned woman who served terrible food and delicious gossip to her customers, mostly local farmers and railroaders, some of whom boarded in the few rooms she kept at the back of the café.

Beyond the Red Star was an open stretch of ground, dry and weedy, then a few livestock pens, apparently used to hold cattle and horses before loading on freight trains. Beyond that, the town stopped abruptly, and the brushy bottom land, like that of their farm, took over once again. Eight miles distant could be seen the faint interruption of the next town on the rail line.

As small as Casilla was—there were hardly more than two hundred souls living there—the town had two distinct sides. In addition to the business along the rail line, the cattle pens, the rail sheds, and the water tank for the trains, there was another, older Casilla, just behind the main street. Facing onto the dirt lane that cut between Wasserman's and the Red Star was a collection of several dozen buildings of raw, brown adobe, or of weather-stained stucco, houses not unlike the Cutters'. A few of the houses had poor little gardens behind unpainted, dilapidated picket or wire fences, though most, like the Cutters', sat on bare, hard plots ungraced by trees or flowers of any sort. Though the main street was deserted at the early hour, there were more signs of life on the side lane. A few dark-featured children played in the gardens and doorways, and chickens and dogs roamed freely among the houses. In front of one house, a place as dirty and uncared-for as the Cutters' had been the day before, a plump, dark-eyed young mother, her jet-black hair in long braids, sat on a bench and nursed a naked infant. Alongside, two more naked children, about Hank's age, played happily in the dirt.

A bit down the lane, just before it reached its end at the main street, a small adobe church stood, distinct as much for its fresh coat of whitewash as for its small, plain bell tower. Next to the church and to the rear stood a small and equally well-tended house and garden, probably the parish house.

"It's a poor town, ain't it, Kate?" Jonah commented as the wagon lumbered along the lane toward Wasserman's. "Reminds me of some of the hollers back home, where folks can't do much but sit and rock."

"That it is. We whites, Anglos as they call us, ain't got much by our standards, but we're well-to-do by the Mexicans'. Least-ways we got some kind of future. Prospects. We may be living in adobe shacks and *jacarals* now, but least we own the land and got the possibility to better ourselves. The Mexicans here don't own land, don't have no way of getting money to do so. The buck a day they can make working for you or any of the Anglo farmers around here won't do much more than buy a bit of kerosene, some beans, and flour. A shame, they're as good a folk as any of us, but that's the way it is around here."

Ruth looked at the poor houses, the dirty children. She reached in her bag, gave a reassuring squeeze to the five-hundred-dollar roll of bills that was their nest egg, their security. It would go toward building the farm, making them comfortable. That bit of money would keep them from winding up as poor as the Mexicans of Casilla. Then she realized how fast it all could go. After all, a good deal of it would be spent that morning. Never before had Ruth felt the thread suspending them above the pit of failure to be so thin. It could all so easily snap and send them tumbling into the abyss. The thought of living like these people, in this kind of poverty, terrified her.

Almost as if he sensed her fear, Jonah offered a bit of reassurance.

"Max said that by the time we get back, he and the men will have at least an eighth of an acre cleared. And once we've got a mule, some chains, and a drag bar, the work will go that much faster. I can't wait to get that first acre leveled and plowed."

Ruth started to work out in her head the mathematics of clearing eighty acres but stopped herself. They could do it; they would do it. And already, today, she had seen Jonah's spirits rise. He was getting over the initial setback, was recapturing his enthusiasm, his dreams. There was no room now for her to be discouraged or afraid.

Wasserman's was very much what they expected: a dark, crowded, but superbly organized store of every item a small farm community could possibly want. When they stepped into the richly textured and fragranced place, they were, for a moment, transported back to Wilkins's store and Jonah's years behind the counter there. Old Wasserman—his shriveled frame and thick-featured face could have been anywhere from seventy-five to ninety-five years old—already knew who the Cutters were when they walked into the store. As they had heard from Kate, there was little in Casilla that Wasserman did not know, since the mercantile was a vital center of news and gossip, rivaled only by Ola's café. The newspapers from El Paso were sold at his counter, and telegrams sent and delivered; his customers were likely to leave information with every purchase. Wasserman acted as Casilla's bank as well. He took cash deposits from his customers, doling out supplies, equipment, or cash as needed, all of which was toted up in a ledger book kept under the counter.

Simon immediately started up a nonstop conversation with Kate and his new customers as he began scurrying around the crowded floor with Jonah's supply list clutched in a clawlike hand. Within minutes, as the list turned into a heap of merchandise on the counter, Wasserman had extracted a good deal of information from the Cutters while telling them a sizable chunk of his own life history, from his birth in the Jewish ghetto of Budapest to his years as a boy wandering through Mexico and Texas with his parents, selling pots and pans from a pushcart. He'd settled in Casilla before the town even had a name, when it had been nothing more than a few adobe buildings and the parish church.

"Wild, very wild it used to be here. Gunfights and stabbings and lawlessness. I been here since 1850. Many people I seen come and go since then. Much quieter here now, I'm happy to say, with the new farmers and good, new families like yourselves. I miss the *bandidos* some and the Texas Rangers and Civil War soldiers. But business is good now that the valley is growing, so I can't complain."

Wasserman toted up the Cutters' order. It was a large one—

two cotton mattresses, a plow, mule harness and fittings, a drag
bar, hoes, pickaxes, rakes, a five-gallon drum of kerosene, various kitchen and household supplies. The bill came to a steep
one hundred and fifty dollars. With some reluctance, Ruth took
the roll of bills from her bag and handed them across the
counter to Simon, some to pay the bill, most of the rest for
safekeeping.

After Wasserman's, the only remaining chore was to buy a
mule. Kate took them to the blacksmith, who gave them a
choice of several, all of which stood passively swatting the
morning air with their tails in the small corral behind the
smithy. They paid forty dollars for a handsome, furry-eared
creature named Jake, tethered him to the wagon, and headed
back to the farm.

Jonah had been right that work on clearing the land would
go faster once they had a mule. In fact, Ruth and Jonah realized
that if it had not been for Jake, they never would have gotten a
crop in the first year. The first day of clearing, when Jonah and
Ruth came back from Casilla with supplies, Max, true to his
promise, had cleared an eighth of an acre, and a large pile of
brush behind the house stood as proof. But the cleared land was
pocked with the clumped roots that the machetes could not get
at; a man could have dug them out with a pickax and shovel,
but a single mesquite might have taken the better part of a day.
Jake was quickly harnessed to a pair of chains with large steel
hooks on the end. The hooks were set deep into the thick mat of
roots, and as Ruth guided Jake, Jonah hacked at the stubborn
roots with a pickax. Jake, his muscled flanks straining, would
pull against the tenacious network of growth until, with a crack
and a sigh, the clump would give way and turn on its side in a
little puff of dust, exposing thousands of scrambling, many-
legged creatures that had had their homes rudely exposed. The
dirt-clotted roots were taken to a pile near the house, next to
the heap of branches. Anna and her brothers worked at the
brush piles. It was their job to sort the wood—one for mesquite,
one for tornillo brush, one for all other scrub. The scrub would
be burned in a bonfire, while the mesquite and tornillo would be
saved for use as firewood. Some would even be sold for extra
money.

The clearing was a filthy, boring job, made even harder as the midday sun warmed the air to an almost summerlike heat; by midafternoon the daily sandstorm had swept across the valley, and the work that had in the morning been hard drudgery now became a battle against brutal nature. Hands that were sore and bloody from thick thorns that pierced even quilted work gloves reached up to wipe brows coated in mud formed from sand and perspiration. Eyelids were closed to mere slits to keep out as much of the sand as possible but to no avail—the sand still clawed at tender membranes, tears flowing down muddied cheeks.

Finally that first brutal day had come to an end, only to be followed by another and another, into March and April. Again and again the Cutters had risen at dawn, bodies still aching from the last day's work, and taken themselves out onto the land to begin the hard routine over again. Again and again, each day like the last in a blur of half forgotten drudgery, they had walked, weary and silent, back to a simple meal and the welcome respite of exhausted sleep.

As April crept into May Ruth sensed a change creeping into their lives. It was not just that their bodies were getting used to the physical work, though that was certainly the case. It was not that they could tolerate the climate better, for though the spring sandstorms had stopped, the early desert summer was already upon them, and each day brought the thermometer reading to ninety degrees or more. The land was changed, certainly—thirty acres had been cleared of brush, and gentle, powerful Jake now spent his days pulling a drag bar to smooth and level the acreage for planting. Each day Jonah and the hired men took the irrigation ditch a few yards closer to the river, and each day they came closer to that long-awaited goal: the first furrow, the first planted seed. More than anything, though, Ruth saw the change in Jonah. The shame and embarrassment that had been in his eyes those first weeks were gone now, replaced by a confident, spirited enthusiasm. When she looked at her husband now, she saw strength and assurance that had never been there before. Now, as they worked inch by inch toward their first cotton crop, Ruth knew that coming to Casilla had not been a mistake after all. Jonah had blossomed so here. It was all too obvious to Ruth that he had always needed to strike out, to try something new and big. There were even times when she felt guilt that she had, with her conservative ways, held him back all those years in Kentucky, that she had thrown too much practical cold water on his dreams. To be sure, they all had worked harder than they ever could have imagined, but now Ruth could see that they were to have their reward for taking the chance and for toiling to make the chance work out.

Certainly Ruth still had her concerns, some of which she shared with Jonah. Casilla was a tiny place with only a few families in town and scattered around the neighboring farms. Anna and the boys had few chances to be with other youngsters. Sundays allowed them a bit of contact with others, at the simple church service in the back room at Ola's, where the local Protestants sang a few hymns, said a few prayers, and made up their own sermons, since there was no minister to talk to them except once a month when a traveling preacher came through. The local Catholics, mostly Mexican families, at least had Father Hernando to minister to their daily spiritual needs. Max and Kate had been loyal friends, but with planting season, the Mirkovskys, like all the farm families, were too busy to be very social. The best times had been the occasional Sunday afternoon picnics by the river, shared with Max and Kate or with the Pettuses and Wilkersons or some of the other local farmers, but these times were too brief and too few, and many Sundays, if the week's quota of land had not been cleared, the Cutters missed church and afternoon outings altogether and instead worked on the farm. But Ruth reassured herself that the work, with time, would lessen, and that Anna and the boys, in spite of their hard work, seemed happy with their lot.

There was another, very private change that came with their move to the farm. It was in Ruth and Jonah's private moments, their lovemaking. As the farm had progressed and Jonah's spirits had risen, so had his attentiveness, his desire for Ruth. In spite of long days of work, Ruth was often awakened, before dawn, by Jonah's insistent caresses. In all their years of marriage there had never been a time when Jonah had ignored Ruth or been inadequate in a husband's intimate responsibilities. But in the last weeks Jonah had shown a new passion, a drive as fierce and confident as his drive to make the farm a success. At

times Ruth had found herself shocked, even a bit frightened by
Jonah's new way with her, but she had always given herself
willingly to him, and her own responses, to her surprise,
matched his in kind. Many times she had turned her head to
bite into her pillow to stifle long-repressed cries of animal passion; there were mornings when she almost shamefacedly drew
back the oilcloth curtain across the door to their room and went
out to fix breakfast for the children, sure that they had been
awakened by her and Jonah's fierce coupling in the predawn
light.

On those mornings when Jonah had awakened her early,
Ruth expected to be tired for the day's work, robbed as she was
of precious minutes of sleep. Instead she found herself full of
energy; the long hours in the heat of the desert sun were filled
with images of Jonah as he embraced her. Sometimes, as she
worked dragging brush or leading Jake across acre after acre of
dusty land, she could almost feel the warmth of Jonah in her
again, and she would look out across the flat land until she
could see him working in the distance. She would wave and
wait for his arm to sweep up in answer. Sometimes, if he were
not too far away, he would come over to her, his tanned face
marked by a happy, white smile, and he would embrace her,
even kiss her if no one were in sight. She would close her eyes,
lost in the fragrance of his body, the male scent of sweat and
dust. He would tell her how much he loved her. And she would
know with every ounce of her being that it had been worth it
all.

By late June, flocks of noisy brown sparrows hopped and
fluttered in the thirty-acre rectangle of cotton that grew waist-
high in long furrows behind the Cutter house. The plain birds'
chatter provided a continuous accompaniment to the sunup-to-
sunset days of field work put in by Jonah and his family; the
sparrows, in their search for the earthworms and grubs that
lived among the furrows of cotton, seemed impervious to the
near hundred-degree heat that registered day after day on the
thermometer nailed in the shade of the outhouse eaves.

All the Cutters were tanned a nut-brown from their months
in the Texas sun. The broken, oozing blisters that had tortured
their palms and fingers the first months had now hardened into

protective calluses. Muscles that had ached miserably and made a good night's sleep impossible were now painless, hardened, and limber from weeks of ten- and twelve-hour days with hoe and plow.

Ruth and Jonah were enormously proud of themselves. They had come from those dark hours of the first days in Casilla; they had persevered. Now the future, which had seemed so bleak only a few months before, was as bright and clear as the midsummer desert sky. They had actually transformed themselves from inexperienced Easterners to a hardworking, productive farm family. To be sure, they had not done all that they wanted to do their first season in the valley, but then again, Casilla had not been all they had thought it was going to be. It was a tough land, independent, resilient, not used to giving in easily to the will of men and women with plows and dreams. The land was stubborn; it fought back. But in the end, the land had accepted its new masters; it had cooperated, turned green and lush, furrow upon furrow, man's geometry upon nature's capricious contours. It yielded treasures it had hoarded since the dim ages before man had arisen on the earth. The Cutters had made only a tiny mark on the face of the earth, a mere thirty acres of green land, but those thirty acres were a monument to man's will, to man's determination. It was their Eden, their Eden in a desert land. And the land, so often more opponent than friend, had earned their undying respect as they, in turn, had earned the respect of the ancient land.

The second week of September, the cotton harvest began. It was something of a communal effort for, even though each farmer was responsible for bringing in his own crop, it was necessary for the farmers to work together to allocate the local laborers, who worked only seasonally, and the extra wagons and mule teams needed during the weeks of intensive harvesting activity.

For the Mexican population of the valley the cotton harvest was the one time of the year when they could be sure of steady work. Only the youngest and oldest, and those unable to work, stayed home. All able-bodied men, women, and children went to the farms to pick. Every morning, before dawn, they could be seen walking in groups of a half a dozen or so along the dusty roads that cut between the dark fields of cotton. Here and there groups or individuals broke off here and there to head toward a farmhouse where the owner waited to send them out into his fields. Other laborers rode in the large slat-sided wagons that lumbered from Casilla out to the farms. With few exceptions the laborers were Mexicans, since most of the Anglo families in Casilla either owned their own farms or had other businesses.

The peons—some as young as five years old—worked from sunup to sunset in the fields. Most wore the traditional loose-fitting white cotton *camisos* and *pantalones* since the garments were cooler than American-style clothing and didn't bind when the wearer bent over for long hours. Almost all wore straw hats, some the large-brimmed *sombreros* of Mexico, others Western-style hats. A few wore sandals, though most were barefoot. Every picker was given a large burlap bag to carry with him into the field. The bag would be dragged along behind the peon as he moved through the furrows and pulled the opened, ripe bolls from the cotton stalks. At the end of the day each worker took his bag to the cotton wagon where the farmer or foreman weighed the bag on scales hung from the side of the wagon. A penny a pound paid to the picker. The best workers went home with as much as three dollars a day, two thirds of a bale of cotton, though only the fastest and ablest could pull in this much. Most made a dollar or a dollar and a half by sunset, while many of the children and old women rode back to Casilla with a quarter or half a dollar in their hands.

As little as the pickers were paid, the cost of harvesting was the biggest single expense the farmers had to bear during the season, and on smaller farms, like the Cutters', the owners themselves had to pick in order to keep down labor costs.

"It's killing work," Max warned them the day before the Cutters began their picking. "Much worse than plowing and hoeing, worse even than clearing brush, if you can imagine that! It's not the hours, so much, or the heat—we're all used to that by now. It's not even the handwork—plucking cotton bolls ain't near as bad as handling a hoe, at least as far as wear and tear on the hands. It's spending twelve hours bent over, dragging that sack through the field, staring at the dirt. It's degrading work, walking through a field, up a row, down a row, hour after hour, bent over like that. Can't look at the sky, can't look a man in the face."

"May be," Jonah came back with a grin. "But you're forgetting one thing, buddy. We're bringing in our first crop. Seven months ago we thought we'd never see anything but desert out there. Now we got thirty acres of the prettiest green cotton, all covered with white fluffy bolls, that you ever seen. I'd walk on hot coals to pick that stuff."

Jonah's pride and self-satisfaction were obvious to Max. His friends had done a remarkable job with their new land; they'd worked like Trojans since coming to Casilla. Amazing, for townfolk not used to that kind of physical labor. Jonah had a right to be a little puffed up over the success of his first season. He just hoped Jonah appreciated what a lucky man he was to have a wife like Ruth and a daughter like Anna, who had worked as hard as any men.

Jonah hired six laborers, all from one family that lived in a little adobe house in the land behind Wasserman's. A father—they only knew that his name was Jose—his two oldest sons, both in their mid-teens, short, wiry boys both, and two daughters, pretty, dark-eyed girls, one about Anna's age, the other J. J.'s.

And there was a skinny, toothless old woman with them, her leathery face wrinkled and drawn. Her hands were twisted and knotted with arthritis, hardly hands suitable for working the fields.

"*Quién es?*" Jonah asked the family.

"*Nuestra abuela,*" the older daughter replied. Our grandmother. Then the girl, apparently the only one who spoke English, continued, "Our mother could not come today. She have a baby boy yesterday night."

"You mean she was going to come just before having a baby?"

"*Porqué no?* My sister who is married is working now at Acala. She will have her *niño* maybe next week."

Ruth looked at Jonah.

"The grandmother looks too feeble to work. We can't send her out to pick. Can't we just give her half a dollar and send her home?" she said.

"I suppose we should," Jonah answered. The family seemed a bit uneasy about all the conversation, not well understood, about them.

"Tell your grandmother we'll pay her, anyway, but she should go home. She is too old to work."

The girl translated into Spanish, and the old woman, after a few hurried words with her son, gave the girl a reply in a hoarse voice.

"She says, please, to let her stay and work. She can do good, even though she is very old. She work hard for you. Please, *señor,* we need the work to make the money."

"What do you think, Ruth?"

It was a painful decision. Ruth tried to picture her Grammy Stratton being sent out to do field work.

"Suppose we should just let her, if they feel that strong about it," she answered, then added to the girl, "All right, but tell *su abuela* not to try to keep up with the rest of us. We won't mind if she works slower. We'll pay her as much as the others, anyway."

The girl cheerfully translated, and the old woman gave a grateful, if toothless, grin. Without another word the family turned and headed out into the field, one person to each row. With their first steps into the furrows of waist-high cotton they bent over, sacks dragging the ground, and pulled the fluffy white bolls from the cotton plants.

The Cutters followed their hired laborers into the field and were soon stooped over the furrows with their hands rummaging among the dark green leaves to pluck the bolls hidden among them. Max had given them detailed instructions on how to pick, especially in gauging the ripeness of each boll. Their fingers must quickly reach for a boll, grasp the clump of fibers, and pull it from the opened casing of the green pod in which it had grown. Max had shown them how to judge if the fibers were still too densely packed and deeply set in the boll, indicating that the cotton was not yet ready for picking; their fingers soon became sensitive to the exact texture of a ripe boll, which could be pulled and put, almost sight unseen, into the sack they carried. Max and Kate had been right about the nature of the work: It was lonely, boring, relentlessly tedious. The minutes turned into hours as they went about the repetitive tasks; the cool morning air, heated by the rising furnace of the sun, turned hot and stifling. Their back ached unmercifully from the unaccustomed posture, and the backs of their necks were seared from the steady onslaught of the sun's rays. The cotton sacks held a pitiful clump of cotton deep in their recesses. As foot after slow foot was moved down the furrows, it seemed that it would take days to fill even one sack; months, years, to harvest thirty acres. By ten o'clock, J. J. and Hank had been sent back to the house—Ruth couldn't imagine letting her young ones work through the whole day in this heat, though she well knew that there were many boys their ages picking cotton that day in the valley. They had done enough, she told herself. Perhaps they could come back for a while later in the day and work some more. Ruth had asked Anna, too, if she wanted to go back to the house for a few hours.

"I'm big enough to work all day, really I am," she replied without standing up from her labors.

At noon the Cutters and their laborers took a half-hour lunch break. They walked back along the furrows they had harvested that morning and sat under the vague shade of the cottonwoods by the house, welcoming what little respite the trees offered from the broiling midday sun. The Mexican laborers sat with the Cutters, carrying on a conversation as best they could in mixed English and Spanish, while they shared a simple light meal of *frijoles* and *tortillas*, cold beans and baked flour patties, which Ruth had prepared the night before.

By Jonah's reckoning they had covered about two acres that morning, a good pace. With luck they could cover the farm for the first picking in a month, then make a second, faster sweep to pick the remaining cotton that had ripened in the meantime.

The morning's cotton that was weighed and dumped in the wagon before lunch made a two-foot-deep pillow for Hank and little Juancito to play in after their meal. Their boyish chirping as they rolled and buried themselves in the sea of cotton were the only sounds that broke the midday stillness.

At twelve-thirty they were back in the field again, bent over between the waist-high plants, burlap sacks dragging behind them; the first enthusiasm of the morning had worn thin, and the hot September sun beat down on the silent field hands, scattered here and there among the fields. As the afternoon heat peaked the air became still and quiet. Even the locusts, which had sung their cacophonous song during the morning, became quiet. The only sound to be heard was the soft rustle of leaves as the *braceros* moved from one plant to another.

To the north, as on almost every afternoon during the summer, a bank of thunderheads rolled above the horizon. A great central tower of cloud flattened into an anvil shape by some unseen wind five miles in the sky. The great central tower was flanked by two smaller companions, like a tower with two vast wings. Beneath the white, roiling edifice, the clouds' flat underbelly were a fierce, purple-gray. Darker, more sinister-hued streaks slanted to the ground.

Rain.

The stillness of the afternoon was interrupted by muffled thunder, like the distant echo of a Titan's battle.

Still, the storm was distant, far out over the desert. Not even the faintest breeze ruffled the fields in the valley. The Cutters continued their rhythmic task, heads down, hands rummaging amid the greenery.

Then, like an invisible herald, a hot wind swept down across the valley off the desert plateau. As it swept across the valley it brought a stinging cargo of sand and debris, swept up from the desert floor.

Ruth and Anna, working next to one another in the middle of the field, stood up and looked at the sky. The great bank of thunderheads was close now, almost overhead, even though the sun still burned through the hot, sandy wind that stung their skin.

They looked at one another, a wordless, uneasy exchange.

Anna squinted, trying to shut out the painful sand; she raised her hands instinctively to her face to shield it. The sky took on an odd, yellowish glow, a pallid veil between the threatening clouds and the earth below. The veil was pungent with the scent of ozone, the unmistakable odor of summer storms.

Anna sent her mother an anxious look. All around them— Jonah a dozen yards away, the *bracero* family scattered about— faces looked up at the glowering sky.

"Should we go in?" she asked her mother.

"Wait." Ruth's brow furrowed, concerned. More often than not, summer thunderstorms passed quickly over the valley, to pour out their fast fury on the desert to the south.

Within seconds light drops of rain speckled their skin and

clothes. The rain built steadily as the dark, low canopy moved over them, blotting out the sun, turning the midafternoon an ominous gray.

Without another word the women began walking fast along the furrow toward the house. The rain increased and came down in a stinging, hard stream. The leaves rustled under the sharp, penetrating shower.

Curious, Anna thought as she hurried back along the row she had so laboriously picked that afternoon, but the rain is almost painful.

She bent down, to lower her face from the driving force of the storm. She looked at the ground. White. Small specks of white on the ground.

Hail.

The storm came full force, with a gust of wind and an onrush of noise. The hailstones were bigger now, the size of pebbles, flung mercilessly out of the sky. A rustle, almost a hiss, came from the cotton as the hail ripped into and through the tender leaves.

Thunder boomed from the blackness overhead, and the cold cold stones fell in a relentless, flogging torrent on her head and back. Arms went up to shield but to little avail; eyes closed against the storm's fury left her blinded, with only the furrow to guide her to safety.

Within minutes the ground was frosted with hail, and the cotton danced in the storm; each stone, millions upon millions, cut and tore their way through tender leaves, breaking, shredding, cutting.

Blinded, her skin torn and bruised, Anna slipped on the icy ground. For an instant she felt the cold stones against her body, then she regained her feet and ran on, knowing only to run on, toward a safe haven.

A burst of light and a terrible explosion from somewhere very near.

Still, she ran on, the thunder ringing in her ears.

A hand grasped hers, through the storm.

Her mother.

Together, reaching across the unseen barrier that divided them, they stumbled, beaten, toward home.

After the storm passed Jonah walked for hours alone through his ravaged fields, until his boots were thick with mud and shreds of the leaves and cotton torn from the plants by the storm. Ruth tried to go with him, to offer some consolation, but he rejected her company and her sympathy angrily, and left her with the children to deal with her own shock and pain.

Max came as soon as he could get away from his own farm, though it was after sunset. Jonah was standing forlornly in the dark field when Max found him.

"Bad, Jonah?"

Max knew the answer; he had just walked the length of what had been Jonah's first crop.

"All gone. Everything. Pounded into the mud by the god-damn hail."

Jonah didn't ask how Max had fared. Just as well, Max thought. He would have found it hard to tell Jonah that the path of the hail had left his farm almost totally undamaged except for the fringe that bordered Jonah's land. That was the quirky thing about hailstorms. They'd cut a swath a hundred yards or half a mile wide, ripping everything in their path to shreds and leave what was on either side untouched.

Max reached out a reassuring hand and touched his friend's shoulder. There was no response.

"It's getting late, Jonah. You've got a hell of a tomorrow. Best get back home and have supper. Get a good night's rest. Besides, Ruth was looking pretty wrung out when I saw her, and Anna was doing her best not to cry, and the boys, of course, are kind of scared and confused by all this. I think you need to be with them a bit. They've got as big a stake in this place as you do."

There was a long silence before Jonah spoke. When he did, Max heard the voice of a changed man. Beyond despair, into anger and futility. Jonah had hardened, as hard and cold as one of the hailstones that had ripped through the sky.

"What I need is a drink. A couple of drinks. That saloon in Alamo Alto stays open late, don't it?"

Max answered in the affirmative. He tried to keep any encouragement out of his voice.

"Come on, buddy, let me buy you a whiskey."

Jonah turned a cynical, half-frozen smile on his face. He

clapped the larger man on the back. "It may be my last dollar. Might as well spend it on a good cause."

Max walked beside Jonah toward the distant horse and wagon. He didn't want to do this; he didn't want Jonah to, either. But he couldn't let Jonah go on a drunk all alone.

"I didn't see Max for three days when we lost our first crop," Kate chirped to Ruth with a forced cheerfulness. "Men are that way sometimes. Just got to run away from their troubles. Not like us women, who like to stick close by things when they go bad, to see them through. Max's over his drinking and running-around days, I'm happy to say. He's out more than anything to keep an eye on Jonah, make sure he doesn't get in any sort of tight spot. They'll show up in a day or two."

"It's not so much them being out on a drunk, Kate. I suppose every woman's had to put up with that a time or two in her life. But we've got so much work to do. I don't want Jonah to be away so long."

Kate studied Ruth's face, as she had often in the day and a half since the storm, hardly any emotion showing, just a mask of quiet control. That was Ruth's way, she supposed, especially when life got tough. She knew enough about Ruth, about a woman's nature, to know what must be going on underneath. She knew Ruth was bothered by a lot more than how much work wasn't getting done with Jonah plumped over the bar in Alamo Alto. She knew Jonah had not spoken two words to Ruth since the storm. That was what was eating away at the woman behind that cool facade. She needed Jonah to be with her, needed it more than anything in the world.

"Give the man time, Ruth. Go see about your business as best you can. Welcome him back with open arms. What else can you do?"

Ruth nodded in agreement. What else could she do? What else would she do, no matter how long he stayed away?

"But what do I tell the children?"

"The gospel truth. Young'uns are a lot more grown-up sometimes than we think they are."

"And there's the crop. It's sitting there, drying in the mud. Oh, I know most of it's lost. But Max, even Pete Wilkerson, told me some of the cotton could be salvaged. Sold cheap as low-grade. At least we can save something out of the mud."

"Why didn't you hire your pickers today, then?"

"That's Jonah's decision. That's why I hope he's back soon."

Kate didn't know whether to grin or grit her teeth. For a schoolteacher Ruth could be a durn fool sometimes.

"It's your farm, too, Ruth Cutter. You've worked this thirty acres as much as Jonah. Hell! Don't sit home whimpering and feeling sorry for yourself. That's what your fool husband is doing in that saloon right now! You got as much right as anyone to say what goes on here."

Ruth didn't answer Kate. Her eyes focused on the soapy dish rag in her hands. Her hands were as suited to field work as a man's. She'd proven that. Her mind might be as suited to farm work as a man's too. Just maybe.

Jonah showed up at the farm the next afternoon, rumpled and unshaven, with bloodshot eyes and a splitting headache. He went straight to bed after only the briefest of greetings to Ruth and only got up the next morning after nine. The house was empty, though the faint odor of breakfast still clung to the room. With eyes that still ached at the morning light, he peered out the front door. The wagon was there with Jake tethered to the wheel, slowly swishing away flies with his tail. No sign of Ruth or the children. Still a bit wobbly from three days he couldn't remember, Jonah went across the front room and looked out the small back window that looked west across the fields. The light brought back the hateful afternoon of the storm. Thirty acres that had been lush and green, now the ugly brown of dry, cracked mud. The once-lush crop was now torn and ragged, some plants broken down completely, others denuded to bare stalks. A few wisps of white, fluffy cotton clung here and there to stalks, a mockery of what had been a promising first crop.

How he hated this place! Every goddamned inch of it! What a damn fool he'd been to ever try. The one time he finally broke away and tried to make something of himself, and he had to pick this godforsaken corner of the world to do it in. It had been doomed from the beginning. To hell with Casilla, with farming. He looked like a fool for all his hard work.

Something caught Jonah's eye at the far end of the field toward Max's place. Figures, half a dozen or so, in the field. Moving slow, like they were picking cotton. Wondering what was going on on his farm, Jonah staggered outside into the brilliant September sun.

As he got close to the figures one of them saw him and broke away from the group and hurried toward him.

It was Ruth.

She hurried along the furrow toward him, arms outstretched in welcome.

"At last," she called out without the slightest hint or reprimand. "Of course, I was a bit worried that you'd be laid up in bed a day or two. Sorry I didn't know you were up, or I would have come in to get some breakfast for you."

Smiling, grateful that Jonah was home safe, Ruth reached out to embrace him. He pulled roughly away from her.

"What the hell is this? What the hell is going on here?"

Ruth recoiled at this unexpected anger. Confused, she studied his face. The bloodshot eyes flared venomously.

"I don't understand." There was genuine confusion behind the pain on her face.

Jonah gestured at the fields.

"This!"

She understood now.

"We're trying to salvage what we can. It's not much, but it will help."

"Damn you, woman! You should have asked me first."

Jonah's second burst of anger goaded Ruth to anger too. Her gray eyes narrowed, angry, on guard.

"I couldn't wait for you to come home to decide. It would only have made the loss worse. Besides, what would you have decided, other than to do what we're doing?"

"I would have said to forget the whole thing. There's nothing out there to save. There never was."

"No, Jonah, you're wrong." Ruth had regained herself again, gotten some of her senses back. "All the other farmers said we could salvage a few bales. At least we'll have a few dollars to show for our work. To put toward next season."

Jonah turned away from her, kicked a clod of dirt hard with his boot toe, sending it in dusty fragments across the field.

"There's not going to be any next season. We're getting out of here."

Ruth was too stunned to reply. He guessed her disbelief. He turned his unshaven face away, still handsome beneath the growth of beard. She thought she detected a quaver of vulnerability behind the angry mask.

"You heard me. We're getting out of this place."

He kicked the earth again, then walked fast, hands shoved deep in his pockets, toward the house.

"We can't leave, Jonah. We can't," she called out to him.

"Why not? Nothing here," he shouted over his shoulder.

She ran, caught up with him, took his arm firmly.

"Jonah, we've got to try."

"No."

"Got to. There's no place for us to go to."

He stopped suddenly, confronted her with an insolent, mocking face.

"Who cares?"

She pulled back, astonished at his insensitivity.

"I do." Her voice was full, controlled. "I do, Jonah. And, I wouldn't want to leave here even if we did have someplace to go to. This is our home now."

Jonah shook his head at her foolishness and, without a word, started again for the house. Ruth moved to follow him, then stopped herself. Kate's words came to mind.

Of course, he was being like most men, running away from his troubles. He'd be back, though, to face reality, and she'd be there, waiting, when he did.

She went back toward the stooped figures with their cotton sacks. Her children were there working. She had to go to help them. There was so much to be done.

Chapter Four

LATE EVERY OCTOBER FOR THE FIFTEEN YEARS HE HAD made Casilla his permanent home, Don Alonzo Lopez y Ruiz hosted a grand fiesta at Casa Portillo in honor of San Lorenzo, the patron saint of the local parish, whose feast-day two months prior marked the beginning of the harvest season. In a quiet, hardworking farm village like Casilla, social events of any magnitude were rare; the grand affair at Casa Portillo was even more special, more eagerly awaited because it threw open the doors into a rarely seen world of tradition, beauty, and wealth.

Don Alonzo himself, though rarely seen in Casilla, was one of the most-talked-about men. Everyone had stories about Alonzo, from Simon Wasserman and Ola down to the poorest peon. Stories about his wealth, his ancient and noble Spanish lineage; stories about his cultured and refined tastes, about his treasure-filled homes. Everyone had an anecdote concerning his kindness and generosity, and tales of his tragic and lonely life. For a man whose status in the community was almost that of legend, Alonzo was a relative newcomer. His life for the most part had been spent on the vast estates his family held in Chihuahua and Sonora, where the name Lopez y Ruiz carried a baronial weight, befitting the lineage of a conquistador who had attended Montezuma's death. Alonzo, a man of sixty-five, could have chosen to live out his autumnal years anywhere in the world, whether in the venerable and palatial *haciendas* on the Mexican estates or in villas or country homes of any of the favored spots of the rich and powerful in Europe. Yet he chose Casilla and the relative modesty of Casa Portillo for the simple reason that the two-hundred-year-old *hacienda*, situated near the Rio Grande two miles from Casilla, had been the birthplace and childhood home of his beloved, deeply mourned Davida.

Alonzo and his wife had only occasionally visited Casa Portillo
during their marriage—their life was centered around the estates in Mexico—but after her death, Alonzo had left Mexico,
forever, so it seemed, to live in the house where the person he
had loved most in the world had been conceived and born,
where she had passed the years of her childhood and youth,
until Alonzo had met, loved, and wed her, and taken her to the
life of secluded luxury in the vast wastes of northern Mexico.
When Alonzo had made the decision to move from Mexico to
Casilla, it had been on the surface a rational decision. After all,
his only daughter, Alessandra, had married the American army
officer John Bradley and lived with him and their son, Bart, in
El Paso, a mere thirty-five miles from Casilla. But in the end it
was Casilla itself that was the attraction for him. Even though
he was an agnostic, Don Alonzo somehow felt that the spirit
and soul of his beloved Davida lived on in the rough adobe, the
cool tiles, and the thick beams of Casa Portillo; the house was
very much of her.

When Alonzo had first proposed an annual *fiesta* at Casa
Portillo, open to all, Father Hernando, the parish priest, had
questions why, if it were to be dedicated to San Lorenzo, the
fiesta was planned so long after the good saint's official feast
day.

"Better to celebrate the successful completion of the harvest
than its hopeful beginning," Don Alonzo had offered by way of
explanation. The true reason he had kept to himself: the date set
in October was the anniversary of his wedding day. The *fiesta*
had become a secret memorial, a celebration of life, dedicated to
the memory of his wife, and though he shared his home, his
hospitality, with everyone, the true reason for the evening's celebration was known to Don Alonzo only.

Ruth and Jonah had both resisted the idea of going to Casa
Portillo at first, though for different reasons. Ruth was naturally shy and reserved around strangers and in large crowds,
and to her it didn't seem quite "fitting," as she put it, that a
family of total strangers should go, uninvited, to a party at the
home of a man they hadn't even met. She never would have
done such a thing in Myrtlesburg, she reminded herself, and she
didn't see why she should start doing it now. Max and Kate had
howled in protest and proclaimed, "This is the West, and folks

don't stand on fancy back-East formality out here, and besides, it's not a regular party but a kind of community get-together, you see." Jonah's reluctance had been harder to fathom, since he seemed the sort to be up for a good time when he had the chance. He refused to explain himself and deferred to Ruth for excuses. He couldn't have told them why he loathed the idea of showing his face at Casa Portillo. It was shame, pure and simple. They would all know, everyone there, what a mess Jonah Cutter had made of things. They'd know that he and his family lived in a dirt-floor shack, more like poor Mexicans than decent white folks. They'd know he'd lost his whole crop, first season out. Know, too, that he had a good-size owing balance at Wasserman's, since anybody with sharp eyes could catch glimpses of Simon's ledger book as he flipped through the pages toting up orders. No, Jonah, for one, would rather sit home and stare at four walls than walk around in a house full of every soul in the county, having them look at him with those damned sympathetic expressions of theirs. He'd seen enough of those since the hailstorm, in Wasserman's or at the Red Star. Every one of them, being so kind, so sorry for him, saying what rotten luck it was he got hailed out. They didn't really care about him, he could tell. What difference did it make to anyone whether Jonah Cutter made a go of his farm or not?

In the end it was the children who persuaded Ruth and Jonah to give in. Not by begging or cajoling but merely by showing their excitement about the prospect of going—along with all the other young ones their ages—to a real grown-up *fiesta*. After all the pain of the last months Ruth and Jonah couldn't deny their children one evening of fun. By the evening of the *fiesta*, as the Cutters bathed and dressed in their best clothes, some of their anxiety about the evening had disappeared, caught up as they were in getting ready, even more so when the Mirkovskys arrived, "duded up," as Kate said, and in high spirits. Max had brought a few bottles of chilled beer for them to enjoy on the ride over to Casa Portillo. As they clambered into the now-familiar Mirkovsky wagon, Max uncapped the bottles and passed them around; Anna and the boys had to content themselves with bottles of cream soda. Casa Portillo was about a mile downriver from the place where the Casilla road dead-ended at the intersection with the river road. There were no farms in that direction along the river, only brushy bottom land. In the distance the yellow pinpricks of light from Casa Portillo came out of the darkness like fireflies on a summer's eve. Max started singing as he guided the wagon through the dark but familiar roads. His voice was as big and hearty as he and surprisingly in tune and musical.

"Alla en el rancho grande . . ."

"Down on the big farm . . ."

After the first chorus they all had learned the Spanish lyrics well enough to join in without too much stuttering, and as they neared the dark grove of cottonwoods that sheltered the *hacienda,* their singing was joined by the muted strains of voices, laughter, and the lively, bright strains of a *mariachi* band. Ruth felt the enormous strain of the last weeks lifted from her as they neared the party. She sang full out, her bright, tuneful soprano joined by Jonah's enthusiastic, if off-key, tenor. She slipped her hand into his, noticing how work-hardened it had become over the months, the hand of a laboring man. He squeezed hers, as hardened as his was, and smiled at her as he sang, the kind of open, youthful smile that was so peculiarly his and that had been so definitely absent for a very long time. *What a silly woman I was, not to want to come tonight,* she thought to herself. *So few occasions to enjoy ourselves here, it would be a shame not to take advantage of them when they come along.* She was feeling very pleased as the wagon turned and drove through the open gate of the adobe-walled *hacienda,* unaware that this night at Casa Portillo would change their lives forever.

Don Alonzo stood at the widely opened doorway that led from the center building of Casa Portillo onto the large, walled forecourt of the *hacienda.* Casa Portillo, like most colonial Spanish architecture, was low to the ground—only the center portion rose to a second story. The walls were of dark, earth-colored adobe, thick and uneven. The windows that faced the outside world were small, deep, and shuttered, revealing little of the beauty within; the truer facade of the house faced the open inner court, down a long passageway that opened behind where Alonzo stood. Only a weatherworn but luxurious carving on the oak doors hinted at the treasures behind the adobe walls. The outer court, which ordinarily was a dusty, empty place used for horses, wagons, and, more recently, automobiles, had been transformed for the *fiesta*. Wires had been strung back and forth across the open expanse between the walls, and they had in turn been festooned with streamers of colored paper and bright paper lanterns. Beneath the gay canopy a throng of several hundred guests mingled about. Where the horse trough usually stood, a bandstand had been erected, and a dozen musicians, in the gaily embroidered *camisos* of northern Mexico, played fiddles and *marimbas, maracas* and guitars. On the opposite side of the court a long row of tables bright with cloths and paper decorations carried a heavy burden of native delicacies. Nearby, a flock of guests hovered near the half a dozen kegs of chilled, light Mexican beer.

Alonzo greeted every guest who came within his range. Most he knew on a first-name basis; others were more distant acquaintances or locals he had heard of but not yet met. He was a tall, thickly built man, whose youthful handsomeness and prowess had aged and mellowed into a rich patina of presence: he was the kind of man who would be noticed when he walked into a room, even though there might be a dozen men there half his age and twice as handsome. His finely shaped large head boasted a full growth of hair, only lately silvered with age; his full mouth, beneath a luxuriant growth of mustache, smiled often and whitely, but his eyes, most of all, captured his audience. Deep, large, and brown, they radiated warmth, humor, and wisdom. It was the kind of face that elicited admiration from the beholder without making the beholder feel inferior.

Alonzo beamed out at the bustling guests, singling out here and there well-known faces. Families from neighboring farms— the Pettuses, the Wilkersons, the Cunninghams, and others, the foundation of the new Casilla, families dedicated to hard work, to progress, to American ideals. There were those of the old Casilla too. Mexican couples in colorful holiday garments, old widows in somber black, fresh from their penances at Nuestra Señora de la Luz, wearing their scapulars only recently blessed by Father Hernando. The good father himself was across the court now, enjoying what appeared to be a second or third mug of beer. There was a third group of guests, faces not familiar to most of the Casillians but known to their host. Elegant couples from El Paso, some Anglo, some Mexican, who arrived in automobiles that roared and sputtered as they pulled up in front of the *hacienda*. These guests hinted at that side of Don Alonzo's world that was as hidden as the inner courtyard of Casa Portillo, a world of money and sophistication, elegance and luxury. And finally there were the most familiar faces, those people who touched Don Alonzo's life more than any others: Maricita and the others of his staff at Casa Portillo, servants who had loyally worked at the *hacienda* since the days when Davida had been a girl. And there were his "buddies" from Casilla; Ola, accompanied by a retinue of her boarders, all looking as if they had begun the celebration early with a jug of whiskey from Ola's special pantry; and Wasserman, silly and endearing, in a bright yellow Mexican-style shirt with ruffled sleeves that fluttered like feathers on his scrawny, birdlike frame.

Across the crowded courtyard Don Alonzo saw yet another wagon pull up alongside the cluster of carts and wagons and automobiles outside the gates. Figures in the darkness, then the familiar faces of Max and Kate Mirkovsky with Max's parents in tow. There was another family with the Mirkovskys, faces unknown to Alonzo. Of course, they would be the Cutters; he had heard the new family in Casilla had become great friends with Max and Kate. A striking family, he thought. A blue-eyed, bantamlike husband, something of the scamp about him. The wife, a tall, handsome, dark-featured woman. A daughter, growing to look very much like her mother, though in a finer, prettier way. And two young boys, as light and dark as salt and pepper. Both were boyish and curious as they took in the sights of the party, though the elder, lighter one showed a gregariousness and confidence that seemed lacking in his more withdrawn, wide-eyed little brother. Yes, a handsome group, Alonzo thought. An air of quality about them that one noticed, even in the bustle of the party. How sad it was about their first crop, a terrible blow for a struggling young farmer and his wife. It was always difficult for these young farmers to make a go of things, trying to put together a farm on a shoestring. So vulnerable to the least setback. Alonzo had known the Cutters were dangling by the slimmest thread financially, even before he had had the fact confirmed by gossip in town.

There was the flurry of introductions, the handshakes and small pleasantries exchanged when near strangers meet. A few words about the *fiesta*, about the weather, about Casilla. Alonzo sensed a certain discomfort on the part of the Cutters. The husband's manner seemed a bit forced, as if he were having to try very hard to appear cheerful and at ease; the wife looked a bit frightened, as if she would be glad to get the introductions and pleasantries over and slip into the anonymity of the crowd. Alonzo had to remind himself that in spite of his congeniality and his genuine friendliness to his neighbors, whether old friends or new aquaintances, to many in Casilla he was something of local nobility, lord of the manor, as it were. He recalled Kate Mirkovsky, several years before, telling him how terrified she had been on her first meeting with the local *honcho*. He certainly didn't want anyone to feel this way about him, certainly not the Cutter family, who probably needed at this time in their lives to feel that there were friends and neighbors who were concerned about them.

Alonzo decided to reassure them, to put them at better ease, but his words backfired. He regretted them as soon as he spoke.

"*Amigos,* I have heard of your recent misfortune. My sincere condolences that the vagaries of fate singled you out. Of course, if there is anything I can do to help—"

"We're fine! We're just fine." Jonah rudely broke into the man's words. He meant his voice to sound offhanded, cheerful, but there was more than a little hostility and anger in his tone.

"We're not the kind to let a little thing like this set us back none. Hell, it's just one crop. It's going to take more than that to get Jonah Cutter down."

Ruth blanched at her husband's words. Why didn't he just say thank you and leave it at that. To her further embarrassment Alonzo tried to smooth things over.

"Oh, I don't doubt that, Señor Cutter. Not at all. I just know how difficult these things can get at times."

Ruth riveted her eyes on Alonzo. Not because she wanted to see his growing discomfort with Jonah's manners but because to look at Kate or Max would have been to see their embarrassment. To have looked at Jonah would have been to see something she didn't want to acknowledge at all.

"We're fine," Jonah continued in the same tone, as if he had some perverse need to make matters worse. "We don't need help. Not help or money. We're doing this on our own."

Alonzo was stunned at the man's words. Of course, he'd
meant nothing of the kind. All he'd meant to offer was sympathy, neighborly concern. Then Alonzo felt himself blush, something he had not done in many years. It was a blush of deep
embarrassment, embarrassment for himself, for the Cutters, for
everyone who might have overheard the conversation.

"Of course," he muttered, trying to keep his eyes from avoiding Jonah Cutter's icy blue gaze. His eyes found Ruth's, saw
there an expression of the deepest pain, of the profoundest sorrow. In that instant Alonzo understood a great deal about
Ruth, about Jonah, about their life together.

Max mercifully broke into the silence that followed the awkward exchange with the suggestion that the Cutters might like
to mingle, see the *hacienda,* and have some refreshments. As
the group turned and lost themselves in the crowded courtyard,
Alonzo felt a sudden, strong need to follow them, to talk to
them. Somehow to make amends for his innocent but offending
remark. But even more than that, he wanted to look again into
Ruth Cutter's eyes.

Two hours later, as the ordinarily quiet rooms of Casa Portillo echoed to the gay sounds of music, laughter, and singing,
Don Alonzo found his chance. The greeting of arrivals was long
over, and Alonzo now had the freedom of the house. He enjoyed enormously the sight of the treasure-filled rooms, with
their dark-beamed ceilings and richly carved oak doors, filled to
the brim with guests. The dark brown adobe-mud walls, usually
so dim, were ablaze with hundreds of candles placed in candelabra and sconces; a large collection of Spanish and Mexican
pottery, some of it very ancient, took on new life when filled
with an abundance of flowers, shipped in by train from Mexico
just for the occasion. The cool, sleek glaze of the tile floors,
which usually echoed only to his own lonely footsteps, and the
quiet padding of his servants now clattered under hundreds of
shoes and boots. *Bueno, muy, muy bueno,* Alonzo thought com-
plimenting himself that he had brought this party into Casa
Portillo tonight. To be sure, his years of solitude in the *hacienda*
had been a great solace, a kind of ongoing communion with the
memory of Davida. But it seemed now, after all these years,
that life at Casa Portillo was becoming too much of a memorial,

an almost monastic existence. This party—this, too, was a celebration of the memory of that woman who had been more alive, more vibrant than any creature he had ever known. Yes, he told himself, there should be more of these parties at Casa Portillo.

Alonzo moved from cluster to cluster among his guests. A few words with Father Hernando and Wasserman, then an encounter with his dear old friends, the Channings, the senator and his wife from El Paso, and their son, Will, just back from the European grand tour after his years at Yale Law School. Alonzo and the Channings stood in the deep lower gallery that circled Alonzo's "Small Eden," the central open court of the house. The court, overlooked by galleries on all sides of both the first and second stories, was understandably Alonzo's favorite part of the house. Though it was open to the October sky, the four enclosing walls protected the garden and allowed a lush, almost tropical growth of plants to flourish, all under the canopied majesty of a vast, ancient magnolia tree. In the center of the court a mossy marble fountain gurgled, attended by a few ornate cast-iron chairs, favored by Don Alonzo for his long, quiet afternoons of reading. Now, across the courtyard, he saw Ruth and Anna Cutter as they walked along the far gallery. Ruth carried Hank, asleep in her arms, and Alonzo guessed correctly that she was taking the boy upstairs to one of several bedrooms that had been set aside as nurseries for the younger children so their parents could enjoy a few late hours of partying. Alonzo excused himself from the Channings' company and hurried across the court to intercept Ruth and her daughter at the foot of the wooden stairway that led to the upper gallery.

"Por favor, señora," he called out softly so as not to wake the boy. "Allow me to help you. It is a long flight, and he is no small fellow."

Ruth at first felt embarrassed, not by her host's gentlemanly offer but by the mere fact of encountering him face-to-face after their awkward introduction. But as he looked down at her Don Alonzo's face was filled with such a warmth and genuineness that her embarrassment vanished. She found herself smiling at him, not a forced, polite smile but one of genuine pleasure. Kate had been right, Ruth thought. Alonzo did have the knack of making everyone like him, or so it would seem.

"Thank you, really, Señor Ruiz. But we'll manage. I'm used to toting the boys around."

"But, please, I insist. This is, after all, a night for my guests to enjoy themselves and not by doing what they are used to." As he spoke Alonzo extended his arms to take Hank's sleeping form. He wondered, as he did, why Mrs. Cutter's husband had not offered to carry their son upstairs, but, of course, he reminded himself, that was really none of his business.

"What do you say, Anna?" Ruth turned to her daughter, allowing herself a bit of coquettishness. "Shall we impose on the gentleman?" Anna nodded with a grin. It was clear that she thought Don Alonzo Lopez y Ruiz was a *very* nice man. Hank was transferred from arms to arms without the slightest ruffling of his sleep. Alonzo stood aside to let the women pass up the stairs; Anna hurried on ahead, anxious to explore the inviting mystery of the upper floor. As Ruth passed him Alonzo spoke quietly in Spanish, then caught himself and began again in English.

"De vero, señora . . . Truthfully, madam, I am sorry that I was so rude earlier. I never meant to offend."

To his relief Ruth riveted him with her opalescent gray eyes. There was no evasion, no hesitancy in them. He noticed that as she spoke she held her head with a particular nobility.

"There is no apology needed or wanted. Only thanks, from my husband and myself, for allowing us into your home, for showing us such a lovely evening. If there was . . . a bad moment . . . it was many hours ago and long forgotten. After all, you did say this was a night for your guests to enjoy themselves. And that they certainly are."

It was a rather formal, controlled statement, but Alonzo liked that about it. The kind of answer one would expect from a woman like Mrs. Cutter. Her nobility showed more than just in the way she carried her head. Alonzo followed her up the long wooden flight of stairs, holding her sleeping son close to him as he watched her straight, slender figure move above and before him. The contours of her body moved with a controlled grace beneath the simple, unadorned silhouette of her long, dark evening dress. A sensation, small but sharp as a pinprick, jabbed Alonzo deep in his belly, then slowly but relentlessly grew, moved through him. He closed his eyes, as if to will away the feeling.

"Abuelo! A dónde vas con el niño?"

Alonzo opened his eyes, looked up toward the familiar figure that stood at the top of the stairs. He called out something in rapid Spanish, which neither Ruth nor Anna understood, and the voice above laughed heartily, a rich baritone that echoed out across the court, even above the sound of the revelers below.

Anna saw him first, and though she did not intend to, she involuntarily stopped in her tracks, held in midstep by the apparition of a man that stood a few feet before her. Her mother had much the same reaction an instant later, for the man who had called out unexpectedly from the top of the stairs was, quite simply, the most extraordinarily handsome man she had ever seen. He was young, though his face, broad, strong, masterfully sculpted, had the kind of presence that is never really young or old. His hair was dark, clipped short in military style, and his skin, though not tanned, had the full-blooded flush of one who is used to the outdoors. His mouth, thin-lipped but formed with a sensuous, almost sculptural line, fell easily into a broad, white-toothed smile, beneath a thick, carefully groomed bristle of mustache. His chin and jaw, darkly shadowed with beard, were strong, angular, almost aggressively masculine; below, a thick, muscular neck gave way to the easily recognized blue-gray wool of a West Point Academy uniform. There was little doubt, from the broad contours of the uniform, that the body beneath was of a oneness with the head and face above. But one feature above all was the cause of the women's reaction to the sight of him: his eyes. They were a rare green, shot through with gold, clear and deep, yet with an almost metallic sparkle and sheen. They were, in their opaline brilliance, both piercing and guarded, the kind of eyes that seemed to look into one's very soul, one's innermost secret thoughts, while revealing little of the man behind them. Ruth and Anna were far from the first women who had found themselves frozen by her gaze; even men sometimes found the man's brilliant, seductive eyes discomforting.

"Ah, perfect timing," Alonzo called out to the young god. "You must meet our new friends and neighbors."

The smile broadened, blazed. The eyes acknowledged each one in turn, surveying them like conquered nations.

"This, *queridas señora y señorita,* is my grandson, Mr. Barton Bradley. I'm feeling a fortunate old grandfather tonight, since Bart has come all the way from New York, from the military academy, to pay me a visit."

Anna, now swept up in profound shyness, heard Alonzo call her name in introduction. Her gaze had fallen to the floor in a young girl's instinct to avoid the gaze of an attractive man, but good manners forced her to look up at him again, to be held, fixed, in the powerful beacon of his eyes. She had only half heard that this was Don Alonzo's grandson, that his name was Bart, that she was introduced as his neighbor. She was too caught up in a feeling, new and inexplicable, a feeling that began with a hot, relentless sinking sensation in her belly, a feeling that then spread slowly throughout her body to the tips of her fingers and toes. It was a frightening sensation, both warm and cold at the same time, as she had felt the time, years before, when she had fallen through a thin patch of ice on one of the creeks back in Kentucky and been plunged to her neck in dark, freezing water. She wanted to say something as Alonzo introduced them, but her throat was tight; no words could be forced out. She managed only a nod of the head, after which her gaze plunged once again to the safety of the rough wood of the stair tread.

Bart watched with some amusement at the uncomfortable girl who had stumbled so awkwardly through their first introduction. He was used to girls Anna's age gawking at him. They were all the same, first staring at him with sad, intent calf's eyes, then turning suddenly shy and staring at the floor. Bart, who in all his young years had spent more than a little time with older, more assured women, the kind of women who could meet and challenge his gaze, still enjoyed the vanity-satisfying encounters with youngsters like Anna. Pretty girls, plain girls, they all were struck by his handsomeness, and he well knew it. It was fun, really, to see them reacting, all very much in the same schoolgirlish fashion. He liked to toy with them, tease them a bit, to capitalize on the discomfort that arose from their attraction to him. He sometimes imagined himself as a powerful young mountain lion playing with a terrified, quivering young jackrabbit. The lion could easily have killed the prey at any moment but instead chose to play with it, bat it with massive, padded paws, hold it firmly in its jaws with only a hint of piercing tooth. Then, let the terrified little creature go, to run away to some hiding place in abject terror.

Often, when introduced to girls in these circumstances, Bart would coolly, deliberately address them as "Young lady" or "Little Missy," and compliment them on how grown-up their frock was, or some such comment designed to point up the immense gap between the adolescents and the man they were so uncontrollably attracted to. It all seemed a harmless enough game to Bart, and he meant no harm by it, though he did often hurt these helpless, well-meaning creatures. He had been about to do the same to this young Anna Cutter, whoever she was, from one of the new farm families, he supposed, when something stopped him. He saw that she was pretty and that one day the girl of thirteen might be a beautiful woman. But Bart had seen many pretty young girls before, girls who might become beautiful women, and he had not been stopped from playing his vain little game with them. It was something in the girl's gray eyes. A flicker of some deep, womanly emotion, powerful though hidden. It was something of a shock for the self-assured, almost arrogant young Bradley, to be brought up by something so small as an expression or an imagined expression in a girl's eyes. Yet it was there; he felt it, and though he couldn't quite touch what it was exactly, in those eyes, he suspected that the young, shy Miss Cutter was, or someday would be, a woman to be reckoned with.

It was over in a few seconds. He had exchanged a few pleasantries with Mrs. Cutter and his grandfather, the girl had slipped by him on the stairs without another glance in his direction, and he hurried downstairs to rejoin the party. It was a beautiful October evening, and all the better for the *fiesta* at Casa Portillo. How good it was to be home, even if it was for just a short break, after the long years at West Point, traveling in Europe and back East. Not the least of the pleasures of being back in Casilla was seeing the Channings, and his best buddy Will, after such a long time. As he looked for Will in the crowd —his grandfather had told him they were downstairs, late arrivals—Bart kept thinking, though he had no desire to do so, about the strange look in that young girl's eyes.

Alonzo leaned over the small bed and laid the sleeping form of Hank Cutter on the white-sheeted mattress. The room was only faintly lighted, and half a dozen or more children slept here and there on beds and pallets brought in for the purpose. "He's a handsome boy, *señora,*" he whispered to Ruth as he straightened after laying Hank down. Ruth bent to tuck her son in, as Alonzo admired, not Hank, but the milky white contours of Ruth's long neck. "He reminds me a bit of Bart as a child. I often carried him up those stairs to put him to bed. As you can see, that was many years ago."

"And what a handsome creature he turned out to be," Ruth said directly as she stood and walked toward the door, Alonzo at her side. "God certainly smiled when he was born."

"De vero, Señora Cutter. His parents were both of extraordinary beauty, so it is only natural that he be so gifted. Alas, though, I sometimes am afraid, here in my old man's *cuerpo,* in my heart, that his beauty may, like great wealth, be a gift that carries a heavy burden in it. He can never be seen as just an ordinary man."

"In that case," Ruth replied with a good deal of common sense, "he's no ordinary man, is he, and therefore shouldn't be seen that way."

"A good point, but still, it causes problems. Already, even at his young age. He is bright, talented. A brilliant future awaits him in the military or in politics, if he wants it. But he is vain."

"Understandable. I would be too."

"But well you should be, *señora.*" Alonzo regretted the words as soon as they were spoken. He had been too forward.

Ruth shrugged off the compliment.

"What a gentleman you are, Señor Alonzo. "You really are very kind and attentive. And so gracious to help carry Hank upstairs."

"Bah. It was nothing. And as I said, I too rarely have the opportunity to hold and carry young children. How I miss that. When I was a young *hombre,* I thought that by the time I reached my age I would be surrounded by and besieged by children and grandchildren. Unfortunately, not so."

Ruth felt a sudden surge of compassion for the man. He was dignified, mannerly, gracious, and bore all the hallmarks of a gentleman of refinement and intellect. But she sensed in his voice a strain of loneliness and sorrow. In an instant Don Alonzo became a figure both noble and tragic.

"I somehow had never guessed you had a family," she added with real honesty. "I suppose I assumed you were a bachelor, since no one ever mentioned relations."

Ruth wasn't sure, but she thought she heard a quiet sigh escape her host's throat.

"No, I am not a bachelor, though I must confess I am as lonely as any bachelor ever was. My wife died, you see, years ago. We had only one child, a lovely, fragile creature named Alessandra. She was Barton's mother."

"Was?"

"Sí, señora. Porque la vida es cruel y dolorosa."

Ruth guessed that Alonzo was not even aware he had lapsed into Spanish. She understood his words. *For life is cruel and sorrowful.*

Alonzo continued, "Alessandra married an American, an army officer. He was a fine, handsome man and loved my dear daughter beyond words. Oh, I had such hopes for their lives! But dear Alessandra was tubercular most of her life, and her blossom faded even as it bloomed. She finally faded away when she was only twenty-five, leaving her son, a *niño*. Her poor husband. It was as if the very heart had been torn out of him, as it was for me. For my daughter died only a few years after my wife, leaving Bart to be raised by two well-meaning but inexperienced men. How sad for the boy to have spent his childhood so cut off from the softening and sweetening forces of femininity! Then his father, too, taken from his son, killed at San Juan Hill. So you see, there are only the two of us now. Bart is the last of my line, the sole survivor of a dying breed. Even the name of Lopez y Ruiz is gone forever, though at least through Bart their blood will pass on to future generations."

Ruth thought of Alonzo's words about Bart, how his physical beauty might be more of a burden than a blessing. It was not much different with Alonzo's wealth. From the outside the master of Casa Portillo could easily be envied, for he seemed to have every advantage. Yet, as he had now revealed, his life was lonely, sad. Curious that she, living in her dirt-floored adobe shack, should have so much more. She had her children—lovely, happy, healthy children—and her husband, a man to share her life with, a man to give her his love. She suddenly felt very rich.

They reached the upstairs gallery where Anna sat quietly to one side in a deeply carved oak chair as she surveyed the crowd in the courtyard below. Alonzo was about to offer to see mother and daughter downstairs when he saw, across the court, Jonah Cutter coming up the stairs, obviously looking for his wife and daughter. Alonzo watched Ruth's face closely as Jonah approached; he studied what was to be seen and revealed there. No question, he told himself, for as Jonah approached, a light seemed to radiate from Ruth Cutter's face, subtle, yet all too clear to the perceptive observer. It was the light of love.

After Jonah had fetched the women downstairs Alonzo stood for a while on the gallery, silent and alone. Then he found himself speaking softly, almost prayerfully, to an unseen force.

"Davida, *mi querida esposa.*" Davida, my dear wife. "How many years, oh, for how many years I have loved you, have mourned you. For how many long years have I known that I can never love again. Until now. She has come to me tonight. So different from you, yet so much the same. Oh, *madre de dios,* the tragedy is that she is as far from me, as impossible for me to have, as you, dearest departed one. I think that I could love her, yet I know she can never be mine."

Don Alonzo, his face dark with love and pain, leaned against the wall of the gallery, his head against the rough surface as if listening for something.

"What am I to do?" he whispered.

The wall was cold and silent.

It was very late. The crowd at the *fiesta* had begun to thin out a bit, though the house was still crowded and noisy. Anna was alone now. Her parents were, the last she had seen of them, mingling about with Max and Kate, seeming to have a whale of a time. Hank was still upstairs asleep, and J. J. had mercifully lost himself with some of his friends, up to boy mischief, no doubt. Anna had spent some time with a group of the girls she knew from Casilla and the other farms, but she had soon grown bored with them. There was nothing really wrong with the girls she knew. It was just that there were none her age or of her temperament. The younger ones were all silly and childish, and the older ones very much taken with themselves, and silly in their own ways. Her mother often encouraged her, at times even pushed her, it seemed, to mingle more with the girls of Casilla, but Anna was just as happy spending time by herself, alone with her own thoughts.

The *fiesta* had not been an easy night for Anna. The prospect of going to a party, a real, grown-up party, had been as exciting to her as it had been to her brothers. Yet once they had arrived, Anna found herself wishing that they had never come. Or, she corrected herself, wishing that she had never come. Her brothers were having a grand time, she could tell that; they had spent the evening scampering about, J. J. with a group of boys his own age, sneaking beers from the tables, and poking into corners where they shouldn't have been. Her parents, too, were enjoying themselves; she could tell that. And it was good to see them laughing, joking, drinking. They never seemed to laugh much anymore. She was the only one who didn't seem to fit in. She didn't want to scamper around with the young ones, and they wouldn't have wanted her, either. Yet she didn't fit in with the grown-ups, either. Had she tried to hang in with them, they would have sent her off to be with the other children. She felt very lost, very lonely, as if she were visibly, conspicuously out of place in the crowd of merrymakers. Even the music of the gaily dressed *mariachis,* who had seemed so gay, so happy when they arrived, now sounded harsh and mocking. It would have been much better if she had stayed home and done embroidery. There wasn't much time for embroidery these days, with all the farm work. As she walked through the halls and rich, crowded rooms of Casa Portillo, Anna's sense of loneliness, of isolation, grew, festered, until it filled her with a deep, burning pain. With each minute her need to be away grew, until she doubted that she could bear the party one more instant. Something else boiled up inside her, too, something that confused her, troubled her, something that was more behind her anxiety than she understood: the image of Don Alonzo's grandson, standing above her on the stairs. His eyes, or rather, the memory of them, still cut into her, stirred things up in her, feelings and thoughts that

were new and frightening. Slowly, without consciously deciding
to, Anna made her way across the courtyard, toward the back
of Casa Portillo where she sensed the kitchen and back rooms
would be. Perhaps there she would find a quiet, empty room,
away from all these people who were enjoying themselves. Perhaps she would find a back door, leading out to the open land
between Casa Portillo and their farm. Her parents would know,
wouldn't they, that she had decided to go home early?

Past the dining room with its oak banquet table laiden with
silver and candles and mountains of food, she found a long
passageway that led past serving pantries and a large, low-ceil-
inged kitchen. Both rooms were busy with cooks and servants,
none of whom paid any mind to the quiet little girl walking
along the passage. Farther along the hall narrowed. The adobe
walls were scarcely wider than her shoulders; the oak-beam and
rush-mat ceiling was low and dark with age, and the tile floors
of the main rooms had given way to hard-packed clay. The
passage was deserted and lined with doors, some opened, some
padlocked shut on their rusted iron hinges. Pantries and store-
rooms, Anna guessed. Surely there would be a back entrance
here somewhere, so she could slip out into the silence of the
night air.

A sound startled her. Not a loud sound, just the quiet thud of
one object against another. Then a low, human sound. A word
or a moan. She felt frightened all of a sudden. After all, she was
wandering by herself in a strange house, in places where she
might not be wanted. Of course, she had been foolish to come
back here. Her parents and Don Alonzo would be furious and
rightly so. She stopped, stepped into a shadowed recess along
the passage. Perhaps, she thought, she might go unnoticed and
could slip back into the party, or outside, without being caught.
Long minutes, waiting quietly. No more sound from down the
passage. She eased along the corridor again, as quietly as possible, toward a large wooden door with an iron handle, which
looked as if it might lead to the outside. There seemed to be a
strong draft coming under it. Just before the door, ten feet or so
away, the corridor opened out into another passage. Anna
stepped quietly to the edge of the opening and saw that it was
an alcove, cluttered with cartons and mops and pails, all bathed
in the blue light of the moon that streamed in through a high,

wood-grilled window. At the end of the alcove two figures moved against the wall. A man and a woman. Her back was to the wall, and he faced her, pressed against her. Her arms were around him, and her hands clutched and scratched against the bare flesh of his back. In an instant, though she had never witnessed this before, Anna understood what was happening.

There was a low moan, a deep, animal kind of sound. Anna could see clearly in the moonlight that the man's face was against the woman's neck, his lips on her flesh. He moved somewhat to one side, bent to lower his head to her shoulder. As he did, Anna saw that the woman's dress was opened. Her breast, full and round, gleamed like marble; the man's hand moved freely across the blue-white flesh; his fingers toyed with the dark circle of nipple. The woman gasped at his touch, and her half-naked body twisted against his in a kind of sinuous, reptilian movement. The man turned again to get better access to the woman's flesh. As he did, his profile was fully revealed to Anna.

It was him. The dark, thick head of hair; the long, elegant nose; the strong, slightly pointed jaw above a thickly muscled neck. Anna held herself against the wall, her limbs suddenly sluggish, numb like the arms and legs of one who has just awakened from a deep sleep. Her breath became short, her heart thudded in her chest. Then a curious kind of warmth trickled slowly through Anna's body, as if the moonlight itself had turned into a warm, blue-white sea.

The woman, even as Anna watched, moved her hand down to Bart's trousers and caressed him slowly, without any hesitation. He made low, catlike sounds of pleasure as she touched him. Then she lowered herself to the floor, pulled him after her until her body lay smothered under his. She fumbled to lift her skirt and petticoats until her smooth, white flesh was exposed to him. With sure, fast movements he went into her. Her head arched back in a gesture of pleasurable pain as her hands clawed into the broad expanse of his back. Then he began a steady, rhythmic thrusting of his loins, eagerly met by an upward thrust of her own.

In Anna's mind the scene before her blended into the familiar spectacle of stallion and mare, in the fields and corrals of the farms. Coupling with that same wild, muscular intensity in the middle of the afternoon, nostrils flared, eyes inflamed, sputum flying from their gasping mouths. Anna wasn't sure how long this coupling went on before her. A few minutes, an eternity, with her frozen in flushed silence against the wall.

Then there was a wilder, more impassioned moment. The hall filled with the unmodulated sounds of animal abandon as Bart mounted her with a faster and more forceful fury. He gasped out as his body seemed to be seized with a profound spasm; at the same time the woman cried out, a high, whimpering cry that echoed into the night.

Anna, stunned by their harsh, almost brutal release, recoiled as she realized that her own hands had, without her being aware of it, found their way across her own body, sought out her own breasts and loins. She felt a tingling firmness in her nipples; her groin was inflamed, sticky with its own moisture. Frightened now by what was happening to her, she bolted toward the door, heedless of the noise, not caring about the clatter as it opened and slammed behind her. She was only glad to be outside, in the darkness behind the *hacienda*. She ran, blood still pounding in her head, across the open land toward home.

Chapter Five

THREE MONTHS AFTER THE FIESTA AT CASA PORTILLO, Ruth Cutter arrived early one morning at Wasserman Mercantile. It was a bitter, nasty January day. A storm had swept south from the Great Plains, bringing with it freezing temperatures and leaden skies that more than hinted at snow. The valley was unaccustomed to these frigid winter storms, and when they made their rare journeys through the area, Simon had noticed over the years, folks tended to stay home, bundled up in their unheated houses, rather than venturing out on errands. Simon had been fully prepared to go the entire day without seeing a single customer in his store.

He could see at once that Ruth was agitated, even though she still moved in her usual stately way; he could see it in the drawn lines of her face. It was an expression he saw in her face most of the time these days as she came in to buy a bit of food and a minimum of household supplies. There was always that moment of embarrassment when the sale was written up, adding to the ever-growing red-inked deficit in the Cutter account. Simon always reassured Ruth that he was more than happy to extend them credit during the lean winter months, that she shouldn't hesitate to charge whatever her family needed. But each time she signed the ledger book, it was clear that the increasing debt pained her to the very marrow.

Ruth was already at the counter by the time Simon had scurried down from his stepladder at one of the crowded back shelves. As he greeted her cordially—Ruth was one of his favorites among the farmers—his eye was drawn down to the counter in front of her. Three objects lay on the bare wood. Two gold rings, plain wedding bands, one larger than the other, and a brilliantly jeweled brooch of garnets and pearls clustered around a single handsome diamond.

Simon understood everything in an instant. His face was suffused with a wise, sympathetic warmth as he studied the woman who had been brought to such desperate measures.

"Dear, dear, Mrs. Cutter. It isn't necessary, this isn't. How many times I have told you, have I not, that you are welcome to credit here? Please, kindly put those back in your pocket, and tell me what you need to buy today."

"But it is necessary, Simon. We can't go on like this much longer. Running up more and more debts." There was more pain, more vulnerability in Ruth's voice than Simon had ever heard before. How desperate they must be, he thought.

"It isn't just you, Simon," she continued. "We have other bills, at Ola's, the smith's. And now we have to get enough cash to try to get another crop in this spring. It's bad enough that we've been borrowing from you to have food to eat. We can't borrow to buy seed and tools too. No, please, I'd rather get this over with, get a fresh start this season."

Simon had often wondered if the Cutters, given their situation, would pull up and leave Casilla. He was secretly very pleased to hear that they were going to try to stick it out.

"Does Jonah know you are doing this?"

Ruth nodded yes. Simon asked himself why it was not Jonah who had come to the store to sell the jewelry, but he knew the answer to that at the same time. He picked up the two rings, looked at them briefly but with a sharp eye, weighed them in his palm.

"I must be honest," he said to her. "The gold rings I can use. Gold is gold—it always has bullion value, easily sold. I can take these, weigh them exactly on a little scale I have in back and probably erase your debt and give you a small credit, to get started with."

Simon exaggerated. The two rings were worth perhaps a quarter of the Cutters' debt to him, but Ruth never need know that. He almost reverentially reached down and picked up the brooch. He instinctively knew that it was a very good piece and probably a very old one, perhaps even eighteenth-century. None of the stones was especially large, but they all were of beautiful hue and perfectly matched and set in a fine lacy filigree of silver.

"Now this is a different matter. This is valuable, worth more than I can afford to pay you. Five hundred, maybe more, I'd guess. Certainly it will bring enough to finance your next season of farming. But this is not for Simon to buy—I do not collect jewels, nor can I sell them easily."

"That's really quite a lot, Simon!"

When Ruth spoke, her voice was excited, anxious. It was clear that the value of the brooch was more than expected. If she was forced to part with it, at least the cash it brought would be enough to really help them through the next season on the farm.

"Can you tell me . . . where to go? El Paso, perhaps? There must be jewelry stores, even . . . pawnshops who would want something like this."

Simon screwed his leathery face into a prunish configuration as he thought.

"Yes, yes, perhaps. Though old Simon's afraid places like that may take advantage of your need to sell fast. Most people are greedy, you know. I have a better suggestion, so I think. You should sell this lovely object to a collector, to someone who loves beauty, fine craftsmanship. Someone who will give you a fair price."

Ruth looked at Simon, her gray eyes dark in thought as she waited for his conclusion.

"Don Alonzo."

Ruth was struck by Wasserman's suggestion. It made sense, of course, since Alonzo was wealthy and an avid collector. That was what struck her—that she had not thought of it herself. She remembered Don Alonzo's words that night at the *fiesta,* his offer of help. She remembered, too, Jonah's childish, angry reaction to Alonzo's words. Perhaps that was why she had blotted out Alonzo as a possibility for buying the brooch. There was another reason, too, lurking under the surface, a reason Ruth could only half acknowledge: the embarrassment of the whole situation. She had endured enough these last months, running up bigger and bigger bills with Wasserman. He already knew her situation; perhaps that was why she could bring herself to offer him the rings and brooch. But to call on Alonzo was to reveal the terrible truth: that she and her family were destitute. A pawnshop, a jewelry dealing in secondhand goods, that was more acceptable to her because at least those people would be strangers who had never seen and would never see Ruth Cutter again.

"I don't think I should." She stared down at the counter as she spoke, avoiding Simon's eyes. Her voice was thick with hesitancy.

"Dear lady, forgive my busybody, old-man's ways, but I think you should, you must. You are doing this to make money, so don't go to someplace where you will get half of what this brooch is worth."

"It's my pride, I suppose," she whispered, with a faint smile of self-recognition. Simon saw that there were tears in her eyes.

"Old Simon learned many years ago that there are times when pride is the biggest luxury in the world. This is one of those times, Ruth. Go to Alonzo, sell him the brooch, and by doing so, do the best for your family, your farm. He will treasure it, I'm sure, for it is very beautiful."

Ruth nodded meekly as she took the brooch and put it back in her dress pocket.

"I'll go see him today."

Simon added a few words of approval as he took Ruth's shopping list and began filling it out. A few minutes later, as she left with her parcel, she turned to Simon and spoke without really understanding why she did.

"If you don't mind, Simon, would you not mention to Jonah that I'm going to see Alonzo? I think it's just as well he thinks I sold everything to you."

"Of course, of course." He nodded, understanding more of what was behind Ruth's words than she did.

Ruth returned to the farm before noon, feeling enormously relieved that her difficult morning was over. Once she had forced herself to go to Wasserman and to Don Alonzo, letting go of the jewelry had been easier than she had expected. She knew that was due in no small part to the fact that her account at the mercantile was paid and now carried a small credit, and that her small needlepoint bag bulged with six hundred dollars from Don Alonzo, enough to comfortably see the Cutters through to the next harvest, provided they were careful about where every cent was spent.

It was clear that Alonzo was surprised by her visit, but he was consummately well mannered. She told him straightaway that she needed to sell the brooch to finance the coming year, and he, to her gratitude, did not ask any further questions. When she showed him the brooch, he said, "But, *señora,* this is a very fine piece. Early- to mid-eighteenth century, I would guess, and probably French workmanship. Not an easy task to part with something so beautiful."

She volunteered the history of the pin. How her grandmother's grandmother, before the Revolution, had lived on a plantation in tidewater Virginia, the only daughter of a prominent, landed family. How the young girl had met and fallen in love with a handsome, titled British officer garrisoned in the Colonies. Their courtship led to an engagement, and she was destined, so it seemed, to be a titled woman, living on an ancient estate in Yorkshire. But the Revolution intervened: her family were ardent patriots, and her groom-to-be a Tory officer. The marriage was forbidden by her father, and once the Revolution began in earnest, she never saw her lover again. After he was killed at Yorktown she had only her memories of him and the fine brooch she had been given as an engagement gift.

"A lovely story, and I suspect every word true," Alonzo

commented after the tale was finished. "Certainly a piece this fine could only have come from a family of means. So it has been passed down for over a century in the female line. *Qué lástima! Señora,* it must be difficult to part with this."

Ruth nodded. "Difficult but necessary. And for the best, I suppose. I don't lead the kind of life that needs jewels like this. Better that the money go toward something more important and practical."

Ruth meant what she had said, but there was still that sense of having lost something special, something magical that had been a part of her life since she was a girl.

"I will treasure it always," Alonzo said as he got up from his desk to go to his wall safe. "And I will also watch with pleasure the great rewards you will reap from this sacrifice as your farm becomes more and more fruitful."

And to himself he added, *And I will treasure this memento of you, Ruth Cutter. Because it has been so loved by you, so it will be loved by me.*

Once again, before she left, Ruth felt an instinctive urge to ask Alonzo not to mention that he had bought the brooch. Somehow, for reasons she couldn't quite understand, she knew Jonah would not be pleased by her meeting with Alonzo. So, when she got back to the farm and found Jonah sitting out the sharp chill of the winter air wrapped in quilts and blankets, she merely said, "It's done, darling, all finished. And Simon gave us a very good price for everything."

"How much?"

"Seven hundred dollars. One hundred on account; the rest I have in silver and gold coins."

"Hot diggety, Ruthie! We're back in the farming business!" Jonah leapt up, throwing off his covers, and did a little jig around the cold room in his long johns. The dance finished with an enthusiastic hug and kiss for his wife. Jonah's enthusiasm lifted Ruth's spirits, for she had not seen him in such a good mood, so much like his old self, since they had lost the crop. She saw that familiar bright light in his blue eyes, a light as bright as that of any jewels.

"We're going to make this one, Ruthie. I can feel it in my bones. It's going to be a damned beauty of a crop. Tall and green, just falling down with them fluffy white cotton bolls. No rain, no hail, just sunshine and a mountain of baled cotton come next October!"

Jonah disengaged himself from her arms and went to the corner chair where his clothes lay in a heap. He began dressing hurriedly, with as much enthusiasm as he had shown in dancing around the room.

"Wait till old Max hears the good news, just you wait. The old fellow's been worried that we was going to pull up and leave, just give it all up. He ain't said nothing, but I can see it in his eyes. Yes, sir, he'll be pleased as hell to hear we're going to be around from now on."

Jonah was dressed and booted in seconds, at the door where his sheepskin coat and wool scarf hung on hooks. He was breathing deeply from his exertions, and wisps of frosty mist were exhaled with every breath. His eyes flashed with childlike excitement.

"You won't be needing the wagon for a while, will you? The kids have a ride back from school with Pettus, don't they? I think this calls for a celebration—I want to take old Max over to Alamo Alto for a drink. Sort of to thank him for all his help."

Ruth was silent, hurt by her husband's insensitivity. First he had cajoled her into going by herself to sell the jewelry, since "I'm no good at that kind of thing," as he'd put it. Now that she was back and they were both feeling in high spirits because of their newly gained money, Ruth wanted to spend the afternoon with Jonah, just the two of them while the children were at school. Together they could sit down, plan the year, budget the money to the best advantage. It seemed so childish, so frivolous of Jonah to go off now, in the middle of the day, to have a few drinks; she even doubted if Max really would join Jonah at the saloon; that was not his style.

Jonah sensed her wounded feelings.

"Aw, come on, Ruthie, don't look so down-faced. I'll just be gone for a few hours. I got nothing better to do this afternoon, anyway. Remember, in a couple of weeks, once we get back into the fields, I'll be working sunup to sunset. This is my last chance to have a little fun."

She did not resist him but gave him a kiss and told him not to stay out too late, not to get Max too drunk. After he had gone, though, as she sat down to go over the stack of bills and lists that had accumulated in the drawer of the table, her anger began to burn in a small but white-hot core deep in her belly. It was anger, not at Jonah but at herself, and her inability to say no to him. She began to loathe this weakness in herself, yet she knew that she could never change it. She could deny him nothing.

"Aw, come on, Max. Don't be such an old woman. You can't be that goddamned busy."

Max couldn't help but grin at Jonah's insistence. The man was determined to go out and tie one on.

"Well, I am that damned busy. The skunks dug under the fence in the chicken coop and killed two hens last night. Awful mess of feathers, and that hole to fill in. And all the harnesses are getting dried out and stiff from this cold. Got to saddle-soap and oil them before they start cracking. Still, Cutter, I'm right glad you got the dough to put in another crop, and I'll sure as hell let you buy me a round Saturday afternoon."

When Jonah had gotten to the Mirkovsky farm, he had found Max in the large toolshed workroom, bundled against the cold, as he cut a length of chicken wire rolled out on his worktable.

"Can't blame a fellow for wanting to celebrate, can you?" Jonah offered with a logic that couldn't be faulted. "I can feel it in my bones: Cutter's farm is going to have one bang-up season. If it hadn't been for that damned storm last year, we would have done it. Now there's nothing going to stop me."

Max thought of several things that might have stopped Jonah's successful crop—hailstorms, floods, laziness, Jonah's foolishness—but he kept his thought to himself and offered only encouragement.

"No question, Jonah, you'll pull in a bale and a half, easy, if you don't have any problems you're not counting on. It's good land you've got over there, and you and Ruth have done a good job of it. After last year I'm sure you'll make a fine comeback."

"And a hell of a little profit, too, buddy."

"Making it big on that farm means the whole world to you, don't it, Cutter?"

"It's the future, Max," Jonah answered a bit pompously. "Sure, we're small now, just getting a foothold, but it's just the beginning. I'm going to do big things with that place of mine. Hell, in ten years we'll be living in a *hacienda* three times the size of Casa Portillo, just sitting there giving orders to a whole crew of foremen."

Max couldn't help but grin at Cutter's wild, and, to his mind, unrealistic picture of the future, but he held his face down so Jonah wouldn't see his amusement. He knew his friend well enough now to know that he needed enormous amounts of encouragement but didn't take well to criticism or disagreement. Still, Max felt he had to caution.

"I got to admire your enthusiasm, Jonah. Always have. You're a bit reckless, going after something like this farm that you knew next to nothing about before you started. Kind of like a pup going after a porcupine when he's never seen one before. Just don't get too big for your britches. You got big ideas but a little farm. You lost one crop, nearly did you in. You got a second chance now, but you'd better not count your chickens or weigh your cotton, before you've plowed your first acre."

Jonah shot a sharp look at Max. It was clear that he didn't like the drift of the conversation.

"Too big for my britches, huh? I got to think big, got to outgrow these britches. Otherwise I'll never get anywhere."

Max realized he had hit a raw nerve. He eased up a bit.

"Jonah, there ain't nothing wrong with having dreams. Thinking about making the big time, striking it rich. I guess we all got a bit of that rattling around in us somewheres. Just don't let yourself be a duck in a shooting gallery, always setting yourself up just to get shot down again. Look at Kate and me. We been here a lot longer than you and Ruth. Built ourselves up a good little farm. But we're still working our asses off and don't do much more than make a decent living out of it."

Jonah was silent for a moment after Max's speech. When he finally spoke, there was a vulnerability and an honesty in his voice that Max had never seen before.

"I'm thirty-seven years old, Max. I been poor all my life. Never had nothing as a kid or even after I growed up. What little comfort I had—a decent house, nice furnishings, a bit of savings—was all because of Ruth and what she got from her folks. Don't you see, Max? This farm is my last chance. My last chance to be something besides an illiterate wagon driver who married the schoolteacher. Something besides a clerk in a mercantile. Damn it, Max, I'm tired of being nobody."

"You are somebody. Jonah Cutter."

"Yeah! And that don't amount to a hill of beans, if a man don't have something for himself. Hell, I can't even keep this place going without having to sell our wedding rings and my wife's jewelry. I can just imagine what folks say about me."

Max shook his head at Jonah's false ambition and pride. The damn fool should have considered himself· lucky—no, more than lucky—*blessed* to have Ruth, to have her support, her devotion. Yet Max sensed that Ruth's help was a thorn in Jonah's side.

"Don't worry about what folks say, Cutter. Just go about your business." Max broke the mood with a brotherly clap on the shoulder, afraid that if they continued the conversation, he would tell Jonah some things he didn't want to hear. Things about what the future might hold.

Jonah grinned. His face showed no trace of the seriousness that had escaped for a few minutes.

"Well, Max, buddy, this farmer's getting on about his business of having a drink at the Red Star. If you're hide-bound and determined to work yourself to death, then I'll have a drink for you. And I heard from one of the rail men that there's going to be a little private party there tonight. I'll have a little something for you there too."

Jonah's grin twisted into the slightest hint of a leer as he hurried out of the shed to his wagon. Max went back to his work, feeling sad and discouraged.

In the boarder's room behind the Red Star Café, Jonah Cutter, like the other five men clustered around the table in shirtsleeves and suspenders, did not have his mind on poker.

"Where the hell is that bastard?" Mickey Hutchinson complained as he folded his hand and went to the window that looked out onto the empty lot next to the café.

"Hell, he probably had to go all the way to Mexico City to find a clean one." Another of the railroaders snickered from the table.

Jonah asked to be hit twice and chewed nervously on his

cigar, a good Havana brought by one of the train men from Houston.

"What's the matter, Cutter? Cat got your tongue? Or just scared of taking something home to your old lady."

"Shit, no. I know how to take precautions," Jonah shot back with a distinct slur in his speech. "I'm just pissed as hell at Mirkovsky. That son of a bitch is a goddamned old maid, if you ask me."

The others laughed.

"He sure gave you a hard time, that's for damned sure, telling you you ought to be home with the family seeing as how it's only a day or two until you start spring planting."

It had been less than half an hour since Max had unexpectedly knocked on the door, looking for Jonah. He had pulled Jonah outside and urged him as strongly as he could to go home to Ruth instead of drinking and whoring with the railroaders. He had left in something of a huff when Jonah had firmly and loudly rebuffed his advice.

"For Christ's sake, fellas, I got six months of ball-busting ahead of me once we plant, working up a sweat every goddamn day. I'm sure as hell going to work me up a good sweat tonight, just to get in practice."

More laughter and a few questions to the lookout at the window for any signs of arrival.

"Aw, Max's okay. Just a hardworking son of a bitch, not much one to have fun," one of the card players said in defense of the subject of conversation. "Though given the way that mousy little wife of his looks, you'd think he'd be the last one to leave here tonight."

In spite of the whiskey and the unbuttoned atmosphere, Jonah began to feel a little self-conscious about all the put-downs aimed at Max. After all, though he was sometimes parental, Max had been a good friend to Jonah since he'd been in Casilla. He had not only taught Jonah a lot of what he knew about farming but had put in many hours of work on the Cutter place himself.

"Old Max, now, he claims he taught me every last thing there is to know about cotton farming," Jonah explained, disguising Max's real help in a half-truth. "He's such a nervous nellie about my farming because he figures that if I don't make a decent crop two seasons in a row, it shows him up in a bad light. Hell, I brought in a hundred twenty bales last year. I can easy beat that without missing a card game this year."

"Shhh!" Hutchinson's voice silenced the poker players. "He's out there and not alone."

The man at the window suppressed a giggle.

In a few seconds, as the hand in progress was quickly brought to an end, the door leading outside opened, and another of the railroad men appeared with a young Mexican girl at his side.

"It's about time, goddammit."

"What'd you do, stop off for a little tryout before you got here?"

"Keep it down, you bastards. Ola'd have our hides if she knew we was bringing whores in her rooms."

The girl and her procurer stepped inside. Even through the haze of cigar and cigarette smoke it was easy to tell that she was young, pretty, and full-bodied. She looked young and innocent, until she smiled. A hard, artificial smile, designed to titillate the customers. Her olive-complexioned cheeks were rouged; her lips as well.

She pulled back her shawl to reveal a full-breasted body underneath a thin blouse already opened halfway down. With a snicker of delight Hutchinson reached over and undid the last two buttons.

She didn't resist.

He pulled open her blouse to reveal her tawny, dark-nippled breasts. His white hand cupped the heavy flesh, squeezed the nipple between thumb and forefinger.

"All right, men, who dropped the most tonight?"

"I did," Jonah said amid a few false claims muttered in jest.

"All right, buddy. Here's the consolation prize!"

Still that hungry, artificial smile on her face.

"Come here, honey," Jonah said as he leaned back and patted his thigh. "Get your hot little taco over here. I got a yen for some Mexican food tonight."

Amid the urgings and teasing of the others she moved toward Jonah. In their enthusiasm for what they were about to see, they didn't notice that she had lost her smile—the seductive mask she had worn before had changed to a look of sullen, angry boredom. And in their enthusiasm the men did not notice a change in Jonah Cutter's face as well. The fraternal, high-spirited, sexed-up spirit in his face was gone. It had happened, unnoticed by all but Jonah, when he had touched the girl's flesh, the first time he had touched a woman besides Ruth in a sexual way since he had married. The girl was pretty, her flesh warm and exciting, and the men egged him on to his task. And why not? he asked himself. Most of the others in the room had wives somewhere; most men were unfaithful. There was no reason why he shouldn't do what seemed to come naturally to men. But the image of Ruth's body, the remembrance of it forced itself on Jonah as he caressed the young whore. He wanted the Mexican girl, wanted to take her forcefully, anonymously, in the hot, smoky room as the other men watched. He needed the thrill, the admiration, his performance would bring him. It had been so long since he had felt proud, cocky. But he knew that, even as he went on with his performance, that Ruth's eyes would be on him just as surely as the men's were.

Ruth lay awake, listening to the sound of the storm. The snow that the day's clouds and chill had promised had arrived instead as a hard, driving sleet; the heavy-oiled paper that covered the windows bowed and flexed under the onslaught of the wind-driven ice. Max had left over an hour ago, looking sad and embarrassed. But she was glad he had come by. At least she knew Jonah was safe, playing cards in town. She was at least spared a night of worrying that Jonah was hurt or trapped out somewhere in the freezing weather. That was a relief, true, but no consolation. Once again the pillow next to her, where Jonah's head should have lain sleeping, was moistened with her tears.

Chapter Six

ANNA WAS FEELING IN HIGH SPIRITS AS SHE WALKED along the dusty white road toward Casa Portillo. It was a fine May day, clear and warm, fragrant with the smell of newly irrigated cotton fields that stretched out on either side of the road. Mrs. Grice, in an unexpected gesture of generosity, had let class out early, to let her charges go out and enjoy the fine afternoon. For Anna, like most of the schoolchildren of Casilla, a weekday afternoon free was a special treat, since, as the weeks moved into high season, Saturdays and often Sundays were taken up with long days of farm work. She had walked her brothers as far as the turnoff to their farm, then gone on toward Casa Portillo. Earlier in the week, after school, she had gone to the *hacienda* for the first time by herself, to accept Don Alonzo's invitation of riding lessons. The unexpected offer had come a few weeks before in the form of a letter from him to her parents, in which Alonzo explained that for any farm child, an ability to ride and handle farm animals was an important one; he had a groom, named Paco, who was a skilled horseman and who would gladly teach riding to Anna and her brothers in turn as they reached the right age, as he had done for many other farm children in Casilla in years past. When Anna heard of the offer, she had shown an excited enthusiasm beyond her usual, rather quiet self, making it clear to Ruth and Jonah that the prospect was thrilling to her. Anna had seen at once that her mother was reluctant, and her father dead set against it, and she found herself begging and pleading with all the energy her fourteen-year-old self could muster. A few days later her mother gave permission. As thrilled as she was about the outcome of the episode, Anna sensed an all-too-familiar tension in the house, and she guessed that her parents had argued long and

hard over the issue. She had felt badly about causing trouble
between her parents at first, then reminded herself that there
seemed to be trouble over everything these days, as far as they
were concerned. But she, at least, could learn to ride; she could
spend lovely hours alone with a handsome animal, riding
through the deserted fields and along the shady riverbanks. It
would be glorious, to be away from schoolrooms and chores,
little brothers, and her parents' arguments.

Anna went directly to the stables, a low, sprawling adobe
building that stood about two hundred feet east of the main
house. She hurried across the open, well-packed expanse of the
mud-walled corral, empty save for a few wandering chickens
and scattered pads of manure.

"Paco! *Dónde estas?*" she called out as she went through the
dark archway leading into the tack room. She knew she didn't
really have to call out—Paco was always in the stable. But she
felt she should at least warn him that she had arrived.

"He's up at the house," a voice boomed out from the hay-
and leather-perfumed shadows of the tack room. "Who's
there?"

A figure stepped out of the shadows, caught in the sunlight
that fell through the arch in a bright beam.

It was Bart Bradley.

He was half naked, stripped to the waist. He held a bridle in
one hand, a wax-soaked rag in the other. His torso, thick and
taut with muscle, was covered by a thick mat of black hair; skin
and hair both glistened with a sweaty sheen.

"Oh, hello," he said when he saw her. "You'll have to forgive
my appearance. I wasn't expecting company." He grinned un-
selfconsciously. There was no hint of embarrassment at her seeing his body so exposed and no hint of asking forgiveness. Anna
once again found herself riveted in his presence. She knew she
had to say something; she couldn't make a fool of herself once
again by being struck dumb at the very sight of him. Fortunately Bart leapt into the void.

"Come on in," he offered in a casual, offhand voice. "Paco
will be back in a few minutes." He moved as if to turn and go
back into the tack room, then stopped himself and narrowed his
eyes a bit as he studied Anna's face.

"I know you, don't I?"

She stared at him, helpless, and managed a nod.

"Of course, from the *fiesta* last fall. On the stairs with your mother."

She nodded again, despairing of ever saying a word to the man.

"You've changed."

Bart remembered more clearly now the shy, rather unhappy-looking girl at the party, awkward in her little-girl party frock that she even then had outgrown. She seemed much more comfortable, much more herself now, in a loose cotton blouse and a pair of well-worn denim pants. But it wasn't just the change of costume he noticed. It was the breasts, firm and full under the blouse, and the elegant curve of waist and hip. A lot could happen in half a year. The adolescent awkwardness and shyness that had been so amusing on the stairs at the party was no longer awkward or adolescent. The shyness was still there, but it was more than a little attractive. His eyes, which had been on her the whole time, became more intent on her, and more calculating.

"I've got to confess that I don't remember your name. I'm terrible on names."

"Anna."

Bart started to tease her about the fact that she had finally said something to him, but he thought better of it. He remembered now that the same thing had happened to him at the party. It wasn't that this Anna was merely attractive or sexy. He could easily imagine putting his hand on her neck, running his hand down her chest to touch her breasts. Oh, yes, he could very easily imagine that. Her pale, firm young flesh, ripe, virginal. But he could imagine that with many girls he saw; he had done it with more than a few. This was different, though, a sensation he couldn't quite put his finger on. She attracted him, but she unnerved him too. Something strange, intense, coming out of those deep, serious gray eyes.

"Do you want to wait here for Paco, or can I help you with something?" Bart found himself thinking how nice it would be if Anna did stay awhile, if Paco didn't show up for an hour or two.

Anna began to stammer, then, by sheer will, forced herself to speak slowly and smoothly. She couldn't let herself seem any more of a fool in front of this man.

"I—I think I should wait. Paco is going to teach me how to ride horseback. Don Alonzo said he could."

"I don't approve."

His words, spoken with a naughty grin, took Anna aback. Once again she felt profoundly uncomfortable in Bart's presence. He turned, slung the harness over a broad, sweaty shoulder, and began walking slowly back into the depths of the tack room. As he turned he added, "At least I don't approve of Paco giving you lessons when I'm around. He's a good stable hand and knows a lot about horses. But he can't hold a candle to me in that department."

When Bart realized that Anna was not following him, he stopped again, motioned for her to come after him.

"Come on, Anna, don't be so shy about everything. Or didn't you get my point—I'm going to give you your riding lesson today."

It was cool and fragrant near the river. The afternoon was still warm and windless, and the sun, lowering bit by bit in the sky, had begun to play games of flickering light and shadow among the pale green leaves of the towering cottonwoods, to the rasping accompaniment of the millions of locusts hidden in the grass and brush. Anna had been out with Bart for over an hour now, riding along the chalky white ribbon of the river road. In Anna's mind, however, the beauty of the afternoon was gone; the lovely scene along the river was obscured, as if seen through a dark gray lens. What a fool she had been to let herself be taken out riding with Bart! She should have said no the minute he mentioned the idea, only she had been too tongue-tied, too confused to say much of anything. It had been great fun the day before, when Paco had begun showing her the rudiments of saddling and bridling, familiarizing her with horses and stables, riding gear and grooming. She had looked forward so to this afternoon, her first real time out on horseback, all the more wonderful because of the long afternoon after the early recess. Now it was all ruined by Bart. He had been nice to her, she knew that, friendly, charming, and polite in that arrogant, teasing sort of way he had about him. And there was no doubt that he was an expert horseman and knew how to convey his knowledge to his pupil. Anna even knew that, had they known, every other girl in Casilla would have been wildly jealous that she had spent an afternoon with the handsome young officer. Yet, for Anna, every moment had been agony. Even as Bart had guided her carefully through the rudiments of horsemanship, posture, balance, the feel and handling of the animal, her mind had been flooded with images of Bart on the night of the *fiesta*. The movements of his body, fully clothed now, reawakened the images of his body, awash in the blue-gray moonlight, as it flexed and coiled in its couplings with the woman. She tried desperately to blot out the images, but her efforts were futile. He was too close, his presence too overwhelming. Though he wore a shirt now, the loose drape of the cotton cloth as he moved and gestured only reminded her of the movements of his arms, his muscled torso, as he had caressed and mounted her that night; the outline of his thighs and hips through the fabric of his trousers echoed the images of his naked legs, his aroused manhood. Anna felt almost criminal because of her intimate knowledge of his body. There was a certain shame in her memories of it, and a hot flush of the forbidden.

Eventually they came to a place almost two miles downriver from Casa Portillo, a quiet, deserted place, beyond the civilized area of farms. Bart suggested a short rest beneath the trees before the ride back to the *hacienda* and chose a spot where salt grass, newly green, spread an inviting carpet beneath the trees. Bart dismounted and quickly threw himself down, legs outstretched, arms behind his head, while Anna followed a bit behind and, not knowing what to do, finally sat on the grass a few feet from him. The horses, oblivious to their human concerns, munched a bit of grass, then helped themselves to a drink of muddy river water. Anna plucked a strand of grass and began poking it among the other blades, desperate for something to distract her. She avoided looking at him, in hopes that would help clear her mind. She sensed that he was looking up into the canopy of the trees, probably wishing that he had not committed the folly of bringing a silly girl out for the afternoon.

"You did really well this afternoon, Anna. Are you sure you haven't ridden before?" Bart's tone was natural, easy, his eyes focused above him.

"Just a few minutes yesterday, at the stable with Paco. And my brothers and I have jumped up on our mule a few times, bareback, but we could never get him to go anywhere."

Bart leaned up on one elbow. His eyes, green and gold, the colors of the afternoon light, caught hers, held them in their hypnotic gaze. He smiled a bit, but it seemed to Anna to be a genuine smile, not that mocking smile he so often showed.

"Well, then, you must be a natural rider. You're comfortable, seem to have a sense of how to handle the animal. It's clear you're not afraid of horses. That's good—they can smell the fear. They always say, too, that women understand horses better than men, have a better rapport with them. Maybe it's true, though I've seen women who were total ninnies within ten feet of a piece of horseflesh. Not you, though."

Anna wondered if he could smell her fear, her nervousness. It seemed to her to be radiating out of her like a dense fog. She didn't know what to answer to his compliments. Words were still hard with him.

"I'm kind of sorry I'm not going to be around to watch your progress. I suspect you might even take well to English saddle, even jumping."

Anna felt a pang at his words. He was so damnably arrogant. Taking for granted that everyone had the luxury of time and means to pursue rich men's sports, to own expensive full-breed horses and high-priced equipment. She, who lived in a house with dirt floors, who could only ride because his grandfather had offered the use of a horse and saddle. Perhaps he was just baiting her, trying to make her feel bad. Still, she realized, he had said he was sorry he couldn't watch her progress. She despaired of making any sense of him, of the afternoon, of her feelings.

There was a bit of silence, broken only by the locusts and the faint murmur of the river. Finally she spoke, both because she felt she should try at least some conversation and because she was curious. Though she wished she were not with him right now, something disturbed her at the thought of him going far from Casilla.

"Are you going away? I thought—at least Kate Mirkovsky said—that you had been assigned to Fort Bliss. At least she said you would be there after you graduate the academy next month."

"That's what I'd like, of course. That's in part why I came home on leave, to try to pull some strings to get myself assigned to Bliss. After all, El Paso is my hometown. I even have a house there, my father's house, that I inherited when he died. And I'd like to be close to grandfather and Casilla. I spent a lot of time here when I was a boy. I love this place."

Anna saw and heard a different Bart as he spoke about his family, his home, Casilla. He was gentle, warm, genuine.

"But, darn it, the army doesn't give a tinker's damn about those kinds of considerations. The greater good of the army and the nation is what they worship, and as the cream of the military crop, I'm expected to follow suit. So now it looks like I'm to be garrisoned at the Presidio in San Francisco starting in June. There's one hope, though. That mess in Mexico is really heating up now. Villa and Carranza are pretty much doing what they please in the whole north, and I suspect Washington's going to beef up the cavalry along the border, just in case the *revolucionarios* get too big for their britches. If that's the case, especially since I'm half Mexican and speak the language and know the country, I stand a good chance of getting assigned here. But I can't count on that. You'll probably have a hubby and several kids by the time I get back to the valley."

Anna did not understand why, but his suggestion of her having a family seemed lewd somehow. Like most girls her age, she had pictured herself settled and happy with a husband and children, but when Bart conjured up the scene, it was shot through with images of the animal coupling she had witnessed at the *fiesta*.

"I'm too young to think about that," she managed to say.

Bart lifted himself upright. He was suddenly much closer to her, and she had to look up to see his face.

"How old are you?" The warm smile that had been on his face faded, and the light in his eyes deepened, intensified. Once again Anna felt an uncomfortable flush, smelled the musky, masculine fragrance of his body. Her eyes darted down to the green carpet of grass, though she knew his still drilled into her. The images came back, his nakedness, his movements.

"Fifteen," she lied. She was still almost a month from her fifteenth birthday.

"That isn't so young. Though, truth is, you look older. I thought you were nearer seventeen. You're certainly more of a woman than a girl, at least to my eyes. 'Sides, there are plenty of women who get married at fifteen or sixteen. Plenty."

Anna riveted her gaze on the ground as she fought an intense desire to bolt and run. There was something nasty and calculated in his voice. Again and again the images of his naked body flashed in her mind with a rhythmic, thrusting pulse, like the throbbing, animalistic pull of his loins.

"Look at me, Anna."

It was a command. She felt compelled to obey.

"Have you ever been kissed by a man?"

She flushed crimson at the humiliating question. What did he want from her? Did he want her to tell him there had been boys who had flirted with her, pressed their lips against her cheeks, her mouth? She was stunned, immobile, like a terrified jackrabbit held in the ruthless claws of a predatory hawk.

"Never mind," he said with a grin. "You haven't been kissed by me." With one hand he reached out and easily pulled her up to him in a sure, viselike grip. His lips were on hers, moist, hot, somehow hard and yielding at the same time. His breath streamed across her face; his tongue probed her mouth. She tried to pull away, but his hands and lips immobilized her. Her body would not obey her commands. He pulled her closer, until she felt the hard contours of his chest against her breasts. Then, somehow, she knew that the ground was beneath her back and the vast weight of him half on top of her. One arm held her tight while the other caressed her waist, her hip, her thigh. She felt her body trembling as he touched her. She could not resist him. Then, as his hand moved up to her breast, the trembling exploded into something else, something new and powerful. She felt a deep ache in her breasts, tightness in her nipples; her groin, with his thigh pressed hard against it, felt moist and hot. She felt a need to move against him, to give in to him.

It was a terrifying feeling. She understood now what that girl had felt that night at Casa Portillo. There had been this deep, moist fire of arousal burning in her, just as it was now burning inside Anna. So this was the secret that adults carried with them, this fire that bonded man to woman. She knew now how easy, how very easy, it would be to give herself to him, just as that woman had. Her physical body was already in his power; only a tiny kernel of her mind resisted the force of arousal. She moaned at the pleasure of his body against hers.

Then something deep in Anna rebelled, cried, "No." She was frightened, frightened of being that woman in the dark of the hallway, frightened of what it meant to give herself to a man. She jerked, writhed, somehow pulled away from him, and managed to get to her feet, gasping, her arousal turned to anger and fright. Bart, his face flushed with excitement, sat halfway up, his eyes full of anticipation. Their green-gold fire beckoned her to come back down to him. She tore away from his gaze and ran, crying, toward the waiting horses. She could not look at him again, for she knew if she did, she would be his.

The encounter between Bart and Anna that afternoon under the cottonwoods remained their secret. The next day Anna was back in the schoolroom, passing the hours in exactly the kind of routine that filled most of her hours, while Bart was in his barracks at Fort Bliss, packing his trunk for transport to his new assignment in San Francisco. Outwardly nothing had changed in their lives. Perhaps Anna seemed a bit distracted and dreamy to her family and friends, but after all, it was spring. Perhaps Bart was a bit withdrawn and preoccupied, but he was embarking on the first major assignment of his military career, and it was understandable that the young soldier would not be himself.

For Anna, that afternoon marked her entry into the world of adulthood, the world of grown-up passions and pains. Bart's kiss had awakened the dormant form of womanhood that lies sleeping in every girl, and though Anna had run away from the frightening new creature that had risen within her, the creature was still awake, still stirring. She would never see the world in the same way after Bart had touched her; she would never feel life in the same way. She had felt that afternoon the first flicker of a woman's desires and a woman's love, and everything was changed after that.

Bart, too, found something new in himself that day. At his proud young age he considered himself a worldly, accomplished cocksman. He had intended that the dark-haired girl who met him in the stable would be nothing more than another of his conquests, a mere afternoon diversion. Yet something had happened with Anna, something he would least have expected from a mere girl. Though she did not give in to him, she aroused a new and strange emotion in Bart. It was an emotion grounded in a physical attraction but which went beyond it, which rose above it. It was a deep feeling, disturbing yet exciting. He did not want to label the feeling, for to label it might be to destroy it. Yet he knew the word, even though he could not admit it to himself: it was love.

Other matters were soon to occupy Anna's waking and sleeping hours, diminishing the time she had free to agonize over her confused feelings about Bart. Four hundred miles to the north, in the high, pine-covered mountains that sit astride the border of Colorado and New Mexico, it began to rain. It was a soft, gentle rain, the kind that often falls in the high western mountains in spring, nourishing the soaring pines and the high, grassy meadows. As the life-giving water fell from the sky, it fell upon the long-needled pines and the soft meadow grass, dotted with wild flowers. The rain that wasn't taken in by thirsty nature ran onto the soil, down gentle mountain slopes; it gathered, drop by drop, into tiny rivulets that trickled into dry brooks. Now gaining new life, the brooks bubbled down hillsides and into creeks, rocky and broken as they cut down mountainsides. The creeks roared merrily, their courses so seldom as full as they were now, and willingly carried their gift of water out of the high mountains and down into the dry, gully-washed desert below. The gullies, in turn, played their part, and the rains that had fallen on the fragrant pines five thousand feet above were carried, now brown with sand and clay, into the Rio Grande.

The rains that began in Colorado that night as Anna slept four hundred miles south under a clear spring sky, continued for a second day and a third and a fourth. On the fifth day the keeper on the bridge that spanned the river between El Paso and Juarez noticed that the level of the muddy water was up but paid little attention: the river was only dangerous in the early spring when the snows in the headwaters melted and were carried down the river, or if the desert around the valley itself were struck by severe thunderstorms, when flash floods quickly filled the arroyos branching out from the river as it moved south. But it was a sunny day—no thunderstorms in sight, and the spring runoff had come and gone a month before.

On the fifth day Jonah went down to the river early in the morning to open the wóoden sluice gates that let the river water flow into the lateral ditch alongside his fields, where the siphon hoses would pull the water over the low dikes and into the furrows. He noticed the rise in the river but didn't think much about it. The river had been lower than usual the last two weeks, and at the last irrigation, the water level had barely been high enough to fill the bottom of the ditch. In places he had had to hoe out deep spots in the ditch to make places deep enough to cover the siphon tubes. Today, the sight of the muddy brown water coursing to the brim of the ditch was a welcome sight.

But nature is capricious and inconsiderate. The large storm front that had hovered over the Colorado Rockies that week roiled up and became restless. It began to move south, out over the desert highlands of the New Mexico Territory. The spring warmth of the broken land below the high Rockies gave the storm new strength, and its sullen gray face became angry and turbulent overnight. It held back its rain as it moved south along the valley toward Mexico, until the vast, stormy canvas held a year of torrents behind its lightning-streaked face.

On the sixth day the gray face loomed over the valley, bringing an unexpected chill to the spring-warmed fields. The storm hovered, quiet but menacing, over Casilla and the other farm towns for the day, as if undecided—stay or move on. During the day work at the farms went on as usual. Little was said of the gray slate spreading overhead, but eyes often turned anxiously upward, waiting for a sign.

Finally, after sunset, the rains began. For the first hour they were gentle, caressing the newly sprouted cotton with moisture. Then, as if by an unseen cue, the downpour began.

Sitting at the table, the Cutters listened silently to the ominous rattle of torrents as they struck the roof in waves. Without a word Jonah got up and walked to the window that looked out the back of the house, toward the fields. Rain, driven by a fierce wind, splattered against the screen and onto his face. He stood there a moment, the moisture gathering like perspiration on his face, then walked back to his seat. He resumed eating again without a word.

The rain continued. One hour, two, three, four. There seemed to be no bottom to the reservoir of rain the storm had gathered in its journey south. Each wave of water was followed by another and another.

At ten o'clock Max and Kate put on oilcloth ponchos, drawing the hoods close around their faces, and walked through the growing mud and spreading puddles to the arroyo that cut roughly between their farm and the Cutters'. When they reached the gulch, ordinarily as dry as a roadway, they saw water, dark and ugly, boiling five feet deep below them.

Max turned to Kate, putting his hand on her shoulder, and said, "I think we'd better make the rounds."

They started back toward the house, leaning down into the wind.

By midnight Max and Kate had ridden to all the houses in the area, warning their neighbors of the fast-rising arroyos. They, in turn, had ridden to other homes and into Casilla. Houses that would ordinarily have been dark at the late hour were lighted and bustling. Bedding was rolled up and put on top of chests. The chests were then lifted onto tables. Chairs were hung on nails driven into the walls, near the ceiling. Women packed sacks with tins of food and moved what they couldn't pack to high places—windowsills, shelves, tabletops.

Ruth and Jonah were awakened by the sound of pounding on the door. At first they thought it was thunder, but it continued in a steady rhythm.

"What do you think it is?"

"Don't know." Jonah groped for his trousers in the dark. "Something to do with the storm, I'll wager."

"Could it be bandits?"

"They don't knock first."

Ruth sat up anxiously, remembering the revolvers in the drawer. But when Jonah got to the door, it was Kate, swathed in her poncho, her face dripping wet.

She came in, breathless. By now Ruth was up, a dressing robe around her.

"Max and I were down to the arroyo. It's rising fast. The

river's likely as not to break banks within an hour or two, even if the storm lets up. There's already three inches of water in low places in the road."

"Casa Portillo?" Ruth knew that in the event of flooding in the area, the inhabitants were to gather at Don Alonzo's. Though near the river, it was the most substantial house in the area and the only one with a second floor. She remembered Wasserman's story of the flood of '98. The water had stood five feet deep over most of the valley.

Ruth lit a lamp as they talked. As the light flooded the room the children stirred.

"Anna! J. J.! Quick! Up and get dressed. Anna, you get Hank ready."

"What is it?" Anna sat up, groggy.

"The storm. We may have a flood."

J. J. looked startled. "We going to drown?"

"Not likely, J. J." Kate smiled. "But you've got to get to Don Alonzo's house in case the water level gets high—"

Jonah interrupted. "Should I ride over to any other houses?"

"No, I think Max has gotten a relay going through town. You're the fifth place I've been to myself. Best get things above the floor as much as possible; gather some dry clothes and whatever food you can carry and get to the *hacienda* quick."

"We'll be there in half an hour." Ruth had already begun pulling clothing out of drawers as she talked.

"Got to go. Lina's setting things up for us, but she and Vassily can't get over by themselves."

Kate went over to Ruth and kissed her on the cheek. She whispered, "Don't worry. It won't be all that bad."

Ruth hugged her but didn't know what to answer. She was, to be honest, terrified. Not for her life—but for the farm and her future.

Kate patted Jonah boyishly on the shoulder and left, pulling the door behind her.

Ruth continued to rummage through the drawers while calling out instructions to the children. Suddenly Jonah's arms were around her from behind. She stopped still.

"I'm scared," was all he said.

Ruth and Jonah made what precautions they could quickly. The furniture was stacked, the linens and food piled on top, and bags of clothes and provisions hurriedly filled. Jonah put on a slicker and dashed out to the lean-to behind the house to where the animals passively waited out the storm. Within a few minutes he came back in, leaving the mule harnessed to the cart outside the door.

There was little time for displays of emotion. After a brief flurry of last-minute checking, Ruth and Jonah bundled themselves and the children against the rain and hurried out to the cart. The hard-packed clay earth in front of the house had already softened into a mire. Their boots stuck as they dashed through the torrent. Covered with a tarpaulin, hats pulled close, they started off through the night, the harsh, cold rain beating down on them.

Water had already collected in vast, shallow puddles in low areas. The rain broke the sheets of water into frantic ripples as it fell. The road leading to Casa Portillo and the river was muddy. Its usually dry ruts ran like small rivers into the distance. They could only see a few feet in either direction as they jerked down the uneven road. The rain enclosed them like a curtain. Behind that curtain, Ruth and Jonah both thought to themselves, were their fields of cotton.

The lights of Casa Portillo cut through the black storm like a beacon, guiding weary pilgrims. When their cart lumbered into the courtyard, covered in an inch of water, there were already a dozen or so carts packed closely together, and another twenty mules or horses tethered to rails, nervous in the rain and from unexpected late-night movement.

The central door of the house stood open, safe from the rain in its deep recess, and in its warm yellow light figures could be seen moving inside. Jonah carried Hank and, with the others, dashed across the court to the entrance. Inside, they were welcomed by Miriam Wilkerson, Mabel Pettus, and some women they didn't know. In the adjoining room Maricita's tiny voice could be heard talking rapidly and authoritatively in Spanish.

Their wet wraps were taken, and voices welcomed them. The women were efficient and hurried but cheerful.

"Not a fit night!"

"Wait, here's a cloth to dry your faces."

"Well, Hank, aren't you growing up fast. What do you think of all this weather?"

They worked like an assembly line, pulling in the new arrivals, sending them to their assigned posts.

"Good to see you again, Ruth. No time for catching up now."

"We women are manning the coffee and food brigade and watching the animals as best we can. Half the men are on a run to Casilla. There's a carload of sandbags on the rail there."

"Max is about to take another cart to town for more bags and shovels. The men going with him are meeting in the library—no, Mrs. Cutter, the other way."

"Anna, you'll best be with the women in the kitchen."

Amid the flurry of orders and comings and goings, the Cutters were scattered through the house, now awash with activity. As Anna hurried down the main corridor she heard the next group of refugees greeted at the door. When they reached the main courtyard, the rain was still pouring down into the heart of the house.

Jonah found Max Mirkovsky, Wasserman, and most of the other farmers talking in quiet but anxious voices. After they exchanged greetings Jonah learned that the men were planning a line of defense against the rising waters. Jonah had thought that Casa Portillo was a refuge, a place of safety in case the river broke banks. It was to be that, but a nerve center for flood-fighting as well. A stranger, a thin, talkative man who was introduced to Jonah as a county land officer, had charts of the Casilla land plots spread out on the library table. He marked the lowest points in the terrain with broad strokes of a red grease pencil. As he marked he kept up a running commentary on the local geography.

"Okay, now, Wilkerson's stretch down at the sixtieth plot is in good shape, but we've got to watch this low spot—about seventy acres' worth—downriver from that. The river used to run a big horseshoe loop through there, so that piece is as low as the river bottom itself. Likewise up here, above Mirkovsky—Anderson and Pettus land. Those loops both got cut off thirty years or so ago. " 'Nother damn flood. Don't rightly know what to say about the arroyo lands. Can't imagine there's enough sandbags in a hundred miles to fill up the mouths of those arroyos when they're running ten feet deep."

"Nope," Max added, "no stopping those gullies. Best concentrate on the plots open to the river that lie low and close to the banks. We can't save every damned acre in the valley."

The men began to break up into groups, forming teams of men with assigned tasks and areas to try to shore up with sandbags. The one thing that was not mentioned in the room was the new cotton crop that was about to be devastated by the flood.

The atmosphere in the vast kitchen was lively. It reminded Anna of the Sunday get-togethers at the Mirkovskys', with the women chatting as they busied themselves over pots and plates. Their talks were of local news, family events, and, of course, the downpour that brought them there.

"Thought we'd ridden right into the river, the road was so full of water!"

"We had to ford the small arroyo up by the junction. Thought the team was going to balk at dragging the wagon through three feet of water."

"Didn't know what to do with Biddy. Her litter's only a week old. Jessie just bundled her in my wicker linen basket and hauled her into the cart."

"My sunflowers will be a mile high with all this water."

The one topic not mentioned was the fields and crops. The women, like their husbands, knew there would be more than enough time spent on that difficult subject the next day.

Not long after Ruth and Anna had joined the other women in preparing food and urns of steaming coffee for the sandbagging crews, a small door leading off the kitchen opened, and Don Alonzo entered. His hat and poncho drained rivers of water onto the floor, and his boots were thick with dark mud. Ruth brought him a mug of coffee and a crisp, warm towel to dry himself with.

"We were wondering where you were," she said as she watched him dry his face and neck.

"I was down by the river, seeing how she is going to treat us tonight."

"And?"

"Not well, I am afraid. She is angry. Just pray that the sandbags and shovels and strong shoulders of the men can keep her from unleashing her full fury on us."

Alonzo saw the look of pained recognition on Ruth's face as he spoke. She could no longer pretend or hope now: their farm was to be destroyed. How he wanted to take her in his arms, to hold and comfort her, to reassure her in some way that everything would, in time, be right again. That the rains would be gone, the land dry, the fields tall and green once again. He rubbed his face. He looked tired and very sad.

"De vero. I am sorry, Ruth. I am sorry."

She looked him straight in the eye, her dark, rocklike strength flowing out of her with the force of the river itself.

"Thank you for taking us in," she said quietly. "It makes—everything—much easier."

Alonzo reached out, took her hand, and held it firmly with a gentle strength that spoke volumes. Then he turned to the rest of the refugees in the kitchen.

"Ladies, my thanks for all your hard work here tonight, and for that of your husbands and sons. It does an old man like me much good to see such cheer, such companionship, such effort in a difficult time like tonight. I have just seen your men outside, and they are almost finished in loading the wagons for the assault on the *río.*"

The women rushed to get their provisions ready, packing the food in baskets along with dry clothing and towels. Then they began carrying the provisions out the back entry and into the courtyard where the carts stood waiting in the steady rain. The men, more than fifty of them, stood in their rain-glistening ponchos and slickers, like somber soldiers. When the women arrived at the door, they took the boxes and baskets and carried them to the carts, putting food and coffee in each, next to the shovels, pickaxes, and high piles of sandbags.

A sheet of water now covered the entire outer court, spluttering in the rain and the footsteps. A few quick farewells were said, and the men broke up into their teams, mounting the carts for the journey to the river.

The first hour after the men left, Casa Portillo was quiet. The women went back to the kitchens to brew coffee for themselves and to relax after the flurry of activity. They realized now that they were tired; most had been up since dawn, and it was now

way after midnight. They knew they would probably see another dawn before sleeping again. Weary, the women grew quiet
and introspective. Ruth found a chair next to Kate, who sat
rather mannishly astride the chair, her head resting on her
folded arms on the chair back. They didn't talk. Lina, without a
word, went from woman to woman, refilling cups of coffee,
offering a bit to eat from her tray. Across the table a lean,
leathery-faced Mexican woman from town—Ruth remembered
her name as Consuela—sat with her two serious-faced daughters, both in their twenties. The three women fingered their
rosaries quietly, waiting.

The room was filled with the steady, hypnotic sound of rain.
Ruth looked to where Mabel Pettus sat reading from a small
Bible. Ruth closed her eyes, remembering the strong young
seedlings, thrusting their first leaves above the sun-warmed soil.
That had been this morning. Her eyes still closed, Ruth visual-
ized the pages of her own Bible, a passage well-remembered
from her childhood:

> And the waters prevailed exceedingly upon the earth; and all
> the high hills, there were under the whole heaven were cov-
> ered . . . and every living substance was destroyed which
> was upon the face of the ground.

Anna sat beside her mother and Kate, absorbed in her own
thoughts. She ate moist, warm biscuits, fresh from the oven,
with preserves, and washed them down with strong, dark coffee.
She had only been allowed to taste coffee at home—had never
been given a whole cup—but tonight the distinctions between
adult and child were blurred. She felt numb and distant. The
whole course of the night seemed like a strange, vivid dream—
the rain, the late-night awakening, the pilgrimage to Casa Portillo, the odd hubbub in the middle of the storm. She wondered
to herself if there would be a flood and tried to imagine the
turbid water flowing through the house, around the beds and
table legs, through the doorways. As she daydreamed she felt
something wet seep through the sole of her boot. She looked
down. A wide, muddy stream spread across the tile of the floor
from under the far door. As if hypnotized, she watched the dark
stain snake across the floor. Then she snapped into reality,

stood up, and shouted, "Wake up! Everybody wake up. The water is here!"

Jonah fell, gasping, against the back of the cart, his breath coming in painful, burning gasps. His poncho, cumbersome for heavy work, had been discarded an hour ago, and his shirt clung to his slim frame. His hair was drenched, plastered against his bare head. The water swirled around him, as far as he could see by the light of the lanterns hung on poles on the cart; it was now above his knees, cold and turbulent. A few yards behind him men shouted to one another in the dim light. He could make out, in the lessening rain, the dark shapes of two cottonwood groves. Between them was the even fainter line of sandbags he and his companions had struggled to stretch across the low place between the two clumps of trees. The line of bags, two and a half feet high, was only visible a few inches above the water that engulfed it.

The river had won.

Still gasping, Jonah looked up to see Vassily pushing a bag off the dwindled pile on the cart, urging it toward him.

"No. No good." He tried without success to clear his face of water. "Max says got to stop now. Water too high. Not enough bags. River getting higher."

Vassily understood enough now to know what Jonah was telling him. He nodded sadly.

"Go back?"

Jonah nodded yes.

"Got to lead horses on foot. Won't pull carts in deep water."

Vassily climbed down, taking time to clap Jonah on the shoulder. He made his way through the eddying water around the cart to where the horse stood, flinching nervously. He began undoing the harness.

Jonah stood leaning against the cart, his breath less strained now. He still tried to wipe the endless rivulets of water streaming down his face, through his eyes. The rain was salty and warm. He realized that he was crying.

He watched passively as a few branches swept by in the chill water. Caught in the crook of one branch was the long, silvery shape of a drowned rattlesnake. The branch and its cargo disappeared into the night.

Suddenly the cart jerked and pulled away from him. He plunged back into the water, feeling the cold river engulf him. He struggled, taking a few, panicked seconds to regain his feet, still not sure of what had happened. Behind him he heard a sharp, wordless cry. He turned to see the cart slipping through the flood, the lanterns bobbing wildly in the dark. The horse had bolted. Then the sudden realization that the cry had come from Vassily. In the dim light he thought he could see the old man's head and an arm above the water.

God! he screamed to himself. The old man's caught. He's being pulled along.

Jonah started to run, stumbling against the deepening current.

"Max! Max!" He heard himself screaming, now left alone in the watery darkness as the lights moved away. "He's caught! Max! Hurry! The horse is pulling him into the river."

As he struggled toward the faint line of the dike, he heard other voices shouting in response. The two faint points of light bobbed in the distance, almost pinpricks, then went out. It seemed like an eternity to cross the few yards to the fallen defenses. Finally he felt the engulfed sandbags against his legs. He groped out and found the damp wood of the cart. Then he slumped down, only to feel hands pulling him up.

"Jonah? What happened?"

It was Max.

Jonah gasped out the essential fact.

He heard Max's anguished voice.

"The cart's against the levee, and the horse has pulled loose. Papa's been dragged into the river."

Jonah struggled to his feet as Max jerked away and shouted out.

"Rope. Quick. Papa's pulled in there."

Other men were around, shouting, struggling in the water that now pulled at their hips. Max vaulted over the low, submerged wall of sandbags, into waist-high water.

"Papa! Papa!"

Jonah thought he heard a faint response. Perhaps only a branch breaking, or the wind.

"Quick, fellas," Max cried, "we've got to move downstream. Along the bank. Hold the rope, and watch for deep spots."

Somehow Jonah managed to follow the others, as near to collapse as he was. They waded, holding the rope, along the fallen barricade, through tangles of branches. Slimy, cold things brushed against them. Snakes perhaps, or fish. Max kept up a steady chant, calling his father. Sometimes it seemed as if they heard a response, sometimes not.

Then, by a faint, light point in the immense shadow that engulfed them, they saw him, out in the raging stream.

"Papa!"

There was no response.

"Thank God! He's not moving. A branch or a sandbar. Hold the rope, find a tree trunk if you can. I'll swim out, holding the end. When I get there, you haul us back. I'll shout when it's time to haul the damned wagon in."

Without another word Max plunged into the water. For a few yards he was on what had the day before been the grass-carpeted banks. Then suddenly the bank gave way, and he plunged under the water, to emerge swimming, a few seconds later. The men planted themselves as firmly as they could in the slippery mud of the overwhelmed riverbanks. The rough, wet fiber linking them with their companions was hard against their hands.

Ruth stood next to Kate on the upper gallery overlooking the courtyard of Casa Portillo. The women had wrapped themselves in blankets to ward off the predawn chill.

The rain had stopped a few minutes before. Below them, the lush tropical foliage of Don Alonzo's tropical garden waved gently, moved by the current of water that flowed three feet deep through the lower floor of the house.

Both women watched, as if hypnotized, by the eerie sight below them. Finally Ruth spoke.

"What will we do?"

It was a few seconds before Kate replied.

"Start over."

The men stood in the dark, holding the rope. The current pulled the line steadily downstream. Finally the line seemed to tighten, and Max's voice could be heard in the distance.

"Pull! Pull!"

They began drawing the line in, slowly, feeling the weight of
the men against the current. They were all exhausted, too tired
to exult in saving Vassily's life. The rain had lessened as they
stood, chest-deep in the flood, and then stopped. The night was
still now, the only sound the rush of water around them,
stretching to infinity.

Finally they could see a ripple in the river and a spot of flesh
in the darkness of the water. They pulled faster, spurred on by
their nearness to success.

Out of the darkness emerged Vassily's face, half conscious,
the rope tied around his chest.

He was alone.

From the window upstairs Ruth and Kate saw a group of five
men struggling through the water. Two were supporting
Vassily, the others leading horses. Seeing that Vassily was in-
jured or collapsed, they went and got Lina from the schoolroom. When Lina heard that Vassily had to be helped to the
house, she insisted on going downstairs to meet the men, even
though Kate didn't want her to get into the flood waters that
coursed through the house. But she insisted, and the others,
including Anna, began a strange procession down the stairs and
into the cold, deep water.

With Lina in the lead the women reached the front door
where several of their neighbors stood, helping the men into the
house.

"Kate! Lina!" one woman called out. "Just in time. Here's
Mr. Mirkovsky now. Look's like he's had a rough time of it.
Ruth, Jonah's there too."

They moved to where the great oak door stood open, letting
the water in.

Ruth saw that Vassily was only half conscious, held up by the
others. Jonah was behind them, walking by himself, his arms
trailing limply through the water. He looked down at the
swirling water as he lumbered through it.

"What happened? Is he all right?"

There was a flurry as Vassily was helped through the door.

"Horse bolted with the cart. Pulled him in." Ruth didn't
recognize the man who spoke, but the others seemed to know
him.

Kate and Lina pulled the limp old man to them out of the men's arms. He managed to smile at them weakly.

"Papa!" Lina embraced him, pulling his mud-streaked face close to her.

"He's all right. But it was rough. He was in the river for a good five minutes before we got to him."

Ruth and Anna slipped behind Kate and Lina when Jonah reached the door. He fell against them, his wet body clammy against their dry faces and arms.

"You're safe!" Ruth cradled her face against her husband's cold neck.

Jonah whispered one word.

"Max."

Ruth jerked away. She knew instinctively what Jonah meant. She looked up at him, her face frozen with alarm.

"Couldn't find him. Went in after the old man. Got him out, all right, but didn't get out himself. Couldn't help him. God, Ruth, I think he's gone."

Ruth twisted away, looking to Kate. She hoped she hadn't overheard; she didn't want her to know.

But Kate was looking at the Cutters. She had heard.

Jonah slumped against his wife, breathing hard. She could feel his heart beating against her body. He was alive. She looked at Kate, not knowing what to do, what to say. Kate, her good friend Kate, stood looking at her, her face impassive, firm.

Finally Ruth spoke.

"We'll get a rescue group out. We'll find him right away."

Ruth turned, searching the faces of the men around her.

They murmured in agreement, but she knew there was little optimism in their faces.

Then Kate said, "Max was a good swimmer. Strong. He would have made it, if he could have."

Someone volunteered another note of hope: "There's lots of trees and high places out there. Probably got to high ground."

Kate shook her head in disagreement.

"Ruth," she said quietly, almost in a businesslike way, "will you help Mama upstairs? And try not to let the girls know anything is wrong. There's plenty of time for all that later."

"Of course. Anything."

"I want to go out there. Can any of you come along?"

Kate looked up at the men, towering over her diminutive frame.

"You shouldn't, Mrs. Mirkovsky."

"Bullshit. I'm heading out."

The men moved to join her.

Before they left, Kate went to her mother- and father-in-law, embracing the old couple. She whispered something to them that the others didn't hear. As they embraced Ruth could see Lina's face over Kate's shoulder, her pink, wrinkled cheeks wet with tears.

Then Kate waded outside, the water deepening around her.

"She shouldn't go," Jonah muttered, still holding his wife and daughter close to him. "Bad out there, still rough."

Ruth started to agree. Then she realized that her husband was still with her, alive, close. Kate wasn't so lucky. She watched Kate's diminutive figure moving through the water, her arms held almost winglike above the flood, her body swaying from side to side as she moved against the current.

She made up her mind.

"Anna, take your father upstairs, get him dry and to bed. I've got to go with Kate."

"Ruth, no," Jonah protested.

"I've got to. We'll be all right. Anna can take care of things here."

Ruth pulled away from them. She kissed Jonah, aware of the odd taste of mud on his lips. Then she hurried, as fast as she could, against the barrier of water, after Kate and the men.

It was more than an hour before they found him, not more than five hundred feet below where Vassily had been pulled from the river. Since the rains had stopped two hours before, the river had slowly subsided, though the water still ran three feet over the banks. The receding water had exposed a tangle of barren branches—what had been a clump of mesquite before the flood had stripped the leaves away. Amid the dark tangle was a darker shape, twisted like the drowned mesquite, oddly decorated by the debris borne by the receding flood.

They knew, though somehow they hoped to be proven wrong, that it was Max there in the branches.

As they neared they could see his limbs twisted among the

branches, his feet caught in the roots. His clothing was half pulled from his massive body; his head, thrust up and back, as if in defiance of the river that had taken his life, was streaked with the same brown earth that had given him his livelihood. His limbs, twisted as if in a grotesque crucifixion, dangled in the same water that had nourished his farm. His eyes, glazed now with death, were wide-open, looking up at the blue of the Texas sky.

Kate reached him first.

Without a word to the others she began tearing away the branches that held Max in their deadly grip. As she tore them loose she cast them into the water that still flowed around them like a shallow sea. As the branches floated, one by one, down the swift, eddying current, Max's great, earth-bronzed frame loosened and finally fell into his wife's arms.

It wasn't until after Max Mirkovsky's funeral, the third day after the flood, that the unreal, dreamlike air that had enveloped the valley began to drift away.

The first two days were spent waiting for the waters to recede. Casa Portillo was still the temporary home of almost a hundred men, women, and children, and the *hacienda* was active, with large communal meals and the inevitable problems and emergencies that arise with so many crowded into one building. But the air was subdued, in spite of the crowding, for all the refugees in Don Alonzo's house were respectful of the bodies that lay in state in the small chapel adjoining the main salon downstairs.

Max was not the only victim of the flood; a family of five had died in the river when the roof on which they had taken refuge gave way, cascading the helpless people into the flood that raged below.

Anna was downstairs, helping in the mammoth task of cleaning the silt and debris out of the *hacienda*, when the bodies were brought in, bloated from a day in the sun. She recognized the faces, in spite of death's distortions, from last year's harvest. The whole family—she didn't even know their names—had come on the cotton cart to work the Cutters' fields.

When Ruth saw the bodies brought in, she went over to her daughter and tried to get her to turn away.

"No, Mama, please!" Anna protested. "It doesn't bother me. I have to see this sometime."

And later that same day Anna insisted on helping Kate, her mother, and the other women clean and dress the dead. Somehow Anna didn't find it troubling to see Max's body, naked, on the long refectory table. There was something spiritual and reassuring about the quiet, solemn business of preparing the dead.

Alonzo was the quiet, firm force that held the ravaged community together. He met with the men, coordinating plans to begin cleanup operations as soon as the roads were easily passable and the houses were dry. He led small groups of farmers and Casilla residents on rounds to assess damage from the flood, and he, himself, rode to Casilla, where the priest at the small church had gathered one group of refugees, to ask the priest to come to Casa Portillo to administer last rites to the drowned family. And on a lighter note he brought out his large stock of wine and beer kegs for refreshment when the supply of drinkable water stored in earthenware crocks ran low. For Anna and many of the refugees it was their first experience of inebriation.

Kate sloughed off any excessive displays of sympathy, reminding her neighbors that there was "lots to be tended to," and she and Lina both worked long hours, caring for the children, cooking meals, and shoveling and mopping the eight inches of silt that had been left in places on the lower floor of Casa Portillo by the retreating floodwaters.

Vassily had recovered quickly, after a day in bed. Like the others in his family, he refused to let heartbreak make him idle. On his first day out of bed, dressed in borrowed clothes, he insisted on helping the men haul mud and debris out of the house. If someone chanced to console him on the loss of his son, his only comment would be, "Better me dead than Max. Better me."

The day after the flood Jonah was weak and listless, exhausted from the night's ordeal. Ruth and Anna both checked on him frequently, between their chores elsewhere in the *hacienda.* By nightfall he had gotten a chill and spent a restless, feverish night. Don Alonzo had warned them of the possibility of typhoid from the contamination the floodwaters might have picked up.

Jonah's fever wasn't typhoid. Luckily no cases developed in the lower valley, though Don Alonzo, on one of his forays to Casilla, heard a rumor that several cases had developed nearer El Paso. He was grateful that there had been enough water, beer, and wine in the house to keep the refugees from having to drink river water.

That third day, when the water had receded in all but the lowest places, leaving behind a vast, drying mud plain, plans were made for funerals for Max and the other flood victims. There was to be a memorial mass at the church in Casilla; the roads were still mired but at least passable by early morning. Then Max was to be taken to his farm for burial, along with the others, to the small, barren cemetery on the edge of town.

Six pine coffins, built from lumber ripped from Don Alonzo's horse stalls, were loaded onto carts brought into the courtyard, their wheels sinking even deeper into the sticky brown mire with their sad cargo. Then, like refugees from the Ark, the people of Casilla left Casa Portillo, filing solemnly out of the water-stained oak door and into the bright, cloudless June sky.

The Cutters took their own cart, making their way through the vast flats of mud, broken by large, scattered puddles and occasional tangles of uprooted branches. The mule made his way through the mire easily, though his hooves were clotted with mud. As they made their way from Casa Portillo the river could be seen, now flowing serenely in its banks. The road was still there, too, though rutted and washed out in places. But on either side, where four days ago had stood fresh, neat fields of cotton, there was nothing but mud and debris. In places the sun had already dried the mire and silt into cracked, broken shapes.

As their cart moved past the turnoff to their house, sitting forlornly in the flat, brown waste, no one spoke except Hank.

"Why don't we go home?" he asked.

"We will, Hank. Soon." Ruth reached out a reassuring arm to her son.

Anna, from her seat in the back, thought she heard her father mutter something, but she wasn't sure.

Anna found the funeral service sad but somehow boring. During the eulogies and the Latin mass, which she didn't understand at all, she found herself thinking of Max. He had always been so lively, so cheerful, that this solemn, long service seemed totally unlike him and, to her, not very appropriate a way to mark his death. She remembered that day when they had first come to Casilla, when he had taken her for her first walk by the river—the river that was to claim his life—and had showed her the young cotton plants in his fields.

She imagined, as she listened to the priest intone the ritual in the distance, that Max would have preferred them all to go home and start planting their crops again.

After the funeral, when they had watched in silence as the coffin was lowered into the muddy soil behind the Mirkovsky house, Kate insisted that they all go back to their own farms and "get to work." Ruth offered to stay, but Kate wouldn't even take Ruth's help. So the Cutters rode back to their farm for the first time since the flood, leaving Kate and Max's parents to put their lives back together as best they could.

The Cutters found their house muddy and damp but not damaged much beyond stained walls and some washed-out places in the plaster.

"One good thing about a mud house," Ruth had said cheerfully. "A little more mud just makes the walls thicker."

But there was a great deal of shoveling and mopping and scrubbing to be done. They worked far into the night before they could take the furniture down and set up the beds and tables in their accustomed places. And the plaster, inside and out, had a three-foot-high border of mottled brown left behind by the receding water. The dirt floors were still soft and had to be covered with dried reeds. Don Alonzo's housekeeper, Maricita, had given them a bundle of reeds before they left Casa Portillo, to keep them from gouging footprints into the muddy floor every time they took a step.

Finally, late in the evening, the Cutter children were put to bed, weary from the last days, aching deep in their muscles, their heads full of the sorrow and upheaval brought about by the flood.

Anna lay awake in the dark after her mother kissed her and turned down the lamp before going into the next room with her father. The house, in the night shadows, looked the same, the furniture all back in the accustomed places. But the room still smelled of the river, and the dampness from the floor and walls seemed to soak through the covers and into her skin, making it clammy and chill. Soon, above the steady breathing of her sleeping brothers, she heard voices from the other room, soft but intense. When she finally fell asleep, the sound of voices still floated around her.

Jonah sat on the edge of the bed, his shoulders slumped forward. His eyes were fixed on his feet as they toyed rhythmically with the dried reeds on the floor next to the bed. Ruth stood next to him at the foot of the bed. She trembled slightly, and her hands held tight to the curved pipe of the footboard, her knuckles white with the strength of her grip.

It seemed to her that she and Jonah had been arguing for hours, circling around and around the same irreconcilable difference.

"I . . . we . . . have to leave, Ruth. There's nothing for us here now. I admit that it's all my fault. I never should have brought you here. I'm sorry for that now. But we've lost everything twice now. There's nothing else left to lose."

Ruth felt the cold metal of the bedstead against her palms. She squeezed even harder.

"We can't just walk away. We can't. We have the land, we have debts. Obligations. And no place to go." Ruth heard herself speak the same words again, for the fourth or fifth time in the hour. The circle of argument again. "Do you really think we can just pack up a few clothes and walk away from here?"

Ruth hung between rage and pain. She so wanted to feel only rage at her husband, rage for bringing them there, rage for wanting to leave, rage for giving up; pain for what she had lost, for what she was about to lose.

She heard him say again, as many times before, "But I just can't start over again. I just can't."

His words cut deep, like a sharp knife. He had asked her to start over, and she had. Now he was asking her to start over— again.

Suddenly she said what she had never said to Jonah before, in these last, difficult years on the farm.

"Jonah, we gave everything up once, to come here. Please don't ask me to give up everything again." Her voice sounded harder, colder than she would have liked. There was a distance in it.

He gave a short, ironic little laugh.

"What's to give up? Eighty acres of mud? You don't have any more jewelry to sell, you know."

His foot scraped aside the reeds, gouging a furrow in the mud underneath.

"We've got the farm."

He laughed again. "Like I said, eighty acres of mud."

Jonah stood up, turning to her. There was less than two feet between them. Their eyes locked, steady and fixed, looking out but revealing nothing behind their gazes.

Ruth knew in that instant that the gulf had come between them, not two feet but two thousand, two million, miles.

"I'm going, Ruth. I have to. Will you bring the children and come with me?"

The choice was to be hers. Jonah still held her with his eyes, his familiar clear blue eyes now hard and unwavering. Images flashed through Ruth's mind: the crisp white house under the elms in Kentucky; the train snaking through the desert; her children; her grandmother; the empty, decrepit hut under the cottonwoods; the hot summer sun; the seedlings pushing up between the brown clods; the rains and the flood; Casa Portillo.

Ruth tore herself away from her husband's terrible stare. She turned, leaning against the damp wall, the plaster cold against her forehead.

"I love you, Jonah."

"Are you coming with me?"

There was a vast, endless silence. Ruth felt tears held back by her shut eyelids and then her voice, barely breaking through the hot tightness in her throat.

"No."

"But you said you love me."

"I do, Jonah. But I can't come with you."

"I'll pack a few things now," Jonah said, a note of defeat in his voice. "It's almost morning, anyhow. Do you mind if I take a few dollars, just to see me over the next few days?"

She nodded assent, her forehead still against the rough plaster. The sharp edges cut into her brow.

"Ruth . . ."

Jonah's fingers touched her elbow lightly.

She pulled away. There had been a tone of reconciliation in his voice, of tenderness. She didn't want to hear it.

Without looking at Jonah Ruth threw herself on the bed, her face turned to the wall. She listened during the long minutes as Jonah went through the bureau, packing his valise. She was aware of a light sky through the window when he finally slipped out of the room.

Anna was awakened by the sound of someone in the room. She assumed it was her mother, starting to prepare some kind of makeshift breakfast with what food was left from before the flood. She sat up in bed and was surprised to see her father, fully dressed, eating a piece of bread hurriedly.

He held up a finger to quiet her.

"Shh! Don't wake the boys."

She gave him a puzzled look. Her mother was usually up half an hour before her father.

"Got to get into town early. To Wasserman's, to get supplies and things. Lots to do around here today."

Anna nodded in agreement, still half asleep.

Still munching the bread, her father stood, grabbed his hat from the peg beside the door, and opened the door to let himself out. Then he turned and came over to Anna. He bent down and kissed her forehead, then gave her head a good-natured rub.

"Go back to sleep now. I'll see you and the boys later."

Anna nodded, then fell back into the warmth of the bed. Just as she slipped back into the nothingness of sleep, she heard the faint, familiar sound of the door as it opened and closed.

It was hardest of all for Ruth to tell the children.

After sleepless hours in hell Ruth had come out of her room, determined to go about the day's business as best she could, not knowing what course of action she could take but knowing that she had to do something, anything, to keep herself from slipping into the dark abyss that opened before her.

"Where's Papa?" J. J. asked in all innocence, rubbing his sleepy eyes when his mother's stirrings awakened him.

"Gone to town," Anna answered. "Heard him leave early this morning."

"Why didn't he take me? He always does when he goes. I wanted to see what the flood did to town."

"You'd just have been underfoot as usual," Anna returned in her most sisterly tone as she straightened the covers on her bed. "He'll get more done without you hanging on his heels."

Their conversation, normal, childish, everyday, was like a knife in the pit of Ruth's stomach. Yes, indeed, their father had gone to town and beyond, and how true, how ironic were Anna's words: "He'll get more done without you hanging on . . ."

She tried, as she fussed over the fire, once, twice, to get the words out. Nothing came from her throat. She screwed up her determination, bringing all her will to bear.

"I have something important to tell you. Very important but difficult for your mother to put into words. Yes, your father has gone to town but not for supplies. He's gone on a trip, you see. A very long trip."

Ruth studied their faces. Perplexity, a bit of apprehension. They questioned her with their eyes.

She was surprised to hear the clear, lucid, distanced way in which she spoke. But behind each slow, almost schoolmarmish phrase was another wrench of the knife, as if she were hearing the painful news for the first time herself.

"You all know what a hard time we've had of things here since we came West. It's been hard on all of us. Sometimes, though, rough times are harder on some than on others. Your father is that way. He wanted so for things to go right for us here in Casilla, for us to do well. Have a successful farm, make a decent living, have a good life. So, you see, when it didn't work out that way, even though he worked hard—we all worked hard—well, it sort of killed something in him. Made him hate this place and the farm. It's like the dreams you have, that's what this farm was to your father. It was a dream that all of a sudden turned into a bad dream, a nightmare. And you know that when you're having a terrible dream, full of frightening and ugly things, sometimes what you want more than anything is to wake up and not be in the dream anymore.

"That's what has happened to your father. He just needed to get away from here—not from you or from me. Because he still loves . . . us . . . very much. But the nightmare was so terrible that he had to wake up somewhere where he'll be happy. So he's gone away from Casilla, and we're going to be on our own for a while."

J. J., his chin quivering, asked the inevitable question.

"Papa's coming back, isn't he?"

In an instant her defenses crumbled, as easily as dry adobe in the flood. Her hands went to her face to hide the tears, her reply half hidden by a sob.

"He'll be back. I'm sure of that. Oh, my God, children, I'm so very sure of that."

Then they all were lost, finding little comfort in each other's arms.

Part II
THE YEARS
OF PASSION
1916–1919

Chapter One

IN JANUARY, ON A RAW, BLUSTERY DAY, A STRONG WIND from north of the Plains turned the sky a heavy blue-gray. A gusty wind whipped through the mesquite and sage, down off the desert into the valley, shaking the bare-branched cottonwoods and the stubble of cotton stalks that poked through the naked fields. On such a day the twice-weekly train from Ciudad Juarez to Chihuahua City, two hundred and fifty miles south in Mexico, pulled into the *pueblicita* of San Ysabel.

The poor little collection of adobe huts was nothing more than a water station for the train. Only rarely did a passenger get on or off at the stop. On this day, while the boiler hissed and steamed as the cool water from the tank hoses struck the heated sides of the boiler tank, a group of several dozen Mexican men, more men than lived in the whole hamlet of San Ysabel, appeared from behind the quiet, apparently lifeless buildings. Some of the men were on horseback, others on foot. All were armed, carrying rifles and Colt revolvers, their ragged cotton shirts and rough wool jackets crisscrossed with heavy leather straps punctuated with rows of gleaming bullets.

The Villistas boarded the train, stern-faced, unsmiling, moving swiftly down the aisles, asking questions of the passengers. Whenever they came to an American, they gestured with their guns for him to stand and get off the train.

When the revolutionaries had combed the train, there were eighteen Americans standing nervously on the hard-packed earth beside the tracks. They were all mining men, en route from the mines of southern Chihuahua and Coahuila to the United States.

The solemn Villistas lined the miners against a convenient nearby wall, a group of three or four searching the men, taking their watches and chains, their pocket change, and the sizable rolls of cash most carried.

When the *gringos* had been stripped of all that was valuable to the Villa men, the Mexicans, without a signal, opened fire. The sharp, irregular staccato issued forth from two dozen repeating rifles and almost as many pistols, piercing the quiet, cold morning air of San Ysabel.

Some of the men were knocked back against the adobe wall, their blood spattering against the dried mud, then soaking into the adobe. Others crumpled, fell forward, spilling out their blood onto the dusty Mexican earth.

From inside the train there was only the silence of shock and fear.

When, after less than a minute, the loud, horrid sound of the gunfire had slowed, then stopped, the eighteen miners lay dead beside the tracks, and the Villistas slipped back among the houses and to their waiting wilderness.

Will Channing craned his goggle- and scarf-encased head out of the forward cockpit of his Curtiss-Wright as he banked her over Casilla. He had followed the straight line of the Southern Pacific tracks on his short flight down from El Paso until he was over the familiar rooftops, and he would now turn and fly along the road that led to the river until he reached the Cutter farm. In less than a minute he was over the small house and collection of outbuildings beneath the two tall cottonwoods; he circled once, then came in for his landing on the hard, flat dirt road that cut arrow-straight between two brown, fallow fields. He made a smooth touchdown, cut his engines, and taxied as close as he dared to the house without scaring the animals.

Anna was on the front porch of the house, a shawl thrown loosely around her shoulders to ward off the January chill, as she waved at her guest. Will removed his leather helmet, goggles, and scarf, and tossed them in the seat of the cockpit, then stripped off his heavy, padded aviator's jacket. Underneath he wore a rather incongruous dark business suit and vest. He hurried across the hundred yards or so of open space to where Anna stood. He embraced her warmly, kissing her briefly but intensely.

"Sorry I'm late, darling. Hope it didn't hold you up."

Their arms around each other's waists, they went into the house.

"Not at all, Will," she answered. "I've had plenty of accounting and paperwork today. Mama's up in Fabens. There's a mule auction up there, and she wanted to try to get another team if the price isn't too high. Lina's only just now getting lunch ready."

Inside, the Cutter house was transformed, unrecognizable from the dirt-floored two-room adobe Will had seen on his first visit to the Cutter farm. The previous fall, with part of the solid profit Ruth Cutter had made on her crop, she enlarged and rebuilt the house. Four generous rooms had been added on to either end of the house. There were now separate bedrooms for Ruth, Anna, and the boys, connected to a bathroom that held a gleaming white ceramic tub and matching washstand; a shallow well was dug in the room, with a hand pump, to provide easy access to wash water. The smaller of the original house's rooms, where Jonah and Ruth had slept, was now a well-equipped kitchen, presided over by Lina Mirkovsky, who came in daily to prepare meals for the Cutters and their laborers. Among the amenities were a large enamel-topped worktable, a bright iron-and-chrome wood-burning stove, and a handsome oak icebox with brass latches. At the other end of the house was a new office, a large, sunny room with three exposures and a connecting door to the original main room, now the sitting room. Ruth and Anna had stocked the office with solid new furnishings—desks and tables and swivel chairs; the windows overlooked the near fields and the sheds and stalls for tools and animals. The whole long facade of the extended house had been unified by a pitched tin roof that sloped into a deep porch the length of the house. Come summer, the porch would be spotted with rockers and gliders, for leisurely viewing of the large picket-fenced garden, which was just now being laid out in preparation for spring planting.

Will and Anna, as was their habit, went to the burgundy horsehair settee that presided over the neat but slightly cluttered sitting room, with its antimacassars, lace curtains, and scattered rag rugs. The room had a particular smell Will loved, the scent of fresh wax, which was applied frequently to the gleaming new oak floors of the house, floors of which Ruth was understandably very proud. Through the open doors at opposite ends of the room Will saw, first Lina's stout form bustling over the kitchen table, and second, at the opposite end, the now-empty office where Anna's desk stood with open ledgers and neat stacks of papers.

Will and Anna enacted this scene often—his noisy, airborne arrival, their quiet, chatty lunches in the sitting room—since Will took as many opportunities as possible to see Anna when he had to come down the valley during the week to call on clients. It was only after they had sat down that Anna saw that something was wrong. Will Channing, with his boyish, blond good looks, the fine, well-bred features, the bright blue eyes full of laughter and good cheer; Will, with his broad smile and quick and easy manner, had one of the least troubled dispositions of anyone Anna had ever known. When he was troubled, it showed in his face like a beacon. In all the time she had known Will, and especially during the year of their courtship, Anna had learned to read Will's every mood, every thought.

"What is it?" she asked as she took his large, elegant, comforting hands in her own. "You're not going to try to spare me this time, are you?"

Will smiled weakly at Anna's reference of his tendency to keep troublesome matters to himself. But his concern showed plainly through the smile.

"No, not this time. Can't, anyway, since it is already in all the papers in town."

Anna's face darkened, grew even more than usually serious, making her look older than her eighteen years. She moved a fraction closer to Will, tightened her grasp of his hands.

"There was trouble in Mexico yesterday. Terrible; a tragedy. The rebels stopped a train at San Ysabel, wherever that is, and pulled eighteen miners off the train. Shot them all in cold blood, with no provocation. Just because they were Americans working Mexican mines."

Will paused for a moment. Anna detected a faint tremble of his lips. It was clear that Will was more than concerned; there was real pain in his face.

"Three of the men worked for Channing Mines. Including one, a senior foreman, who got started with Mother back in the old days when she worked the first mine by herself. These men had wives and children, Anna. To be cut down like that, for no reason . . . My folks are destroyed, of course. And El Paso is in an uproar. There were riots last night, crowds of men and boys demonstrating in the plaza and at the bridge to Juarez. They threw garbage at the house on Oregon Street."

Anna knew he was referring to the house where Villa and his wife lived in 1914.

"Villa was burned in effigy in the plaza, and known sympathizers to his causes were harassed and beaten, their houses splattered with the contents of chamber pots," Will continued.

"It was still going on a bit this morning, Anna, and I'm afraid it's only the start of something. Now the federal government is bound to step in, and who knows where it will all lead."

"Those poor men," Anna said quietly when Will had finished his story. "So unnecessary, so cruel." The revolution had gripped Mexico during the last years, the fighting coming as close as Juarez, just across the Rio Grande from El Paso. Still, the war had always seemed rather dreamlike and distant to Anna, as it had to most Americans living along the border, whose lives were little affected by the turmoil in Mexico. Now, for the first time, the revolution had affected Anna on a human scale; it had come as close to her as Channing employees. Will's father, and, on occasion, even Will himself, rode the train through Chihuahua to Channing Mines. They easily could have been among the victims of the San Ysabel massacre. The whole world was slowly going mad, so it seemed: the war in Europe, the madness in Mexico. Life was tranquil, steady enough in Casilla, and the larger troubles of the world seemed very far away. But she wondered how long it could last.

Lina interrupted them with lunch, a fragrant, steaming repast of pork chops and kraut, served at the round oak pedestal table that presided over one end of the sitting room. Lina had been working at the Cutter place for two years now as cook and housekeeper, and the cheerful, industrious old woman had made life immeasurably easier for Ruth and Anna during their long hours of work in running the farm. To Anna's mind, hiring Lina was as wise a decision on their part as it had been to lease Kate's farm acreage from her beginning in 1914, when Ruth and Anna had become secure enough with the farm business to consider expanding their cotton acreage. Kate Mirkovsky was happy with the arrangement, too, since, relieved of the burden of trying to manage a farm by herself, the young widow could

devote her full energies to caring for Max Junior, born eight
months after his father's death, and for Vassily, who was now
too feeble for much activity of any kind.

Will and Anna enjoyed a leisurely lunch, a luxury Anna
could only afford during the fallow winter months, and by the
time Lina brought them mugs of steaming coffee, Will's mood
was immeasurably improved. It was always that way when he
was around Anna, or so it seemed to him. She had the ability,
just by her presence, to cheer him, to calm him. Though on the
surface Will seemed to be the most blessed, least worried man
in the world, even sometimes to Anna, who knew he was a
more serious, thoughtful, even brooding man than his surface
good nature revealed. He was a man who took life and its responsibilities very seriously indeed.

Will supposed there had never been a time that he had not
loved Anna, from that early June afternoon when he had arrived, fresh and chipper, from Yale Law School and newly en-
sconced in the family firm of Channing, Allen, & Channing, for
one of his first assignments as a lawyer. It had seemed a routine
enough assignment: Don Alonzo Lopez y Ruiz, old and dear
friend of his parents, was loaning several thousand dollars to a
woman with three children who had been abandoned by her
husband on their failing cotton farm. Alonzo was like an uncle
to Will, his grandson Bart one of his oldest and closest friends.
Will knew well that Alonzo had many times over the years
generously and secretly helped neighbors of his who were having financial difficulties, always with the insistence that the
loans be kept secret.

Will's first sight of the Cutters was still etched in his memory:
the mother, tall, erect, a stately, even noble-looking, woman
with both strength and suffering lurking in the depths of her
gray eyes; the two sons, such contrasts in their physical appearance, shyly watching the strange man in their sad home, their
faces marked with the pain caused by adult problems, yet visited on children who have no means to understand those problems. And there was Anna. Looking back, Will liked to think
that the Anna he saw that day had one foot in childhood, the
other in womanhood. Certainly there was the woman's body,
all too visible within the confines of her girl's dress. There was
her long, dark hair, done in two thick braids, which, even then,

he could easily imagine swept up in an elegant feminine coiffe, which would better reveal the lovely, sculpted lines of her face and neck, which seemed to him to be freshly emerged from the softer, fuller lines of a girl's face. Anna was shy, self-conscious; Will could see that easily enough, yet he could also see that the girl was one who could be transformed into something extraordinary. The delicate bud promised a magnificent rose, and to Will, who was so used to polished, studied women, Anna's naturalness was more than a little charming and attractive.

His first visit to the farm was brief: a quick discussion of the terms of the loan and his part in the deal. Ruth was obviously embarrassed by the very fact that she was borrowing money from Alonzo, and to make her more comfortable, Will carefully and subtly indicated that Alonzo had done this many times before, and that one reason why Alonzo preferred the formality of his attorney's office handling the loan was in part to insure privacy and discretion for the recipients of the loans. In fact, Alonzo need never be brought into the transaction at all; everything was to be handled through the offices of Channing, Allen, & Channing.

In the following months Will had been a frequent visitor to Casilla, and his fellow attorneys noticed that he was more than ready to take on new clients in the valley, until he reached a point that several days a week were spent away from the city. It was also noticed that Will paid special attention to the Cutters and that many of his visits were more of a social rather than legal nature. By the following summer Will was being teased by friends and associates for "being sweet on that pretty young farm girl," and though he joked in return when teased, he never denied his interest in Anna Cutter. Senator Channing, who had watched with great care his son's first year in the firm, was well aware that Will had more than a business interest in Casilla; Alonzo had filled the senator in on the gaps in the story that the senior Channing could not fill for himself. He had been enormously amused when his normally conservative son had taken up the rather faddish sport of airplaning, and he suspected that part of Will's interest in the sport was the speed and ease with which he could cover the thirty-five miles to Casilla.

Will had spent the next three years after his first visit watching as both Anna and the Cutter farm grew, matured, blossomed. After the flood there had been no hope of Ruth replanting the cotton crop, but once she had some capital to operate on, she planted ten acres of corn, tomatoes, and other vegetables to be sold to city markets, so there was at least some income from the land that season. Ruth and her children had done almost all the work themselves, from dawn to sunset that summer. Only in September, when classes began in the two-room schoolhouse in Casilla, did Ruth allow herself the luxury of a few hired field hands. Still, Anna and her brothers worked an hour or more both before and after school. In the evenings a quick supper, followed by homework.

Without intending to Will had fallen into a paternal role as far as the Cutter farm was concerned; he watched every moment of its growing years with the same kind of love-inspired interest that a father lavishes on his firstborn. The second season, through a combination of hard work, conservative living, and good luck, Ruth and her daughter brought in a fine crop, a bale and a half per acre from the full eighty acres of the land they owned. Not only were they able to repay the loan from Alonzo; they could afford to expand, and leased the Mirkovsky land, more than doubling their cultivated acreage. Will watched with enormous satisfaction as Anna emerged as a capable farm manager. Her mother was a good, sound businesswoman, comfortable with figures, but it was Anna who seemed to have the feel for the land, the understanding of the life that sprang, tall and green, from the brown earth.

He and Anna had slipped almost imperceptibly from friendship into romance, in the same way that the green seedlings in the fields grew up into the cotton-laden, mature plants. It began with a small thing—an afternoon of riding horseback up into the desert. They would lay out a saddle blanket on the mesa, a sweeping view of the valley below, and feast on a picnic of cold fried chicken and homemade pickles and corn bread, followed by a slice of Lina's magnificent pecan pie. They would sit for an hour or two with the vista of the river, the farms, and the distant, rough mountains stretching below them to the horizon across the river in Mexico to the south. On those winter afternoons, surrounded by the endless miles of desert waste that extended all around the small strip of human habitation in the valley, Will would talk about his life, his days of schooling in the East, his travels to New York, California, Mexico, Canada, Europe. He talked of Paris, the opera, the Eiffel tower, the promenades along the Seine, Notre Dame de Paris; he talked of châteaus presiding in ancient majesty over the hills covered with vineyards and of the snow-covered Alps. He told her about London, the West End theaters, Mayfair, Kensington Park, the Houses of Parliament, the Tower. He described the Temples of the Nile, seen from a slow-moving river steamer, and the harbors of Rio de Janeiro and San Francisco, seen from the bow of a passenger liner; he described the grass-covered, ruined temples of the Aztecs and the vast, unspoiled beauty of the Sierra Nevada. Anna would sit, mesmerized, listening to Will's tales of the larger world, sometimes asking for more description, more detail, wanting to have these unseen sights, these unfelt experiences, brought even more to life. At these times her world, bounded by the barren horizon, seemed very small indeed.

At times it was difficult for Anna to grasp what was happening between her and Will. It had all seemed so easy, so natural when, during their afternoons or evenings together, he had taken her hand or kissed her gently and told her how much he liked her, how much he wanted to spend time with her. After all, she reminded herself, Will Channing was an Ivy League lawyer, the son of a retired senator, the heir to a mining fortune, a member of one of the county's most socially prominent families. Yet this was not the Will she knew. Her Will was a man of great simplicity, of natural charm and ease. Though he often entertained her with tales of his varied, privileged, and glamorous life, it was with a childlike joy in what he had done, told with the excitement and enjoyment of a boy telling fairy tales. She had been invited on many occasions to meet Will's family, both when they visited their friend Don Alonzo at Casa Portillo and at their home in the city. She had seen the world they moved in, she had felt the almost palpable aura of sophistication and wealth that was their lives, yet she had come away from her meetings with the Channings with the distinct impression that they considered the Cutters their equals. For reasons she did not fully understand, that was very important to Anna, for she knew instinctively that she could not love a man who in his own mind elevated himself above those around him.

This particular afternoon Anna was especially concerned

about Will's frame of mind. They had come to know each other so well in the last years that they were acutely aware of one another's fluctuations in moods. Part of what they found so satisfying about their relationship was the fact that when either of them was "in a mood"—whether it be Will, concerned about a problem in the firm, or Anna, occupied with a problem among her hired hands—they would share the problem with one another. They were friends and confidants. Today, all through lunch, Anna had noticed how preoccupied Will was, and how nervous and fidgety, not at all like her calm, sunny-natured friend.

After Lina brought them freshly brewed coffee and a platter of delicious honey-sweetened pastries, Anna reached over and squeezed Will's arm to reassure him.

"The killing of those miners has you really upset, doesn't it?"

Will nodded. He fidgeted with the spoon in his coffee, deep in thought. Anna sensed that there was something he was trying to say yet had difficulty putting into words.

"Come on, Will," she encouraged. "This is no time to start holding back from me."

Will was silent for a moment, his handsome blond head held down in concentration. Then he broke into a grin, laughing at his own seriousness.

"Yes, what happened at San Ysabel has me upset. But that's not what I'm really wrestling with right now. It's you and me."

Anna felt a sudden flush of embarrassment, concerned that she might unwittingly have done something wrong, something to displease Will. That was the last thing in the world she wanted to do.

"Have I said something . . . ?" she volunteered, hoping that this wouldn't be too painful.

Will threw his head back, laughed that light-filled laugh that was so very much his own.

"You're way off the track, Anna. It's just . . . just that I've been thinking lately about how much I love you and about how long I've been feeling that way about you. I've also been thinking about the fact that I'm twenty-eight now, almost an old man!"

Will studied Anna's face, trying to guess what was going on behind those gray eyes. He could tell that she knew what he was getting at—there was a flash of anticipation in her face—but he could not guess exactly what her reaction was going to be.

"Damn!" he whispered under his breath. "I'm a lawyer, for God's sake, and supposed to be able to get to the point, even when under pressure of courtroom situations. This isn't easy, but I have to get on with it!"

"I promise I won't faint."

"Then I think it's time you and I talked about getting married."

"Yes, I think we should talk about it," Anna replied in a matter-of-fact way.

Will looked enormously relieved and surprised by her reaction.

"You mean, you're not totally against the idea?" Will sounded like a boy who had been told that, in spite of rumors to the contrary, there really was a Santa Claus. It was at moments like this that Anna realized how very much she did love Will Channing. Her mother had often said that he was the most charming and lovable of men, and she had to agree that her mother was right.

"It has crossed my mind," she said, trying hard not to sound too coquettish. "After all, Mr. Channing, I would not exactly be a normal eighteen-year-old girl if I hadn't at least thought that the man who had courted me for two years might eventually ask her to marry him. I think most unmarried girls spend a good deal of their time dreaming of wedded bliss. Oh, Will, I do love you, and I have many times thought what it would be like to be Mrs. Will Channing."

"Then you'll say yes."

Will caught a look in her eye that dampened his enthusiasm.

"I'm sorry, Anna," he apologized. "That was presumptuous of me, to expect you to make a decision like that in two seconds."

He knew Anna well enough to know that she was a careful and thoughtful girl. After all, part of what had drawn him to her in the first place was her seriousness, that maturity beyond her years. It wouldn't have been his Anna if she had said yes right off.

Anna got up from the table and went to the connecting door to the kitchen. She shut it so Lina would not hear too much of their conversation. As she moved across the room, from table to door, then to the settee by the window, Will watched with admiring eyes as Anna's tall, slender body moved under her simple blue wool skirt and jacket. She had the same kind of unconscious grace as her mother but, just as Anna's body was fuller, riper, her movements were more sensual. Will found her enormously attractive, desirable, so much so that he knew, no matter what her answer would be, that he would wait, try again, continue the assault to win her hand.

Will sat beside her on the settee, his arm protectively around her shoulder. It was she who now looked preoccupied, anxious. He apologized for having put her in a mood.

"No, it's all right," she replied. "We've got to talk about all this. You see, I've agonized over all this, hour after hour, myself. I suppose most women would tell me I'm a complete fool for even hesitating a moment at a marriage proposal from Will Channing."

"But you're not most girls. That's the whole point, you see. If you were like the rest of the pack, I wouldn't be here right now. Don't you think I know that, in certain circles at least, I'm considered quite a catch? For years now I've had every silly debutante in the county throwing herself at me with the most outrageous examples of phony flirtatiousness you can ever imagine. Most times their mothers are right behind them, wielding a riding crop, urging their little beauty on to win the race to marry the senator's son—or I should say, to marry the senator's money. I could never marry a girl like that, though God knows at times the pressure has been pretty heavy."

"But I think that is the world you should marry into, Will. Oh, I don't mean some silly little flirt who just wants to marry well. I mean, a woman who is from your kind of life, who has money and social position. A woman who has gone to college and traveled. Who appreciates fine clothes and beautiful houses. Who likes to give fancy parties and use all the best crystal and china. Look at me, Will—I'm a country girl, a farmer. I just finished high school, that's all. I've never been anywhere but El Paso and the little town back East where I was born. I could never fit in your world."

"I think you underestimate yourself, sweetheart. As far as I can tell, you can pretty much do anything you set your mind to.

Remember, you're still young. There are a lot of doors that haven't opened up in your life yet."

Anna was quiet for a moment. When she spoke, there was a note of sadness in her voice. "I don't think they ever will."

"Don't say that! You're making yourself old before your time. You have to remember that you have a wonderful life ahead of you."

"It doesn't seem that way sometimes. All the work on the farm—it's endless. And how can I think of marriage with my brothers still in school? How could I leave Mama with the full burden of raising two boys and running a farm?"

"You wouldn't have to do that. I wouldn't allow it. You see, I don't want a wife who is some kind of hothouse flower, though I won't swear that I won't spoil you horribly. I admire that you're 'the lady farmer' around here. I could never ask you to give that up—it would go against your nature. I don't want you to give up your life for me. I just want you to share it with me."

His words deeply touched her; they were unexpected yet so very much like Will. Perhaps in her mind she had built too strong a case against marrying Will. There was no doubt that his feelings for her were deep and genuine, yet realizing that brought up the frightening thought that perhaps it was her own feelings she didn't trust.

"You do love me, don't you?" he asked.

She lowered her head to his shoulder; felt the reassuring rough wool of his suit against her face.

"Oh, I do, Will, I do!"

"Then isn't that enough?"

"I don't know. My mother and father loved each other, I'm sure of that, but it wasn't enough."

Will touched her hair and brow with kisses.

"True, darling, but I'm a very different man from your father, and you're a different woman from your mother. Our story won't be the same, you can be sure of that."

Anna was suddenly overwhelmed by the sheer wonderfulness of the man. He was like a gift, a blessing, in her life. She knew that she would probably not have made it through these last hard years if Will had not been there to encourage her, advise her, to make her feel happy, to make her feel loved.

He lifted her head, held her face where he could see her

clearly. He asked the question silently, with his eyes, then held her gaze until she answered.

"Yes, I will," she whispered as tears finally broke free to roll down her pale cheeks. "Just, please, be patient. There are so many things to be done, so many things to work out. . . ."

"I'll be patient beyond your dreams, Anna. As long as I can have my life with you. Just wait and see."

He kissed her, a long, deep kiss, full of love and meaning. They stayed a long time on the settee, holding one another in silence, accompanied by the ticking of the wall clock, like a counterpoint to the beating of their hearts.

Finally Will realized the time and, with reluctance, extracted himself from Anna's arms. Once the moment of decision had come, there was little for them to say, except with their eyes, their lips, their arms. As Will stood to go he took a last sip of his now-cold coffee. His face glowed with happiness, a glow that seemed to fill the room with warmth and light.

"Of course, we have to talk to your mother. Got to confess that my folks already know what I'm up to. They think you're swell and wholly approve of my choice of fiancées."

"Mama's going to be pleased as punch, too, I'm sure of that."

Will gave her one last hug.

"Wonderful! Now, just one favor, little miss. If I'm going to have to wait a month of Sundays to marry you, can I at least have the satisfaction of announcing our engagement right away? In two weeks or so Mother is giving one of her big dos. A dinner dance in honor of General Pershing, now that he's the commander of the Fifth at Fort Bliss. It would be a great night to make the announcement and a good chance for you to get your feet wet in the big city social whirl. I'm sure you're going to take to it just fine."

"You're trying to make me into a society matron even before we're married," she teased, "but what can I do but say yes? Announce it to the whole world, and I'll be there in a pretty new dress."

"See, I knew you were going to make me a happy man! It's starting already. Mother will pull out all the stops for this party, you can be sure of that. And we may have a special treat if the workings of the military don't foul up things. Word is that

General Pershing may be bringing one of his aides to Fort Bliss from San Francisco. Some scoundrel named Bart Bradley. If all goes well, Bart will be transferred to El Paso in two weeks and may be in town in time for the party. Old Bart always told me there were two occasions in my life he wouldn't miss on a bet—my wedding and my funeral. It's going to be a great night!"

With that, Will hurried out the door as he called out a thank-you to Lina for his lunch. He trotted across to the biplane parked on the road, flipped the ignition switch, spun the propeller blade until the engine sputtered and roared into life. In seconds he was in the cockpit, waving merrily as he taxied through the barren fields.

Anna waved good-bye, then turned and went again to the settee, elated, exhausted, confused. Will had asked her to become engaged to be married, and she had said yes. It frightened her to have made that decision, perhaps the biggest one she would ever make in her life. It seemed so right, yet there were so many nagging doubts. And now there was the news that Bart was coming back to the valley. It had shocked her when Will had told her the news. Shocked her and made her feel something else, a feeling she couldn't name, a feeling that wrenched her gut. Why? she asked herself. Why should she have these strange feelings? She thought that she was rid of him, of those images of his face, his body, which had haunted her for so many years. He had been like a demon that had to be exorcised, so powerful had those images of him become. She had fought terrible battles with herself as she lay awake in her dark room, as her mind conjured up visions of his naked body coupling with that woman in the dark pantry at Casa Portillo; visions of his muscled, sweating flesh as he greeted her in the stable that afternoon; visions of his face as he lowered himself to her that afternoon by the river. How many nights had she felt, as if it were real, the touch of his arms, his lips, so much so that her flesh tingled and her own hands sought out the curves, the folds of her body.

She had battled the demon, month after month, and won, or so she thought. Her mind was now filled with thoughts and images of Will; he had taken his rightful place in her dreams. Now, at this of all times, Anna realized that the demon still lurked within her. He was still there, to be fought.

Chapter Two

EDNA CHANNING'S DINNER BALL IN HONOR OF JOHN PER-
shing was finally set for a mid-March evening, in order to give
El Paso's most noted hostess ample time to make the elaborate
arrangements she so loved to make for these kinds of affairs.
Mrs. Channing had in part wanted the time to go to even more
than the usual trouble because the evening was also to mark the
engagement of her son to Anna Cutter. Edna had wholeheartedly approved of Will's choice of fiancée: she had spent too
many years watching her son fend off an army of ambitious
girls, looking to make an advantageous marriage, that it was
deeply satisfying to her to see him in love with a girl who was so
very fresh and independent with a life and a mind of her own.
The Channings had also kept a close watch on Ruth Cutter in
the years since they had first met her at Casa Portillo, for they
knew full well of Alonzo's feelings for the abandoned Mrs. Cutter. It was a frustrating business, seeing dear Alonzo so in love
with a woman who, had she not clung so stubbornly to the
misguided hope that her husband would, or should, return,
would have made such a fine companion for Alonzo's autumn
years. Edna and the senator had already expressed the hope
that Anna's engagement to their son might encourage her
mother to open herself up to a relationship with Alonzo.

In the weeks after Will and Anna's conversation over lunch
at the farm, Edna made a great effort to welcome Ruth and
Anna into the Channing family. She and Jack made weekly
trips to Casilla to visit Alonzo, making sure that the Cutters
were invited to the *hacienda* for lunch or dinner. And Ruth and
Anna were encouraged to visit the city as often as their work
schedules would allow. Edna insisted that the women stay as
guests at the Channing house, where they enjoyed the unheard-

of luxury of private baths with gold fixtures and hot water on tap, antique-filled bedrooms rich with damask hangings, and maids only one pull of the bell cord away.

Anna had felt an immediate liking for Will's mother when she had first met her three years before at Alonzo's, and as they came to be on more intimate terms, Anna began to see how Will had turned out to be the man he was: Edna was one of the most honest, direct, down-to-earth people she had ever met.

She was, to say the very least, a homely woman, tall, bony-faced with a rather horsey, buck-toothed smile. But her lack of physical beauty was more than compensated for by her personality. She talked incessantly, in a hearty, if piercing, East Texas twang. Her taste in clothing was impeccable, as was her taste in all other areas as well, and her eye for beauty was an ironic compensation for her own ugliness. Her greatest passion was jewels, which she bought and wore in abundance. Garlands of pearls, coral, garnets, and diamonds, which would have seemed garish on most women, appeared, on Edna, as just enough.

Senator Jack Channing was a complete contrast to his wife. He was a tall, stately, silver-haired man whose refined and handsome features had clearly been the source of his son's good looks. He was a soft-spoken man of dazzlingly good manners, whose quiet and eminently polite speech revealed his aristocratic Virginia birth. The senator was very much the patrician sort. Born of moderate wealth and excessive pedigree, the only work he had done in his life was to pursue a gentlemanly, if dedicated, career in the United States Senate, followed by genteel retirement as the titular head of Channing, Allen, & Channing. The family mining business, which was a vastly successful one, he left totally up to his beloved Edna.

As she began to learn more about the Channings Anna also began to understand more clearly why she and her mother were so accepted and liked by them. Edna had begun life as the daughter of sharecroppers in the cotton fields of East Texas. After the death of her mother from typhus her father had pulled up and moved to New Mexico, where he had staked a prospecting claim. Edna and her father had lived for years in a tent in the desert, eking out the most meager existence. Finally her father had struck a modest copper lode, though, tragically, a few months later, he died in a fall from a rock outcropping.

Edna, a girl of sixteen, had stayed on, working the claim by herself until she made enough from her modest diggings to hire occasional digging help. Her perseverance had paid off, and the modest lode her father discovered proved to be only a small branch of an enormous copper field that had eventually become one of the largest open-pit copper mines in the world, the heart of Channing Mines, Ltd. It was clear that Edna understood and appreciated what Ruth and Anna had done with their farm. They were women cut from the same cloth.

Edna had taken it upon herself to teach the Cutter women the vices of extravagance and luxury, as evidenced one morning when she met them in the egg-yolk-colored breakfast room with its glass cases filled with Sèvres. As they sat down to eat—Anna noted with some amusement that Edna was the only woman she had ever known who wore jewelry to breakfast—Mrs. Channing proclaimed in her ear-shattering twang, "Shop! Shop! I want you ladies to go out there and shop! And come evening, I want this house to be inundated with gowns. Hatboxes. Jewel cases! Spend some of that money! What's all your hard work for if you can't be foolish with your money!"

Though they laughed at her advice, they took it, at least in moderation. It was a thrill, though something of a guilt-laden one, for Ruth and Anna to finally afford themselves some of the feminine luxuries they had so long denied themselves. Edna's harangue had in fact reminded them that, as of this year, their little farm had become profitable, and nicely so. There were no debts, and the bank balance was, by their standards, sizable.

The Channing house stood in white-columned majesty overlooking a full square block of impeccably maintained lawns. Though the house was only five years old and featured every luxury of the modern sort, from electric lighting to an elevator to central heating in pipes, it affected the grand Greek-revival style of the great plantation homes of eight decades before. The main facade with its eight tall, fluted Corinthian columns, presided over a broad paved avenue lined with homes of almost equal grandeur. After their breakfasts with Senator Jack and Edna, Ruth and Anna would walk down the broad brick drive, amazed in a sense even to find themselves in such a home and wait for the bright green horse-drawn trolley that rattled down the broad avenue every fifteen minutes, en route for the center of the city, a mile distant.

Though El Paso was only thirty-five miles from Casilla, the city was still very much a foreign place to the Cutters. They came to the city twice, at most three times a year, usually for an hour or two to buy supplies. Their trips during February and March of 1916 were the first opportunities they had had to spend real leisure time in the city, to enjoy the sights and pleasures of the place. Like all rural people, they found the city both fascinating and frightening, an exotic foreign world. As the trolley jostled along its shiny steel tracks, the majestic procession of mansions that proclaimed the new wealth of this new city that was rising out of the desert gave way to larger commercial buildings, vast structures that loomed over the traffic-clogged streets. The city was growing fast, flexing its muscles of glass and steel and concrete, like some healthy young animal full of its own strength. Everywhere, even more than they remembered from past times there, there were signs of growth: new buildings half built, old buildings half demolished. Cartloads of bricks and mortar rumbled through the streets, and doors and piles of window frames with glass already in place were stacked at construction sites, waiting for the walls to hold them. Some of the newer buildings, to their amazement, loomed twelve and fifteen stories above the noisy streets.

It was on the streets, though, that the peculiar quality of the city revealed itself. The asphalted streets were choked with traffic, vehicles as varied as the city itself. Men rode horseback, threading their way among the horse- and mule-drawn wagons. These, in turn, vied for passage with the sputtering, noisy automobiles, which had been a rarity on the Cutters' early trips to the city and were now filling the streets in almost equal numbers to the horse-drawn vehicles. The people, too, were a jumbled sort. There were the handsomely dressed, stylish Americans, women parading around in their walking suits, their shoulders draped in furs, to ward off any sudden cold that might appear unexpectedly on a mild midwinter day. Men strolled with them in fashionably tailored suits and bowler hats. By contrast, there were the older, more familiar citizens: the rumpled, rough-looking cattlemen with their mud-caked boots and sweat-stained felt hats. And there were the Mexicans, reminder of the fast-disappearing old El Paso, who walked the modern streets in bare feet or sandals, garbed in the simple white cotton dresses and *pantalones* their forebears had worn for generations.

There was one other group that stood out as Ruth and Anna walked along the crowded sidewalks, or strolled through the plaza with its grove of bare-branched elms, or dined in electrified splendor in the dining room of the Hotel Orndorff: El Paso was full of men in uniforms. Singly or in groups, some apparently on their own time, others on official business, the soldiers were there in numbers, no matter what their business. Their dark olive uniforms—jodhpurs, black leather knee boots, high-peaked flat brimmed hats—all bore the distinctive bright yellow shoulder patch that proclaimed the Fifth U.S. Army Cavalry of Fort Bliss. This strong military presence was a reminder that there was a war in Europe, a war that every day threatened to pull in the United States. It was a reminder that there was an endless, brutal revolution in Mexico, which threatened to spill over the border into the American side of the Rio Grande Valley. And it was a reminder of a different kind to Anna, a reminder that in a matter of days or weeks there would be another soldier assigned to the Fifth Cavalry, a soldier that would be there the night her engagement was announced.

Edna Channing had directed them well, for they found the shops and dry goods stores she recommended, where every kind of item a feminine heart could desire was available—for a price. Ruth and Anna, so used to being tight with every penny, slipped more easily than they would have thought into the delight of their shopping spree. Though they did not indulge themselves on the scale that Edna Channing might have, by the end of their afternoon there was a respectable pile of boxes and parcels piled at their feet as they rode the open-air trolley back along the mansion-lined avenue to the Channing residence. There was one particular purchase, the extravagance of which would have pleased Edna Channing no end: the beaded silk Poiret gown, purchased for the staggering sum of one hundred dollars, which Anna had bought to wear the night of her engagement party. The gown was so special, and the evening on which it was to be worn was so special, that neither Anna nor her mother had had any difficulty in justifying its purchase. The

only thing that had troubled Anna about the dress was the
thought that had come into her mind as she tried it on in the
shop. She had wondered whether or not Bart Bradley would
like it.

Three days before the affair at Senator Channing's, an event
took place that sent shock waves through the entire nation and
had a marked effect on affairs along the Rio Grande. On March
sixteenth, the isolated dusty little ranch town of Columbus, one
hundred miles west of El Paso, was attacked by Pancho Villa
and a band of his men. The attack had come without warning.
Seventeen innocent Americans were killed in the unprovoked
raid, several buildings burned, and most of the rest of the town
was damaged. The attack was as much an outrage as the San
Ysabel massacre, with the added insult that Villa himself had
led the raid and that he had crossed into United States Territory. Villa was clearly showing off, being spiteful, because the
Washington government continued to back the established,
Mexico City-based regime of Venustiano Carranza. El Paso and
the border towns, like Casilla, were in an uproar at the news,
and for some days people slept badly for fear that their homes, a
mile or less from the river, would be attacked next. There was a
general sigh of relief, as well as hearty cheers of approval, when
President Wilson ordered Blackjack Pershing to take the Fifth
Cavalry out of Fort Bliss and pursue Villa and his band of
rogues into the Chihuahua wilderness, a "punitive raid" designed to teach the arrogant revolutionary to leave American
lives and property alone. Suddenly the Channing party took on
added significance, for it was to be a send-off for Pershing and
his troops. And, as Alonzo was the first to point out, it meant
that Bart was very quickly to be plunged into his first military
combat situation.

The afternoon of the party Anna made a futile attempt to
have a *siesta* in the guest room she occupied upstairs. She
counted the globes on the electric chandelier overhead, listened
to odd noises and snatches of conversation as the maids and
caterers, decorators and florists, made preparations downstairs
for the evening's event. She made a mental list of things that
needed immediate attention as soon as she and her mother re-

turned to the farm; she reconsidered the wisdom of the French gown she had chosen to wear that evening and wondered what she could possibly say to the hundreds of people who would be meeting her tonight and expecting some kind of intelligent response. Worst of all, she imagined the whole litany of shocked and amazed responses guests might have on hearing the astonishing news that this bumpkin of a girl was to be Will Channing's bride.

Finally she gave up and got out of bed. Ruth, as restless as her daughter, was already up and in the white-tiled bath that separated their rooms. She had already finished soaking in the fragrant water that filled the claw-footed ceramic tub; Anna soon took her place while they marveled at the luxury of hot tap water—enough that they each could have their own fresh tubful —and of a special maid to come and do their hair. It all seemed very dreamlike, a million miles from the cozy, neat rooms of their house in Casilla. An hour later the maid had just left after expertly coiffing Anna and Ruth's hair into great dark coils on the top of their heads. Ruth's hair was adorned with pearls, loaned by Mrs. Channing, while Anna was dramatically bedecked with a spray of emerald-colored feathers, carefully chosen to match the emerald silk of her silver-beaded gown.

The festivities downstairs had already begun when Anna stood in front of the tall gilt-framed beveled mirror to inspect the results of her transformation. The sounds of the salon orchestra provided accompaniment to her posing. And it was indeed a transformation Anna reflected in the mirror. The glistening sheath of the gown, with its deeply cut front and back necklines, enhanced the full, alluring curves of a woman's body; her uplifted and adorned hair revealed a fine line of shoulder and neck, and her face, framed in dark coils of hair with subtle but distinct marks of rouging, had become the face of a sophisticated, glamorous woman. At first the woman in the mirror was a stranger to Anna. Then, as she turned and posed, she did indeed recognize herself in that woman. It was her body, her face, her beauty. She felt a very deep, almost erotic thrill to see for the first time that she could be something she thought she never could. It gave her confidence for the evening to come.

At eight-fifteen Will rang up on the house phone to ask if she and Ruth were ready to be fetched downstairs. There was a last-minute flurry of inspection and adjustment, and they were out of the rooms. As they traversed the broad floral-carpeted expanse of the upstairs hall toward the broad double landing of the stairs, Ruth took Anna's arm and pulled her daughter close as they walked.

"You look very beautiful this evening," she said, "and I'm very proud of you. Will is a fine man and will make a good husband for you. If my mother's instinct is right, you'll have many happy years together. I only wish your father were here to see you this evening."

Anna held back a sudden surge of anger at her mother, at the mention of Jonah. How she wished her mother would stop speaking of him in that reverential way, as if he were some hero on the battlefield who was kept from his family because of the forces of fate. How much she wanted to cry out to Ruth, "Four years! He's been gone four years! And he'll never come back!" But Anna knew too well that she could never say that to Ruth; the illusion that Jonah would one day return was often what had kept Ruth going during those hard years when, lonely, depressed, and exhausted, she had gotten up at dawn for yet another day of labor in the fields. Anna still rankled with anger at the thought of her father's abandonment; it was a deep wound that she suspected would never heal. But at least she had no illusions about the man. If she had wanted him to be there that night, it would only be to have shown him what a fool he'd been to run away, to show him how very much indeed he had underestimated his wife and children.

Anna's anger at her mother for mentioning Jonah at this, of all times, faded quickly. It always did. For as much as Anna admired her mother's strength, she pitied her loneliness, her self-deception. How sad, Anna thought, that Ruth was going downstairs to meet a man who loved her, who wanted more than anything to make her happy, yet to whose love she was blind.

Will met them on the broad landing, in front of the jewel-toned stained-glass window with its scene of an Arcadian glade. He was looking handsomer than ever in his dinner clothes, and as he bent to kiss their hands, first Ruth's, then Anna's, Anna suspected that from the broad smile on his face, the happy light in his eyes, he was very pleased with the ladies he was about to escort into the thick of the evening.

Jack and Edna Channing were in the foyer at the foot of the broad first landing, greeting the steady stream of guests who made their bejeweled and befurred way through the wide-open front doors. Beyond the portico, through the doors, Anna could see the sleek, dark sides of the cars and carriages as they paused in the carriage drive to let off their cargoes of partygoers.

"Oh, darlings," Edna called out when she saw them, "you're just *visions. Visions,* the both of you." She kissed them both with a considerable rattling of necklaces and bracelets, then added with a wink, "And your gowns just take the cake. You must promise to reveal your couturier to old Edna." The senator, next to his wife, was glowing every bit as much as his son was. He kissed Ruth's hand, then took the liberty of kissing Anna on the cheek.

"Welcome, my dear," he said in his softest drawl. "It's going to be just lovely having you with us. Will's made me promise to wait until midnight, so not a word to anyone until then!"

Will steered his guests into the heart of the affair. The main floor of the house was a series of vast rooms glowing with light from dozens of chandeliers. The light, in turn, was reflected in tall, beveled mirrors, glittered off ornate gold frames. The finely carved paneling with its deep, intricate moldings and fluted pilasters, was hung with a collection of fine canvases. Underfoot, the floors were of inlaid marble or rich golden-brown parquet, half covered with fine Persian carpets of many hues.

The guests were as extraordinary as the house. Richly dressed, heavily jeweled, the women vied with the decor of the house in extravagance. The men, by contrast, were tailored, elegant in their black dinner suits or medal-laden uniforms.

As they worked their way through the crowded first salon, many guests turned to greet Will, in both English and Spanish, as they eyed the woman, unknown to most of them, whose arm he held. They stopped at the refreshment table, a long banquette of white linen laden with flowers and glittering with crystal, attended by an army of white-jacketed waiters, each stationed in front of a tub of iced champagne. Will handed a bubbling glass to Anna, then took one for Ruth. It was then that they noticed they had lost her in the journey across the crowded room. They looked back to see her in the thick of the crowd, deep in conversation with Don Alonzo.

Anna smiled at the sight.

"I think she cares for him more than she's willing to admit."

"I think you're right," Will answered, keeping the glass intended for Ruth for himself. "I'll lay money they won't be out of each other's sight all night."

Anna wrinkled her nose; nodded in agreement.

"What do you think so far?"

"About the party?"

"And about becoming a social butterfly, living the high life in the big city, all those things you swore you weren't cut out for."

"The party's wonderful."

"Yes, Mother does have that knack of throwing together a 'do.' All the local social bigwigs. Lots of politicians—that's for father's end of things. Her club friends. They *all* talk a lot, if you ask me. And these days, a lot of refugees from Mexico. The money crowd from down there. And she always throws in a few of the more intellectual types. Writers, artists, professors from the college. And a few old buddies from her mining days— they're the ones in the baggy borrowed evening clothes. Mother never deserts a friend."

"What's her secret to making it all work?"

"Get them all drunk, so she says. Seems to work. And, to that noble end . . ." Will raised his glass in a toast.

"Before I salute you, darling, you must finish answering my question. The part about becoming a social butterfly."

"Oh, Will, I do love you!" she said, giggling.

"Shhh! I said to answer my question, not tell me what in the world I most want to hear. Now . . ."

"Well," she mused in mock thoughtfulness, "I'd say that, after the first fifteen minutes, it's just great."

"Music to my ears," Will said as he clinked the rim of his glass to hers. "In that case, here's to *us.*"

The champagne, as cold as it was, seemed to have a warming effect on Anna. She soon felt more relaxed, caught up in the energy and spirit of the evening. She found herself in animated conversation with Will, walking through the groups, being introduced to the various mistresses and *señoras,* misters and *se-*

ñors; it seemed that Will introduced her to a hundred different people. She recalled brief slips of conversation: a dark, almost Oriental-looking woman, all in black, asking her where she found the stunning gown; a burly sunburned man talking about the unexpected good yield on his cotton acreage this year and the surprised look on his face when she commented on her own yields. She vaguely remembered talking intently with the stranger about the effect she thought the European War would have on cotton prices; there was a conversation about the quality of accommodations at the hotel with a Mexican couple she recognized from the hotel restaurant; even a dialogue with the senator about the effect of irrigation on the new dam upriver in the valley. All the while Will was beside her, shepherding her through the whirl of new faces and sensations, enjoying himself, enjoying her.

When the orchestra began playing, Will and Anna went right away to the large French-windowed room that stretched across the entire back of the house, opening onto broad terraces. There, as other couples moved onto the polished floor, she and Will began dancing. Anna was hesitant at first. She had only danced before in Casilla, practicing steps with some of the other farm girls, as teenage girls always do, or dancing on summer Saturday evenings with the awkward, silly Wilkerson boys. But as soon as Will put his arm around her waist and lifted her hand up in his, she found the movement to the music, the steps around and around the room easy and soon exhilarating. She had no idea how long they danced, but it seemed like a very long time. They stopped from time to time for another glass of champagne and then danced again. Sometimes Will talked while they danced. He had to put his face close to her ear, to be heard above the music, and when he did, she felt his warm breath and the lightest touch of his mustache.

As they whirled around the floor, caught up in the movement and the music, Anna watched the other guests, those dancing and those standing to the side, as she whirled past them. Occasionally she would see them looking at her and Will, but she wasn't bothered by it.

On one turn through the room Anna saw over Will's shoulder a group of men in uniform. She knew in an instant that one of them was Bart. Perhaps it was just the music, but it seemed that they were dancing faster all of a sudden, circling the room. On each turn she saw Bart. He was watching her, a small smile clearly visible on his lips.

Will must have seen Bart, too, as they turned.

"There's Bradley. He must have just gotten here." The mustache brushed her ear again. "Want to say hello? I'm sure he's anxious to talk to you after all these years."

Anna replied quickly, "Let's finish this dance. It's such a nice tune to dance to!"

"And I was hoping it was me and not the music!"

Will guided her around the room, again and again. She couldn't help but notice Bart each time he came into her line of vision. Sometimes he watched her, sometimes he talked with his companions. Anna threw herself even more into dancing. The steps came easily, fluidly, her body moving in graceful, swanlike gestures to the lilt of the music. She knew she was dancing well; the energy of it coursed through her, feeling the ebb and flow of her body against Will, the rhythmic counterpoint of her feet to the floor, the fabric of her dress moving against the movement of her body.

When the music stopped, Will took her, breathless from exertion, to where Bart stood. He held out both hands to her, taking hers in them.

His voice boomed out cheerfully, a smile breaking out.

"So this is our little Anna. Will, you secretive rascal, you should have told me she'd grown up so much."

"I thought you'd be surprised."

"I should think you'd be surprised if I hadn't changed. It has been almost three years." Anna found it easy—much easier than she would have thought minutes ago—to talk to Bart. She seemed to be floating, feather-light. He had changed too. Taller, broader. His frame carried more weight, visible under the meticulously tailored uniform. His black hair was sleek and brilliantined, a sharp contrast to his skin, pale from the San Francisco winter. The added maturity of the past years had only emphasized the fine sculpted structure of his face.

He seemed genuinely glad to see her.

"And grandfather has kept me up to date. Tells me things are going well and that you're quite a businesswoman now." Bart looked to Will and said conspiratorially, "If this is what a few

seasons of running a farm will do for a woman, I think we
should get a law passed not letting men within a mile of a
cotton field."

Even though there was a teasing tone in his voice, she was
flattered.

"Careful, Bart, you'll spoil her."

"Shh. Let him go on, or spoil me yourself."

"Gladly." Will gripped her arm gently.

"No," Bart cautioned, "we'd better ease up, or we'll have just
another one of these spoiled debutantes on our hands."

Anna affected a little coquettish curtsey. "Why, Mr. Bradley,
I'm a farmhand. I'll be behind a mule team come seven o'clock
tomorrow morning."

Bart made a move to leave the group. He clapped Will on the
shoulder. "In that case, Channing, you'd better not keep Anna
up too late. The fields need tending. Just leave one dance open
for me before it's time to harness the mules."

Will chuckled. "I don't think Anna's going to be anywhere
near a farm tomorrow morning. Most likely she'll be taking a
leisurely breakfast, the world at her feet."

"Or taking a leisurely ride beneath the cottonwood trees."
Bart's eyes narrowed a fraction. "You do still go riding by the
river in the afternoons, don't you?"

She felt the little jab from Bart and shot back, "Only when
I'm bored."

He threw back his head and roared, the thick cords of neck
muscle working as he laughed.

"I can see that you've learned to flirt as well as to farm."

With that, he excused himself and slipped back into the
crowd of guests.

Hours later the buffet supper was over and cleared away. The
orchestra played again, faster and louder, the champagne
flowed colder and freer, and the chandeliers glittered brighter.
Anna danced again with Will, Don Alonzo, Jack Channing,
with Bart. He held her at some length, their bodies not touching
as hers and Will's had, but his huge hands were like iron vises
where they gripped her at hand and waist. He didn't speak
while they danced, and she was left to her own imagination as
to what lay behind his rather distant, but amused, expression.

Then she was dancing with Will once again and then with a

short, cheerful fellow, a friend of the senator's, whose name she couldn't remember. There were others who danced with her or caught her in conversations at the refreshment table or in one of the quiet drawing rooms that opened off the great room. It was so easy for her now, to fall into casual, offhanded talk, to laugh at jokes, to chatter amiably about the city, the party, politics, farming, the music, the dinner. She saw her mother, too, from time to time, floating among the guests, on the arm of Alonzo or the senator or Mrs. Channing. Ruth was enjoying herself, too; Anna could tell that easily, and she was glad to see her mother, so handsome, so elegant, in this beautiful and elegant surrounding.

Then she was missing Will. He had been gone for what seemed like a very long time. She searched the main rooms but with no success. But there was Bart, across the ballroom, going out the doors to the terrace. They had danced only once. Perhaps her would ask her again, if he saw her.

He was standing at the end of the terrace, by the stone rail that overlooked the neat hedges and lawns below. As she walked up to him he was lighting a cigarette.

He didn't seem surprised to see her.

"Cigarette?" He held the silver case to her.

She declined.

"So you're not a totally modern woman, eh? They say that soon as many women will be taking tobacco as men. Thought you might be out here in the night air to indulge in a little smoking."

It was a cool, crisp spring night. The chill made her suddenly feel the warmth from the party and the dancing.

"No, I just can't find Will. I was in the mood for another turn on the dance floor."

"You *have* changed." He exhaled, the silvery coil of smoke curling between their faces and up into the darkness.

"How so?"

"I think you know. Certainly more than I can describe in a word or two."

His voice was calmer, less boisterous than it had been before, inside. He was a bit solemn, even moody.

"I didn't mean to tease you before about learning to be a flirt. And mentioning that day by the river . . . it wasn't really fair

of me, not a Texas-gentleman, army-officer kind of thing to do.
I'm sorry if I embarrassed you in front of Will."

"Thank you for the apology, but I don't think Will understood what you were getting at. It was a private joke, after all."

"Don't underestimate Will. He's no fool."

"I know that. But he knew nothing of that afternoon and has
no reason to. It was a long time ago. A childish sort of incident.
I'm frankly surprised either of us remembered it."

Anna had intended her words to make light of the incident,
to push it into the safe distance of the dim, youthful past. But as
she spoke Bart's eyes narrowed, intensified, glowed with that
same green-gold light that had hypnotized her years before. The
memory of that afternoon, the feel of his hands and lips on her
body came back once again, as they had so often over the years.
The flesh of her back and neck bristled, as if she had been swept
by a quick chill.

"I do remember it—very well," he said quietly, with a
thoughtful half smile on his face. "I've often asked myself why.
After all, you were just another pretty young girl who ran away
when I made a pass at her. I'm sure there are plenty of those
incidents I've forgotten. But you were different, Anna. And I'm
not just saying that to flatter you or to set you up for another
pass. I've often pictured you, in your pants and shirt, the way
you looked that afternoon by the river, your face all pink and
flushed with excitement when you pulled away from me. I've
wondered how you grew up. Remembered the shape of your
body, the curves of it, tried to picture how they had filled,
ripened."

Anna wanted to tell him to stop talking that way. It was rude
and inconsiderate to talk about her body like that. But she
couldn't say it; his eyes held her immobile as he spoke. The
tingle in her flesh had deepened to a warm, aching flush.

"It's really been a source of irritation to me, why some
damned farm girl has haunted me all these years. Now, after
seeing you here tonight, I understand. Even then there was
something about you that captured me. Something very desirable in you. It's even more desirable now."

The flicker of excitement that she felt, that the champagne
had allowed her to feel, suddenly turned to fear. He still riveted

her with his eyes, and though he had not moved one inch, there was a tension in his body like that of a leopard about to spring.

"Please, Bart, don't talk like that. It isn't fair. I'm here with Will—"

"Yes," he interrupted sharply, "but you came out here to talk to me, *followed* me out here, I should say. Followed me out here just because you did want to hear some of the kinds of things I've been saying. You'll at least admit that, won't you?"

She tried to evade his point, but it was useless.

"You're talking nonsense, Bart. I came out here because Will had to go upstairs with one of the guests who was sick. I really was in the mood to dance some more, it's such great fun. I thought perhaps we could have another dance."

"Don't be coy, Anna! It's beneath you. Coy girls are the sort that I make passes at and then forget about."

His face had intensified as he spoke, almost to the point of anger. Of course, she could not pretend with him or with herself. She had been drawn to him all night, had fought the terrible desire to be with Bart even as she danced with Will. Perhaps the champagne had made it easier, but she had eagerly seized the opportunity to follow Bart onto the terrace. The tall, broad, uniformed shape of his body had been like a magnet, drawing her after him.

She did not tell him the truth, but he saw it in her eyes.

"You came out here because you wanted to be alone with me, didn't you, Anna?"

She nodded, defeated in her attempt to pretend.

His hands were suddenly on her bare arms, his lips hard against hers. His mouth was warm and full against her lips, fastening her to him, holding her suspended on tiptoe between the cold stones of the terrace and the hot, deep cavern of his mouth. His body moved against hers, pulled hers easily up against his. The rough wool of his uniform was coarse against her bare chest and arms; she could feel the heat of him through the thin silk of her dress.

He held her there until she gave in to him, returned the kiss freely. It was the answer he wanted, the answer he knew he would get from her. Then, just as he felt her give in fully to him, she changed, fought, pulled away.

She was breathing heavily as she looked up at him, passion,

arousal blended with anger and confusion in her eyes. He thought her extraordinarily desirable and beautiful at that moment.

"You told me what I needed to know," he said quietly as he took out his cigarette case and lit another cigarette.

"No," she said, gasping, "I didn't! You don't understand."

"Your message, lovely creature, was loud and clear."

"Will—"

"It's all right," he interrupted smoothly, his old arrogant self-confidence regained. "We're childhood friends, remember? We've kissed the same girl many times. He's a good sport about that sort of thing, or at least he used to be."

"You don't understand. Tonight, in just a few minutes, Will's father is going to announce our engagement!"

There was a long silence as Bart's face was transformed. The eyes receded, darkened; the face tensed and froze into a hard mask. When he finally spoke, his voice was tight and controlled.

"I'm sorry. I owe you an apology. And congratulations. Will's a great guy, and he'll make you a great husband. Too bad I won't be around to cheer you on to wedded bliss. I'll be leaving in a few days on the expedition into Mexico with Pershing. At least that will keep me from getting myself—and you—into any more trouble. Good night, Anna."

He turned abruptly and hurried down the stone steps into the dark of the garden. Anna felt the chill of the night air now and went back into the light and warmth of the house. It was almost midnight, and Will would be looking for her.

Chapter Three

IN THE FALL OF 1916, WHEN THE LAST OF THAT YEAR'S crop was sold to the cotton brokers, Ruth Cutter commented to Anna that the last three years of peace in Casilla had made them prosperous, but that the war had made them rich. Ruth's comment was not an understatement, for the fifteen hundred bales of cotton that Cutter Farms sold on the market that season, at the high wartime price of forty-two cents a pound, brought them a gross income of well over three hundred thousand dollars. The success of the Cutters was a remarkable achievement for a single woman and a teenaged girl who had begun with eighty acres and a pile of debts in 1912; by 1915, with five hundred acres in cultivation, they had become the fourth largest farm in the valley. The following year, with the purchase of a new tract across the Casilla road behind Casa Portillo, Ruth and Anna became the second largest cotton farm in the Rio Grande Valley and an economic force to be reckoned with. In earlier years more than a few farmers had joked about the "lady farmers" from Casilla. Now Ruth and Anna were among the most successful business people in the valley. Beyond that, Ruth was friend and confidante of Don Alonzo Lopez y Ruiz, and Anna was engaged to Senator Channing's son. There were few, if any, jokes about mother or daughter. The women who had looked askance at the field-hand mother and daughter, while offering them a patronizing sympathy for their hard lot as women alone, now sought them out for their social gatherings. The same women's husbands, who had made the jokes, some of them crude, now openly sought out the Cutters for advice about their own farm business.

More and more, as the 1916 crop had come to maturity, the valley farmers realized the impact of the European War on their lives. Prices on the Memphis cotton market were at all-time highs, and still rising; all along the Rio Grande, parcels of land were being snatched up, either bought or leased, in anticipation of an even greater demand for cotton the following year. Cutter Farms was at the forefront of the rapid expansion of the cultivated land in the valley. In addition to the one hundred and sixty acres they leased from Kate Mirkovsky, in 1915, Ruth and Anna had bought another one hundred and sixty acres adjoining the original farm. Anna turned eighteen in May of that year, and Ruth, on the occasion of her birthday, signed over a one-fifth share of the farm to Anna, making her a legal part owner. One of Anna's first acts, once she had reached the legal age for business transactions, was to sign the papers of purchase on the new land. Anna was now one year out of school—she had graduated from the upper grades that met in the second room of the two-room school in Casilla a year early because of her top grades—and once she was free to devote her full energies to the farm, it soon became clear that she was taking more and more responsibility for the running of the farm. Ruth, like her daughter, was an enormously hard worker; she had spent more than her share of twelve-hour days in the blistering, hot-summer fields. But as the farms grew, as Anna took on more and more a position of leadership, Ruth pulled into a quieter position on the farm. She spent most of her time in the new office in the expanded house, and her world became that of the ledgers and files. She was a conservative comptroller and watched every penny with an eagle eye. It was her conservatism in such matters that freed Anna to expand the operation in those years of growth.

"Anna is the *farmer*," her mother always said with a firm emphasis on the last word, and it was a true statement. Anna was the one with the feel of the land, the sixth sense about what to do with earth, with seed, with water. And she was clever, as her sense of timing in the expansion of the farm showed. Beyond that, she had a natural flair for working with others, a flair that did not come so easily to her more reserved mother. The men and women who labored on the Cutter farm found their employer kinder, more interested in them than any farmer they had seen or heard of in the valley. Many did not speak English, so she mastered Spanish. Many had young children who needed attention, so Anna had hired a woman to look after the young ones so their mothers would be free to work in the fields for much-needed money. When the farm expanded to the point that permanent housing was needed for year-round workers, Anna built better adobe *casas* than any other farm around. And at midday, as the workers took their midday meals in the midst of the fields, Señorita Cutter sat with them and ate beans and tortillas.

As simple, as hardworking, as Anna's life was at the farm, she afforded herself one great luxury. That was her time with Will Channing. The announcement of her engagement to Will in the spring of 1916 had been a matter of some note in the valley, and Anna read with a mixture of pride and embarrassment the extensive notices the event warranted in the newspapers. She began to lead a double life: five days of dawn-to-dusk work during the week and two days of relaxation, luxury, and society in the city, at the Channings' house. Will had been sincere in saying he wanted to change her life, to open new worlds to her. As the future Mrs. Will Channing, Anna found herself more and more caught up in the whirl of the Channings' world of wealth, sophistication, excitement. To her surprise, though not really to the surprise of any who really knew her, the world was as comfortable and as natural to her as the simple world of the laborers lunching in her fields.

Hovering over the excitement and expansion of these months, however, was the dark cloud that had begun spreading over the world with the assassination of Archduke Ferdinand at Sarajevo in 1914. Indeed, the war was bringing a new prosperity to the valley, to the Cutters, but the war itself was drawing closer to America as 1916 drew to a close. It seemed only a matter of weeks, at best months, before the United States would be among the warring nations, and the prospect of that dimmed the brightness of the prosperity.

As Anna had pointed out to Will on more than one occasion when they were sharing a particularly glorious time together, they were able to lead their lives, to be together, in part because her farm was making bandages, his mines making bullets.

In a sense their relationship was molded by the times as well. Anna had told Will that she had too many responsibilities to think of marriage anytime soon; if anything, the success of her farm only increased those responsibilities. Will, too, was caught up in the fever of the times, more and more involved in the Channing Mines and their frantic output to meet wartime needs. He and Anna had reached a tacit agreement that marriage was out of the question until the war was over, until their lives had settled in to something more resembling normal lives. In the meantime there were those glorious days and evenings to be shared together, respite from the responsibilities that the larger world—and their own ambition—had placed upon them.

Three days after the engagement party at the Channings', Bart went to Mexico with Pershing and the Fifth Cavalry. He was to be there for eleven months. The so-called "punitive raid" that President Wilson had ordered against Villa and his troops

turned out to be an embarrassment for the American cavalry.
As hardy and disciplined as the men were, once they crossed
the border into the desolate mountainous wasteland of Northern Mexico, they were lost, strangers in a strange land. Pershing, with his natty uniforms and his Dodge touring car and
his smartly turned out horse and foot soldiers, were no match
for the wily revolutionary bandit, who for months on end frustrated the American expedition by merely disappearing into the
wilderness without a trace.

"It's a punitive expedition all right," Bart wrote in one of the
few letters he managed to get to Casilla during the eleven-
month campaign, a letter that was eagerly read by those who
were anxious to have word of him. *"We're* being punished by
marching all over this hellish country, chasing ghosts. We've
seen rocks, rattlesnakes, and rabbits, but no revolutionaries.
Old Pancho must be laughing like a son of a bitch as he sits up
there in some hidden canyon watching us stumbling across the
arroyos and sand hills. Watching us pull the general's car out of
the mud when it rains. Watching us pull the cactus spines out of
our butts when we fall on them, which is often."

Anna followed the course of the Pershing expedition as
closely as she followed the course of one of her growing seasons.
That strange, confusing scene on the terrace the night of the
engagement party had come back to haunt her time and again.
She was ashamed of what had happened, of course, and there
was scarcely a time with Will, as he bent to kiss her, that she
didn't remember with shame how Bart had done the same, how
she had allowed him to, only minutes before Will was to declare
his intentions toward her in front of everyone. She had agonized
over Bart, over the hold he seemed to have on her, and she had
in her own mind constructed a long series of rationales for the
power this man seemed to have over her thoughts and dreams.
He was handsome, he was a soldier, he was now in danger;
these were all reasons she sorted through to explain to herself
why Bart forced himself into her thoughts, yet she knew,
though these rationales might explain her preoccupation with
him on the surface, they were inadequate to really explain the
hold he had on her.

As 1917 began it was increasingly clear that the entry of the
United States into the war was imminent, and finally, on April

6, the declaration of war was official. The cause of France and England against the Austro-German powers had always gotten the sympathy of the majority of residents of the valley, even when in the rest of the country there had been strong feelings for American nonintervention in the war. The reason was only in part because El Paso was a military city. Stronger reason for border residents to want their country to join the Allies were the overtures Germany had made to Mexico. More than once in the last years it had seemed a real possibility that the Mexican government, a great source of trouble to the United States, might take sides with a friendly, powerful, and wealthy Germany.

At the time of the declaration of war, President Wilson announced the appointment of John Pershing as the commander of the American Expeditionary force. The appointment was naturally big news in the valley—"Black Jack" Pershing was already a local hero—not only because it made the general world-famous overnight, but also because it meant that the men of the Fifth Cavalry would be recalled from the prolonged and embarrassing fiasco in Mexico. After eleven months of Pershing's "Punitive" expedition, Villa remained unpunished, as brash and powerful as ever. The defeated American cavalry, now facing a far bigger and more serious business in France, were more than happy to turn and march out of the Mexican wasteland and leave Villa's country to him.

General Pershing's rising star included Bart in its constellation. As one of the general's aides, he was to be in the highest echelon of the American Allied command. There was a price to pay, though, for only hours after arriving back at Fort Bliss after his return from Mexico, Bart was dispatched to Washington to pave the way for his commanding officer to assume his duties at the head of the American forces. Only Don Alonzo had the chance to see Bart before he left, a tender but frustratingly short meeting in El Paso, each man knowing that, given Alonzo's age and Bart's career, the meeting might be their last.

Within a month of the American entry into the war, Will had enlisted in the army, as did so many of the men from the valley. It was the first sacrifice Anna made to the war; the prospect of her Will being away for months, possibly years, made the future seem gray. Her only consolation was that, after his training at

Camp Hood, Will would probably be stationed in Washington doing legal work for the War Department. His life, at least, would not be in danger. With Will gone Anna had even more time to devote to that greatest of distractions: hard work. To make sure that she had no time to brood on Will's absence—and with an eye to the profits to be had—Anna convinced Don Alonzo to lease Cutter Farms a tract of two hundred acres of land, previously uncultivated, which lay to the East of Casa Portillo. With the leasing of the new land, which was soon being cleared by a small army of laborers housed in tents on the land, the Cutters became the largest farmers in the valley.

By the end of the summer of 1917, the effects of the war were being felt in more and more ways, even though American troops were still mobilizing and would not see their first combat until late October. In July President Wilson put in effect embargoes on crucial supplies being sent abroad—food, fuels, metals, war materials—and channeled them instead into the American military. Certain foods began to be in short supply, meat and dairy items among the most missed. There were other, more humorous, changes. The farmers and train men still congregated at Ola's café, though at breakfast she now served French instead of German toast, and her Wednesday specials included Liberty Cabbage instead of sauerkraut.

For Cutter Farms the shortage of supplies and labor during wartime, coupled with the continued expansion of the farm operation and the urgent need to produce every possible bale of cotton for the war effort, presented enormous logistic problems. Ruth and Anna calculated that they would need over two hundred workers during the picking season, half that many during the regular growing season. In the best of times the number of local men and women available to pick cotton would have been barely adequate to fill their needs, but with many of the younger men conscripted or volunteered into the army, the labor situation threatened to become critical. There were only so many women and children able to work the fields. If their laborers had to be brought in from other areas on a temporary basis, the Cutters would have the additional problem of feeding and housing the migrants—no easy task, considering that they might have to provide as many as six hundred meals a day. The valley farmers decided that their only hope of a large enough force of pickers was to scour the countryside, to send out word that every man who wanted to come to Casilla for a month would be housed, fed, and paid decent wages for a hard day's work. Word was also put out among the locals who worked the farms that they would be paid a bounty for every healthy worker they brought to the farms to pick. The campaign worked. The week before picking was to start, men and women, mostly Mexican, began arriving in groups of two, three, as many as ten or twelve. Most spoke no English, but they knew of one distant relative or friend of a friend in Casilla who would bring them to one of Anna's foremen, who did the hiring every morning at a table set up in the small tent city that had sprung up among the Cutter fields. The workers came from as far as Sierra Blanca, fifty miles east, or Las Cruces, seventy miles upriver. Many simply appeared from nowhere, and though no questions were asked, it was assumed that they had swum across the river during the night, anxious to earn the high wages the *Americanos* were paying.

Ruth and Anna were fortunate, given the sheer size of their work force, that they had two full-time workers who showed real leadership and talent on the farm. Juan Gordo, so called because of his ample girth, and Pablo Sisneros, a quiet, handsome youth with a crippled leg, had both worked for the Cutters since they were teenagers, in the days when they came from Casilla to work during the harvest. They had been among the first Ruth had hired when she was able to afford full-time workers, and in the intervening years, the two men had come to know almost as much about their farm as she and Anna did. The men were smart, dependable, reliable, and provided an excellent liaison between the Cutters and their Mexican laborers. It was only natural, then, that Ruth and Anna discussed the possibility of making the two men farm foremen with official management responsibilities. It was a novel idea, for at that time there was not a single Mexican foreman on an Anglo-owned farm in the valley.

Ruth had naturally wanted her sons to be foremen. She and Anna had discussed it often as they realized that their operation was becoming too large and complex for them to manage themselves. It was logical that the Cutter sons take on a management role on the farm, but Ruth herself agreed that it was out of the question until they were both out of school. J. J., at seventeen, had only one additional year before graduation. Hank, at twelve, was years away from taking on a man's job. In due time, of course, Ruth's sons would come into their own. In the meantime, during weekends and summers, they worked on the farm, encouraged by mother and sister to learn as much as possible about the operation.

Anna was secretly relieved that her brother J. J. was still in school for another year at least, for there were serious doubts in her mind just how good a farmer he would make. Anna had known for years that her father's abandonment had taken a serious toll on J. J.'s outlook and personality. He had always been a high-strung, feisty boy, and more than a bit spoiled by his father. Since Jonah had left and J. J. had gone through those always difficult adolescent years, he had become a difficult and demanding youth. He did badly in school, played truant often, and was known for picking fights with other boys. He had an inclination to be boastful, to put on airs, combined with a distinct streak of dishonesty his sister found worrisome. Anna knew that her mother was well aware of these problems in J. J. —she had been forced to get him out of scrapes too often not to notice them—but Ruth seemed patient and indulgent where her son was concerned, as if she felt she should let him misbehave as compensation for having lost the father he so adored.

"He's young yet; he'll outgrow all this," was Ruth's typical remark about J. J. Yet, as he approached a man's age, Anna seriously had begun to doubt whether J. J. would outgrow those unpleasant traits. If anything, in the last year, as she had seen J. J. grow into a man's stature and physical presence, she had sensed a deep, almost frightening anger in him. His arrogance became full-blown, so taken was he with the farm's success, yet he showed a distinct laziness when it came to the hard work required for that success. Even more troubling was his growing and undisguised dislike of Mexicans. To Anna's mind her brother was hardly a sterling candidate for the manager of a farm with hundreds of Mexican employees.

Hank was a different matter, so much so that Anna often found herself wishing that he were the older of her brothers. Hank had always been a quiet, solitary boy, given much to spending time in a secret world of his own. He was as shy as his brother was brash, and that innate difference in the two boys' personalities had made them distant from one another, at times almost like strangers. Hank had not been an especially good student; he seemed to have no great flair for "book learning." On the other hand, since his youngest years he had been fascinated by living things, animals, and plants. He had always said that he *liked* to work in the fields, and in recent years his greatest delight was the neat kitchen garden that grew inside the picket fence around the front of the house. He had made it his domain, fussed over every plant, every vine, like a hen over her chicks. Many evenings he had to be taken away from his seed and farm catalogues and sent to his schoolwork. Free times after school, when most boys his age were playing, he would spend in his garden or tagging along with Pablo Sisneros as he did his farm work.

Hank idolized Pablo, and though the workman was twenty, the two had become great friends. In this respect Hank was night to his brother's day, for Hank was fascinated by the world of the Mexicans who lived and worked around them. At twelve he spoke Spanish as well as English, and it was in fact his preferred language. At school he had chosen to be friends with Mexican boys, garnering loud disapproval from J. J. for doing so. He loved to visit the homes of his friends in Casilla and was accepted as one of them by their families, and he took every opportunity to be with Pablo, following him like a pup, asking endless questions about the farm in his fluent Spanish. On more than one occasion J. J. had tried to cruelly criticize his little brother for "turning Mexican," but his words had merely been taken as a compliment.

When Ruth and Anna made the final decision to make Juan Gordo and Pablo foremen, the problems that had been lurking under the surface with J. J. bubbled up and erupted violently. J. J. burst into Anna's office one afternoon, the time he usually got home from school. Anna had seen her brother's anger often —the youth's wiry, muscular frame tensed, his blue eyes flashing, his fair face hardened. She put aside the papers in front of her, waiting for him to get out what was bothering her.

"I just heard about the new management here." There was a distinct, acid quality in his voice.

"You mean, the new foremen?"

"What's the idea, setting up two Mexicans in cushy jobs when you got your own family shoveling manure and picking tomatoes?"

So that was it! J. J. was furious about not being made a foreman. She asked him to sit down, knowing he'd be a bit disarmed at eye-to-eye level.

"You don't think it was a good idea, as much as we've expanded this year, having some help from Pablo and Juan?"

"I think you ought to give your blood relations some consideration for the good jobs around here, before going off and giving work to field hands. It don't make a man feel good when his own sister passes him over for a Mexican cotton picker."

Anna held back a flash of anger.

"J. J., you know damn well that the men I made foremen are good. They've worked for us since Papa left and know as much about this farm as any of us."

"You just wanted to hold me back. Keep little brother in place. You act like this is your goddamn farm. Big-shot lady farmer. Doesn't even let her brother help run things. Packs mama off to the office to keep her out of the way, *after* she signs over the farm to you."

"That's a lie, J. J., and you know it. Mama signed over a fifth of the farm when I turned eighteen. She'll sign over your equal share when you and Hank are legal age."

"And meanwhile sister has her own little empire, to do with like she damn well pleases. Never asks any of us who've got—or will get—a stake what they think about her way of doing things."

"I am the manager, after all."

"By what rights?"

Her anger finally flared out at his remark.

"By rights of sitting behind this desk. By rights of making a go of this farm when you and your brother were too young to feed and clothe yourselves. When Mama was too torn up inside to take on the responsibilities of a failing farm. By rights of getting up at dawn every day since I was thirteen, working in the fields with my own hands, as hard as any peon. That's why I'm here making the decisions."

"Yeah. And what do your brothers get for all the hours they've put in the fields? Or shoveling shit in the barn?"

"Simple, Jonah." She used his full name deliberately, in the sternest voice she could manage. To her it had all the connotations of false pride and irresponsibility that she associated with her father. "You've got nine months a year, because of me, so you can go to school. You've got a roof over your heads because of me. And food in your belly. And you've lived better for several years now, better than almost any other family in the valley. Better clothes, better food, a better house. And what you're getting for my effort, and for yours, is a share in the biggest and richest farm in the valley."

"I wouldn't stake my life on ever getting my share, or my fair say in running things."

"When your time comes."

"Meanwhile you're giving a job I should have to some smelly peon who can't even talk English good."

Even in her anger Anna was amused by the irony of her brother's bad grammar. But she let it pass and replied as calmly as she could. "That's not the case at all. I gave the jobs to them because they're capable—and because they're not in school five of the eight months that we've got a crop to tend to."

"I don't have to stay in school. You didn't."

J. J.'s wheedling was impossible. Anna thought of the nights when she had sat up until after midnight, studying by herself, after a day in the fields, her hands bruised and sore as she turned the pages of her books.

"You're talking nonsense. I'm in charge of the farm now, J. J., and you've just got to accept that as a fact. You're staying in school, like it or not, for your own good, and when you're finished, you'll have your pick of jobs on the farm."

"Except yours?" His blue-gray eyes were hard.

Anna flinched. She'd left herself open for his cut. But she had to answer honestly.

"Except mine."

Enraged, her brother swept an arm across the desk, scattering papers across the office.

"You grasping bitch. Keeping things from the rest of us. Making it all work out just fine for you. Kissing the damned Mexicans' asses. Next thing we know, you'll be sleeping with them, if you already aren't. You'll marry some spic and give him the farm."

"Get out! Get out of my sight!" She stood, enraged at his vulgar insults. Her fist slammed down onto the desktop, and her eyes burned into him with a gray fire. J. J. shrank back for a moment at his sister's outburst, a look of genuine fear in his eyes. Then he recovered himself, slipped into a smiling, venomous calm. He stood and walked to the door.

"Okay, big sister. I'll get out of *your* office." His voice oozed. "But just remember, I know what you're up to. You can't fool J. J. Cutter. And I'll make you regret this. Yes, that I will."

She stood at the desk, stunned by what had happened, as his back disappeared through the doorway.

The wartime Christmas of 1917 was spent at Casa Portillo. With Will in Washington and Bart in France, Alonzo thought it appropriate that the friends and families of the two men share the holiday season. The Channings came down from El Paso for several days, and Alonzo planned a traditional Christmas dinner for Ruth, Anna, the boys, Kate, Vassily, and Lina. Alonzo and Maricita and her staff of maids had transformed the dark, now almost-empty house. The hall, the court, and the gallery were festooned with bright paper streamers and *piñatas,* and the dining room, with its heavy carved ceiling, its gold-framed portraits, its long, banquet-size table, was gold with the light of a hundred candles and hung with garlands of greens. The walls sported gay Mexican Christmas decorations as well—ornaments of shimmering, cut tin or of brightly painted papier-mâché. The sideboard was covered with trays of desserts: buttery cookies flavored with almonds or lemons; cone-shaped sugar cakes with dark caramel icing; little cakes in the shapes of crucifixes and stars, with pink and yellow icings; and the deep-fried puff balls of *sopapillas,* sprinkled with white powdered sugar. From the kitchen came the smell of half a dozen dishes: beef and mutton, ham and goose, roasted, baked, basted, and stuffed. And there were the by-now familiar, but still exotic scents of chili peppers and *comino, jalapeños* and *solantro,* the rich, pungent smells of the regional foods. Once his guests were seated, Don Alonzo stood at the head of the table, a glass of wine in hand. His face, almost always dark and serious, beamed a genial, but sincere warmth at the friends in front of him. He raised his glass in a toast.

"*Queridos amigos,* as you all know, I am not one for prayers of thanks, but I am one to offer up thanks for what is in my heart. This is a time when we are surrounded by so many troubles. The world, whether it be across the river or across the sea, is so full of suffering and death and ills, and these sorrows threaten every day to become a sad part of our lives. So tonight I am indeed thankful for us all being together, my daughter, my grandson, my dear friends from the city, my dear friends from the valley. How fortunate that we can be together, safe, well, and happy. May it be so every year for many years to come."

Don Alonzo's toast accurately captured the mood of the evening. There was on one level a very real sense of well-being, a feeling of friendship and love among the party gathered at Casa Portillo. But underlying it all was a deep, profound *ostinato:* Things were not very right with the world. At the moment they all enjoyed comfort, financial security, and a sense of belonging —feelings especially important to Ruth and Anna, who had been through such hard times these last years. But in the quiet moments during dinner, as the conversation momentarily waned, it was as if they felt the wet, stinking silence of the stalemated trenches of the Marne and the hushed, sleeping violence of northern Mexico.

Though there was a serious undercurrent to the evening, the talk and the guests' thoughts did not linger along on the darker side of things. It was Christmas, after all, and there were happier things to think about, happier things to do. Though war and revolution wove their way in and out of the conversation, like warp and woof, most of the talk centered around lighter things; a bit of local gossip; talk of the farms and of the city; general ecstasy over Maricita's unbroken record of triumphs in the kitchen; talk of fashions and styles, of art and music, of agues and arthritis, of people and personalities.

Late in the evening Don Alonzo interrupted his guests, by then broken up into small conversation groups, to announce that they should all come upstairs. They followed him to the end of the upstairs center corridor, where, at the end, a shuttered window overlooked the front courtyard. It was a window Ruth and Anna knew well, for it was from there that they had watched Jonah and the other men bring Vassily through the floodwaters.

Once the guests were assembled behind the shuttered window, Alonzo silenced them with a finger to his lips. Then, with a sweeping gesture, he threw open the shutters. Before them was a beautiful and magical sight. *Las luminarias.* The lanterns.

During dinner Miguelito and the other boys of Casa Portillo had, in an elflike manner, made their way across the roof and the walls of the spacious outer courtyard of the *hacienda,* placing at regular intervals small brown paper bags, each with a handful of sand inside, on each handful of sand a small devotional candle. The small lights turned the simple bags into glowing cubes of warm yellow-brown light. Each *luminaria,* in itself, was insignificant, but the boys had placed over a thousand of the lanterns around the *hacienda,* along the roof line, on the sill of every window, along the adobe wall that embraced the outer court like thick, curving arms. In the courtyard the rows of evenly spaced lanterns outlined the geometry of the building, placed in rigid squares along the ground, one square within another. Beyond the house, the drive had been lined with the pinpricks of light, and beyond that, near the river, even the great branches of the cottonwoods had been garnished with light, their gnarled shapes silhouetted in candles.

They stood at the window in silence, awed by the quiet spectacle. The effect, quiet but breathtaking, was of a great, geometric ship, the house, floating in a thousand lights across a sea of darkness.

The silence was broken by the sound of a dozen voices piercing the chill winter air. The house staff, gathered in a corner of the courtyard, singing the odd, repetitive melodies of Mexican *canciones de navidad*—Christmas carols.

As the pure, unaccompanied voices rang out in the cold night air, Anna felt a sudden welling up of love, deep, rich, and profound. It was a full, all-encompassing love, a love of her life, of being. Her thoughts—and love—were with Will, and with Bart, of course, and with the friends and loved ones that stood with her at the window overlooking the fairyland of the courtyard. She realized at that moment that too much of her life had been caught up in struggle, in conflict. Worry and anxiety had been her partners, her closest companions; so much of her brief years on earth had been spent thinking about, agonizing over the final outcome. That night, as the carolers' voices floated up to her with their ancient melodies, a very important thought came to her: just being was enough. The final outcome, the ultimate resolution of her life was something she could not control, just as she could not control the war, the larger forces that had taken Will and Bart so far away from her, from their loved ones. It was futile to predict, to guess how life would go. She could only accept and rejoice in the present. It seemed like a hard task, to relinquish that need for control over one's fate, but she sensed that if it could be accomplished, there was indeed a means to happiness.

Late in the evening Alonzo made the unusual request of speaking to Ruth alone, apart from the other guests, who had retired to the library for cordials around a roaring fire. Ruth waited until the others were all caught up in conversations, then slipped quietly into a small sitting room just off the main salon. Alonzo followed and closed the door behind them. Ruth was a bit puzzled by his request to speak to her alone—they had ample opportunities at other times—and her puzzlement showed in her face.

"Forgive me, Ruth, for being selfish," he said by way of apology, "but I needed just a minute to speak with you alone. It is Christmas and, well, that is a special time."

"And it has been that," she answered with real sincerity. "I think we all needed very much to have an evening like this together."

Alonzo, tall and handsome in his dinner clothes, towered above her. His noble, graying head was deep in thought for a few moments, as if he were digging deep, very deep, for his words.

"I have a gift for you," he said with the slightest hesitation in his voice. "Something I have wanted to give to you for a very long time. But before I do so, I must, *querida señora*, say something. Please forgive a silly old man if what he is about to say is forward and not like a gentleman."

"Alonzo, please, we have been friends too many years for you to talk that way! There is no need for you to hold back anything from me." Ruth reached out, touched his hand in reassurance. He in turn patted her hand with his other, in thanks for the gesture. It was true, though, she thought. The man who had seemed so distant from the world, so lonely, had over these years become a great friend to her and her family. He had been her mentor, her advisor, and, with that loan years before, the savior of her farm. Alonzo, dear, kind man that he was, was both friend and guardian angel, hovering over her life with benign attentiveness. How many times in the last years had she gone to him for advice on her problems, for a friendly ear when she needed someone to talk to? Their lives, which had seemed worlds apart when she had first come to Casilla, were now closely bound up with ties of friendship and love.

"Ruth," he began, "there is one thing, one subject on which we have never spoken. I have wanted to many times, but I knew full well that the subject was one you preferred to keep to yourself. Now, to put an old man's mind at rest, I beg you to let me speak of it."

"Yes, I understand. Please do." It was about Jonah, of course. There was no question.

"It has now been five years since your husband left. Five years in which your life has taken turns no one would have expected at that terrible time. It is not my business, dear Ruth, though it is, to be honest, my concern about what course your life is going to take now. Though I do not know, I sense that there has been no word from him, no sign. In little more than a year, from the standpoint of the law, your husband will be, forgive the harsh terms, legally dead."

"But he is not dead."

Ruth's words were spoken with a calm, unquestioned conviction.

"I am sure of that, Ruth. But my question, my concern is whether you can, after all these years have passed, if you can consider sharing your life with another."

She was silent, but he saw a look in her eye, a confused, anxious look, that he could not quite understand. He knew he must go on, get it all out.

"I am sorry Ruth, but I must tell you. I love you. I want you to be my wife."

So many years, he thought, so many years since Davida had died. It had taken him this long to say the words to another; it had taken this long for there to be another.

Ruth turned her head away, a movement that made Alonzo

deeply embarrassed for his confession. But she still held his hand, and its grip, though trembling now, was firmer than before. Finally she looked back at him, tears in her eyes.

"I—I can't, Alonzo. Of course, I do love you, in a certain way. I have a feeling for you, a very deep feeling, that I cannot even put into words. But Jonah is my husband, and that is a bond of the heart and soul and spirit that I cannot break. Don't you see? I always have loved the man, I always will. I know some people think I'm a fool, waiting these years for him to come back, not filing for a divorce or annulment. But what are five years out of twenty-five, out of a lifetime? I wouldn't be much of a wife if I wasn't willing to wait. That would mean I didn't really love him."

Alonzo looked deep into the darkness of Ruth's eyes. He saw something there that disturbed him but gave him hope. There was a pain, a questioning in her eyes, and a kind of quiet but deep desperation, as if she wanted very much for Alonzo to believe her.

"I admire your loyalty, Ruth."

"Thank you, 'Lonzo. That means a good deal to me. And I hope you understand that as long as I love him—"

She caught herself, unable to complete the thought that had escaped from her mind. In his own mind Alonzo completed it for her. *As long as I love him, I am safe.*

Ruth recovered, evaded the thought. "I know, as surely as I love him, that he is alive, that he will come back."

Alonzo wanted to say that, as sure as he was that Jonah was still alive, he was just as sure that he was never coming back to her. But he held back; that was not for him to say.

"Please, Alonzo, please understand. I wish that I could give my heart to you. Oh, it would be a wonderful life we could have together. But I cannot. My heart is not free to give."

"No, of course. I understand. It is your loyalty, your commitment to love that in part draws me to you. I must now accept that it is also what keeps you from me. Such is the way of this world."

He smiled, bent down, and kissed her hand.

"I will never speak of this again, *querida*. It will be between us as it was before."

Ruth stood on tiptoe, kissed him on both cheeks.

"Thank you for understanding. You are very special."

As she pulled away, Alonzo reached in his jacket pocket and extracted a small, brightly wrapped box, and handed it to her.

"I think it best you open this here, not with the others."

She untied the ribbon, then unfolded the crisp paper, curious but apprehensive about so special a gift that it had to be opened in private. Beneath the paper was a velvet-covered box, a jewel case. Her hand a bit unsteady, she opened the lid. Inside, in a nest of creamy satin, was her great-grandmother's brooch.

Chapter Four

DURING THE SUMMER OF 1918, NEWSPAPERS CARRIED REports of an outbreak of influenza in Europe, which began when a Spanish freighter docked in Lisbon with most of her crew seriously ill. This "Spanish influenza" soon spread throughout Europe with a virulence that had not been known since the great plagues of the Middle Ages. Outbreaks most often began wherever men live in close quarters—on board ships, in military barracks, in hospitals and prisons—but it soon spread to the population at large. The symptoms were not unlike other influenzas that went through the population from time to time— fevers, chills, nausea, head and body aches, congested lungs. But there were crucial differences: the Spanish flu seemed to have a bizarre preference for striking the young and healthy, and it was deadly beyond any influenza ever known, due mainly to its cruel habit of causing the lungs to become seriously inflamed and clogged. The result was that many men and women who had been healthy a few days before lay helpless as their lungs filled with fluids and literally suffocated them to death, their lungs a boiling cauldron of sputum and phlegm.

By August all of Europe was in the throes of the epidemic. Millions fell ill, and tens, then hundreds of thousands died.

Hospitals, already overcrowded with war casualties, overflowed into the streets and parks of Europe, with beds in makeshift wards set up in tents and lean-tos. Patients went untended because their doctors and nurses fell ill themselves. Crucial factories were idle because there were no men to work in them; ships putting in to port couldn't dock because there were not enough longshoremen or crewmen standing to bring them in; entire battlefields fell silent as men from private to general, Ally or Axis, lay feverish in their tents and trenches.

Bodies went unburied in cities and villages because there were not enough well men to keep up with the vast number of graves to be dug or enough to build coffins for the dead.

By the end of August the first cases appeared in America.

In Casilla, as the front pages of the newspapers began to give as much coverage to the influenza as to the war, people clung to the vague hope that the invisible killer might somehow pass them by in its relentless march across the continent. But in late September the first cases appeared at Fort Bliss, and in the poor *barrios* of South El Paso. Like a match to powder, within a few weeks the valley was in the full clutch of the epidemic, and the same scenario was enacted: the overflowing hospitals, the idle factories, the closed stores and schools, the crowded churches and funeral parlors. In the streets the men and women courageous enough to venture out wore gauze masks, in the vain hope that it would filter out the evil air.

The prospect of the epidemic in Casilla, at that time, was especially frightening. Harvest was in full force, and even the smaller farms had their seasonal laborers staying on the land or arriving every day to work. The Cutters had over two hundred men, from as far away as Chihuahua City and Albuquerque, staying in the tin sheds and tent towns set up on the four farms. "Our two hundred children to nurse" as Ruth described them.

But by the time the first cases appeared in Casilla—a young Mexican woman who helped keep house for Father Hernando and two of the railroaders who boarded with Ola—it was clear to Ruth and Anna that they had to plan for the worst: in some places in the East, especially in close quarters, as high as forty percent of the population fell ill. The Cutters might have that many sick men and women on their hands, and they had to admit that they themselves might succumb as well. The more preparations, the better.

Anna set up the largest of the workers' camps, the one on the original farm, just behind the house, as an infirmary; Kate and her helpers began stockpiling compresses and what extra sheets and blankets they could: The workers were used to sleeping in open air, in the tents and sheds, with just their ponchos for cover, but if they were ill and the warm weather didn't hold, a poncho wouldn't be enough.

Don Alonzo's home was pressed into service. Much as the *hacienda* had been refuge during the 1912 flood, it would serve as hospital during the epidemic. Ruth and Kate changed their efforts at war relief to preparations for running a small, ill-equipped hospital at Casa Portillo.

"We can handle most of our sick at the farm," Anna told Alonzo, "at least the milder cases. Those who are bad off should be inside, out of the weather and not in tents. We're bound to have a few serious cases, as well as the other farms."

"Best then, *querida,*" Alonzo replied, "that we plan on having them here in one place, to care for. The terrible matter," he added with a sad, helpless look on his face, "is that there is almost nothing to be done, once they are ill. No medicines, no purgatives or foods, can keep them from going one way or another. And the terrible business with the lungs . . ."

The prospect of the epidemic was dark, terrifying. Across the world war had wreaked its devastation. The deadly influenza seemed to be war's evil sister, carrying death in its own way to every corner of the globe.

By the time it was clear that the influenza had come to the valley, the cotton harvest was about to go into full swing. It seemed that the epidemic was going to take a toll in more ways than in illness and lost lives.

For a cotton picker whose only income for the year may be the money earned during the six weeks of harvest, time and energy are precious. Paid by the pound, each second translates into ounces of cotton, each ounce into pounds and pennies. A good day, perhaps a hundred pounds, a dollar to put aside for the lean months ahead.

When the first laborers began feeling the stiff neck, the tense, aching muscles, it was easy to put that off to the strain of bending over the cotton plants for six, eight, ten hours at a time, though they knew all too well that their bodies were used to the strain. Then, when the chills and fevers came, they could pretend, as they forced their bodies down the almost endless rows of cotton, that it was from the bright fall sun, though it was no brighter or hotter than in years past. Still, each boll they plucked from the plants was money, and, no matter how welcome the prospect of sitting or lying down seemed, they simply could not afford to stop. A few pickers noticed other workers, a few rows away, faces drawn, eyes glazed, staggering, stumbling as they made their way through the fields. It wasn't until late in the afternoon that the first man fell, disappearing into the sea of green. Others close by ran to him. A fever raged, his body almost convulsing with terrible, piercing aches. They shouted for the foreman, then hurried back to work. Perhaps the terrible spirit of the fever would pass them by if they prayed to Our Lady and stayed at their work.

But the first of the Cutters' workers—a man from Chihuahua known only as Juancito—was not the last. Three more fell ill that same afternoon. That night, two more. By the end of the next day there were already ten men and two women in the beds set up in the tents.

Kate sent Lina home to rest while she and two of the girls from Casilla who helped her with housework at the farm stayed up all night, tending the ill.

"Damn," she told Anna the next morning when she came out early with Pablo to see how the sick were doing. "I thought it was a chore watching after the little ones when they were young and laid up. Hell, I never had twelve at once. That wrings a woman out."

Anna went to the beds, standing between a man and a woman. Both lay almost motionless in their beds, staring straight ahead, their eyes glazed; the woman pawed the bed covers, as if to distract herself from the fever that racked her body. One of Kate's helpers changed the compress on the woman's forehead though she hardly moved when the cool rag was laid across her brow. Her breathing was strained, thick, coming in uneven gasps.

Anna reached down and took the woman's hand and gave it a squeeze of comfort. Her flesh was scalding, dry with the fever.

The woman tried to smile, but all she managed was a hard, painful stretching of the lips. A stream of fetid breath floated to Anna's nostrils.

She turned back to Kate.

"They look so helpless, Katie, so damned pained. Can they at least sleep?"

"Sometimes, for a bit. It ain't pleasant when they do, most times."

Anna looked puzzled.

"Not so different than taking care of little ones, like I said."

Kate motioned to a bucket at the end of the row of beds. It was filled with linens, stained a putrid brown, reeking of foul excrement.

"Can't keep control when they's asleep. Kinda unpleasant for the others and me, but we'll get used to it."

Discouraged, Anna put her arms around Kate.

"Thank you for being so good."

The Cutter farms were hit hard by the epidemic, though no other farmer or family in Casilla would have said they got off lightly. Within a week of Juancito's illness, almost a hundred of the Cutters' workers were sick. Twenty of the weakest had been moved to Casa Portillo where the house staff looked after them, along with another dozen cases from surrounding farms who were the worst off, or who, like the spinster schoolteacher, Etta Pringle, had no family to care for them. Work on the farm had slowed to a near halt: pickers had at first continued to work as their *compañeros* fell ill, but as the disease spread, most of the pickers who were still able-bodied slipped away, back home across the river. Fewer than twenty seasonal workers stayed on the farm, hardly enough to keep in full operation.

The rapid spread and the sheer numbers of those ill were a terrible blow to all those struggling, like Anna, to keep some semblance of normality in their lives. But almost every day a new blow would strike, almost like a nail driven into a coffin.

The first death in Casilla was one of Anna's people, the woman she had seen that first morning with Kate. She had been taken to Casa Portillo when her lungs turned pneumonic, but even that was useless. She died a few hours later, simply because her lungs were too full of fluids to take in air. Sad, too, that no one even knew her name—the few friends she had come across the river with had disappeared back into Mexico days before.

They buried her, with a simple cross, in the cemetery in Casilla.

She was to be the first of many.

Even before Miss Pringle was stricken, schools in the valley had been ordered closed; supplies, already hard to come by because of the war, were almost nonexistent: the trains ran almost empty because so many men working at the supply and warehouses in the city were ill or staying home to avoid the influenza. When word got around that Wasserman was down, the news seemed to confirm that nothing of life in Casilla was going to be untouched by the illness.

The first week stretched into the second, then the third, and the epidemic showed no signs of abating. The early victims who were well enough to be up and around were replaced by a steady influx of new cases; Casa Portillo was still an unofficial hospital, with the sick being brought from farms all around the area. Though Anna had fewer of her people sick after a while, she found herself taking in stricken laborers from other farms—along with what help the other farmers and their families could provide—because it made caring for the sick easier with pooled efforts.

The influenza was a quirky disease. Ruth and Anna knew that all too well, an invisible hand that picked its victims randomly and capriciously: two teenage sons from a new farm family in the area died in three days, while the parents and other children weren't touched at all. When the flu struck close to them, as they knew it would, it was capricious as well: Vassy had a light case, recovering like a young man, while Lina, who had been working like a woman half her age, didn't even take ill at all. After three weeks of fine health Kate succumbed, her tiny, energetic frame knocked helpless in a matter of hours. Ruth was with Kate when she felt the onslaught, helped her to one of the beds she had tended so often herself in the last weeks.

Kate had a rough few days; her fever seemed abnormally high, and she was delirious at times, calling out for Max in a pitiful voice. But on the third day her fever broke, and she was able to talk a bit, even take some liquids. Still, she was weak, and Ruth and Lina decided it was best that she go to the *hacienda* for a slow recovery: once she was out of the fever stage, as weak as she was, Kate was furious at herself for having given in, as it were, to the flu; she wanted to be up, right away, and back at her nursing. With Kate down, the burden of work on Ruth and Anna was redoubled. The days were relentless, with no semblance of any order. Anna might find an hour or two to sleep at widely scattered times of day—midafternoon, just before dawn. New cases might be brought in at any hour, or a lull, when it seemed that the sixty or so beds were filled with quietly resting patients, might be broken by a sudden, terrible outburst as a man gasped, spitting and choking, as his lungs filled to capacity. Then Anna, Ruth, anyone able, would run to him, trying to lift the patient up, pounding on his inflamed ribs to try and loosen the choking, suffocating fluids.

There were times when Anna's attempts at sleep were broken by a firm shake and her mother or brothers telling her that another had died during the last hour. Hours would go by when she was on the verge of breathlessness, hurrying from bed to bed, half running down the long path between the twenty tents, each with its six beds, to fetch a stack of compresses, a basin of water, to carry away a bucket of excrement or vomited bile; there was always an urgency among the women tending the tents, always three things to be carried, ten beds that needed immediate attention.

During the endless, exhausting hours, there were two thoughts constantly in Anna's mind. One was that the farm was going completely untended with acres—she wasn't even sure how many, perhaps a hundred—going to rot. There was nothing she could do about it. The second, and it hit especially hard each time they lost a patient, was that Bart and Will were in the middle of this deadly madness, too, that every day hundreds of soldiers died. And that there had been no word for weeks. It was not a thought she could let herself dwell on.

Early one morning, as she and Ruth carried out the kettles of broth that Lina made daily for the patients, one of the boys that she recognized as working for Don Alonzo came to the house. He was out of breath and nervous.

"Don Alonzo, *tiene un dolor. Es muy malo.*"

"Alonzo is sick. He is very bad."

Ruth and Anna exchanged a quick, panicked glance.

"You go, Mother, I'll manage here."

Ruth pulled off her apron, crumpled it on the chair by the stove, and hurried outside, catching Pablo just as he was leaving in one of the wagons. She was grim and silent the whole way, working her mouth nervously, biting her lips.

She let herself in unannounced and went straight up to his room, past the dozen or so people who were going about the business of tending the sick who lay on their pallets in the downstairs rooms. Alonzo's room was dark, the drapes pulled, but even in the shadows she could see half a dozen pallets on the floor, most of them occupied by sleeping bodies. With a start Ruth realized that the figure in the massive, draped four-poster was that of a woman, a terribly thin, elderly creature, sunken-eyed, breathing in shallow, hard gasps. Ruth went from mattress to mattress. No sign of Alonzo. Seized by a wave of panic, she ran out onto the gallery, not knowing where to look for him, who to ask.

She spotted Maricita's stout figure coming out of a doorway on the far gallery, across the court, and hurried around to her. When she saw Ruth, white-faced with alarm, she spoke first in her rudimentary English.

"He in here, Ruth. In this room. Very bad night, much fever. He call you name much." There was a calm but terrifying pessimism in her voice.

Ruth clasped the woman's hand, then went in. Alonzo was on a pallet on the floor, his large frame almost hanging over the sides and ends. His head was turned to the wall; his hands dropped over the side of the pallet and lay on the cold tile of the floor. Kate was kneeling beside him, sponging his feverish body.

"Why is he here, Kate? I looked in his room."

"He's been sleeping here for two weeks now, letting the worst cases have his bed. When he got sick last night, well, he wouldn't let us move him into his room. Insisted that Abuela Morales stay in his bed, since she was so bad."

"The damned, generous fool," Ruth hissed. Ruth glared at Kate, as if she were to blame for Alonzo lying on a straw pallet on the floor.

"Believe me, Ruth. I tried. But you know how stubborn he can be."

Ruth's face softened.

"I know, dearest. I'm just very upset. . . ."

Kate smiled, understanding in her eyes.

"He may be asleep now," she said, "but I think you should go and wake him. He asked for you all during the night, then stopped when we said we would send for you. Said we should wait until morning, so you wouldn't miss any rest."

It was ironic. Ruth had been awake all night and was planning to sleep as soon as she and Anna had gotten the food out to the tents.

Ruth went over and knelt beside Alonzo. She put her hand on his shoulder. The intense fever burned through his nightshirt. She shook him gently.

"Alonzo. Alonzo. It's me."

He was still for a moment, then pulled out of the troubled, painful sleep. With difficulty he managed to turn to her.

"Querida."

He said the one word, then held his hand out to her.

Ruth stayed with him for the day, hovering over him like a benign spirit. She had hoped that he would be over the worst when she arrived, but from the moment she saw him, she knew he was gravely ill. The fever raged on for hours, broken by chills and fitful, nightmarish sleep; the terrible nausea and diarrhea; all the evidence of a strong body devastated by an invisible force.

She was furious with Alonzo for sleeping on the floor out of consideration for others; she was furious with Kate for not disobeying Alonzo's orders and sending for her in the middle of the night; she was furious because there were no doctors to be had, though she knew they could do nothing in any case. But most of all, she was furious because she knew he was dying.

Kate went in on tiptoe through the silence that was broken by Alonzo's troubled breathing. She knelt down beside where Ruth knelt and took her hand. She asked the question with her eyes.

"I think—I pray—he's better," Ruth whispered. "But I can't really tell. I may just be hoping against hope."

Suddenly, from outside the room on the gallery, there was a shattering crash, followed by silence. Both women ran out to see what the matter was. Across the court, where the stairs went down to the lower level, Anna lay motionless.

On November 11, the world received the long-awaited news: the Armistice was signed at Compiègne. The horror of "The Great War," "The War to End All Wars" was over. In a devastated Europe, the end of the hostilities was joy beyond measure; the ten million who had died in the conflict were beyond any such human concerns. In places as remote from the war as Casilla, the end of the fighting was greeted with elation for, though there were the dead to be buried, there were the living to be welcomed home. It was as if a great, dark cloud had been broken apart to let the golden sun shine through once again. From Washington came the happy news that Will, though stricken down with influenza, had recovered and was about to resume his duties; better yet, though the end of the war had left America's military in some confusion as to how to regroup itself, there were indications that he might be home by Easter. From Europe there was the equally happy news that Bart had gotten through the last months of the war unscathed; he had even witnessed the surrender in the railcar in the forest of Compiègne.

There was one, though, who heard none of this good news. For most of November Anna lay near death, her thin, fever-racked body lying almost as if in state in the great baroque galleon of Don Alonzo's bed. It was ironic that Anna should lie so near death in Alonzo's bed. To the superstitious among the residents and visitors of Casa Portillo, it seemed almost as if Anna were giving her life in place of Don Alonzo's. Only hours after Anna had fallen ill, Alonzo had begun a slow, steady, even remarkable recovery while Anna slipped further and further into the clutches of the influenza. Within a few days it was clear that Alonzo would recover while it seemed almost certain that Anna would not. After the first week, as her fluid-filled lungs brought her closer and closer to death, few of those who came to see Anna and to care for her held out any hope for her survival. They had seen cases not at all as serious as hers in which the patient died in a matter of days. Ruth could see the hopelessness in their eyes, though she refused to believe it. Ruth's heart clung with a fierce determination to the fact that her Anna was going to live.

"She's strong, she's strong. She's always been strong." Ruth recited the phrase over and over again, a litany at her daughter's bedside. Yet, for days on end, as the world saw great events, Anna lay with only the slenderest thread connecting her to this world, barely conscious, barely alive. Hank, devastated by the inevitable loss of his beloved sister, spent hours wandering alone in the bare winter fields; Kate, that pillar of optimism and high spirits, fell into a quiet, sullen depression; Alonzo, who had in a matter of two weeks regained much of his former strength, stood by Anna's bedside and cried out for all to hear that he would gladly go in Anna's place. Even J. J. had been seen, when he thought no one was looking, to be crying tears of genuine grief over his dying sister.

She lay in a half world, slipping back and forth from darkness to light, from consciousness to dreams. The pain, the profound helplessness of her body were well-known, well-accepted companions by now. She had no idea of time; there was only the strange shapeless being that was her existence. There were dreams that might be people and people that might be dreams. There were faces or spirits that hovered over her: her mother, her brothers. Kate, Alonzo, Vassily, and Lina. Maricita and the other servants of Casa Portillo. Wasserman, Ola. Her friends from school. Her father was there, smiling. And Jo Ellen, her best friend from Myrtlesburg, with her hair in pigtails. There were faces she did not know; perhaps they were angels, for sometimes it seemed very likely that she was dead. Sometimes Will's face was there with his dear smile and lovely blue eyes. And finally, one day, she saw Bart's face hovering above her, dark and serious and full of love.

Bart stayed with her for a day and a half after he arrived at Casa Portillo before he could be persuaded to go to bed, get some rest himself. He sat in a chair beside her bed, with a bowl of cool water and a stack of fresh compresses in his lap and bathed her feverish body hour after hour with the cool, moist cloths. Though he deferred to Ruth and the others when they came to be with Anna, it was clear that first day that he had become Anna's guardian angel. In that dark, sad room, smelling of death and sorrow, he hovered over her, a powerful, and all-caring presence. Ruth sensed that presence and respected it, for when she had stood in the room and watched him beside her, she had seen that the room was filled, overwhelmed, with love.

Bart had not even known that Anna lay near death when he arrived in Casilla barely two weeks after the Armistice. He had leapt at the chance to come back to the valley when Pershing had needed someone to go back to Fort Bliss to pave the way for the Fifth Cavalry's triumphant return home. He had telegraphed to his grandfather that he was coming home but had not waited for any news to arrive from Casilla in order not to miss the first available ship for New York. He had not known about Anna's illness, in fact, until he arrived at Casa Portillo, breathless from the ride from Casilla on the horse he had rented from the blacksmith, just to get him home the fastest way possible. He had galloped into the outer court in a cloud of white dust, still in uniform, and half run through the familiar, weather-beaten entryway, only to be greeted with Maricita's downcast face and the words, "Oh, Señor Barton, Miss Anna *es muy mala.*"

Death had become a close companion to Bart Bradley in the years since he had gone chasing after Pancho Villa in Mexico with Pershing and the Fifth Cavalry. He had seen it first, there in the desolation of the Mexican desert, then later in the man-made desolation of the trenches. He had seen hundreds upon hundreds die; he and his fellow officers had engineered the deaths of thousands. Death's irrevocable power had earned the profound respect of the young officer and had changed and tempered his view of life. Bart had always been a maverick and a scoundrel, though an immensely gifted one. His growing intimacy with death—first his mother and father, now his friends and companions—had made him realize that his gifts, his beauty, his wealth, his intelligence, all were in the ultimate scheme of things, as but grains of sand. He had, in his dark months of surveying the trenches and death-stenched fields of France and Belgium, learned that he, as quickly as anyone else, could lie rotting in the mud of an indifferent earth, and all of his arrogance and pride would be nothing, nothing but the merest wisps in the vast wind of eternity. Only one thing, one force seemed to have any strength in the face of the madness of existence, and that force was love.

"Mama says it was all your doing. Says her strength had run out, that she had lost me. Until you got back. That changed everything."

Bart watched Anna as she spoke. Her face was turned up to the warm, late January sun that streamed into the courtyard of Casa Portillo. The winter days had been mild, almost springlike, causing the pale, dormant foliage in the sheltered courtyard to turn fresh and green in an early renewal. Anna's face, after her long convalescence at the *hacienda,* had begun to take on the flush of renewed life too. There was more spring in her eyes.

"No," Bart said in protest. "It was no more any of my doing than anyone else's. We all hovered over you then. I just hovered a little harder than most anyone else."

She laughed, a high, silvery laugh, light and full of life.

"Don't be falsely modest, Bart. It isn't a bit like you. Why, if you're not cocky and conceited and inclined to think too much of yourself, I'm liable to start believing it's some handsome impostor the Germans sent over as a spy or something."

"I'm a changed man, Anna."

He tried to make it sound joking, self-mocking, but there was an intensity and sincerity in his tone. She saw behind the greengold magic of his eyes that there was a depth, a darkness that was never there before. She knew indeed that he was changed and thought she sensed rightly that it was a change that was born of pain, of experience; it gave Bart Bradley a quality of humanness, of vulnerability that he had lacked before. She knew she had always been drawn to him—she would have been a fool to deny it—but that attraction had always been something of a physical, animalistic kind. Now, for the first time, she felt a need to comfort him, to protect him. It was a new and, in its own way, very frightening way of viewing the man.

It was Anna, now, who turned serious.

"I know now that just a few weeks ago I was dying. In fact, I know I had already crossed over, slipped into the other side, whatever that is. Something—or someone—brought me back, pulled me out of that place across the line between life and death. And I know it was you, Bart, who brought me back."

She reached out a pale, thin arm to him. His own strong, brown hand took hers, held it securely in its massive warmth. He began to speak slowly, his words carefully chosen. As he spoke, the fingers of his other hand caressed the back of Anna's frail arm.

"If you knew, if you only knew how much I had thought about you when I was in France. It was almost as if I were haunted or possessed. The oddest times, the oddest places. While inspecting the men, writing my reports, eating breakfast on the edge of my cot, while reporting to the general. Why, why, I kept asking myself, do I keep thinking about, seeing images of this girl, this woman I hardly know? A woman I've kissed twice in my life, neither time with much success. There have been, there could be, so many other women. Why this one? I couldn't understand it, yet you were there the whole time. If anything, it was you who got me through those black, terrible days over there, when the killing and suffering were more than I thought I could stand, when I was ashamed to be a human being, to be alive. And when it was all over, all I could think about was getting back here—of course, because I wanted to be back home, to see my friends, my grandfather, but also because I wanted to see you, to find out more about the woman who had been with me through the war. When I got here, to find that you were dying . . . I don't know, Anna, I felt almost as if you were dying to save me. That I had survived the war because in some crazy way you were sacrificing your life. I know that's not a grown-up man's way of thinking, but it was what I felt."

"Then, in a sense," she said after a moment of thought, "we have done the same thing for each other. We have exchanged favors."

She turned her face from him, rolled her head to one side until it almost rested on her shoulder. It was a delicate, almost birdlike gesture, all the more so because of the expanse of thin, bony neck and shoulder it exposed above the neck of her gown and robe. Her chest began to heave, almost like it had when her lungs were so inflamed, and in an instant Bart realized that she was crying.

"No, Anna!" he cried as he leapt to his feet. "We've got to

stop talking about this. Nothing—nothing can upset you. I won't let it."

"We have to," she said as she turned to him, her tears under control now. "It's just that I'm confused."

"It's Will."

"It's Will," she confirmed, "Will—and the fact that I love you."

"Don't say it, Anna! Don't say it!"

His fists slammed into his thighs; his lips drew tight across his clenched teeth.

"But I have to!"

"Then, damn it, don't expect me to hold back. Don't expect me to pretend."

He knelt down next to her chair, leaned to her. His arms took her in an embrace as delicate and controlled as it was powerful, and his lips pressed against hers, finding the long-awaited touch and taste and smell of her. He pulled away, his lips close to her ear, and whispered, "I love you, Anna. Oh, God, how I wish I didn't, but I love you."

Their lips met again, and her body, frail and warm, arched up to meet his, melding in a oneness that had transcended the years, the oceans that had kept them apart. With an understanding that needed no words they rose from their place beneath the newly budded magnolia tree. He swept her carefully up into his arms and carried her across the court to the stairs where they had first met. It was a quiet afternoon. Don Alonzo was away; the maids were all in the far end of the house, having their *siesta*. Bart took her up the stairs, then along the gallery, to his room. No one would hear them; they would be alone.

J. J. Cutter opened the front door of Casa Portillo quietly, slipped through the crack, then pushed the massive carved slab back into place without a squeak. No one minded if folks just walked into the *hacienda;* that was the way Alonzo was about his place. J. J. hurried down the long, low-beamed corridor toward the court. Anna would probably be there; that was where she usually sat during the afternoon, reading or doing her embroidery. It was humiliating, really, how his mother and sister had kept him doing errands for them since Anna had been recuperating at the *hacienda*. Every afternoon, or so it seemed, he had to ride over to the place to take a packet of papers or bills to his sister. What a crock, him being eighteen and out of school and acting as messenger when he should have been managing the farm himself. But his mother wouldn't hear anything of it. She was soft, real soft, where Anna was concerned.

There was no one in the courtyard, just the splash, splash of the fountain and what looked like a fresh pot of tea sitting on a little table next to the chair where Anna usually sat. He heard some noise upstairs, footsteps on the gallery, and leaned out to see beyond the upper rail.

J. J.'s eyes glittered when he saw them, too much caught up in their business to see or hear him. He watched as Bart carried Anna along the passage and into an upstairs room. The court echoed faintly as the door closed behind them.

He waited a minute or two, then crept as quietly as he could up the stairs and around the gallery until he was a few feet from the door they had gone through. He stood there a long while, hearing only the faint trickle from the fountain below and the muffled cries of passion from within.

In the dark mustiness of the bedroom Bart held her close against him, the sweated, muscled nakedness of his body hard against her own naked flesh. She could not guess how long they had been there; she could not remember how the clothes had been torn from her body. There was only the heat of him against her, the probing fullness of his lips, his tongue. His arms held her tight against him, his hands explored, aroused the curves, the folds of her body. Anna found herself instinctively pulling up against him, her loins against his, as a deep, glowing fire welled up in her. She knew that the moment was near, that threshold from which there was no turning back. She felt his maleness against her belly, felt its mysterious weight and warmth, probing, insisting. He said nothing to her as he pulled himself up over her. He knew he was to be the first, but she did not want him to hesitate or hold back on that account. Her body was to be his, fully, willingly. She was no longer the girl resisting his kisses. She was a woman giving him the purest gift a woman can give.

Then he paused for a moment, a proud, male animal above her, and with a single thrust, he penetrated her to the very depths. There was pain, if a liquid fire welling up inside, burning, consuming, can be called pain. She cried out but not in protest, not in agony, and her cries were met with his own moans of sweet, agonized pleasure. Then the liquid fire bubbled up, overflowed, until they both were lost, oblivious to time and place, caught up only in the power of their coupled bodies. It was a mysterious, rich world that Bart's body led her into, yet her own flesh instinctively found its way. Still, when the final moment came, the explosion ripped through her with a force beyond comprehension. She had ceased to be a woman, he a man: they had become a force.

Chapter Five

"IT WAS EASIER THAN I EXPECTED, HANDING IN THE RESignation. Oh, Pershing looked hurt and disappointed in his own way, as much as any tough career military man can feel those things. I think he genuinely liked me, wanted to make his protégé into a general in his own image. Me deciding that I hated armies and that everything having to do with war and militarism just wasn't in his battle plan."

Anna cuddled up next to Bart, felt his skin, naked and damp from their lovemaking, close against her own. It was warm and fragrant on the April-green grass by the river, and the little amphitheater of trees that had been witness to so many of their afternoon meetings in the last two months seemed as comfortable with their presence as they were.

She toyed with the curls of dark hair that matted his chest, watched them as they caught glints of sun that filtered through the newly leaved trees.

"I suppose he asked you what you were going to do next?" She smiled, anticipating correctly the question and answer.

"Yes," Bart replied, "and he didn't look like he believed me when I told him, 'Nothing.'"

"Very unsoldierly."

"Very."

Anna sat up next to Bart, pulled her blouse around her naked breasts. The curves of her body were firmer, fuller now, the color of her skin pink and healthy. There were few signs of the ravages of her illness.

"You don't think you're making a mistake, do you?" she asked as she closed the long row of buttons from waist to neck. "It is all you've ever known, after all. With the war and everything, maybe there's too much temptation to chuck it all overnight."

Bart stretched, luxuriated in the grass, not caring that he was half naked, shirt off, trousers open. He looked as relaxed, as carefree as he ever had, as happy as a truant schoolboy on a warm spring afternoon.

"Just the problem. That's all I've ever known. I was raised to be a military hero. First, following in my father's footsteps, then, after he was killed, forced to be a substitute for him."

"Who forced you?"

"Me."

"And now, darling?"

"My life's an unwritten book. Lots and lots of blank pages. Just one thing I want to happen in the rest of the story—"

He caught himself and stopped.

"I'm sorry, Anna. I promised not to bring it up."

Anna began pinning up the long, dark coils of her hair. Bart reached up and pulled out a few stray strands of grass that had gotten caught up in it.

"No, it's all right," she said with a calmness in her voice that confirmed her words. "I've made up my mind, Bart."

"No, please, Anna. I told you I didn't want you brooding about this, wearing yourself down again. I refuse to pressure you or to let you pressure yourself. It isn't fair to you . . . or to anyone."

"Bart Bradley," she said, teasing him, "how did you manage all those years to hide from every man, woman, and child the fact that you were a nice man and an honorable man?"

"Took a lot of work."

"Suppose so."

She leaned down, her face over his. His skin was brown now from his long afternoons in the sun, and his beard showed a full day's growth. His skin exuded that faint masculine smell of sweat and cigarettes and talc. She kissed him long and deeply, a kiss full of meaning.

When she spoke afterward, her voice was calm, controlled, but dead-serious.

"Will is coming back in two months. I got a letter two days ago. No matter how beautiful a day it is, no matter what has happened between us these last weeks, Will is going to be here in two months. It won't be any easier to face then than now."

Bart looked up at her, and though his face glowed with warmth and love, she thought she detected a trace of fear in his eyes.

"Do you love Will?" he asked.

"Yes."

"Do you love me?"

"Yes."

Bart rolled away from her until he faced the other direction. She could not see his face, but his voice was distinct, an outward tone of humor thinly disguising anger and frustration.

"Isn't this the point where I'm supposed to knock you around in a jealous rage, give you a black eye or two, then storm off, get drunk, and wake up tomorrow morning with a strange, painted woman?"

She would have laughed had the image not rung so true.

"You asked me if I love Will. I answered honestly. Will is the only man I've ever known except you. Of course, not in the physical sense. You know you were the first. But I was a girl, really, when Will came along. He changed my life, showed me so many wonderful things. And you know Will as well as I do, perhaps even better. Know what kind of man he is. How could I help but love him? I loved him enough to become engaged to him."

Bart turned back toward her again, looked at her when he spoke. For that she was grateful.

"That's the way it should be," he said quietly. "Will is the kind of man you deserve; he'll give you the kind of life you should have."

"You're right. Totally right. Except for one thing. It would be dishonest and unfair. Dishonest because I would always be thinking of you; unfair because I could never give myself totally to him, as long as there was you."

Bart couldn't answer, though there was so much he wanted to say. It was cruel and malicious of fate to have brought Anna into his life, for she had brought with her the one thing he thought he could never have, yet she was not really his; he could never really possess her, totally share with her.

She saw the conflict in his eyes, saw that she would have to be the one to resolve it. She sat up tall, a kind of nobility in her features, mature beyond her years.

"I want to go with you Bart, wherever that is. My life is yours now, if you want it that way. I've made my decision. I'll have to live with what I've done to Will. But it would be foolish of me to give up what we have, what we can have, because I can't tell a man that I love another more than I love him. I have to do it for me, for us."

Without a word he pulled her down to him. Their bodies meshed, flowed together, until the beauty of the afternoon was forgotten.

J. J. Cutter had a plan. It had grown, like the mighty oak, from the small, hard acorn of disgust that he had felt at the very idea of his sister having an affair with Barton Bradley. His intention was not to be cruel or to destroy lives; in fact, such ethical issues had not even crossed J. J.'s mind. From that afternoon when he had accidentally discovered that Anna was seeing Bart, J. J. had nurtured only one overriding thought: drive them apart and smash any hope of their having anything more than an afternoon's rutting.

J. J. was not motivated out of concern for his sister's virtue or for her well-being, let alone her happiness. His motives were simple enough, both base and basic: J. J. Cutter could not stomach the idea of Anna marrying someone of Mexican blood. Bart, to J. J.'s way of thinking, in spite of the fancy Bradley name and pedigree, was as brown as any peon hoeing cotton in the Cutter fields. That old spic dog, Alonzo, J. J. told himself, had been sniffing around his mother enough since his father had left. J. J. wasn't going to let Alonzo's half-breed grandson do the same to his sister.

Lurking behind J. J.'s self-admitted bigotry was another concern: Anna's engagement to Will Channing. J. J. had secretly gloated as Senator Jack's son had fallen for Anna. It was a dream—an unsurpassed opportunity for J. J. and his family. The Channings were a catch: rich, prominent, powerful. Once Anna was securely married to Will, the Cutters were set for life. No more concern about dry years or wet years. About hailstorms or floods. No more getting up at dawn or sweating all day through the hot months, like some smelly Mexican field hand, in the vain hope of a decent profit at the end of the year. That kind of life wouldn't be his anymore once Anna was legally a Channing. Sure, the Cutter farm was doing well without an advantageous marriage but at the price of backbreaking work and year-to-year anxieties. The Channings, on the other hand, had so much money that they didn't have to work. They led comfortable, luxurious gentlemen's lives.

No, J. J. told himself, he wasn't going to make the same mistakes his father had. A man didn't have to break his ass on a farm to make good. Not if he played his cards right. Not if his sister married the right man.

It was at this point in his life that J. J. Cutter became a grown man. He crossed that important threshold, as all men do, when he decided to take responsibility for achieving something in his life that he wanted. It was not enough now to let others take care of his needs, as he had always let them. Now he had to act, to do something in order to get what he wanted. But because he was both lazy and ambitious, he chose the easiest route. J. J. saw his opportunity—it was as if Lady Luck had handed it to him on a silver platter. To achieve his ends J. J. had only to get rid of Bart Bradley. Simple enough, he realized, because here opportunity and timing were right. J. J., clever youth that he was, saw Bart's great vulnerability: he was going to Mexico incognito, going into the desolate, uncivilized heart of the Revolution-torn North, into a land where he and his family were not just unwelcome but hated. In Villa's land Bradley was vulnerable; the desert was full of enemies. The fact that he had to go there under another name was proof enough of how dangerous it was for Bart. Yet Bart had made a fatal mistake: He had assumed that his enemies were only in Mexico, not close to home in the midst of the Cutter family. He talked openly with them about his trip to Chihuahua, omitting, as J. J. smugly noted, any mention of his upcoming plans with Anna.

It was easy enough for J. J. to accomplish his end: a simple matter of a one-day journey to El Paso on a trivial pretext. While there, he spent an afternoon drinking at one of the south-side bars known to be frequented by Villa supporters and hangers-on. Everything fell into place beautifully. It was easy for the eighteen-year-old farmer to get the ear of the hard-eyed Villistas after dropping only a few hints that he had information of interest to them. By sunset J. J. was at the station, waiting for the evening local to take him back to Casilla, feeling satisfied that Bart Bradley would not likely be coming back from Mexico anytime soon, now that the bandit revolutionaries knew that the last of the Lopez y Ruiz family was within their grasp. J. J. had made only one mistake in the afternoon's negotiations: When he had told the *bandidos* that he knew the when and where of Bradley's trip across the river, the Mexicans had asked him how much he wanted for the information. Youthful fool that he was, in a rush to get the all-important deed accomplished, he had told them he wanted nothing.

Bart lay awake on the bare, musty straw mattress of the long-unused laborer's hut. His body ached from the long day's ride across the miles of desert from Chihuahua City to Hacienda Rosada, and he longed to be in one of the large, comfortable featherbeds in the big house a hundred yards up the hill. But it was much more sensible to sleep out in the hut, quietly, in the dark, instead of in the *hacienda*.

For Bart, being back in Mexico again had an unreal, dream-like quality to it. The last time he had been in his ancestral land was with Pershing and the Fifth Cavalry in their ill-fated, futile expedition through the wild mountains of the Sierra Madre. Now, for the first time since he was a teen, he was back at Hacienda Rosada, the Rose House, the place where his grandfather had been born, and his fathers before him for many generations. The vast *hacienda*, three hundred years old, was more like a small, mud-walled city than a private home, yet it had been built by the *conquistador* who had founded the Lopez y

Ruiz line in the New World, as the seat of power for all future
generations of Lopez y Ruiz in the centuries to come. For Bart,
with his half American roots from his father's side, the *hacienda* and its fifty thousand acres of kingdom had always been a
place of magic and mystery in his childhood and youth. His
mother, the last one born to bear the name Lopez y Ruiz, had
been born and raised there. He, the last male to carry the family
blood in his veins, had been conceived there. Yet Hacienda
Rosada had, to Bart, never been more than a place of legend. It
had never been his home, as Casa Portillo had been. And now,
as he slept in the abandoned hut outside the dark, hulking
shape of the *hacienda,* he knew that he would be the last Lopez
y Ruiz to set foot in the *hacienda.* The house, the world that
created it, were dying. He was here only to say farewell.

He had arrived on the rancho that afternoon, only to find the
place abandoned, and fairly recently, from what he could see.
He had expected all the men to be gone, off joining one or other
of the ragtag regiments fighting for or against Villa, for or
against Carranza. The word that the men were leaving the estate had reached Alonzo in Casilla, which had precipitated
Bart's unexpected journey to Chihuahua in the first place. With
the men and boys running off to become soldiers, there was real
concern that the estate was being looked after properly. When
Bart had arrived at Hacienda Rosada, after the train ride to
Chihuahua City and the horseback ride beyond there, he had
expected to find at least the women, children, and old men
living out their lives at the *hacienda,* much as they had for
generations. To his surprise and anger, the vast, sprawling pile
of adobe and stucco, the ancestral home of Lopez y Ruiz, was
dark and deserted though, fortunately, not looted. The signs
pointed to recent departure of the forty-odd souls who had lived
on the estate, a warning sign that, though the men might have
gone off to fight in the revolution, the women and children had
probably run from the revolutionaries or from the thieves and
ruffians who hovered around the events of the revolution. Bart
had not seen a soul for almost the entire day, so he had little
fear of seeing one in the middle of the warm, empty Mexican
night. Still, it paid to be cautious.

In one sense Bart did not mind the nuisance of the trip to
Chihuahua: he was conveniently out of sight when Anna left for

her holiday in the mountains. They had decided to break away clean, to strike out suddenly and completely on their own. Bart had suggested that they slip away together to the mountains a hundred miles north of El Paso in New Mexico. His parents had left him a small, rustic cabin there. There in the high pines, five thousand feet above the desert, he and Anna could settle to start their life together. There was a justice of the peace in the village near the cabin who could marry the eloping couple. Then the problems in Mexico had thrown a hitch in the plans, or so it seemed at first, until Bart realized that it might be easier for both of them if they left Casilla separately, met secretly in the mountains a week later.

Anna had been nervous, of course, about Bart going into Mexico alone. But he assured her that it was a simple matter. He had not spent time at Hacienda Rosada in almost ten years, had not even set foot in Mexico since the ill-fated eleven months of the Fifth Cavalry's Punitive Expedition against Villa.

"You're just being a nervous bride-to-be," he had teased her when she had expressed her reservations about the trip. "The Villistas may hate my guts because I'm from the now-crumbling wealthy class, hate me even more because I was an American cavalryman chasing after Pancho himself, but they also do not really know who I am, what I look like. The man passing through Chihuahua next week will have a different name, a different identity than Barton Bradley."

It had been a sad day, seeing the ancestral estate of Lopez y Ruiz abandoned to the dust and the wind. It had never been home to him, but still, Hacienda Rosada was filled with memories: memories of childhood visits with his parents, when the great house had been a rich, colorful fantasia of treasures and mysteries, the visitable, tangible link with the world of the *conquistadores* and *padrones,* the world of his mother's family. All was changed now as everything in the world seemed to be changed. It was a surprise to Bart, in fact, that Hacienda Rosada had survived as long as it had, for its world was a world of two, three hundred years before. The house and all it stood for had outlived its time. He had arrived too late to do anything about Hacienda Rosada; there was nothing to be done about the place. The tide of history was against him. All he could do was walk through the ancient rooms, look here and there for a few

last mementos to take back to Don Alonzo in his last refuge of
Casa Portillo.

Bart had difficulty sleeping. The hut was musty, warm, the
mattress uncomfortable. And he was anxious to get his business
here over with, so he could hurry back to El Paso, then on to
the Sacramento Mountains and his rendezvous with Anna. The
vast emptiness of the Chihuahua desert engulfed him, made him
more than ever want to spend his first night with Anna next to
him in the bed. That would be one of the great luxuries of the
cabin in the mountains: though they had made love many times
in the last two months, they had never slept together through
the night.

There was a noise outside, a soft rustling in the dark, moonless night. Raccoons, he thought. Finishing off the tin of meat
he had tossed outside after his supper, Bart stretched, tried to
find a more comfortable position on the rough bed.

Then it happened. A flash of light as a torch was thrust
through the open window at the end of the room; a thud as the
rough wood door was kicked open. Bart leapt to his feet, still in
his traveling clothes, and fumbled for his revolver.

"Cáyate, cabrón," a rough voice called out from behind the
torch light. "Hold it, bastard. Don't touch the *pistola."* Blood
pounding from the shock of the intrusion, Bart sensed that he
should heed the warning. Three men, brown-faced and unshaven, stepped into the room. The gray steel of rifles gleamed
in their hands.

"All right, you son of a whore," one of them called out in
Spanish. "We've found you now. Thought you could hide from
us, eh?"

One of the men, smelling of stale sweat and beer, came over
to Bart. He grinned a yellow, snaggletoothed grin. The point of
his rifle dug hard and cold into Bart's neck.

"Me llamo Jorge Maldonado," Bart said in rapid, perfectly
accented Spanish. *"Me voy a Torreón."* He told them his alias,
for which he had false papers in his pocket, and that he was en
route to Torreón.

"Don't give us that crap, *gringo,"* the ruffian shot back in
Spanish. "We know damned well who you are, Señor Bart, you
rich traitor bastard."

Bart started to protest that there was some mistake; he was

just sleeping in the hut while traveling across the desert. But the man's rifle slammed into Bart's rib cage, winding him.

"Get your lousy half-gringo ass outside. General Villa himself is going to want to put one of the bullets into your lousy rich-boy carcass. The general doesn't like *Americano* soldiers who think they can chase after our glorious army and get away with it."

Still gasping for air, Bart stumbled out into the night air.

Chapter Six

ANNA LEFT CASILLA BY TRAIN FOR HER SOLITARY HOLI-day in the mountains. Bart had left a week before for Mexico, and they had made arrangements to meet at the cabin the third day after Anna arrived there. They would spend perhaps a week at the cabin, be married by the justice of the peace. After that they would make an announcement to their families, then spend two weeks traveling, probably to California, before their return to Casilla. Beyond that, their lives were a clean slate: Bart had made no decision about his career, Anna none about her continued involvement with the farm. For the first time since she was a girl Anna felt free. For so many years she had been burdened with responsibilities, with obligations. Now all that was going to be behind her. The farm was successful, but that was in good hands with her mother, brothers, and their foremen. She had earned her freedom, and most glorious of all, that was to be with Bart.

In El Paso she changed trains onto the Santa Fe and North-ern, which traveled north up into the New Mexico desert, through Albuquerque and Santa Fe to Colorado. As the miles of flat desert sped past the train windows, she reflected on her relationship with Bart. How ironic it was that a man who had frightened her so, had overwhelmed her so, would now be her husband. Yet now this creature, this man who had seemed more like a god, loved her, desired her, possessed her. It was as if her life had suddenly become enchanted, blessed with a kind of magic.

It was brutally hot in the middle of the desert, far worse than the valley, which at least had the river and the cottonwoods to soften the heat. Behind her, across miles of flat, empty desert, the bare bones of the Franklin range guarded the desert from El Paso in a long, unbroken chain. Ahead were the Sacramentos, a great, brooding range, even at a distance, seen through the shimmering waves of summer heat. The rounded flanks, rising behind bare, rocky foothills, were dark with forests, flourishing in the benign atmosphere thousands of feet above the desert floor.

The single-passenger car on the narrow gauge was almost empty: a couple with their children, all dressed in summer whites and straw hats, the seats piled high with hampers; an old couple with dark, leathery faces and inky-black eyes, sat in the back of the car—Indians going to the Mescalero reservation in the mountains. On larger trains they would have sat in the separate car reserved for coloreds and Indians; in the single car of the small train they had their own seats behind a line in the rear.

Aside from them, Anna was alone.

The train started across the desert, a slow climb of some miles, until, though the terrain outside had not changed, the buildings of Alamogordo were distant and below them. Soon the flat, sandy desert was broken by outcroppings of rock, and the barren, reddish arms of the hills rose up on either side of the tracks. The train slowed as the incline steepened, and the rusty earth soon gave way to rocky, broken cliffs of ocher and russet, streaked with sulfurous yellow. In places the cliff faces were split and fractured, showing deep crevasses filled with tumbled boulders; an occasional gnarled bush found a foothold in the fissures.

After half an hour of climbing slowly through the rocks, on one side of the tracks the cliffs fell away into a deep gorge, sharp and narrow, the bottom not visible from the window. Across the narrow gash in the mountain the sheer cliffs were a brilliant palette of colors from the raw minerals of the rocks:

russet and gray; yellow and coppery green; a touch of vermilion and turquoise. Here and there a hardy cactus or stunted oak clung to a fracture in the rocks, its spines or branches growing out over the precipice.

The train continued to climb; wheels screeching as they inched around sharp curves snaking up the sheer mountain face. The gorge suddenly opened up into a wide valley bristling with firs and pines: they had climbed to the timber line. The train suddenly turned and seemingly moved out into midair over the valley; on either side only open sky could be seen, with the tops of the pines pointing up from the valley floor a hundred feet below.

It was the last leg of the trip before reaching the mountaintops: a narrow, high wood trestle that spanned the canyon the train had climbed through from the valley. It was a spectacular last leg to the journey, almost as if the train were flying toward the green forest on the other side.

When the train reached the other side of the trestle, it plunged into the dark shadows of the pines. Anna turned and looked behind for a last glimpse of the desert, four thousand feet below, through the narrow, *V*-shape of the canyon's mouth.

The train picked up speed, moving across the flat, forested crest of the mountain. Overhead the pines made a lush, dark canopy; alongside, their reddish-barked trunks stood like sentinels, a vast army marching into the distance. Sunlight occasionally trickled through a gap in the trees, dappling the undergrowth of ferns and honeysuckle.

Anna cautiously held her fingers out the open window. The breeze that touched them was moist and far cooler than inside the train, which was still warm with the air from the desert. She leaned close to the open pane, letting the draft flow by her face. The air was moist, sweet, and cool, fragrant with the fresh, pungent scent of pine. There was something familiar about the air, the half remembered scent of cool summer evenings in Kentucky, the memory of an atmosphere laden with moisture and the perfume of trees and flowers.

It was difficult to remember that the desert was only an hour in the past.

The train slowed, then halted, and the conductor came in and announced Cloudcroft—what a magical name, she thought.

The family and the Indian couple bundled up their possessions and Anna hers, and left the train, the Indian couple walking off without a word into the woods. There was no platform to speak of, only a flat place covered with cinders. About fifty yards from the tracks was a lodge, a low, rambling, log affair, nestled on a low slope beneath the trees with a deep porch running its length. A man and woman were coming down the path toward them, pulling a small wooden wagon. They identified themselves to the family and Anna—as the Jenkinses—and greeted the train crew. The old codger—he was much older close-up than his lively gait had revealed from a distance—said with a tobacco-choked mouth, "You'll be Miss Cutter. Mr. Bart said you'd be up t'th' cabin a spell."

Anna confirmed and shook Jenkins's bony hand.

"Wife Sarah," he pointed nonchalantly. The wife smiled a broad, gummy smile. "We was up t'other day. Cleaned out a bit, stocked in some vittles. Yuh ride, dontcha?"

Anna answered yes.

"Well, let's getcha some coffee or whiskey, if'n you're so inclined. We got purty good stock, cas'n it get's illegal like it may and gets hard t' come by."

An hour later, after a few shots of whiskey, a cup of coffee to counter its effect, and a change to riding clothes, Anna left Mr. and Mrs. Jenkins, who seemed to keep up a pretty steady intake of "likker," and left on the saddled mare Jenkins had provided for her.

Anna had been amused, if a bit taken aback, by their straightforward invitation to "come down for a shot or two if'n you and Mr. Bart gets too lonely up there."

At least two other people knew about her and Bart!

The cabin was about three miles farther up in the mountains, by Jenkins's reckoning, just below one of the highest points, almost nine thousand feet up. Jenkins told her the trail up was good but little used. Within minutes after she'd waved good-bye to Jenkins, Anna could see no sign of man's hand, except for the faint trail that wound through the trees. Tall, straight-trunked pines with an open, almost brushless forest floor, surrounded her. Here and there the carpet of yellowed pine needles was broken by a cluster of fallen pine cones or spindly seedlings growing at their elders' feet. The path wound up and around the flank of the mountain, in places quite steep, where the mare had to pick her way through gullies and rocks; at times the path would turn, and the forest opened into a sunny little meadow with tall, rippling grass spotted with dandelions and wild iris.

Finally, after a steep, scrabbly climb beside a narrow brook, Anna saw a dark shape through the trees. A bit farther and it took the form of a low, rough cabin. The path came up behind and alongside the cabin, and it was only when she got close that she could see the meadow it faced. It was a large meadow, flat and grassy, ringed on three sides by majestic trees. On the far side, opposite the cabin, the meadow fell away, down the slope of the mountain, revealing a broad sweep of sky and a panorama of the lands below.

The door was unlocked. Inside, a single room. Long, small-paned windows. Blue-and-white-checked curtains, a cluster of hanging pans above a wood cook stove. A small stone fireplace, a crotchety rocker made from bent branches. In one corner a painted iron bed, piled high with quilts and blankets. Odds and ends collected over the years—hunting rifles, baskets of pine cones, a bit of Indian weaving. The room was neat and dusted in spite of the clutter—Mrs. Jenkins's work, no doubt—but still stuffy from long disuse.

After settling in and having a quick wash in the icy cold water from the hand pump in the corner, Anna relaxed in the cozy corner window seat, piled high with pillows and lap robes. From the window the view stretched across the meadow, now a blazing emerald in the late-afternoon sun. On a branch just outside, two blue jays quarreled noisily against a gold western sky.

Casilla seemed a million years ago, a million miles away. There was nothing but peace and solitude here; the air seemed to breathe happiness. In three days Bart would arrive, to find her rested, peaceful, loving.

What a wonderful spot, she told herself, to be in love.

The next morning, after a long walk in the clear, fragrant mountain air, she sat at the table by the window of the cabin and began the difficult task of writing to Will. She had deliberately waited until she got to the mountains, knowing that in totally new surroundings she could think more clearly, be more

honest, away from all the associations of her life in Casilla and
her relationship with Will. It was perhaps the most painful task
she had undertaken, for she knew that with every word she was
hurting a man who loved her. Still, there was no way to get
around it. She was honest, direct; emphasized again and again
that Will had been nothing but wonderful to her, that she had
shared many beautiful times with him. But the unavoidable fact
was that she had to follow the dictates of her heart, even though
she knew she would be hurting the one man in the world who
least deserved to be hurt. Yet, as she explained with an honesty
that she knew Will would understand, to continue her relationship with Will, to follow it to the logical conclusion of marriage,
considering how she felt about another man, would be even
crueler than breaking the relationship off at this point. Still,
when the twenty-five pages of cream-colored paper were folded
and slipped into the envelope, Anna felt ashamed for what she
was doing to Will. The task was made all the more painful
because she had to tell Will that it was as close a friend as Bart.
She knew very well that she was far from the first woman to
have to write such a letter, but that companionship was little
comfort. Through all this she was sustained by her deep conviction of the rightness of the decision. Honesty is not always the
least painful course to take.

She slept well that night, her task completed. The letter, addressed to Will in Washington, stood propped against the salt
and pepper shakers on the table, waiting to be postmarked and
mailed when she and Bart left the mountains as husband and
wife. The cabin was cold in the high mountain air, and she
made a warm cocoon of quilts and blankets. As she drifted off
into a deep and dreamless sleep, she was immensely happy,
knowing that tomorrow night Bart would be with her there in
that bed. Now, at last, they could begin their life together.

Midafternoon and Bart still hadn't come. Anna busied herself
in the cabin, brewing coffee, straightening pillows and linens
that had already been straightened, checking her hair in the
mirror, taking it down and pinning it up again, all the while a
hard knot of uneasiness sitting heavily in the pit of her stomach.

By four a wind came out of the north, across the ridge of
peaks that glowered high over the slope on which the cabin sat.

The wind, first in small gusts, then in stronger ones, caused the pines to shake and whisper, the high, soft, whirring sound broken occasionally by the sharp sound of a pine cone breaking loose and falling, helter-skelter, through the branches to the ground a hundred feet below.

A few wisps of white clouds appeared over the top of the ridge, scudding fast and low to the mountaintops. They were soon followed by darker clouds, until the bright afternoon sun was shadowed and blotted out by a heavy, close-hanging wall of leaden gray. From somewhere behind the mountains could be heard the rumbling of thunder, echoing and reechoing through the high dells and ridges.

Her emotions pulled taut to the point of breaking, a strip of elastic stretched too far, she went outside into the gathering storm. The warm summer air had turned suddenly cooler, pungent with the scent of ozone and damp pines. She stood for a while in front of the cabin door, feeling the first light sprinkling of rain blown into her face, feeling the gusty wind tugging at her clothes. Then, anxious, impatient, she walked, face to the wind, across the carpet of dry pine needles, breaking under her steps, toward the rough path that led from the cabin down into the gully between the hills. It was the only way for him to reach the cabin; perhaps, if she walked down the path a bit, she could meet him sooner, halfway down that last steep hill that led to the cabin.

Anna was suddenly swept by a terrible, stabbing thought: What if he didn't come?

Hours late already, he should have been there by midmorning. Something was wrong—the uncontrollable images of accidents flashed through her mind, terrible, ugly. Then, even worse, the thought of him not coming at all, because he chose not to.

She felt the burning sensation in her throat, the tightness around her eyes, preludes to tears. *No, Anna,* she told herself, trying to regain that distance, *don't let go, don't break down now. He'll come, he'll not do this to you. Be ready for him. Be happy and full of love when he arrives.*

She walked amid the gathering rain and the whirring and cracking of the trees, her arms pulled close in, protectively, around her body. When she was out of sight of the cabin, down the gully, and around an arm of the mountainside, she stopped and stood for a long time, watching the empty path in front of her, devoid of any life beyond the coming storm.

She stood for a long moment, feeling the heavy, random raindrops against her face, a feeling of utter hopelessness, of utter aloneness sweeping over her.

She turned to go back to the cabin, leaning into the steep slope of the path up the hill. The thunder was loud and close now, rumbling through the ground with a sharp, palpable crack as the full sky flashed brightly around her.

"Anna! Anna!" the wind seemed to cry out to her.

She turned back, climbing up the empty path.

"Anna! Anna!" The wind cried out again, sharper, louder. She kept walking, trying to shut out the mocking cry of the storm.

"Anna!"

She whirled, looking for the source of the sound.

A movement, there among the thick growth of trees. She ran toward it, down the path a hundred yards or so. Even as she ran she could almost feel his arms around her, his lips on hers. In her mind a picture of their lovemaking, there under the trees in the rain. She knew they would not even wait to go into the cabin; they would fall in a heated, rain-soaked jumble with only the forest as witness.

She came to the place where the sound of her name had come from. Nothing. Nothing but the still-quivering branches of a rotted tree that had been felled by the wind. She kept walking, farther and farther down the hill, until she was blinded by the rain mingled with her tears. Then she saw him, through half open eyes. A moment of fear as she realized the man half stumbling, half running up the path was not Bart. Then puzzled relief as she realized that it was her brother.

J. J. ran toward her, gesturing wildly, until he got to where she stood. He was soaked to the skin and breathless, as if he had run up the mountain in the storm.

"Anna! Finally!" he gasped as he embraced her. "The storm caught me. Scared my horse. Left him at the bottom of the mountain."

Anna knew that her face cried out to know why he was there.

Oblivious to the rain, J. J. panted a few deep breaths. There was a wild light in his eyes.

"I had to come, Anna. Don't be mad at me, sis, but I knew why you were here. I knew Bart was coming to meet you. That's why I had to come get you! So you would know before you got back home."

"Know!" she cried. "Know what?"

As if to punctuate her alarm, the sky cracked with thunder, shuddered with the recoil of the explosion.

"In Mexico," J. J. gasped. "Three days ago the damned rebels found Bart. Found out who he was. Anna, I'm sorry, but they've killed him. A firing squad. Shot him down in cold blood!"

The words tore through her like lightning through the stormy sky. There was the flash, the terrifying surge of power. Then she remembered nothing.

Part III
THE YEAR OF PAIN
1922–1923

Chapter One

"I WONDER WHAT THE OLD BASTARD WOULD HAVE thought of this."

J. J. Cutter spoke the words aloud to himself, pulled his canary-yellow Pierce-Arrow runabout to a roaring dust-clouded halt halfway down the still-unpaved drive to the new house. On either side of the broad drive was a row of newly planted cypress trees, the largest that could be brought by train from California, though they still needed a good few years of growth to give them the stately height, the effect of architectural columns that was intended. At the end of the drive loomed the tall, hipped-roof facade of the new house, still under construction. Silhouetted against the clear blue sky were the shapes of half a dozen workmen, standing and kneeling as they laid in place the glazed terra-cotta roof tiles.

"Hell, it sure is nice being rich," he continued in his dialogue with himself as he brushed the white caliche dust from the tufted black leather of the empty passenger seat. He reflected with a certain satisfaction that his new car, the trademark by which he was becoming known as one of the gad-abouts of the valley, had cost almost seven thousand dollars. And the house his mother was building on the farm was costing well over a hundred thousand dollars. When it was finished, the house would be the largest in the area, bigger than the McNary mansion in El Paso. Ruth Cutter had spared no expense: She had hired the Mizener brothers, who were designing all the mansions for the Palm Beach millionaires, to draw up the plans for the Cutters Italianate villa; most of the skilled craftsmen in the valley were working on the job, directed by half a dozen master carpenters and stonemasons brought over from Italy just for the job. And even though the house was still a good two months from completion, there were already crates of furniture stacked in the unfinished rooms, brought by train and boat from New

York and Europe; bolts of hand-loomed damask were daily being cut and sewn by Mexican seamstresses into drapes and hangings for the house's one hundred and twenty windows.

J. J. remembered as a boy, back in Myrtlesburg, when he would walk home from Wilkins's store with his father. How Jonah would always comment with admiration and envy on the big houses on the hill overlooking town! Kind of a twist, J. J. thought, that the old man had shipped out, left them high and dry, just when things were about to get good. Who knew where he was now, ten years later. Remarried, another family. Or in some flophouse somewhere. Who knew? He'd be sorry he ever left—if he ever came back. He'd find the family he abandoned living high on the hog, rich, respected. Powerful. Living in a house so big, so grand, it was already nicknamed Casa Grande. Big house.

J. J. leaned out and glanced at his reflection in the chromed reflector mirror attached to the windshield. He unnecessarily smoothed down his already slick, brilliantined blond hair. His twenty-two-year-old face was tanned, lean—a bit too lean, perhaps—but thought handsome. J. J. freed his eyes from the rubber motoring goggles, vainly pressed away the pink creases they caused, then studied his own gaze in the mirror. Clear blue eyes, intense, sparkling. Much admired by women. But something in them made J. J. flick his gaze away from the mirror. Something that made him nervous. For an instant he had seen his father looking at him.

The moment passed quickly as J. J. turned the ignition and jumped out to crank the engine. The day was half over, and he had things to attend to. A call on the foreman to make sure they kept their lazy asses in line; a look in on the workmen and his mother awash in a sea of blueprints. With Anna out of town he'd have to spend an hour with his boring little brother and that damned crippled Pablo his brother was so tight with. Then, most important of all, the drive to El Paso to send a telegram and, on the way back, a stop in Clint to pay a call on that foxy little Mary Ella, with her short skirts and her hard, pointy breasts. Mary Ella just loved rich blue-eyed farm boys. There was nothing she wouldn't do for them.

For several months now Ruth Cutter had set up her workstation on the broad landing of the stairway of Casa Grande. It was a perfect place for her to supervise her domains. At the long table made of planks laid on sawhorses she could sit, surrounded by stacks of papers, blueprints, and renderings, both rolled and unrolled; before her cascaded the broad flight of steps leading down to the marble-floored hall, a vast, two-story box lined with ornate balconies and arcades, the labor of the Italian stonemasons and crowned by a great dome of multicolored leaded glass, a floral profusion created by Tiffany in New York and shipped by rail to Casilla. The great hall, now nearly finished, was the heart of the house, the ideal spot to see the comings and goings of the contractors and workmen she supervised so carefully.

Behind Ruth were three great arched windows, fifteen feet high, that overlooked her other domain, the farm. In the distance the windows framed a western view of the mountains and the city; nearer they framed a memento of another life: the simple white stucco box of the old farmhouse, soon to become farm offices.

On the table where Ruth worked her ten- and twelve-hour days was another memento of the past. A small double frame of silver with two faded sepia photographs. One, of the white tree-shaded frame house in Myrtlesburg; the other of the young Jonah Cutter.

It had not been an easy morning for Ruth, though the farm and the construction brought its problems every day. But there had been several serious problems this particular day. First the pink marble lavatory, carved to Ruth's specifications in Italy, had arrived in its crate shattered in several pieces. It would take months now to have it remade. Then Hank and J. J. had had another one of their fights after breakfast. As a mother she would expect that two brothers of such different temperaments would have occasional fights. But with her sons the arguments had become too frequent and too intense; there was an ever-widening gap between them. Her dream of having a tight family-run business was clouded now. Whenever the boys had to work together on farm business, they instantly disagreed on everything: what equipment to purchase, when to begin planting or thinning or picking, how to allocate labor crews. True,

Hank was already the better farmer of the two; his childhood interest in plants and gardening had insured that. But J. J. was far more aggressive and extroverted, more likely to ride hard on the foremen or argue with the mill people and merchants over shoddy baling or short-shipped supplies. It disturbed her profoundly, given that their talents and dispositions complemented each other so well, that they could not work better together. What Ruth was beginning to feel, though she refused to openly admit it to herself, was that her sons had grown to hate one another.

For the moment these concerns had been pushed aside by the letter that had arrived in the morning mail. From the large, distinctive handwriting on the blue onionskin paper, she had known immediately that it was from Alonzo. He wrote regularly, once or twice a month, in the two years he had been in Europe. They were chatty, amiable letters, full of anecdotes about his life abroad, in Paris, on the Riviera, in Tuscany and Switzerland. Alonzo's letters always made her happy; they infused her busy, rigid life with some warmth. How different Alonzo's life was from hers with its planting schedules and construction plans, the church doings and school board meetings, the growing number of charities that swallowed up every minute of her free time. The letters always made her think of simpler, happier times, when she had less in material ways but more in other, less tangible ways. It had been a loss to them all when Alonzo had gone to Europe after Bart's death, leaving Casa Portillo dark and shuttered. She had long since pushed to the back of her mind the thought that she was in part—the main part—the reason why Alonzo had left Casilla.

Today's letter from Alonzo had been different from all the others, and it had suddenly reopened old wounds. In it, for the first time in years, he had mentioned the possibility of a relationship between them. As usual with Alonzo, it was simple, direct, and in good taste.

I sit here as I write on the terrace overlooking Lake Lucerne. There is a mist on the lake that obscures the distant shore and mountains. The air is fresh and sweet, and around me, many birds sing in happiness. It's a place and a moment of great beauty, and I cannot help but think how much more beautiful it would be if I could share this with you. Perhaps I am being just an old fool, but in my mind is always the thought that it has been so many years now since your husband went away. Perhaps now you can consider what another man might have to share with you. . . .

She had gotten no farther; the letter had been slipped back into its envelope to be read later when she felt stronger. As she put the envelope down she saw the framed photographs of Jonah, of their first home. They reminded her of what was right, of what she had to do. Perhaps she was a fool not to give herself to Alonzo; many people thought so and had said as much to her face. There were those who had said she should have Jonah declared legally dead.

Impossible, unthinkable. She knew in her heart, as surely as his bright eyes looked out from the sepia photograph, that he was still alive, that he still loved her. He was still her husband, the father of their children; they had shared those years, those many nights together. It was a bond holding them together. Someday she knew it would bring him back. And when he came, he would find her waiting as she always had; he would also find the kind of life, the kind of home he had always dreamed of. Jonah's wife and children had created the life Jonah had wanted so much. They had made his dream come true. It was waiting only for his return.

In some people's eyes—she suspected even in Anna's—Alonzo would have made a fine companion for her life. It all looked good on paper, like one of the architect's finely executed elevations of Casa Grande. There was only one thing wrong with the plan.

She loved Jonah Cutter.

"I'm going to tell them tonight."

Pablo Sisneros sat back at the rough wood table in his adobe foreman's cottage, his bad leg resting up on a stool he kept handy for the purpose. His dark eyes focused intensely on Hank Cutter as the younger man spoke from across the table. Hank's face was somber, more serious than one would have expected from an eighteen-year-old farmer.

"They'll be angry," Pablo warned. "They won't understand."

"I don't care, Pablo. I just can't live with them there in that damned palace. They'll understand someday."

Hank toyed with his half empty beer bottle with a work-roughed finger. Years of long hours in the gardens and fields had burned his skin a permanent brown; he wore a simple cotton shirt and soil-stained dungarees. Few would have guessed that Hank Cutter was one of the wealthiest men in the valley.

Pablo looked concerned. He had known the Cutters for years now; they had taken him in and given him a home, a good job, a good life. And Hank had become a brother—no, more than a brother to him. He had worked side by side with the youngest of the Cutters for years now. He knew Hank, though the quiet one, was as determined, as strong-headed as the rest of his family. Pablo also knew that there was no changing Hank's mind; it was now a matter of facing the consequences of his decision.

"You know, *amigo,* most people in this country would give their eyeteeth to have what you're in such a hurry to give up. Life in a mansion with servants to wait on you. Your own private suite with a bath and shower and hot water pouring out of pipes, a flush toilet. Even telephones."

"You know I don't give a shit about that."

"I know. But the others do, *compañero.* "

Hank shrugged, and a boyish grin crept across his tanned face. "They can have all that marble and stained glass. I want something else. A little corner of the farm all to myself. Just a room to live in. And I want to build a greenhouse. Two or three maybe. A place to grow flowers. Seed vegetables. Maybe learn a bit about hybridizing and cross breeding. There's a fellow up at the college of mines who's working on high-producing strains of long-staple cotton."

"An experimental farm?"

Hank nodded.

"Sounds all right, Hank. You're good at that sort of thing."

Hank paused, gave his companion a deep, curious look.

"So are you. Will you help me set it up? Work with me there?" Hank paused, hesitated. "We can even share the house, to be close to the greenhouses."

Pablo began to understand now.

"The family won't like it, *amigo.* Especially your brother. A Cutter living in an adobe shack with a Mexican foreman?"

Hank made an obscene gesture to dismiss his brother.

"J. J.'s an asshole, Pablo. A bullshitter. I don't care what he thinks."

Pablo lost himself in thought for a minute.

"Do you really want to do this—with me?"

Hank nodded, smiled. His eyes went bright, almost with tears. He put out his hand to the other man.

"Shake on it, *amigo?*"

"*Amigo.*" Their hands clasped in silence.

Chapter Two

"I'M GLAD WE DIDN'T GO TO EUROPE THIS YEAR. THIS IS A wonderful change of scene."

Anna surveyed the plaza in front of the cathedral. It was after three, *siesta* time was ending, and the heart of Ciudad Chihuahua, which had murmured through the last three hours, was beginning to beat faster again. In the last two weeks she had come to love this provincial capital; Juarez, picturesque though it was, always had an edge of seediness about it, the parasite quality of all border towns. Ciudad Chihuahua, though a mere two hundred and fifty miles south, was drenched in a full-blown Spanish-Colonial scent, the historic perfume of cathedrals and *haciendas,* of winding streets and sprawling *barrios,* of wealth and poverty, sophistication and naïveté cheek by jowl.

Will, leaning back in his chair at the terrace café overlooking the plaza, couldn't help but be amused by Anna's enthusiasm for travel in Mexico.

"Chihuahua's a charming enough city," he commented dryly, with some effort at a straight face. "Though not half as charming as Barcelona or Lisbon. I don't understand, darling— you were so head-over-heels about Lisbon last year, I can't understand why you didn't want to run back this year for a few weeks."

Anna was momentarily distracted by a man in the street below, selling brightly colored wooden snakes on poles. He carried several dozen of the jointed creatures. They slithered above him like a Medusa's head.

"Lisbon is so . . ."

"Far away," he completed her sentence.

Anna realized he was teasing her. She wrinkled her nose at him.

"Will you stop ribbing me about that? I mean, you did manage to get me this far from Casilla. Be thankful for that, at least."

Will sipped his daiquiri, savored the frosty sludge in his throat. He watched Anna as she amused herself with the passing scene below. She was looking marvelous these days, more stylish, more sophisticated. The long, dark hair she had always worn coiled or braided up on her head was gone now, sacrificed to a smart, mannish shingle with a long, asymmetrical sweep across her forehead. The bit of rouge and powder she had worn in the years before the war had given way to a more frankly "made-up" face: garnet rouge on the mouth, a streak of blue-gray above the eyes. The long-sleeved blouses; narrow, long skirts; and high collars were gone now, too, replaced by what a decade before would have been suitable only as a slip, a night-dress, a chemise. Anna now wore the classic lines of the jazz age: a narrow, short tube of a dress, bare arms, silk-stockinged legs, generously exposed, all garnished with coils of pearls and thick, noisy ivory bracelets on her wrists.

Will had seen Anna undergo transformations before. First, from the shy, plain farm girl to the hardworking, successful young businesswoman. Then this crude chrysalis was shed to reveal the beautiful young social butterfly. Now that creature had evolved into a chic, sophisticated woman of the world, a woman who for her age and experience knew food, clothes, politics, literature, a woman gifted with an innate sense of style and taste. This Anna was a far cry from the nervous, somber-eyed little girl he'd seen, quivering like a rabbit in a hutch, that first visit he'd paid the farm in 1912.

There was another change in Anna, though, a newer, more

substantial change, which Will found personally the most grati-
fying. It showed most in her face, when she talked, when she
laughed, when she slept. It was that beautiful, mysterious radiance of motherhood, the light of the madonna.

Will had seen it so often in the last year and a half, first
during Anna's pregnancy, and then, since Wilhelmina's birth
nine months before. Anna's single-minded devotion to the farm
had receded, to be replaced by her single-minded devotion to
their perfect little blond, blue-eyed infant. It had even become a
standing joke at home that it only took seven pounds of baby
daughter to lay waste to one thousand acres of farm. The joke
was only half true. Anna's attentiveness to Wilhelmina, or
Mina, as she was soon called, really was no threat to the future
of Cutter Farms: by the end of the war, Ruth and Anna had
built a smooth-running agricultural machine, a large, modern,
efficient operation that did not depend wholly on one person to
maintain itself. With the crew of foremen—Juan Gordo, Pablo,
and the others—Anna could easily be away from the newly
christened Cutter-Channing Farms for days, even weeks at a
time, with little or no effect on the substantial profits shown at
year's end. The joke about the "seven-pound threat" was more
to do with Anna's charming fuss over her daughter. The
woman who had developed a confident stride in building a farm
operation of one thousand acres and two hundred and fifty resident employees, was a bundle of nerves in the nursery. She
constantly looked in on plump, cherubic Mina; whether the
infant was asleep or awake, she worried that the child was not
eating enough or too much, that her diapers were not changed
soon enough, that her toys were not amusing enough, that her
colic was a dire warning. It was a delight for Will to watch
Anna announcing even the most ordinary event in the routine
of infancy as if it were an occurrence of historic importance.

He and Anna had gone to Europe on their honeymoon, then
back again the following summer for a month. They had been
glorious times, full of love and discovery, and the freedom that
happiness brings. The rich tapestry of Europe had been an incomparable backdrop for the charmed fairy tale of their marriage. They were prince and princess, knight and damsel.

After Mina's birth Will had not even considered another major trip a possibility. Anna was certainly entitled to relish the

new role of mother, and there was all the farm business for her
to attend to. And since before Mina's birth, he himself had been
immersed in his campaign for the state legislature. He had
planned on taking the plunge into politics since his Yale days—
a man cannot grow up as a senator's son without either wanting
to be very in, or very out, of politics. But the reality of
campaigning, even on the relatively modest scale of the state
House of Representatives, was a damned hard job. By November, when he had won his first election, Will was exhausted and
desperate for at least a brief vacation from the rigors of the
campaign trail.

Finally Will had insisted on a trip to Mexico, capping it with
the agreement, half serious, half joking, that surely a nine-
month-old girl with a grandmother, two uncles, a nanny, a
cook, and half a dozen housemaids to look after her needs could
manage to do without her mother for ten days.

In the end Anna had to laugh at herself for being such an
overly attentive mother. "I'm just worried about making too
many mistakes," she had said. "A child is not quite like a cotton crop that you can plow under and start over the next year."

To which Will, with the devil twinkling in his blue eyes, had
replied that he was looking forward to planting any number of
new crops while they were in Mexico.

Once they had taken the train from El Paso to Ciudad Chihuahua and had set themselves up in a suite overlooking the
courtyard of the Hotel Victoria, Anna had realized just how
much she needed a vacation. Her duties as a mother had by no
means relieved her of her duties as a farmer, and she had
worked as many hours a week since Mina's birth as she had
during the busiest of the war years. Once she was away from
Casilla, she realized that she was tired—physically tired. She
and Will both had been operating at the peak of their capacity
for months.

At the hotel they enjoyed, for the first time since Europe, the
luxury of nothing to do, the extravagance of being lazy. Anna
discovered the wonderful pastime of sunbathing. In a newly
bought jersey swimming trunk she lounged about the pool while
the fierce Mexican sun turned her exposed face and limbs to a
field-worker brown. Will lay beside her, as scantily clad as she,
in trunks and a tank top, as he read the *Wall Street Journal* or

This Side of Paradise, a new novel by a young American named Fitzgerald. One of Anna's favorite pastimes by the pool was watching the other women, most of them Mexicans, as they admired Will's lean, muscular body, tanned to a golden bronze, and his blond, Anglo-Saxon face. She would catch them out of the corner of her eye, when they didn't think she could see them. They would stare at Will as he lay on his stomach reading, with the perspiration beading on his shoulders and the sun highlighting his curly, golden hair on his legs. She could see them as they undressed him, lusted after him with their heavy-lidded eyes. Just to tease them Anna would reach over and let her fingertips brush casually on his arm, his thigh.

After several hours of lounging at poolside like lizards on the rocks, they would go upstairs to their suite and wash the perspiration and oils off of their sun-tingling skin. The bath had a large, tiled shower with two spray heads, and as they showered and soaped one another's bodies, they would invariably become aroused. They would kiss and caress in the shower, then move to the bed where their damp, sun-warmed bodies intertwined, joined. At times they didn't even leave the shower but made love on the tile floor with the spray streaming over them.

Two years before, Anna could never have imagined that she could be as happy, as fulfilled in her marriage to Will as she was. For months after her return to Casilla from her ill-fated rendezvous in the mountains, she had lived in a world black with anger and despair. Her rage at fate for having cheated her of a life with Bart was at times all-consuming, though on the outside her mood appeared to be more one of melancholy and depression. No woman longs to be deprived of a great love, yet few women get through their lives without knowing the anger of that most terrible of losses: it is a universal experience of womanhood. Anna was no exception, and like all in her position, she found it difficult to imagine that there would ever be a time in her life when she would not feel her loss every hour of the day, waking or sleeping. Yet, as the weeks and months passed, Anna, like many women before and since, found that the wound slowly healed, that her heart slowly grew back. She could trust again; she could love again.

It was Will, of course, who had accomplished that miracle.

When she had returned to Casilla, there was no doubt that all was not right with her, but she had the obvious and very accept-able excuses that she had just undergone a serious illness and that a very old and close family friend had just been killed. Will never pried, never questioned, but surrounded her with atten-tion, with good spirits, with love. As the months passed Anna began to see just how deep and how real the love was that Will offered her and how much she felt it in return. She began to understand how much of her love for Bart had been pure pas-sion, an animal thing, like a rutting mare and stallion in a sta-ble. She had made the foolish mistake of confusing lust and love and had very nearly given up love for lust. Will offered her genuine love—something that went far beyond animal sex—and he had offered it to her all along. She had just been too blinded by lust to see it clearly.

Anna had been nervous about what would happen on their wedding night on the train to New York. She and Will had kissed, had fondled each other during their courtship, but their intimacy had never gone beyond that. Anna was concerned that Will would suspect that she was not a virgin. She also worried that intimacy with Will would be difficult for her. In the months that she and Will had been engaged and had sat "neck-ing" on the porch or parked in Will's Ford under the trees by the river, Anna had constantly battled the powerful ghosts of her lovemaking with Bart. As Will kissed her Bart often forced his way into her mind; and on many occasions she had come within a hair's breadth of letting Bart's name slip out in some endearment she was whispering to Will.

Instead her first night with Will, in the noisy, rhythmic con-fines of the train berth, had been an unexpected revelation. Will had been slow and tender with her, a gentle and considerate lover, but the gentleness of it all had built to a long, explosive climax. Will was an expert lover; he seemed to know every nuance, every need of her body. With Bart there had always been an edge of the wild and the brutal, a headlong, uncon-trolled avalanche. Sex with Will was a spring shower, compared to the violent thunderstorm of Bart, and Anna found this sex with Will immensely satisfying and reassuring.

During the eighteen months of her marriage to Will Anna had come to accept Bart's death. The rage at the loss of him, which at the beginning had seemed like a force that would never be overcome, had gradually calmed and receded, leaving her with a pure, refined memory of the man and what they had shared. Bart had become an icon of passion, and the image of that icon appeared daily in her thoughts. It was not a painful or disturbing presence: she was happy with Will, happier in fact than she had ever imagined she could be after Bart's death, and she had made the conscious decision not to torment herself with what might have been when what she now had was so fine and golden.

It was perhaps a measure of how much Anna had accepted Bart's death that she had suggested to Will that while they were in Ciudad Chihuahua, they should make a few discreet inquiries as to the place where Bart had been buried. The political situation in Mexico was now so much more stable than it had been in the months after Bart's death, perhaps they could find something out now. Anna had discussed the idea with her mother and with Will's parents, and they had all agreed that it should be Alonzo's decision. After all, it might be too painful for the man if the whole tragedy of his grandson's death had been brought to the surface again. Perhaps the anonymity of an unmarked grave somewhere in the Mexican desert was best, after all. But Alonzo had telegraphed from Switzerland that he would be eternally grateful if they could find Bart's grave, for nothing would please him more than to have his remains moved to a grave next to his parents and grandmother in the small, walled family plot at Casa Portillo.

The whole issue of finding where Bart was buried, and of trying to bring his body back to Casilla, had lain dormant for the last three years, since the horrible, tragedy-laden days after the word came from Mexico about his death. The tragedy had been devastating to Alonzo, who had worried about his grandson's trip to Mexico from the very beginning. He had been unable to persuade Bart not to go and had finally trusted in Bart's cleverness, his familiarity with Mexico, his military training, to see him through. Each day of Bart's absence had been a strain on the old man; each day had brought a deepening sense of doom. Then, almost as if expected, came a telegram from one of Alonzo's few remaining contacts in Mexico, a former manager of the Hacienda Rosada stables, now driven off the land

and forced to fight for the Villistas. The telegram contents had been horrifying: The manager reported that there had been intensive rebel activity near Hacienda Rosada during the past days. Bands of radical Villistas had gone from town to farm to town, rounding up anyone suspected of loyalty to the Huerta regime. Though he was garrisoned a hundred miles from Hacienda Rosada, he had heard a terrible rumor; the Villistas had executed almost two hundred men and women by firing squad. Worse yet, the rebels claimed one victim in particular, Bradley, once heir to the Hacienda Rosada estates. The man could not verify the story, but he wanted Alonzo to know it, with prayers that it was not true; a sympathetic telegraph operator had agreed to transmit the message.

The following day, final confirmation came from a different source, the revolutionary tabloids published by the Villa government in Juarez. They boldly proclaimed that a traitor and subversive named Barton Bradley had been captured and executed in Chihuahua while on a secret, seditious mission in aid of the Huerto regime and the crumbling landowning classes, of which he was a part. The tabloid had carried a photograph of a horrible tangle of "traitorous" bodies piled in a dusty courtyard.

The news of Bart's death had devastated the valley, and the outpouring of sympathy for Don Alonzo was matched only by the citizens' rage against the villainy of the rebels. Official complaints were lodged by Washington, but they were as straws in the wind. The Huerta government officially condemned the act by the brutal rebels, who held northern Mexico in iron grip; they privately apologized for the tragedy and said that Barton, like so many others, had been a victim of Huerta's enemies. The government's only reprisal was the continued battle against the northern rebels. The revolutionaries were clearly not interested in apologies. In their papers they described Barton Bradley as "a secret mercenary" of the Wilson government; they also pointed out that the U.S.-backed Huerta regime had executed many American men who had joined the Villa forces as mercenaries; they claimed to be exercising the same political right.

With time the furor had died down, and Alonzo was left to deal with his loss. He knew there was nothing to be done; no complaints, no reprisals, no justice would restore his loss. The cruel land of his birth had taken yet one more treasure from him, a treasure worth far more than any of the *haciendas* and *ranchos* of Mexico. Alonzo had accepted his final challenge: to learn to live with his grief and loneliness. Yet he knew he was not alone in his grief—it was shared. He could see it in their eyes, his friends' eyes. The Channings, Ruth, Anna. They mourned with him.

In the months immediately following the tragedy Alonzo's only action was an attempt, through official channels as well as unofficial ones, to try to find Bart's grave so his remains could be brought back to Casilla and Casa Portillo. But the reports were unanimous. Nothing could be found out for the foreseeable future; the area surrounding Hacienda Rosada was still devastated by fighting, a desolate and dangerous land. There was no one to ask, no one to care. Before going to Europe in his self-imposed exile, Alonzo had faced the inevitable. He had erected a marble tablet in the small family plot behind Casa Portillo, next to the resting places of Bart's mother and father and his grandmother.

Will was careful not to make the business of finding Bart the dominant note of their trip to Mexico. He knew that if they had any hope of finding out anything about that night when Bart had been discovered by the Villistas, it would mean bribing numerous soldiers, government officials, and the kind of petty hoods who specialize in selling information. Will cleverly had gone to the last category of informant first, greased their palms liberally and sat back and waited for information to come to him. Within a few days there were messages at the hotel desk and phone calls at odd hours, all with mysterious leads. Will had responded to each one, with disappointing results. Each contact led him to yet another contact, the next promising that the person he knew was the one who really did know where the victims of that particular firing squad had been buried. It was a frustrating business, and Will held little hope of any success. Still, as long as he kept any of his dealings with informants away from Anna, it did not have any adverse impact on their time together. And if his mission was successful, how much it would mean to all of them!

In Cathedral Square below the terrace café, other vendors caught Anna's eye: one old man, selling tin whistles and bright metal whirligigs on sticks; another with a colorful cart, bearing jars of fruit syrups to be poured over scoops of shaved ice in little paper cups. She made a note to go down after lunch and buy a whirligig for Mina, to be added to the growing bundle of gifts for the child that was accumulating in the hotel.

"Hard to believe only three more days," Will commented lazily as he stretched his arms. "I'm almost wishing I didn't have to go to Austin in January."

"You're just saying that because the daiquiris have made you sleepy. You know you're itching to get out and rewrite half the laws on the books."

Will made a disinterested face.

"Maybe, but I'm sure as hell not looking forward to spending so much of the year away from you and Mina."

"Are you really, darling?" Anna was only half teasing at this point. "I thought all married men looked for an excuse to get away from the wife and family."

"Not me. I love you too much."

Will said it with the utmost simplicity, a bare statement of fact.

The campanile of the cathedral struck four, the deep tones of the bell reverberating across the plaza. Anna looked at Will, studied his bright, open, blue eyes. His tanned face was suffused with a gentle, happy light; it was as if she were bathed in love.

She reached across the table, felt his hand slip into hers. As the last bell sounded, echoed, died, she thought for an instant of Bart, wherever he had lost himself in Mexico. She forced the image out of her mind.

"I love you, Will." She smiled, squeezed his hand. "You've made me a very happy woman." As she often did in those moments when she expressed her love to Will, when she stepped back and thought about what a wonderful life she and Will had made together, Anna told herself that Bart, if he were in some place in eternity where he could see them, would wholeheartedly approve.

A few minutes later Will excused himself from the table when the captain called him to the maître d's station in the interior of the café. He was gone at most five minutes, but when he returned, his appearance had changed dramatically. His face was drawn and tense, and beneath the fresh tan his skin had taken on a sickly, greenish pallor. Anna knew right away that something was wrong.

"What is it, Will?" She leaned forward and took his hand. It was unexpectedly clammy. "Not another attack of the gastritis? I thought we were both over that by now."

Will tossed his head back, laughed a short, delirious little laugh.

"That's not it at all. But I feel just as strange as I ever did with Montezuma's revenge. I don't know quite what to say. Shock, I guess. There was a man in the front of the café. One of those seedy, underworld types. Said he'd heard I was looking for the grave of *el Americano Bradley*. The usual line, 'for a price,' et cetera."

"I hope you didn't pay him, Will. We've already bribed so many of these types, and they never have any truth to their information."

Will focused his blue eyes on her with a strange, sharp expression in them that she could not quite fathom.

"Something told me to give this one a few bills. Some kind of instinct, I guess."

"Do you think he knows where the grave is?"

Will paused, having difficulty in answering her.

"That's just it," he finally said with that odd note of hysteria in his voice. "That's just it, Anna. There is no grave. Because Bart isn't dead. He's in prison, right here in Chihuahua City. He's alive, Anna! He's alive!"

The light, the music of the afternoon vanished in an instant as she fell to the floor beneath her, swallowed by a black void.

Chapter Three

THOUGH IT WAS A CLEAR, SUNNY JANUARY DAY, THE corridor of the presidio behind the capitol was drenched in perennial gloom. The floor of the narrow passage, though dirt, was packed as hard as any tile floor from two centuries of footsteps of jailers and prisoners. The half dozen iron-banded oak doors that lined either wall were bolted shut; not even the small windows that punctured each door at eye level, through which prisoners were passed their single daily meal, were left open to allow the cell inhabitants to communicate with each other. The adobe walls were stuccoed and whitewashed, though the whitewash had long ago degenerated to an excremental yellow; even through the oak doors came the stench of generations of human waste, of unwashed bodies, of rotting food, of suffering.

The two *carceleros* ambled indifferently along the corridor, chatting in slangy Spanish about the latest jail gossip. They both wore pistols belted loosely around their hips; one carried a kerosene lantern. They stopped before one door, lifted the beam that held it shut, then swung open the door.

"*Hola! Gringo cabrón!*" one cried. "Come out, you big white piece of shit. We have a nice treat for you."

The lantern was thrust into the dark, fetid-smelling cell. A surprised rat scurried away from the food bowl and into the open hole in the corner that served as a latrine.

The American was sitting on the pile of hay that served as the cell's only furnishings. His eyes squinted against the unaccustomed light, though he made no move to get up.

"Come on, you smelly son of a whore, get up before I come over and kick you in the balls. They'll be in your mouth when I get through with you."

The guard sounded cheerful, joking; they always talked like

that to the prisoners, as if they were just a couple of buddies kidding around. But Bart remembered all too well his first weeks in jail, in that hellhole of a *cárcel* outside Torreón. For days on end the guards had beaten him just for sport, laughing and joking at his agony. He remembered the pain of the blackened eyes, cracked ribs, the swollen testicles. They had finally grown bored of the sport when he was too weak to fight back, and they had left him alone and gone on to newer, fresher game.

The amazing thing in those dark, brutal days was that Bart remained alive at all. The men who had captured him at Hacienda Rosada had talked of his imminent encounter with a firing squad, yet that moment had never come. To be sure, it had been threatened often, while he ate, while he tried to sleep, when they shunted him from cell to cell, from prison to prison. Bart himself was not sure why he was allowed to live—in the wilds of northern Mexico, courts and due process were easily dispensed with. Perhaps his captors considered him too valuable a prisoner to be shot. For all he knew, the bastards were holding him for ransom from his grandfather, or keeping him as an item of barter in some sort of prisoner exchange. Or perhaps it was the simple fact that a living prisoner is more fun to torment than a dead one.

When they had brought him to this new jail in Ciudad Chihuahua, Bart had worried that the guards would start in on their new prisoner, but so far, after a month, he had been left mercifully alone in the cell with the rats and the fleas. He had a brief exercise period each day—nothing more than ten minutes when he could mill around in the dusty, high-walled courtyard of the presidio, exchange a few words with the sixty or so other prisoners before being herded back into his dark, filthy cell. He had been out already today, so the guard's visit was unexpected and unnerving.

Bart got up and went over to them, a bit unsteady on his feet. The food was better and more plentiful in the Chihuahua presidio, and he had begun to recover some of the weight and strength he had lost in the two years at Torreón, but he was still weak and drained after his few minutes of exercise.

They took him from the cell area, through the court, and into a large, high-ceilinged room nearer the front of the jail. There were barred windows high in one wall, and through them Bart could hear the sounds of the street outside. There was a long, rough wooden table with a few chairs to one side where the guards sat, and a small table and basin in one corner. Bart was relieved that the room was near the street. It was less likely that they were going to work him over. When the guards were in the mood to work some poor bastard over, they took him to a windowless room in the back of the jail. Even so, screams could sometimes be heard, late at night, through the thick adobe walls.

"Okay, big *gringo,*" one called out. "Take your clothes off. There's water and soap over there. We have orders to get you cleaned up and beautiful by this afternoon."

"Why?" Bart was confused, suspicious. He felt vulnerable standing in his tattered cotton *camiso* and *pantalones* in the middle of the bright room. The dark cell would have been safer.

"Because the *comandante* wants to fuck you!"

The two guards roared with laughter at their joke. Then one of them turned serious, hard.

"Just get your American ass over there and clean up. We'll tell you why when we feel like it."

Half an hour later Bart stood bathed and in clean *camiso* and *pantalones* for the first time in two years. The guards had given him a pair of *huaraches,* leather sandals, and a small knife to clean and pare his nails. They had given him a small mirror and straight razor as well. He had not seen his reflection since the Torreón jail, but he was pleased to see that his face was less ravaged, less emaciated than he had expected.

With no further explanation the two *carceleros* took Bart down another hallway, a clean, well-lighted corridor that must have been part of the jailers' offices. They ushered him into a large, barren room with a few simple wood chairs and a large table in the middle. The red, white, and green flag of Mexico hung on the wall, and behind the table sat a dark, thin-faced man, in his forties perhaps, with a large black mustache. He wore crossed *carabinero* belts and pistols over his shirt, the universal sign of the revolutionary officer.

"Sit down, Bradley," he said in Spanish with a curt monotone. He seemed bored with whatever their business was.

Bart observed, took a chair in front of the desk.

"I am Capitano Rodriguez, director of this prison and an officer of the Mexican Revolutionary Army. We are under the command of Villa, not Huerta. Our loyalty is in the north."

The *capitano's* story was unclear, but Bart guessed correctly that since he had been taken prisoner, there had been a split between Pancho Villa's forces in the north of Mexico and the central government in Mexico City.

Rodriguez narrowed his dark eyes. His air of boredom darkened to one of anger and cruelty.

"As I am sure you know, you are here now because you are an enemy of General Villa and his government. If it had been in our control, you would still be rotting in the *cárcel de Torreón*. But it seems you have friends in high places, *gringo*. You were not so easily forgotten as we would have liked."

The officer nodded to the two jailers, who opened a door on the far wall behind Rodriguez. A figure appeared through the door, tall, blond, smiling. Bart could not suppress a cry of joy at the sight of Will Channing. He sprang to his feet, but the guards quickly restrained him until the signal came from Rodriguez that it was permissible for the two men to embrace.

Three months after the reunion in Rodriguez's office Bart Bradley's trial for treason and crimes against the Republic of Mexico began. The intervening weeks had been a nightmare of international red tape as Will and Anna had worked endlessly, almost twenty-four hours a day, to secure Bart's release. Alonzo had been telegraphed immediately, of course, and had sailed from Europe to New York, then by train to Chihuahua City. Senator Channing, after many long telegrams to Washington and Mexico City, had finally arrived in Chihuahua, armed with a caseful of letters, documents, and telegrams from any number of officials, from Harding to the State Department, to the ambassador. Senator Channing and the American officials had of course demanded Bart's immediate release, and the government of President Huerta in Mexico City had quickly agreed, since Huerta's shaky regime was too much in need of support from Washington to allow American citizens to be held without trial in Mexican jails. Unfortunately the rupture between the powerful revolutionary political bloc of Pancho Villa and Emiliano Zapata in the north and Huerta's regime in the south had left Villa and his loyal troops virtually autonomous in the northern states. Villa still rankled at the United States' support of the Huerta government, and he was ill inclined to cooperate with Mexico City and the Americans in the affair of Señor Bradley.

Given the fact that Huerta was handicapped in the north and that Bart was, in reality, a prisoner of Villa's government and not the official Mexican government, Huerta could do little more than put pressure on the Villa-controlled officials in Chihuahua to free their American prisoner. In the end a compromise was reached, if such a travesty of justice could be called a compromise: Bart was to go on trial as a traitor and spy. He was being tried as a traitor because he was of Mexican parentage and had fought against Villa with Pershing; he was a spy because he was traveling through Mexico at the time of his capture under an assumed identity.

"We're in a tough position," the senator explained to Alonzo and the others at one point. "In a sense, Bart was safe in that prison. Out of the way, as if he were dead. Prison was merely a substitute—a crueler substitute, if you will—for death. Now Bart is revived, alive again, not only as far as we're concerned, but also as far as the Mexicans are concerned. They can't just put him on a train back to Texas and say, 'Golly, we're sorry about all this.' They've got to save face, and in order to do that, they're going to pretend to the bloody end that Barton is the enemy. They need to make an example of him. And, of course, being the corrupt kind of government that they are, they'll be royal hypocrites. Most likely an official explanation of Bart's imprisonment will be circulated—'It was all the fault of a bad egg in the provincial army, who has now been removed from his position and reprimanded for imprisoning Bart without trial.' That sort of thing. Then they'll point to themselves as being the epitome of justice and fairness because they bring Bart to trial openly and publicly."

Alonzo asked what all this meant for Bart's release.

"Legally, in spite of Washington's efforts, they can order him shot for treason, if that's the judge's verdict. But given the shaky state of political affairs here and the fact that the northern government is beginning to realize that it's in big trouble and has to be a little more solicitous of Uncle Sam's favor, they're going to cooperate a bit. I think."

"They'll release him, then?"

"At best." Channing sighed. "But they may get one last twist of the knife in. They want to make it clear that they're willing to cooperate with the U.S., but they're also going to put up a brave, independent front. I think we've managed to save Bart's life, but whether or not we've secured his release, I can't say."

One of the worst aspects of the situation was the government's stubborn refusal to let Bart's friends and family see him until the day of the trial. Almost immediately after Will's meeting with Bart in Rodriguez's office that day, the Mexicans had realized that Bradley was a controversial prisoner, one who had powerful friends who could stir up trouble for them, and they had quickly returned him to the oblivion of their prison, with no contact with the outside world.

For Anna, the days since Will had told her about Bart as they lunched in the café overlooking the plaza had been a nightmare —days and nights full of joy, anger, disbelief. He was alive, a fact that seemed so miraculous, so beyond hope that she could scarcely believe it, though her heart flooded with happiness at the very fact of it. But there was the fact, the cruel, brutal fact of her situation and of Bart's. Her first concern, once her heart and mind had really begun to believe, to trust that he was alive, was for his well-being, his safety. He was still in prison, still kept from his loved ones, from freedom. And at any moment he might be condemned to death, taken from her once and for all, irretrievably, forever. Every ounce of her energy during those terrible weeks had been devoted to preventing that; she had gone back to Casilla before the trial, not to attend to her daughter or to the farm but to spend every hour she could find in the day, calling, writing, telegraphing, marshaling every possible resource to insure Bart's safe and speedy release from prison. The foremost thought was that Bart must be saved. Behind it, not acknowledged for the moment, was the other concern, a concern that had to be ignored for the moment: What would she do if Bart did survive, if he was free again? That issue, she told herself, would be faced in time. For now, all she cared about was that Bart was still alive, on trial for his life.

The trial, once it began, was over very quickly. In the morn-

ing three hours of testimony in the bare, whitewashed room
that served as Capitano Rodriguez's *oficina* and as the courtroom. On one side a long row of Mexican military men of varying ranks, each with damning testimony against the treasonous
Señor Bradley, their testimony given with the mechanical fresh-
ness of a newly memorized lesson. Bart was the only witness for
the defense, helped by Senator Channing as his counsel, with
Alonzo serving as the senator's translator. Seated on the crude
wood chairs behind Bart and his counsel were four others, each
of whom would gladly have given witness in Bart's behalf: Edna
Channing, Ruth Cutter, Anna, and Will.

As the mockery proceeded, under the scornful eye of a fat,
pig-faced judge, a profound sense of doom descended upon the
small group of family and friends of the accused. They hoped
where there was no hope.

At noon the judge called a recess for a *siesta,* a break during
which no one ate, no one rested. Then, at three, the court met
again for sentencing. The pig-faced judge barely concealed a
smug smile of triumph as he pronounced Bart guilty of treason
against the state of Mexico for his participation in the Pershing
Expedition. The charges of spying were dismissed, and the
usual sentence of death by firing squad for traitors was miti-
gated "in these unusual circumstances" to five years' imprisonment.

Bart stood, strong and handsome, as the sentence was read.
His face, his eyes did not betray the slightest flicker of emotion
at the judge's words. Abruptly after the sentencing the judge
and the officers left the room, and the jailers stepped forward to
take Bart once again into their custody. There was only a moment before they took him away for the sorrowful farewells.
The moment, as he kissed and embraced each one in turn, was
too deep, too painful for words. But he spoke to each one in
turn with his eyes: Alonzo, Ruth, Will, Jack, Edna. And finally,
as the jailers pulled him from her arms, his eyes spoke to Anna.

Anna stood in the doorway of the cell, waiting for the jailer
to swing the heavy iron-clad door shut behind her. Now that
she was so close to Bart, just a few feet from where he stood by
the rough bench that ran along the far wall, it had all been
worth it. The fear of coming to the jail alone, her nervousness in

asking to see Bart, in bribing the jailer to leave them alone for half an hour. Gone, too, were the stench of the corridors, the unspeakable horror of the place. All that she could see, feel, think about now, was Bart.

He had called her name out as he jumped up, startled by her unexpected appearance in his cell. The trial was two days over, and he thought he had said his last farewells to Anna, Will, his grandfather, the others, in the crowded public room of the jail. For two days he had lived with the reality that he soon would be transferred to a larger prison, that he would never see them again, knowing what he knew about life and death in the prisons of that country.

They stood facing each other across that expanse of floor littered with dirty straw, not knowing what to do, what to say. Then, as if by some signal, they went to each other without a word and swept into each other's arms. They kissed long and hard, a kiss that spoke volumes about their past, their future. Finally they parted, nestled in an embrace.

"You shouldn't have come," he whispered. "It's dangerous for you here."

"I don't care," she said. "I had to."

He held her face close between his hands, looked at her with his magnificent golden-green eyes, their light now tempered with pain and wisdom.

"Thank you, then, for coming. This will help me through these five years."

He kissed her face softly, almost as a father might kiss a child.

"How you must have suffered, darling," he whispered. "How much this must have hurt you!"

"Of course, Bart! Of course, I've suffered the tortures of the damned! But that's nothing compared to what you've lived through! How can they compare? My world collapsed when I thought you were dead, until slowly, bit by bit, it rebuilt itself. Now . . ."

"It would almost be better if I really was dead, wouldn't it, darling?"

"No, no!" she protested. "Don't ever say that! You're alive! You'll be out of here someday, as soon as we can manage it."

He smiled.

"I'm glad you have Will," he said with a sweet sincerity in his voice. "It's the best thing for you, if this had to happen. Can you imagine if I had been captured after we had gone to the mountains and been married? I almost postponed the trip to Mexico until after the mountains, you know. No, I'm glad you married Will. You have your farm, your home, a daughter, and I'll bet she's a beauty. Go back to that when you leave here and be happy."

"I can't now," she cried. "Not knowing you're here. Before we found you, I had somehow gotten over things. Life seemed to be sailing a smooth course."

He grinned, and though his face was thin and drawn, there was a flash of the old, flirtatious Bart in his expression.

"I always seem to be complicating your life, don't I?"

She nodded, then rested her head against the furred mat of his chest, until she could hear his heartbeat, faint and steady in her ear. Then it happened, what she had known would happen from the moment she had left the hotel to go to the jail. They began to make love, first his lips on her head, her neck, then her lips. Their arms intertwined, their hands exploring. The rest of the world was forgotten, and they lost themselves in one another. He lowered her, still in his embrace, to the straw-covered floor. As he lowered himself onto her she welcomed him, gave herself freely to him. As they made love there was only the incomparable present. Past and future ceased to exist.

Part IV

THE YEARS

OF POWER

1928-1935

Chapter One

NINE YEARS.

How little the world within the confines of a Mexican jail had changed during those years, and how much it had changed outside. Casilla was still recognizable as the town he had left in 1919. Most of the old landmarks were still there: Ola's Red Star Café, Wasserman's Mercantile, Smitty's Blacksmith Shop, the collection of frame and adobe houses scattered along the path of the railway. But the little wisp of a farm town he remembered had become something else: a bright, bustling farm center; an active, fast-growing, prosperous community.

The drive down the valley from El Paso, where he had been met by his grandfather and the Channings—as well as a clutch of reporters and photographers from the newspapers—had been on a crisp ribbon of asphalted highway where the old dirt road had been. The thirty miles of what was now Highway 80, with flat green fields stretched out on either side, was lined with an endless row of creosoted electric and telephone poles. During the forty-minute trip in the sleek, dark green confines of the senator's Packard touring sedan, they had passed a few mule teams lumbering along the gravel shoulder of the road; the wagons tried to keep well off the blacktop to make room for the automobiles speeding along from east to west at thirty or forty miles per hour, many bearing license plates from faraway states.

Bart did not even realize they were in Casilla, so much had the town grown since the war. A collection of diminutive white frame cottages built around a circle of clipped lawn were the first buildings along the highway into town; a billboard in the middle of the lawn proclaimed, TOURIST COURT, ROOMS $1.25 A NITE. Beyond the bungalows stood a row of prosperous-looking new brick houses, followed by an imposing two-story brick schoolhouse, complete with American flag fluttering at the top of a mast. Then a familiar row of buildings. The blacksmith

shop had evolved into a gasoline station, as evidenced by the
bright red cylinder in front of the open doors where formerly
the smith had been seen shoeing mules and horses or repairing
harnesses and wheels. A car was pulled up near the cylinder,
and a black rubber hose snaked into it; a youth—perhaps one of
the smith's sons—enthusiastically wiped the car fenders with a
cloth.

Alonzo and Senator Jack kept up a running commentary as
the buildings slipped by. The Red Star looked much the same,
though an addition in the back had turned the former rooming
house into more of a real hotel; Ola was gone now—she had
been sent to a sanitorium in Dallas when her mind slipped into
senility. A well-off couple had bought the Red Star, aggressive,
ambitious Yankees who raised prices and were generally not
trusted by the locals. Wasserman had died too. Many joked of
loneliness once Ola had moved away, and there was concern
that Wasserman's relatives in California might sell the mercantile shop to the same couple who had bought the Red Star.

To Bart's eyes the whole changed landscape of Casilla was
summed up by the gin and cotton mill that had been built on
the north side of the tracks. It was a vast structure of gleaming,
corrugated tin that loomed over the lower buildings of Casilla
like a Gothic cathedral over a medieval French village. In a
sense the gin was the spiritual center of Casilla, the House of
the God of Commerce and Industry. The farmers of Casilla
channeled and distributed their agricultural wealth through the
gin; the tin smokestacks spewed the sick-sweet odor of burning
cottonseed husks into the clear Texas air; the herd of rust-red
boxcars on the rail siding awaited their cargo of burlap-encased
cotton bales and barrels of cottonseed oil bound for markets in
Memphis and San Antonio. The cotton disappeared along the
rails, in exchange for large bank drafts from the cotton brokers.

It was not just the farmers whose lives were intimately bound
up with the looming tin sheds with their presses and steel-
toothed combing wheels and rattling conveyor belts; the gin
cast a shadow over everyone in Casilla. The men who were not
farmers worked at the gin; after picking season, the Mexican
laborers worked the graveyard shifts to make extra money; the
front office revealed that new phenomenon of the twenties, the
female office worker. And even those who had never set foot in

the gin still reaped the benefits of its productivity: The merchants, the building contractors, the real estate people all fat-
tened in the flow of money that came from the cotton gin. As
the senator's Packard passed the gin Bart reflected with a mixture of admiration and amusement that this cathedral of commerce had been built by a consortium of farmers—headed by
Anna Cutter of Cutter-Channing Farms.

When Senator Channing turned the Packard off Highway 80
at the point where the now-paved lane intersected the highway
between Wasserman's and the Red Star, Bart caught a glimpse,
half a mile down the road, of the secluded great edifice of
Casilla: Casa Grande. The red tiles of the hipped roof glowed in
the afternoon sun; the stucco chimneys cut through the silhouette of the trees and up into the blue sky. Bart, as he had wandered through the long, unchanging months of confinement,
had often tried to imagine what the Cutter-Channing house
would look like. The reality that loomed over the fields was not
unlike the image of Casa Grande that Bart had constructed in
his mind based on what he had learned from the occasional
letters that got through to him in prison: the Italianate edifice
proclaimed, for all to see, that here was the seat of power of the
united families of Cutter and Channing. Bart felt almost like a
knight errant, just released from the dungeons of the Saracen
and returned to his kingdom to find his princess captured and
wed by another knight.

Bart had at first been surprised to hear that Anna and Will
and their children, Wilhelmina, now seven, and Alessandro,
almost five, lived under the same roof with Ruth Cutter and one
of her sons. Then, after some thought, he understood why. It
was Will, with his incomparable, enviable generosity and consideration for others. He easily could have afforded to build his
own home in the city, in Casilla, anywhere he wished. But to
have done so would have separated Anna a fraction too much
from her family, her farm. Ruth Cutter might have built Casa
Grande as a kind of grandiose nest to live in with the mate who
never returned, but as long as the mansion was filled with
Ruth's children and grandchildren, the fact of her loneliness
was less apparent. Yes, Bart mused, Will Channing was the
kindest of men.

The dark, musty rooms of Casa Portillo were an enormous reassurance from the moment Bart set foot in them for the first time in five years. The valley had changed—Casilla, Anna's life, his life—but the *hacienda* was frozen in time, immune to the modern world, or so it seemed. At Bart's request his grandfather had made no special plans for Bart's return to Casilla—he needed a few days of quiet transition back into the world before beginning to reestablish his human, worldly life again.

From the moment Bart had stepped through the gates of the prison into the bright light of freedom, his every waking hour had been pervaded by a sharp, brittle pessimism. First the war, then the years of imprisonment, and above all, the loss of Anna had destroyed all the illusions Bart had ever held about what life might offer. There was no justice, no happy ending, only a sense of the folly of life, the cruel ironies, the broken dreams. Now that he was thirty-five he could look back on his life, back to the time when he had believed in ideals, in higher goals. For, in spite of his restless wildness as a youth, he *had* been idealistic and high-minded. The reality of war and politics had ripped away many of those illusions: how could a man aspire to be a great soldier or statesman when the very nature of those pursuits were rooted in suffering, death, and greed? After the war he had been left with but one illusion: love. For a while Bart Bradley had believed that in the midst of the insanity two human beings might find a safe haven in shared life and love. That illusion, too, had been ripped from him when the Villistas had burst into his room that night in Chihuahua and dragged him into jail. Very little mattered to Bart anymore, very little except Anna.

Of course, it was inevitable that he see Anna; it was the thing he wanted most in the world. But as he had traveled on the train north from Chihuahua, thinking constantly of Anna and the hopeless tangle their lives had gotten into, he began in a sense to dread seeing her again. Their brief reunion in the jail had been chaotic, frustrating—cast in a setting that, even five years later, seemed unreal, dreamlike. When he saw Anna again, in Casilla, married to Will, with their children, he would be faced once and for all with the truth, the facts of her life.

They finally met at dinner at Casa Portillo—Anna had not called, which he appreciated. Bart and Alonzo had discussed

the evening and decided that the best vehicle for Bart's reentry
into society would be the close group of Casilla families—Ruth,
Anna and Will, Kate Mirkovsky, Jack and Edna Channing.
Maricita, who had fussed over him since his return like a nervous hen over a strayed chick, had outdone herself for Bart's
homecoming dinner. Her energy was unabated. She had hardly
changed though she was nearing ninety, except for her hair,
which was now steely gray.

By the time the guests arrived, the dark expanse of the baroque table in the dining room was buried under an avalanche
of damask, china, and silver, which, in turn, was nearly hidden
by mountains of food: *tortillas, enchiladas, pollo en mole,
quesadillas, sopa con aguacate.* The guests arrived en masse after bootleg cocktails at Casa Grande: Jack with a bejeweled
Edna, who, in spite of her physical ugliness, managed to trans-
form herself into a glittering, glamorous, if eccentric creature;
Kate Mirkovsky, as feisty as ever, had made a token gesture
toward fashion by bobbing and marceling her hair and by wearing a fashionably short silk-print dress, which scarcely disguised the old Kate who would have preferred being in her
denims and cotton shirts. Her son Max was with her—a strap-
ping, suntanned blond boy of twelve, big for his years, and a
vision of his father incarnate.

To Bart's eyes, of course, Anna was incomparable; their long
separation had enhanced her beauty, her desirability. She was
with Will, of course, and they seemed to be happy, comfortable
together; certainly they made a striking couple. When they
greeted Bart, it was with the warmth and caring of two old,
dear friends. As his arms went around her, pressed the firm
curve of her body against him, he waited for some kind of signal
from her, a message. It was in her eyes as she pulled away from
their embrace, a lingering look shot through with pain and love.
He was to see it many times in her eyes throughout the evening
as she sat across from him at the table, engaged in the kind of
conversation old, dear friends would be engaged in after a
forced separation of so many years.

Before the dinner was finished Bart was determined that if
Anna could not be his wife, she would be his mistress. It might
take months, years—who could say when they had yet to have
even one moment to themselves? Anna gave every appearance

of being the devoted wife and loving mother he was sure she was. But she also had given herself to him once, in Mexico, in spite of being Mrs. Will Channing, and he knew she would again. He would worry about the ethics, the morals of coveting his best friend's wife later. All he cared about now was that she be his.

The Back Door had become the valley's most famous night spot, even before it opened just before Christmas of 1926. The notice the club had gained was due in part to the fact that its owner was a prominent member of one of the valley's most prominent families, though it was the club's borderline legality that brought the most attention. The Back Door owed its existence to the quirks of two pieces of lawmaking. The Volstead Act of 1919 and the U.S. Mexican-Border Treaty of 1923. The Volstead, of course, meant Prohibition, which caused the saloons and bars that had flourished in hard-drinking El Paso to be padlocked overnight. Drinking retreated into the privacy of homes, amply supplied by the network of bootleggers that had sprung up at the clicking shut of the first padlock, or across the International Bridge, where Mexican *cantina* operators gladly plied thirsty *Americanos* with oceans of booze.

Though many of the drinking citizens of El Paso were more than happy to cross the Rio Grande into Juarez to do their drinking, there were still plenty of citizens who preferred not to face the rather seedy, occasionally dangerous side streets of the Mexican city. Many of these were women freed of the constraints that had been put on the "fairer sex" before the war, who now wanted to smoke and drink in public. It was ironic that now that alcohol was illegal, social drinking had become stylish, popular, and respectable.

The second piece of legislation that led to the creation of The Back Door was the U.S.-Mexican Border Treaty of 1923. The international boundary created by the Rio Grande between the two nations had been a source of difficulty for years, due mainly to the river's habit of changing course during floods. Since the middle of the river was the boundary, a Mexican farmer might wake up after a seasonal flood to find the river flowing half a mile south of its former course, leaving his land and home in the United States; a manufacturer with his warehouse near the river *in* El Paso could, in a week's time, see his inventory and warehouse relocated in Mexico.

The agreement of 1923 attempted to sort out the problem, though it created problems of its own. With the building of the dams upriver in New Mexico, the U.S. Bureau of the Interior had assured that the Rio Grande would be more controlled during flood season. The border nations agreed that the boundary would be the river's course as of that date; if the river changed its course, the boundary would remain the old dry riverbed, not the new course. This brought on a new problem: If the river moved channels, it would leave land on the north side of the river, which was part of Mexico yet not separated from the United States by anything other than an imaginary line.

The river flooded in 1923, as if to show man the silliness of his legislating nature's course, and created several "islands" of Mexican territory on the American side of the river. By chance, one of these pieces of land, where it had been on the south side of the river, was part of the estate Alessandra Bradley had inherited from her mother's family and, in turn, had passed to Bart.

There had been a public outcry among certain groups— mainly the local temperance leaders—when Bart Bradley announced that he was building a large supper and dance club on the island he owned near Zaragossa, halfway between El Paso and Casilla. He had had the genius to realize that a club on the land would legally be in Mexico—subject to Mexico's more-than-liberal drinking laws—yet it would be quickly and easily accessible to his patrons, who would merely have to drive into the parking area to leave the United States and its Volstead Act. The club even merited an editorial in one of the city papers, which decried "a prominent member of one of the areas oldest and most distinguished families who has taken advantage of a loophole in certain laws in order to promote alcoholism and immorality in our midst . . . a sad commentary on the state of the world when men go through little back doors to get at the whiskey barrel."

Bart had read the newspaper's moralizing with great amusement; the editors seemed to think he would care that they had a very low opinion of him and his new business venture. Had the concerned citizens of El Paso known Bart's true feelings, they would have understood that he was opening the club because he genuinely did not care what other people thought.

For every man and woman who raised a disapproving eyebrow at his actions, there would be another who would raise their cocktail glasses in a toast. The one glimmer of hope, the one scrap of illusion that remained was that by some twist of fate, somehow Anna might be free to be his. In the meantime he would thumb his nose at the world, have a good time, and make a good deal of money in the bargain. And he had the newspaper to thank for one thing. They had intended to give him a lecture; instead they had given him an appropriate name for his night spot: The Back Door.

The club was near completion the first time Anna saw it, perched incongruously in the middle of a former cornfield. The former field was soon to be a parking area, though now it was a dusty maze of potholes from months of traffic from carpenters' and workmen's vehicles. Anna had heard about The Back Door from many sources, including Bart himself, who had enthusiastically described the project to them over dinner one night a few months after his return from Mexico. As the construction had begun she had heard reports—of varying degrees of approval— about the ultramodern architecture of Bart Bradley's club. Now that she was seeing it for herself for the first time, she could appreciate why The Back Door was so talked about. The building was a low, wide facade of white stucco molded into sinuous curves, punctuated by a sweep of glass brick and stainless steel banding. The only color on the exterior was the still-unlighted neon sign proclaiming the club's name. Inside there was the sharp contrast of mahogany walls and plush burgundy carpets; a hundred tables still naked in their places; a cascade of brass-railed steps leading down to the circle of dance floor, still being sanded by half a dozen kneeling workmen. From somewhere in the back of the club came the clatter of hammers. Several naked light bulbs threw a garish brilliance into the dark, plush atmosphere of an interior designed for perennial midnight.

Anna had been anxious and uneasy all morning—for several days, really. She had gotten up before dawn, after a fitful night, and paced the floor in her bedroom for hours, sipping continuously on steaming coffee brought up in a silver pot by the maid, so the black night outside her window lightened slowly into the

steely gray of a cold November day. She had no illusions as to
why she was in such a state; in a few hours—by late afternoon
—she and Bart would be alone together for the first time since
he had come back from Mexico.

All those months Bart had waited for her to make the first
move. At the first dinner party, and on every occasion since,
when they had been together, always in the company of family
and friends, Anna had seen in Bart's eyes the truth; his eyes
wouldn't let her pretend. Yet she also knew that he was going to
force her to make the decision. He was too strong, too sure of
himself to give in or to force himself on her. He would wait for
her to come to him.

She had finally given in, a few weeks after Will had gone to
Austin for the fall legislative session. Bart's soon-to-open club
was the talk of the valley, and it only seemed natural that she
call up and invite herself by to see the club. After all, most of
her friends had already gotten a pre-opening tour of The Back
Door. It was all very natural, very legitimate that Mrs. Channing would call Mr. Bradley and ask if she could stop by and
see the new place, get a personal guided tour of the premises.
Even on the phone, though, she had not kidded herself about
what she was up to. Bart knew it too; it came through in a kind
of amused, formal irony in his voice. He made no hints, no
innuendos, but Anna knew in her heart that when she got to the
club, she would give herself willingly, anxiously to him. She had
known all along, since that brief time in the Mexican jail, that
she would give herself to Bart again. She had enacted their
reunion again and again in her mind, rehearsed it to perfection.
The only flaw, the only disturbing note in the performance was
Will and the children, lurking beyond the footlights like critics
and hecklers. As the theater of her imagination built to the
intimate passion she so desired, their voices, their screams of
shock and disapproval always cut into the performance.

Anna was tortured by the thought of being an adulteress, yet
she knew as surely as she knew she loved Will and Mina and
Alessandro that she was going to give her body to her lover.
That, of course, was the core of anxiety that had had her pacing
the floor before dawn: it was the driving force, not only of guilt
because of what she was about to do, but also it was fear of
what might happen, what terrible choices might be ahead.

There would be a few hours of passion, of animal intensity—then what?

She found Bart in the back of the club, in a maze of corridors and rooms being constructed for the musicians and employees. Though it was almost five-thirty he was still with a group of carpenters and painters swarmed around ladders and buckets and toolboxes; he himself was wearing paint-stained dungarees and a collarless shirt, stained and sweat-soaked, and she heard him giving the workers instructions in Spanish for the next day's work. When he saw her, he smiled, and his eyes brightened. She was a bit early, and her appearance in the back had obviously surprised him; there was no time for him to put up the controlled, guarded facade he had worn in their previous meetings.

"Anna, you're early. I wasn't expecting . . ."

"Hope I'm not interrupting. . . ."

"No, of course . . ."

They stammered over the words like two embarrassed adolescents as he came to her. He caught himself as he started to embrace her, then extended an innocent, friendly hand instead.

With the workmen still around they had to be careful; they both knew that. They kept up a busy, self-conscious dialogue as Bart gave her the "grand tour." The tour, of course, ended in the privacy of the raw, unfinished room that would eventually be Bart's private office suite. As soon as the door clicked shut behind them their chatty conversation stopped; there was silence, a long silence, as they came back to the bedrock of their emotions. The only interruption was the faint sound of the last contractor's truck leaving the lot outside.

Anna found herself staring at the raw concrete floor, the unplastered lath, the sawdust and scattered nails. Behind her she heard his breath coming in deep, powerful gasps. She forced herself to turn to him, to give herself up to his eyes. All the pretense was gone, all the barriers. For a moment she held herself back, poised on the abyss. Behind her were responsibility, duty, obligation: her husband, her daughter, her son. Before her, poised on the other side of the chasm, was a man whose power over her transcended time and place; the eyes, the voice, the muscle and sinew drew her, pulled her toward him.

The moment passed, and she went to him, into his arms, and they fell together into the abyss.

Later, in the quiet moments, as their fragrant sweat-moist bodies intertwined, they talked. First, of simple things, of the pleasures of their bodies, of the rich, sensual texture of their afternoon of lovemaking. Finally the real world began to filter back into their hearts and minds, like the gray November light through the canvas-covered windows of the room.

"What now?" Anna finally managed to say.

Bart kissed her, full and deep on the mouth; his hands roamed gently across her body, cupped against her breasts, her thighs.

"We don't have much choice, do we?"

Had it been said in a different tone of voice, his words might have sounded cocky, arrogant. Instead they were gentle and reassuring.

"I can't see doing without you any longer," she confessed. "It's just that . . ."

"I know. Will. Your family."

"I cannot hurt them. They're too important, too good."

Bart snorted his breath through his nostrils, a sigh of anger and frustration.

"Why did it have to be this way, Annie? It isn't fair. It isn't goddamned fair!"

"I can't change it—not now."

She closed her eyes and tried to imagine a world without Will, without her marriage to him. Difficult to imagine being happy without him, difficult to imagine being happy with him now that everything had changed. For one black moment she imagined that it would have been for the best if Bart had died in Mexico. She would have gotten over the pain somehow; it would have receded into the past. Now the pain was part of some indefinite, irreconcilable future.

"I'm a wife and mother, Bart. I can't forget that."

To her surprise Bart pulled away from her and sprang to his feet. He went to a crate in the corner where his clothes had been tossed and fished a packet of cigarettes from the pile. He offered her one, then took one for himself. He lit them, then threw the match carelessly on the floor. Instead of lying down next to her again, he paced the room. His body was tense, a coiled spring of muscle and bone and sinew. The anxious tightness was rather like a panther poised to spring.

"That's just it," he said, breaking the silence and continuing her thought. "I can't forget that you're a wife and mother, either. At least you have that."

"And I can't change that."

"I know that, darling." Bart tried to soften his voice, but she heard the anger and frustration come through all the same. "That's the fucking hell of it. We can't go back. Do you think it's easy for me to see you with your family? See you with your loving husband caring for your every need? You with your beautiful children—the children I wanted to father—running up to you, calling you Mama, telling you how much they love their mommy and their daddy."

"You can have that."

Bart's anger surged.

"The hell I can! What do you expect me to do? Marry some woman I don't love and ask her to bear the children that should have been yours and mine?"

Anna protested that she hadn't meant that at all.

"What did you mean, then? My choices aren't the best, darling. Marry a woman I don't love. Live a lonely bachelor's life. Or become the lover of the state congressman's wife."

Anna sat up, pulled back her damp, disheveled hair. She noted the large wall calendar with the photo portrait of Calvin Coolidge dourly surveying their naked confrontation.

"Is that what you want, Bart?"

He didn't hesitate.

"Yes, if it's the only way to be with you."

"It won't be easy for me."

"Or me, either. Remember, I'm the spoiled one. The man used to getting his own way, having what he wants."

He came and knelt beside her, covering her face with his hands.

"Do you think we can manage it, Anna? Being secret about it, hiding our feelings, our goings-on?"

"We don't have any choice, do we?"

He nodded in agreement as he moved close to her again, wrapped her protectively in his strong hair-roughened arms.

"Just be patient, Anna," he whispered. "Just understand that when I get moody or angry, it's because I'm being kept from being with you fully, the way I want to."

"Will it be that hard?"

"It already is. A few weeks ago, the day we went to the airstrip to watch Will test-fly that new mono plane of his, I remember feeling like I had been stabbed in the back watching young Alessandro running on his boyish, energetic legs toward Will as he got out of the plane. Watching as Sandro ran to him, calling out, 'Daddy, Daddy, I love you.' Watching as Will picked the boy up in his arms, kissed that curly, dark head of his and carried him back to where you were waiting on the runway. It's times like that when it's almost more than I can take, Anna. I'll never have what Will has with you. I'll never have our little boy to carry to you in my arms. I'm constantly reminded of how things could have been. Reminded that I could have had a son like most men my age, if only God or fate or Lady Luck or whoever runs the show hadn't cheated me of it."

There was a long silence. The empty, unfinished room, the scene of their lovemaking turned maddenly cold and ugly, a raw, unfinished place.

Anna shut her eyes to blot out the room, the truth. But she could escape neither. She forced herself to open her eyes and look at her surroundings, to look into Bart's steely gray eyes.

Then she told him.

"Alessandro is your son."

Chapter Two

IN AUGUST OF 1929, ALONZO UNEXPECTEDLY SUFFERED A heart attack. The attack was serious, though it was what Dr. Henderson described as "not devastating."

"He's lucky and he's strong," Henderson told Bart as he left Alonzo's room at Casa Portillo some hours after the attack. "A man Alonzo's age usually has just one coronary and that's it. Or worse, he has a stroke and lies helpless until his body decides to die, which can take years."

Bart asked about his prospects. After all, his grandfather was almost eighty, though he still looked and acted like a man twenty years younger.

"Alonzo will be with us for a while, Bart. But if he runs true to pattern, there will be a series of attacks—small ones, enough to lay him flat for a week and enough to do more and more damage to his valves and arteries. I know it's hard to think of Alonzo this way, given the kind of man he is, but don't get your hopes up that he'll ever be out of bed for long. And consider yourself lucky if he's here a year from now, though I hope I'm wrong."

Henderson sensed Bart's pain. It was the kind of news no one likes to hear or give.

"Sorry, Bradley," Henderson went on with his most reassuring bedside tone. "I know he's the only family you've got left. So enjoy him as much as you can while there's time."

Within two days Alonzo was well enough for visitors. Ruth, Anna and Will came first but only spent a few minutes in the dim, darkened bedroom. Alonzo was weak—he was only able to raise his hand with effort to embrace them, and his face was drawn and ashen. But by the following week Alonzo was sitting up in bed, talking briskly with them, urging them to stay more than the allotted hour maximum set by the doctor.

Alonzo, of course, passed the attack off as nothing, "a mere incident of the circulatory system." He was full of good spirits. He talked politics with Will, advised him what politics *he* would adopt if *he* were in the legislature. And he insisted that Mina and Sandro climb up in bed with him and gave them a whiff of oxygen from the black rubber mask attached to the tall metal oxygen tank next to his bed.

By the time Will had left for Austin for the opening of the legislative session, the third week after Alonzo's attack, Alonzo was venturing downstairs into the courtyard where he held court in robe and slippers for the steady stream of visitors that came to Casa Portillo.

Then, very late one night, Anna was startled from her sleep by the phone ringing. Her instinct told her it was not good news, instinct confirmed by Bart's anxious voice on the wire.

"It's Lonzo. Another attack, I think a bad one. Henderson's on his way."

Anna's natural reaction was to ask what she could do.

"He's asked for Ruth. I know it's late, but do you think she'd come?"

Anna checked the clock. It was one o'clock. But her mother would want to be there. "Of course . . . no question."

"Will you come too?" he asked with just a hint of the frightened boy in his voice. "I need you here tonight, with me."

A quarter of an hour later Ruth and Anna let themselves in the front door of Casa Portillo, relieved to see Dr. Henderson's black Ford parked outside. Bart met them in the gallery. His unshaven face was stern; his hands were jammed deep into the pockets of his wrinkled trousers. He didn't give them a chance to ask.

"Henderson's still up there, so I don't know anything yet. But I think it's bad—as bad as the first one. And on top of the damage already done . . ." Bart paced along the gallery, his movements tight, stressed.

"He's conscious—he was through the whole thing. But he couldn't even call out, the pain was so bad. Teresa was in with him, but she was dozing. She only knew when he rolled off the bed from the pain and knocked over the table. God, why does he have to go through this? It just isn't fair." Bart turned and walked to the far end of the gallery where he stood and leaned his forehead disconsolately against a wood post.

Anna had never seen Bart like this. He was always one who took every emergency in stride; he was so strong, so above it all. Now he was agitated, even rattled. She wanted so badly to put her arms around him, to hold him.

Anna caught her mother's eye. There was a look of concern, of conflict in it. Then Ruth smiled.

"Go to him, Anna," she whispered. "He needs you right now. It's all right—I understand everything. I'll go upstairs and wait for Dr. Henderson to come out."

Anna was stunned by her mother's words. She stared at Ruth, waiting for some confirmation that she had indeed mis-

understood Ruth's meaning. A feeling of nakedness suddenly
came over her, though her mother's eyes were warm and understanding.

"Anna, this is no time to talk about this."

"But you know?"

"Of course. A mother always knows these things. It's in her
blood and bones. It's her right, her instinct. It's also her duty to
keep quiet, too, to know her place. So be assured, it's as much
my secret as yours. I wouldn't even have mentioned it now,
except I was afraid you wouldn't go to Bart out of fear I'd see
too much."

"But how much do you know?"

"Shh! Enough, child. I know very little, but enough! Now run
along. He'll be wanting you with him now."

Ruth turned and went up the stairs to the upper gallery.
Anna waited a moment, then ran to Bart. She didn't know if
she should feel afraid or relieved that someone else shared her
secret.

"He asked to see you—alone," Henderson said as he faced
Ruth on the gallery. The doctor, his face tired and grave, put a
cautionary hand on her arm. "Ruth, he's very bad . . . weak. I
think there's slow hemorrhaging. This may be the end. Don't
let him talk. Just be with him, hold his hand. Only a minute or
two."

Only a minute or two! How strange, how sad, Ruth thought
as she eased open the heavy oak door, that so many years of
interwoven lives had to be summed up in only a minute or two.

A single lamp illuminated the dark, heavy-beamed room,
dominated by the tall, tapestry-hung bed. Alonzo's figure,
swathed in white linens, lay motionless, as if he were already
lying in state. Ruth shuddered as she approached the bed.
Alonzo's face was death-gray, his eyes closed, the lips tight but
slightly parted. Only the faint movement of the sheets across his
chest revealed any life.

He must have heard or sensed her. The heavy-lidded eyes
opened slowly, and the faintest breath of a smile crossed his
face. He turned one hand slowly, palm outward, an invitation
for her to hold it.

Ruth took his hand, moved closer to the bed. His hand was cold in hers, limp and heavy.

Alonzo opened his lips, tried to form words.

"No," she cautioned in a whisper. "Don't try to talk. Just rest."

His eyes closed again for a long moment, then opened slowly, as if with great effort.

"Please." The word escaped him with the barest sound. "Want to say something . . . to you."

Ruth clasped his cold hand, felt a faint response from his.

He began, enunciating each word slowly, almost inaudibly: "So sorry, Ruth. So very sorry. Wanted everything different."

Ruth tried to swallow the hot, painful lump that rose in her throat. She knew what he was going to say; she knew she owed it to Alonzo to hear it.

"I wanted so much to have a life with you. Together. I understand, though, why you could not. I was very happy anyway, just to love you in my own way."

He paused again as the eyes closed, as if under a great weight. "Thank you, Ruth. Thank you."

Alonzo slipped into a quiet sleep, his hand still in hers. The faint rhythm of his breathing ebbed and flowed under the sheets. Ruth stood beside him, fighting back the terrible tightness in her throat. It was a terrible struggle, to hold it back, not because she was afraid of tears. Far from it; for at that moment she wanted more than anything to cry. She fought to hold it back because she knew what filled her chest, what burned in her throat was not tears but a scream—a scream of terror and despair at the folly of her own inability to give him her love.

The death of Don Alonzo Lopez y Ruiz merited a front page obituary in the *El Paso Times*. The obituary described Alonzo as "a man of great culture and taste, as renowned for his generosity as for his charm," and "one of the last descendants of one of Mexico's most prominent and ancient Spanish land-grant families." The article mentioned in passing that according to the will of his late daughter, Mrs. Alessandra Lopez y Ruiz Bradley, many rare and valuable Spanish Colonial artworks from her estate, which had been held in trust for her father during his lifetime, would be donated to the new art museum being organized by Senator and Mrs. Channing of El Paso, along with other artworks and artifacts Don Alonzo had left directly to the fledgling museum. The article concluded: "The death of Lopez y Ruiz marks another final step toward the end of an era in the history of Southwest Texas."

Alonzo had requested that a funeral mass be held at the venerable mission of Nuestra Señora del Carmin at Ysleta, below El Paso, built by Pueblo Indian converts under the supervision of zealous Spanish missionaries in 1680.

"I don't want a mass for anything having to do with God," he had told Bart several years before, when his will had been drawn up. "I'll be dead and couldn't care less. But my friends may want to mourn me, *un poco,* so why not give them an appropriate and traditional setting?"

Anna was surprised by her own reaction to Alonzo's death. After the first attack she had prepared herself for his death. She knew she would feel deeply the loss of the man who had been father, protector, adviser to her and her family. Yet, in the days immediately after that long, sad night at Casa Portillo, Anna found herself feeling angry, irritated, short-tempered. She had difficulty sleeping, which angered her even more, since the harvesting was just beginning and she needed every ounce of her strength to manage the dawn-to-dusk workdays.

She knew what the problem was. It was Bart. Bart, as always. Alonzo's death had triggered something in her, triggered a coiled spring that she had let wind tighter and tighter these last years. The night of Alonzo's death, when she had comforted Bart in her arms, she had felt a oneness, a unity with him. As his grandfather died Bart had turned to her, shown his need for her. Then, as always, there were the interruptions, the separations, the deceptions that were part and parcel of their relationship. She wanted so much to be with Bart during this period, but even on the day after Alonzo's death, the house was already filled with friends and mourners, and she had to restrain herself from the slightest gesture of affection. The funeral would be the same—Bart would be by himself, she would be with Will. And after the funeral the same thing for days, for weeks, for years.

That was what made her so angry. The dishonesty of it all— the dishonesty and the frustration and the pain. She had married Will out of honest motives, out of a very real regard for him—what many would call love. But Anna knew she would never be able to give herself totally to Will, not so long as there was Bart. And she and Bart were paying the price for what ill-fortuned fate had sent their way. No one was to blame for the trap they had been caught in, but that was little consolation since they were nevertheless trapped.

It had been a valuable lesson for Anna to see her mother at Alonzo's death. What a pity it was that Ruth had never let go of the fantasy that Jonah would return and be united with her in some sort of blissful fairy-tale life. Jonah had been gone fifteen years, fifteen years that Ruth had lost forever. Perhaps Ruth really did not love Alonzo, but Anna doubted that. No, Ruth was just protecting herself from another hurt by raising the drawbridge and filling the moat of the lonely castle of her heart. By telling herself that Jonah would come back, she was giving herself the best excuse in the world not to face the reality of a relationship with Alonzo. She would never have to take a chance on being hurt again.

What a waste! Anna thought. What a waste to let those years of possible happiness slip away forever because of fear of possible hurt. It was sad, seeing the enormous energy that Ruth channeled into her pursuits: the charities, school, entertainment. All good things in and of themselves, but they all added up to an enormous distraction from Ruth's self-imposed loneliness.

What troubled Anna was the idea that in some way she might be making the same mistake her mother had made. Their situations were very different, to be sure, but wasn't Anna clinging to Will and their marriage to avoid the pain and hurt of leaving Will for Bart? She was running the same risk that Ruth had—that she would let too many years slip by before she faced the reality of her love for Bart and the painful decisions she would have to make because of it.

She thought of her children. One Will's, one Bart's. She felt the mother's instinct to protect them. After all, children could not understand the complexities of adults' lives; they only felt the rejection and the hurt that adults' problems passed on to them. She was trying to protect Will too; she knew that. It would have been so easy to hurt him if Will were not who he was. But he was such a good man, such a loving man, she couldn't bear the thought of hurting him.

Yet, she asked herself, is that fair? Didn't Will deserve a more honest relationship? A relationship with a woman who could fully give herself to him? There was no way to avoid the mess—and it would be a horrible mess—of leaving Will. But in the long run, once the dust had settled, once the wounds had healed, it would all be for the best.

She would have to be careful, take her time. Perhaps in a few weeks she could bring herself to face Will, to tell him the truth.

She shuddered at the thought: it was hard to imagine the words coming out of her mouth. Anna imagined herself saying them: "Will, I want a divorce. I'm in love with Bart."

Will Channing's Curtiss-Wright soared through the pass at Sierra Blanca at six thousand feet. Below the broken, lava-strewn terrain dotted with brush sped by while the peak of the extinct volcano rose another two thousand feet to the left. As the pass was cleared the valley came into view, with the Franklin Range forty miles northwest marking the site of El Paso.

Will checked his watch.

Two-ten. Damn, but why did he have to have that flat on the runway at Austin this morning? It had cost him a good forty-five minutes, what with trying to find the damned mechanic who was sleeping in the toolshed behind the hangar.

As the high desert plateau gave way to the Rio Grande Valley, Will recognized the landmarks of his home turf. The river to the left, the distant patches of green that marked the farms of Tornillo and Casilla and Fabens; the parallel ribbons of the state highway and the Southern Pacific Rails unrolled in an arrow-straight course toward the city.

The valley basked in a brilliant September sun, but to the right, along the ridge of the valley, a vast bank of thunderclouds reared their noble white heads into the stratosphere as they moved south toward Mexico. Will knew their habits; he had so often over the years stood by the fields and watched the summer storms in their sweep across the valley.

The Curtiss-Wright, still in sunlight, heaved and bounced as the first turbulence from the approaching storm caught the fuselage.

Will banked and turned south, toward the river, to put more distance between himself and the storm. He was only twenty minutes from the runway at Ysleta, plenty of time to land and get to the funeral before the storm hit.

Et nomine Patris, Fili, et Spiritūs Sancti. Amen.

From the gilded splendor of the altar the priest intoned a final blessing over the flower-draped casket of Don Alonzo. The nearly six hundred souls who jammed every corner of the narrow, lofty nave echoed "Amen."

Their voices were barely heard against the fury of the storm outside. The waves of rain lashed against the stained-glass saints who looked down on the proceedings. Thunder, like the very voice of God, had boomed out again and again during the mass, until the ancient timbers, carved by the pious Indian converts, seemed ready to crack and tumble into the chapel.

The crush of mourners stepped back to open an aisle for family and close friends. Bart and the staff from Casa Portillo, the Channings, the Cutters. Ironically Anna had sat next to Bart through the service with only the small space left open for Will between them.

Anna was naturally concerned that Will hadn't arrived, and it was tragic for him to have missed the service. With this weather, though, he might have been forced to land at McNary or Casilla, for he could have been held up driving to the mission, since thunderstorms as heavy as this one often flooded out low places in the farm roads and engines stalled. She slipped into the small office off the vestibule, where she had noticed a telephone, and asked the operator to ring up Casa Grande, collect. The operator clicked on and off a few times, then came back and said the lines to Casilla were down in the storm.

She thought a moment, then asked if the switchboard had a number for the airstrip at Ysleta. Will had said he would fly in there, then call for a taxicab to bring him to the mission.

A few buzzes and a man's voice came on the line. She identified herself and asked if Will's plane had landed there.

"Just a minute," the voice said.

There was a long silence, then another man's voice came on. "Are you Mrs. William Channing. Of Casilla?"

She answered.

"Mrs. Channing, this is Deputy Kendall, Sheriff's Department. I'm sorry to have to tell you this, but there's been a crash. It happened when your husband was coming in on final approach to the strip."

A numbing shock wave surged through her.

"Mr. Channing is alive, but he's hurt pretty bad. They just took him to Southwest General. We tried to call you in Casilla but couldn't get through. Where are you now? I'll send a car to get you."

The receiver hung limply in her hand. She couldn't find the words to answer him.

The antiseptic smell of the hospital. The cold walls and floor, the uncomfortable wood chairs lined up against the walls of the corridor. Through the slats of the blinds on the single window at the end of the corridor the last ruddy glow of sunset had faded into dusky gray.

Nurses, with trays and carts, and occasional white-jacketed doctors moved along the corridors. Since this was a surgery floor, the hospital staff moved about their business with a brisk, serious air. Little notice was given to the friends and family of surgery patients who waited outside the steel doors that led to the operating rooms.

Anna sat silently next to Ruth with Jack and Edna next to her. Bart paced quietly by the window, staring out the window as if he expected to see something of importance.

It had been over three hours since the surgery began. Surely, Anna thought, they would be finished soon. There had been such a rush after the funeral, when Anna had gotten the news. J. J. had taken the children back to Casilla; Bart had told the priest to hold Alonzo's burial so they could rush to the hospital; Dr. Henderson, following them from the mission in his own car to the hospital; his hurried conference with the surgeon, before the two disappeared into the operating room.

The surgeon—his name had escaped her—with the litany of injuries.

Ruptured spleen . . . a liver and right lung puncture . . . possible spinal injuries . . . minor head lacerations . . .

The hours had dripped by, second by second, waiting, waiting.

Will might die. The injuries were serious; the surgeon had not pretended otherwise. How could it be otherwise? How could it be otherwise when his plane had been caught in a sudden, squally updraft fifty feet above the landing strip, thrown nose-down onto the runway and skidded a hundred feet before stopping.

"Damned lucky he was low on fuel or the thing would have burst into flames," the deputy had said. "Damned lucky."

There was nothing lucky about it, she thought as she pictured Will's broken body as the doctors and nurses struggled to repair the broken veins and arteries, to stitch the lacerated organs.

Her poor Will, thrust so suddenly at death's door.

She looked toward the window where Bart, his back toward her, looked restlessly out. Just hours ago she had come to the edge of decision: to leave Will. Now she was praying to God for Will to live.

Perhaps God was going to make her decision for her.

The steel doors facing her swung open, and Dr. Henderson and the surgeon came out. The faces were somber, tired. There was blood on their white gowns.

Anna shot her glance to Bart; his eyes met hers. They understood that their fate hung by the slenderest thread.

"Anna," Dr. Henderson said solemnly, "I'm afraid I have some very bad news."

Chapter Three

"OH, GOD, SANDRO, DON'T BE SO SERIOUS ABOUT EVERY-thing. You just don't know how to have any *fun!*"

Mina Channing wrinkled her nose at her little brother, to show her displeasure at him for his stubborn refusal to go riding with her. It had been storming for most of the afternoon, and Sandro and Mina had been cooped up in the sun room, amusing themselves halfheartedly with their grandmother's discarded mah-jongg set. Now that the thunderheads had blown south and left the valley wet and fragrant with ozone, Mina was itching to get out of the house for a good gallop on Charity. Like most horses, Charity got lazy in the summer, apt to poke around, but after a good rain, she was as frisky as she ever was on a brisk November day.

"Sure I want to have fun," Sandro countered to his sister's remark, though the expression on his face was, in fact, as serious as she had accused it of being. "I just . . . don't feel like riding right now."

Really, Mina thought, thirteen-year-old boys are the earth's most impossible creatures, and her brother was an especially bad example of the type. She didn't ask much from Sandro, aside from the usual favors one would ask of a brother, such as not telling his friends which boys she had crushes on and not squealing when she snitched cigarettes from the compartment of Uncle J. J.'s truck.

"I just don't know about you, Sandro," Mina added with as much *hauteur* as she could muster. "You *are* bizarre sometimes. All you want to do is hang around this gloomy house like Bela Lugosi or somebody strange and play the piano."

Mina made another face indicating distaste, as if she had gotten soap on her tongue.

"So what's wrong with playing the piano?"

Sandro's gray eyes flashed defensively, and an adolescent squeak crept into his voice.

"Well, nothing, I suppose, if you're a *vampire!* A vampire who would rather play all that silly Mozart crap rather than learn to ride a horse really, really well."

Sandro gave his sister a frank, no-nonsense stare, punctuated with a meaningful "Um!" Mina knew as well as he that Sandro was easily as good or better a rider than she, in spite of being a year younger and less inclined to ride daily. She had seen him clear a four-foot fence in English saddle. Sandro knew Mina was just being ornery, and he knew the reason.

"You're just teed because Mama won't let you go to Uncle Bart's club with the grown-ups next week. I know it's true. You've been on a tear ever since she told you no."

Mina gave a slight toss of the head, a gesture she had practiced often in the mirror. As she made the move she realized that it was much more effective when her hair was down and flowing instead of in pigtails as it was now.

"I *am* old enough to go out to clubs," Mina countered. "Lots of women my age do."

"You're fourteen, Mina," Sandro added dryly.

She drew herself up, trying to reassure herself that the physical development she monitored so carefully in the triple mirror in her bathroom was as apparent to Sandro as she would have liked.

"Lots of females," she pronounced with the air of a true authority, "are adults at my age. You know, married and stuff."

Sandro narrowed his eyes wickedly. His sister was so grand sometimes that he couldn't resist an opportunity to deflate her.

"Yeah, sure. Enough of that 'stuff' and you'll *have* to get married. Whether your tits have popped up yet or not."

"Oh, you little brat!" Mina protested in a sudden fury. "I'm going to tell Mama you talked vulgar to me."

She went for Sandro, grabbed him by the shoulders as if to give him a shake. He came back by digging his fingers into her ribs. They fell back onto the chintz-covered cushions of the sun room divan as their mock fight dissolved into a bout of tickling and wrestling. A minute later they collapsed, breathless from laughter.

"Go on, then." Mina gasped holding her sides. "Play your old piano. I'm going to give Charity a good workout. I'm just as happy riding by myself, anyway."

"Why don't you call Mirkovsky's and get Max to go with you? He's your riding teacher, after all."

"He can't do it today. He had to go over and help Miss Deane move into her new bungalow."

Sandro caught the slight, venomous hiss in his sister's voice. He knew Max Mirkovsky had been to several barn dances and picnics that summer with the pretty young second-grade teacher.

"So that's it. You're just jealous because Max can't spend the afternoon with you the way he usually does."

"Maybe."

"Maybe," Sandro parroted. He got up from the divan. The

sun was fully out now, and he knew a lovely warm light would be streaming through the French windows into the music room.

"Aren't you a little young for Max?"

"Maybe," was her reply.

Bart was sitting in one of the deep, overstuffed chairs by the window in the music room when Sandro came in. His feet were up on a footstool, and he was glancing over the previous day's paper that had been left folded on the chair when he came in. While he waited for Sandro he had been reading about the latest in what seemed to be Roosevelt's endless stream of New Deal agencies and programs. There was a kind of grandiose, self-righteous optimism coming out of Washington now that Bart was rapidly finding a bore; he often wondered if things wouldn't straighten themselves out if just left alone. Bart was much more interested in hearing Sandro's daily piano practice. He always sat with him during practice when he had the chance, but since the thunderstorms had blown over and it was now sunny out, he thought Sandro might have decided to let the piano wait and instead go out to play.

"Uncle Bart!" Sandro exclaimed when he saw him. There was a genuine pleasure in the boy's voice. "I didn't know you were still here; I thought you left after lunch."

"Can't get rid of me that easy, kid," Bart answered. "You know I'm getting to be your biggest fan."

Bart usually managed to sit in on Sandro's music practice once or twice a week, which they both enjoyed. Sandro was for the most part shy about playing for an audience, and he would sometimes get "a case of nerves," even when playing for his mother and grandmother. For some reason he didn't understand, though, he always felt perfectly comfortable with Bart there.

"You don't mind if I listen, do you?" Bart put his paper aside.

"Sure. I mean, sure I don't mind."

Sandro went to Bart, felt the older man's arm around him in a reassuring, fatherly hug. He then hurried to the ebony expanse of the Steinway that presided in somber majesty over the paneled, damask-draped room. He sat at the bench, then leafed through a pile of dog-eared music on the score rack until he found the volume he wanted.

"Don't try to skip your scales and arpeggios, son." Bart warned with obvious humor in his voice. "You know I'm one of Miss Careth's secret agents and am duty-bound to report you when you get lazy."

Sandro made the kind of face piano students, even talented ones, make when faced with the distasteful task of technical practice. Then he dutifully plunged into a series of scales in octaves, note-perfect and with a technical proficiency beyond his years.

Bart leaned his head back against the antimacassar as the sound of Sandro's practicing echoed through the room. Hearing Sandro play was always special for Bart; he felt a deep, rich satisfaction in his son's talent, and true fatherly pride as well. There was always the emotional wrench because he could not acknowledge that he was Sandro's father, but that in no way took away from the pleasure he experienced in his son's accomplishments.

It had been fascinating to watch Anna's children growing up in the years since he had come back from Mexico. They were both beautiful children, as he would have expected Anna's children to be, but they were as contrasted, as opposite as two siblings could be as well. Mina was Will's child, no doubt about it, as one glance at her blond hair and aquamarine eyes confirmed. She had her father's sunny, extroverted charm, too, though there was another quality to Mina, a rather flighty and irresponsible side that Bart knew had not come from Will or Anna. Bart was terribly fond of Mina, and he loved watching her at the threshold of what promised to be a beautiful womanhood. With her looks, her natural charm, her talents, she promised to develop into an exceptional adult, though he could see she was going to have the potential of being a heartbreaker. There was also no doubt that she was spoiled; she was charming and she knew it, and she used it often to get her own way. It was this part of Mina that had come from her grandfather; it was the fatal Cutter charm.

Sandro was a different case. Anna always insisted that he was Bart without the cockiness, that she had managed to give birth to a perfect copy of Bart, minus only the rough and headstrong edges. She was teasing, of course, and being falsely modest to boot. Any fool could see that Sandro was Anna all over again. Their son, now that he was burgeoning into manhood, might resemble his father in height, in broad-shouldered muscularity, in the fine, chiseled strength of profile. But these were merely physical resemblances. The real Sandro, the Sandro Bart liked to see developing, was very much Anna's son.

Like his mother, he was quiet and reserved, almost to the point of shyness; unlike his sister, he did not take quickly to the company of strangers or to society. But Bart knew that the qualities Sandro shared with his mother were not signs of weakness. Like his mother, Sandro had a deep inner drive, a firm self-determination that operated beneath the reserved exterior. Bart remembered well when Anna, hardly older than Sandro was now, had plunged headlong into the work of the struggling Cutter farm. She had been shy and awkward in some respects then, but underneath had been real drive and determination. Even as a girl she had shown that when faced with adversity, as when her father left, she would not look back but would keep going, headlong, until she succeeded.

Bart had seen much of the same attitude in Sandro. He was not as quick and clever as Mina—she had that knack of breezing through her lessons, getting better than average marks with little effort. Classes were hard for Sandro, and he had to spend many long hours studying while Mina played with friends or practiced her riding with Max Mirkovsky. Yet Sandro's hard work paid off, and he consistently had better report cards than his sister. Sandro even approached horsemanship in the same determined way. Mina was a natural horsewoman and, like all young girls, worshiped the gentle power of horses. But she rode for fun and spent hours daily after school riding for the sheer physical pleasure. Sandro, on the other hand, had less of the natural talent, but he took his riding very seriously, in the same way he took his arithmetic lessons; he might go through a jump dozens of times in one afternoon until he had gotten it just right. And given his love of reading, he backed up his riding lessons with hours of study of the history, care, breeding, and handling of horses.

In the last two years, as Sandro approached his teens, Bart had seen the youth take a deep interest in the farms, as if in preparation for his birthright and ultimate responsibility. He and Mina had both been raised in luxury, and unlike many farm families, it was simply not necessary for the Channing children to work. But Sandro, almost like a young lord of the manor, had asked to learn about the farm, and he had spent the last few summers and many after-school hours "palling around" with his uncles and with Pablo Sisneros, Juan Gordo, and the other foremen. He had planted, weeded, irrigated, chopped, hoed, and even picked cotton; he had ridden the farm's new bright red John Deere tractors, which roared and smoked like dragons and smelled of diesel smoke; he had even learned to drive one at age twelve. He had also spent more than a few hours in the back office with his mother and grandmother as they balanced books, filed invoices, and telephoned the mills. By the time he was thirteen, as he began the spurt of growth that was to send him toward the six-foot mark and beyond, he had already been dubbed "The Little Farmer."

But it was Sandro's love of music that showed the most distinctive and individual side of the boy. The music the Cutter family knew was the lean, solid church hymns; the lively but simple "fiddle music" of Scots-Irish hill people; and the popular sentimental ballads of the turn of the century. When Will Channing had first met Anna, he had introduced her to the "art" music of Brahms and Beethoven, Mozart and Chopin, on the tinny hand-cranked Victrola at the Channings' house. Though Anna found she enjoyed the music, it always remained somewhat foreign to her; it had come into her life too late to be taken to heart. Classical music had much the same effect on Ruth, and when she had included a handsome boiserie-lined music room in the plans of Casa Grande, complete with a Steinway imported from New York, it had been for the most part because every grand house of the era was required to have a music room. In a sense it had been almost a premonition or at least a stroke of luck, since Sandro, at an early age, had shown such a strong interest in the piano. At age three the dark-haired child had shrieked with delight as he banged away at the keyboard, producing horrendous chords. By six he was asking for lessons to learn to make "pretty music." Once he began study with the dour Miss Careth from Fabens, he showed real talent and progressed rapidly from able beginner to accomplished student.

In the years after Sandro began lessons, as he practiced an hour or more daily, his fellow inhabitants at Casa Grande got a crash course in European music between the eras of Bach and Brahms, whether they liked it or not, though as he progressed from the dull, square compositions for beginning pupils to real music, his resident audience began to appreciate to one degree or another the works of Chopin and Haydn, the Three Bs, and all the rest of the great names in European music. With time the music room at Casa Grande became a kind of cultural center for the valley, host to many recitals and musicales performed not only by Sandro but by other students and even by musicians from the city and from the college.

Now Sandro dutifully whipped through his scales and arpeggios, then went on to a Beethoven sonata. Bart could not remember the number, but he recalled hearing it at Aeolian Hall in New York with his mother and father when he was about Sandro's age. Since he was practicing, Sandro stopped and started, played some passages fast, some slow, went over figurations until he got them right. Once he had begun, his concentration was intense; he seemed oblivious to the man's presence in the room; to Bart it seemed almost as if some sort of hypnotic force had taken control of his son's mind.

After the Beethoven, Sandro went through two modern-sounding pieces, works Bart didn't know or care much for; finally, as if to signal that the practice hour was over, Sandro played a Brahms intermezzo, a piece he played well considering his years. It was a composition he knew to be one of Bart's favorites. When the last pianissimo chord had died out, Sandro let his hands drop, then dutifully closed the keyboard cover and put the music back on the pile he'd taken it from.

"Bravo!" Bart called as he applauded. "Come on, take a bow."

Sandro made a face. "Aw, come on, that's silly."

"No, it isn't. An artist's always got to acknowledge his audience's applause."

"I was just practicing."

"No, no! That's not the attitude a great performer takes." Bart said it in the manner a managing agent takes in encouraging a reluctant performer. "You've got to get used to bowing, for the days when you'll play Carnegie Hall."

Sandro grinned, his eyes shyly grazing the floor.

"You know that if I get to Carnegie Hall, it's only going to be in the audience."

"Now, wait," Bart said, scolding him, "don't tell me you're not going on the concert stage?"

"Me?" Sandro's voice fell into an adolescent crack as he spoke. "Not a chance. I'm going to be the biggest cotton farmer in Texas. Besides, I'm too chicken to play in front of all those people."

"Why not do both? Alessandro Channing, the Cotton-picking Pianist. It's bound to go over great in the cultural capitals of Europe."

"Yuck."

"Yeah," Bart confessed. "Not such a glamorous idea."

He got up and went to where Sandro still sat on the bench, and tousled the youth's dark, wavy hair, so much like his own.

"Thanks for the music, son. I've got to get to the club now. I'm late as it is."

Disappointment registered in Sandro's face.

"Aw, do you have to? You never get to have supper with us anymore. Can't your club make it without you just one night?"

"I wish I could, Sandro. Believe me, after six years of late nights at the club one more doesn't seem like so much fun as it used to. But remember, fella, we're in the middle of a depression, and a man's got to make a living. Right? Especially since drinking is legal now and there are plenty of new clubs around to give The Back Door competition."

"I understand, I guess. Mama keeps telling me that just because our farm is in good shape moneywise, I can't forget that most other businesses are having a hard time. Like Grammy Edna and Grandpa Jack when their mine stock went down to fifty cents a share."

"You got the idea, buddy. I'm one of those peons that has to work for a living now. The stock market crash didn't exactly leave me sitting pretty, either." Bart was exaggerating purposely. He had certainly lost on the exchange, but the large cash income from the club during the Prohibition years had left him with drawers full of gold coins, cash, and a large amount of paid-for real estate in addition to what he had already owned. He was more concerned that Sandro would not learn the value of money or the reality of life away from the security and luxury of Cutter-Channing Farms. Sandro was one of the lucky ones: his mother and grandmother had wisely avoided speculating in the market, and they had whenever possible run the farm on a cash basis. Thanks to that, the farms had weathered the Depression with hardly a leak or a crack. But they were the exceptions: every day the valley saw dozens of homeless drifters, men, women, and children, as they drove, walked, or hopped freights, heading west from their dust-bowl-ravaged farms toward the promised land of California.

Sandro looked at Bart with a face full of innocent, boyish concern. It was at times like this that Bart wanted more than ever to put his arms around his son, tell him how much he loved him.

"Gee, Bart, if things get real bad at the club, I'll come and help out. Not for pay or anything. Maybe I could play piano, though I'm not so good at that kind of pop music. Maybe I can wait on tables or something."

Bart couldn't help but laugh at Sandro's generous offer.

"Well, that sounds great, but it's not that bad—yet. Besides, you're still a bit green, from a legal point of view, if you know what I mean. The club has had enough scrapes with law enforcement around these parts. I'd better be careful about hiring underage help."

"You mean, I've got to wait until I'm twenty-one?"

"Maybe not *that* long. Drinking age in Mexico is eighteen, though no one's going to say anything much as long as you look like you shave every day."

"I do that now—almost."

"So we'll talk business when you can leave off the 'almost.' "

They went out into the marble cavern of the domed stair court. The afternoon sun streamed through the myriad-colored Tiffany-glass ceiling and turned the pale terrazzo floor into a festive carpet of hues. The four dozen potted palms that stood around the court like sentries were freshly watered, and in the summer heat they gave off a musky, hothouse aroma. The court was very beautiful and very grand, Bart had to admit, but he had always found it rather empty and severe, more capable of intimidation than anything else. The sheer scale and importance of the architecture reduced human beings to lonely entities. He would take the rougher, more human-scaled spaces of Casa Portillo any day.

"Bart! Sandro!"

It was Will's voice. Its clear, cheerful tone boomed out from the upstairs gallery and echoed through the court below. Bart and Sandro looked up and saw Will smiling down on them from one of the arched openings of the gallery that lined the court on three sides of the upper level. His face was only just visible above the marble balustrade.

"Hi, Dad," Sandro called out. "Could you hear me practicing?"

"Sure did," he called down. "Didn't realize Bart was sitting in. Hope he wasn't too critical."

"Not a bit," Bart interjected. "I'm a fan, remember."

"I thought you were going back to the city after lunch," Will said, "though it's just as well you're still here. I could use a hand."

Bart hoped Will didn't mean anything about his staying on after lunch. Will had often told Bart to come and go as he pleased at Casa Grande, to use the place as a second home when he was in Casilla, to consider himself "Uncle Bart" to the Channing family.

He asked Will what the problem was that he needed help with.

"The damn elevator. Stuck again, the second time this week. It's this highfalutin modern technology."

Will seemed to take the elevator breakdown in good humor, as he seemed to take everything.

"I was about to call down to the office to have J. J. come up to the house and give me a hand. Hated to bother him, though. He and Anna have enough problems today with that seepage in the feeder ditch over by the Mirkovsky line."

With Sandro close on his heels Bart bounded up the broad central flight of steps, across the windowed landing, then up one of the paired second flights that led to the upstairs gallery. Will, in slacks and shirt, sat in his wheelchair halfway along the carpeted gallery. He smiled warmly as Bart and Sandro approached.

As they did, Will was struck, as he always was, by the lack of envy and resentment he felt toward Bart. In the youthful years

of their long friendship Will had often asked himself why he
was not jealous of Bart, who had the greater looks, the greater
magnetism, the greater abilities. Bart, whose life seemed to be
writ large, as some men's lives are, was to most men the most
enviable of characters. Yet Will, his closest friend, had not envied Bart Bradley for a very long time. Even in recent years, as
Will had come to know and understand the hidden relationship
Bart had with Anna, he had not been hurt and angry as he once
would have predicted he might have been in the circumstances.
An inner voice had said, "Of course" to him at the thought of
Bart and Anna's relationship. "Of course they love one another
—it seems only right and logical and natural, given the circumstances and who they are," the voice said. Will listened to that
voice and accepted that Bart gave—and always had given—
Anna a kind of love, a kind of passion and fulfillment he could
not. There had been times—difficult times—when Will had suspected that he might wake up some morning with the demons
of jealousy and envy and inadequacy gnawing at his guts. But
that morning never seemed to come. In fact, just the opposite;
in the years since his accident, Will had come to appreciate and
even admire Anna and Bart for their consummate discretion
and consideration of his feelings.

At times Will even found himself feeling somewhat guilty for
being the undeniable barrier between the lovers and any real
consummation of their love. Will knew Anna could never leave
him as long as he was in his wheelchair, and they both knew he
was to be in that chair for life.

In recent years Will had at times even felt sorry for Bart.
Sorry that one who had been so blessed by the gods at his birth
had been so cursed by them during his life. Will, of course, had
his own reasons to curse the gods, but he at least had certain
compensations that were denied to Bart. Will, though he shared
Anna with another man, at least had the fullest, richest life with
her. And even though Sandro was not his own son—a fact
never so apparent as now, as the boy and his real father came
toward him on the landing—Will at least had the satisfaction of
raising Sandro as if he were his own son. Bart, cheated by fate,
had the terrible task of watching his own son being raised by
another man, unable to acknowledge his own lineage, his own
immortality. At the thought of this Will Channing realized that

he would not have changed places with Barton Bradley for all the strong, healthy limbs in the world.

"This is a damned nuisance," Will said cheerfully. "I think from now on, as long as the elevator is going to break down on a regular schedule, I'm going to keep two chairs in the house—one upstairs, one down. That way I can get myself up and down. All I've got to do is slide out of the chair up here, onto the floor, then ease myself down the steps crabwise and right into the chair at the foot of the stairs."

Bart reached down and in a single stroke lifted Will from the chair. The crippled man lifted one arm and hooked it around Bart's shoulder for support, as his body was cradled in Bart's arms. The useless, dead legs hung down limply.

"I don't think that's such a good idea," Bart cautioned as he started down the stairs, Will in his arms, Sandro beside them, pushing the vacant wheelchair. "You'd always have dirt on the seat of your pants. Not to mention, old buddy, that you might slip on the stairs and break your neck."

"I've already broken my back," Will returned with a wicked little smile. "It wouldn't make a helluva lot of difference now if I broke my neck. Anyhow, that's not likely to happen as I crawl downstairs. How far can a man fall when he's sitting down?"

"Got a point there. But I think you'd best let someone help you downstairs, anyway, just to play it safe."

As Bart carried his burden step by step down the last flight, he remembered those months after the plane crash, first as Will had laid in the hospital bed fighting for his very life, then, once the critical, life-threatening period had passed, the long, slow battle from bed to wheelchair as Will struggled heroically to adjust to life with only half his body.

Since the afternoon of the accident, when Dr. Henderson and the surgeons had appeared in their blood-spattered robes with the news that if Will survived his internal injuries, he would be crippled for life from the waist down, Bart had been forced to accept the cruel irony of the situation. If Will had not been crippled in the crash, Anna might have been able to divorce him with a clear conscience. And, if Bart was honest with himself, he knew that if Will had died on that rain-soaked airstrip, the tragedy would have meant freedom for him and Anna. Instead, fate had chosen a middle course, what seemed to Bart to be a glass-walled trap for him and Anna. Their lives were lived close together, as if in adjoining compartments of the trap, but they were kept apart by a glass wall; they could see, they could talk, but they could not touch. And the glass wall was cemented in place by nothing more than conscience.

It was conscience that had made them decide, after the accident, to break off their affair. They had shared almost two years of a secret happiness, but they both knew that the longer they were together, the more involved they would become, the more difficult it would be to look Will Channing in the face.

"I can't do it, Bart," she had told him. "I can't help him out of bed or massage his legs or draw the epsom baths or push the wheelchair—I can't do those things when I've been sleeping with you. It would make me feel so dishonorable."

Bart knew it had to be this way. It had been hard enough to live with his conscience when he was having an affair with his best friend's wife. But an affair with a crippled friend's wife was beyond him. In the end they had settled on one of life's painful compromises. They knew they could never separate their lives entirely—they were too intertwined. After all, they had a son, and to have deprived Bart of the pleasure of seeing his son growing up would have been inhuman. So Bart had taken the only role open to him. He became friend of the family, "Uncle Bart." In the six years since the accident he and Anna had made some sort of peace with the arrangement; they had played their roles beautifully, without a slip, without ever stepping out of character. Bart Bradley had become best friend to Mr. and Mrs. Will Channing and beloved uncle to their children. Yet in his heart he always carried the truth.

Chapter Four

ONE AFTERNOON IN MARCH OF 1935, IN THE MIDST OF A
fierce sandstorm that scoured across the valley, there was an
unexpected knock at the front door of Casa Grande. Teresa,
who long ago had given up worrying about the sand that
filtered in through shut windows, was watering the dozen palms
that stood around the perimeter of the court, as if to console
them for the dry, dusty March air they were having to breathe.

The knock surprised her, since she was unaccustomed to anyone knocking at Casa Grande during daylight hours, especially
at the front door. As large and formal as the house was, it was
essentially run on informal lines. If friends or tradesmen
stopped by during the day, they usually walked in the back
door, unannounced, and chatted with the cook and maids while
helping themselves to coffee.

Teresa put down her watering can and hurried to the door as
the knocker sounded again, more insistent this time. She wondered who the stranger was; it had to be a stranger, not to know
to use the back way. The door swung back, admitting a stinging
blast of sand.

She screwed up her face to keep the sand out of eyes and
mouth. She saw the figure of an old hobo in tattered, ill-fitting
clothes. A shapeless hat was pulled down to ward off the sand.

"*A detrás*. To the back."

She motioned in a circle to indicate that the bum should go
around the house to the kitchen door. Teresa wasn't bothered
by the hobo. Scarcely a day went by when two or three didn't
call at Casa Grande asking for food or water. They were harmless enough folks, single men, or sometimes even whole families,
driven by the dust bowl to walk or hop freights to the promised
land of California.

When the stream of migrants had begun pouring through the valley, Ruth and the Channings had given the girls who worked in the house instructions to show concern for the migrants, to keep a platter of sandwiches and some bottled drinks to give the ones who were hungry.

"We can't let them in the house," Ruth had cautioned. "After all, they are strangers. But we have plenty and can't let the unlucky ones suffer needlessly." As she said that, Ruth remembered her Grammy Stratton, back in Myrtlesburg, giving leftovers to the two or three town bums who lived on the courthouse square. During bad weather she and Anna had even stretched their rule enough to let migrants, the Okies and Arkies, take shelter overnight in the sheds behind the big house. And they knew that Hank and Pablo, since they were at the end of the farm nearer Casilla and the tracks, saw even more hobos and often let the wanderers pick vegetables from the fields to make a pot of soup by the roadside. Whenever they could, the foremen gave the migrants a few hours of work to give them enough pocket money to get to the next step along their sad pilgrimage. It was especially heartrending to see the mothers, the emaciated, toothless madonnas with their pale, hungry children and naked, unwashed infants. Ruth and Anna both wanted so badly to take them in, to give them homes, but it was impossible with so many of their own laborers to support. The best they could do was give them a bag of food and five or ten dollars to help them on a bit.

Teresa motioned again to the hobo outside in the sandstorm. *"A detrás.* Go to the kitchen, *señor.* We have plenty food there for you."

"Ruth Cutter. Where's Ruth Cutter?"

The stranger's words startled her. None of the hobos had ever known the *señora*'s name. She began to feel uneasy when he slipped by her through the door.

"Whew!" The old bum whistled appreciatively as he surveyed the sweep of marble stair under the stained-glass dome. "Will you look at this place. This is really something!"

"Señor! Por favor." Teresa tried to sound firm. The old man's indifference was making her nervous.

"Go find Mrs. Cutter. She's gotta be around here somewhere. Go on, be a good girl and get the lady of the house."

Teresa skirted around the stranger, toward the stairs. She knew Ruth Cutter was upstairs in her sitting room. The man swayed a bit as he stood, and Teresa could smell stale alcohol. A drunk.

"Por favor, señor," she asked, trying to mask her uneasiness. "I don't know you. *Su nombre, por favor."*

"Never mind. Just tell Ruth there's someone come to see her."

"It's all right, Teresa!"

Ruth's voice called out from the landing as she turned and started down the second flight. Ruth walked calmly toward the stranger with the same demeanor she would have shown to any guest at Casa Grande.

"I heard you ask for me. Don't mind Teresa being a bit cautious. We don't have too many strangers calling this time of day. What can I do for you?"

The bum took his hat off and walked toward her, his gait unsteady.

"I ain't no stranger, Ruthie. Ain't no stranger at all."

The drunk smiled at her toothlessly. His grizzly, unshaven face was the ravaged, puffy landscape of the drunkard. Wisps of unwashed gray hair fell across his furrowed brow, and a pair of faded blue eyes looked at her with an unsteady, glazed look.

Ruth confronted the stranger, met his gaze. What did this man want with her—

"It's me. It's Jonah, Ruthie. I come to see you."

The face grinned, a pitiful drunk smile, an old bum begging for a kind word.

No, she wouldn't believe it. It was impossible that this pitiful creature was her Jonah Cutter. It was a bad joke, a cruel joke. Someone had told this old beggar to do this, given him a few dollars to walk to Casa Grande and play a cruel practical joke on her!

"Gosh, Ruthie. You look real good. Real prosperous too. I guess having a lot of money keeps a body young and good-looking."

Jonah sheepishly looked down at the floor as he fingered his hat. When he looked up at her again, his face was a mask of pitiable self-loathing.

"I know I don't look so good anymore, Ruthie. I ain't had a very good life since I left here. I drink a lot now."

Ruth's eyes darted to Teresa, who stood confused and curious as she watched her employer confront the stranger.

"Teresa, it's all right!" Ruth tried to hide the edginess in her voice. "I know this man. Go on back to the kitchen."

There was a long, awkward moment after Teresa left them alone as Ruth tried to comprehend what was happening. It was Jonah; she knew that now. The shape of the head, the fine jaw, the slightly upturned nose. But what ravages the years and the alcohol had wrought. The mouth was drawn over a snaggled grin; the nose was swollen and traced with purple capillaries. More than anything, the eyes had died: the once-clear, lively blue of Jonah's eyes had faded into a glassy, dull gray. The spirit had left them.

She knew she had to say something—but what? She couldn't run to his arms, couldn't imagine touching the unwashed body. A shiver of revulsion ran through her at the thought.

"I don't know what to say, Jonah. This is such a surprise. . . . If you'd only . . ."

The five feet of marble floor that separated them was a vast desert. She made no move to bridge it.

Jonah grinned and shrugged. There was no hint of his old, irresistible grin. This was a sad, self-deprecating grin.

"Don't try to be polite, Ruthie. I know you'd just as soon never seen me again."

The irony caught her. For all these years she'd dreamed of the moment when she would see Jonah again. Now that it had come—like this—she wished it had never happened.

"Don't worry none. I'm just passing through, heading back to California. I took real sick at Memphis, went to the doctor at the clinic up there. They told me my lungs is shot. My liver too. Said I'd probably not last another year. So I decided I might as well sit it out in California. 'Least the weather's nice."

Suddenly the man became a pathetic, sad creature. This was not the Jonah she loved, but it was a man for whom she could feel only pity and compassion. Ruth reached out her hand to him.

"Jonah."

He stepped back to avoid her.

"No! Don't just try to be kind to me. I'm just a hobo now. I ain't had a bath in three weeks. You don't really want to touch me. Nobody does. Can't blame 'em."

Ruth retreated, stung, back into her shell.

"Why did you come?"

Jonah worked his hands nervously as he began; his eyes roamed around the cavernous marble court. It was as if he were a schoolboy, called upon to give his first recitation.

"It's kinda funny. I hadn't thought about this place much in years. Then, when I took off from Memphis, I hopped a freight. When I was getting on the car, I saw a whole loading dock piled up with bales of cotton. Hundreds of 'em. And every damn one had Cutter-Channing Farms stamped on it. Cutter-Channing Farms. Casilla, Texas."

Jonah smiled wanly and shook his head at the memory.

"So I said to myself, 'Well, Jonah, Ruthie must still be farming after all, and doing good at it. Funny, but I figured you and the kids woulda gone back to Kentucky years ago."

"We stayed." There was a pained pride in the words.

"Who's Channing? You got a husband?"

"Anna's husband."

Ruth didn't want to volunteer any more information; she felt suddenly very protective of her family.

"And the boys?"

"Grown, of course. Still single. We all work on the farm here." She hesitated, then added, "Jonah, I don't think you should see them. It would stir up too much from the past."

Jonah looked passive, accepting.

"Sure, that's all right. Bet they'd not be too happy to see how their old man turned out. I'd kinda like to see J. J. Bet he turned out to be a fine young man!"

Ruth thought of her bitter, angry son, who had never forgiven his father for leaving. She nodded in agreement. Let Jonah have his dream.

"And Anna," the old man continued. "Bet she turned out to be a good looker—like you."

Ruth fought back a sudden wave of nausea. She shuddered to think that this man had held her in his arms, kissed her, made love to her, fathered her children.

"Yes," was all she managed to say.

"Ruthie, I was wondering if you could help me out a bit. You know, a bit of cash. I don't want to bother you none, but if you can spare a bit, so I can get me a room when I get to California. I don't want to die in the freight yards. I'd kind of like to be in a bed."

Ruth stumbled through her answer, hardly knowing what she said, her mind was so jumbled in sorrow and revulsion. In a confused trance she made her way upstairs to her desk where she kept her ready cash, then down again to where Jonah stood waiting.

Her hands trembled as she unfolded the bills.

"Here. Here's five hundred. That's all I can get now."

Jonah stared blankly at the thick pile of crisp bills.

"Jesus," he muttered. "I thought you'd slip me fifty bucks or so."

He grinned at her, and for a moment there was a flicker of the spontaneous charm that had been so much a part of the Jonah Cutter she'd loved.

"Thanks, Ruthie. Thanks a million! You always was a good woman."

Jonah was visibly elated as he stuffed the bills into his pocket. Then his elation crumbled as a fit of deep, tubercular coughing racked his thin, wasted frame. When the spasm stopped, the flash of the old Jonah was gone, and Ruth saw only the old derelict.

"I'd best be going now," he said. "I can hop the next freight to El Paso and get a room with a bath somewhere. That'll be right nice after sleeping on a pile of rags for so long. Thanks again, Ruthie," he said as he turned and shuffled toward the door. "You're a right generous woman, to give me a hand after all these years."

When the door had shut behind him, Ruth went back upstairs to her room and sat numbly on the edge of her bed. She looked up at the silver-framed photograph of Alonzo that stood among the collection of family images on her night table. His full, handsome face, though serious, radiated warmth and love.

"What a fool, I am," Ruth said aloud as she studied Alonzo's face. "What a damned, sad fool!"

Then she threw herself face down on the bed and cried for the first time since Jonah had left her so many years before.

The family was well aware that Ruth began changing in the spring of 1935. Though she had never been a woman to wear her heart on her sleeve, this tendency became more pronounced, so that now Ruth Cutter could only be described as withdrawn and preoccupied. She became prone to long silences and spent more and more time alone in her upstairs sitting room. The changes in Ruth were gradual, so they went almost unnoticed for some months, until the summer, when Will, with a note of amazement in his voice, told Anna that he'd been told that morning by the superintendent of schools "how sorry he was that Mrs. Cutter had resigned her position on the school board."

"The hell of it is," Will then told his wife, "is that Williams heard that Ruth's dropped everything. Resigned as president of the Women's Club. Told the Junior League she won't chair the Christmas Ball. Same with the Cotton Festival Committee. I felt like a fool, not knowing a thing about this when Williams told me. He asked me if Ruth was sick, and I had to say I didn't know."

Will and Anna had understandably felt hurt by Ruth's secretiveness, but far more, they were concerned as to what could cause Ruth to give up those activities that had meant so much to her. It had been a decade since Ruth had given over management of the farm to her children, but she had done that in part because she wanted, after so many years of hard work, teaching and farming, to have more time to devote to what she called "good works." All the more puzzling, then, that she should give it up so abruptly, without telling them.

Will and Anna confronted Ruth with it—there was no reason not to, since the announcements that Ruth was stepping down from various positions, "for personal reasons" would be appearing in the papers in a matter of days.

Anna would never forget the look of stony impenetrability in her mother's face during their conversation; it was frightening to see the wall that had gone up between Ruth and the world.

"But why so suddenly?" Anna had pleaded. "It doesn't make sense, Mama, unless there's something wrong."

"I'm tired," Ruth had replied with a profound flatness.

"You weren't tired two months ago, Ruth," Will offered.

"That's why we're worried there's something you're keeping from us."

Ruth had managed a weak smile, intended to reassure them, but it was clearly hollow.

"Will, there comes a time in a woman's life when she wonders if anything is worth it anymore. I've just come to that point, that's all, and I just want to sit and be alone for a while."

It soon became clear that they were not going to get anywhere with Ruth; they knew her stubbornness all too well.

In the coming weeks Anna alternated between pain and anger as she watched her mother fade into a kind of pale spirit that roamed the vacant rooms of Casa Grande. All the life seemed to have left her—the spirit and strength that had seen Ruth Cutter through so many hard years had evaporated, blown away, as if by one of their spring storms.

Hardest of all for Anna to accept was her mother's withdrawal from her grandchildren. Ruth had always been attentive to Sandro and Mina, encouraged them in school and in their activities. She had made it a habit to go out to the corral to watch Mina ride every afternoon after school, and she usually sat in the music room and listened while Sandro practiced his daily two hours. Now, when Sandro and Mina got home from school, Ruth was already upstairs in her sitting room where she would stay alone until dinnertime.

During that summer the family's concern over the change in Ruth's behavior changed to alarm when she began to lose weight rapidly. Her appetite dropped, and she frequently vomited after eating. This went on for some weeks—Ruth passed it off as "some sort of summer influenza"—until eating became so difficult for her that Anna and Will insisted she see Dr. Henderson.

The afternoon of Ruth's appointment, Anna received a call from Henderson in her office at the farm. He told her he was admitting Ruth to Southwest General the next day for tests. Ruth of course pooh-poohed the whole idea, called Henderson "an alarmist," but she went to the hospital in any case and underwent a series of gastrointestinal examinations. Within the week Henderson confirmed that Ruth had a number of inoperable stomach and intestinal cancers and that she might have at most nine months to live.

Ruth took the news remarkably well; she even seemed to be less distant to the family. It seemed to Anna that, as ever, Ruth was not happy unless some great, difficult challenge lay before her. She was a woman who thrived on adversity.

"I've lived my span, had a better life than most," she told Will and Anna the day the diagnosis was confirmed. "At least now I can tidy my life up a bit, tie up the loose ends, and get into bed with a stack of good books."

Will admired Ruth's stoic attitude—who could not admire such a matter-of-fact approach to approaching death?—but he confided to Anna that one thing bothered him about it all.

"She decided to die. I feel it in my bones. She just made up her mind to die."

If Ruth had overheard Will's comment, which she did not, she would have been forced to admit that her son-in-law was right.

Chapter Five

IN LATE OCTOBER WILL'S PARENTS INVITED WILL AND Anna to dinner at their house in the city. They would have preferred not to go, since Ruth had just started into a particularly bad period, when the intestinal pain had become more severe, so much so that she had to be totally bedridden and sedated with morphine. But this particular dinner was being held in honor of Governor Ferguson and her husband James, and when Will's father had called with the invitation, he had made it clear that the Fergusons wanted Will and Anna to be there.

Will had never respected the Fergusons' politics, though he did admire them for their high-flying political savvy. After all, one had to stand somewhat in awe of a governor who, driven out of office by the rampant corruption of his office as Ferguson had been in 1917, could in turn get his wife elected governor in his place. Though "Ma" Ferguson had achieved an almost mythic status by the time she had been elected governor of the largest state for the third time, it was no secret that Jimmie Ferguson and his powerful political machine wielded the power behind her gubernatorial throne.

The evening was one of those glittering, sophisticated affairs that had been part and parcel of the Channings' lives for so many years. For the twenty-four guests seated at the damask-draped table amid a forest of candelabra and roses, it was as if 1929 had never happened. While conversing with the governor or the mayor, the dean of the college or the commanding officer of the base, as the Mexican footmen passed silver trays laden with oysters or Beef Wellington or Coquille St. Jacques, it was easy to forget that Jack Channing, though straight and hand-some as ever, had difficulty following conversations now; it was easy to forget that Edna Channing, though as witty and talk-ative as ever, found it hard to hold knife and fork with her arthritic hands; it was easy to forget that Ruth Cutter, who never would have missed one of her beloved Edna's dinners, was at Casa Portillo dying of cancer; it was easy to forget that Will was in a wheelchair and would never walk through the glittering rooms of his parents' home again.

And for Anna, as she mellowed with the wine and the candle-light, it was easy to forget that Bart would never be wholly hers.

The underlying feeling of the evening was summed up when Edna Channing stood as the brandies were passed, raised her snifter, and toasted, "Zur Götterdämmerung—to the twilight of the gods."

After dinner, as the guests retired to the small drawing room at the back of the house, Jimmie Ferguson asked Will to stay at the dining table with him, "for a little bull session." Once the other guests were gone and the maids had cleared the table, Ferguson offered Will a cigar—a fine Havana—and leaned back in his chair as he savored the aromatic tobacco.

Will made no pretense of small talk: though he didn't know Ferguson well, Will had learned enough from their few meet-ings when Will had been in the legislature at Austin to know that even when Ferguson suggested something as casual as "a bull session," he was intent on serious business.

Ferguson stared at Will, his gaze like a leopard before leaping to the kill. He waited for Channing to flinch, the sign for the leopard to spring, but Will held firm; his own gaze was as steady as the other's.

Ferguson smiled appreciatively. He'd been right: Will Channing might be in a wheelchair, but he was no cripple. He'd do just fine.

"I'll get to the point, Channing," Ferguson began in his hard, East Texas accent. It was a slow, calculated voice of smoke-filled rooms, not the chicken-in-every-pot voice of the campaign podium. "I don't care much for your kind of politics, and I'm damn sure you don't care for mine."

Will nodded in agreement.

"Good. We understand each other on that point. I got some interesting news—kind of a secret, just between us boys for now. Ralph Gillespie died on Tuesday."

Will was surprised by the news. Gillespie was one of Texas's more popular representatives in Washington. If he'd been dead four days, why hadn't it been in the papers?

"It hasn't been announced yet," Ferguson continued, picking up on Will's unspoken thought, "because we had a mite of housecleaning to do before the late United States representative's unfortunate demise can be announced to his devoted constituency."

Ferguson grinned, as if enjoying a private joke. "You see, Channing, Gillespie croaked Tuesday night in a whorehouse in Washington. In the loving arms of a Negress. A very attractive but very underage Negress so I'm told. And at the time Congressman Gillespie was wearing a garter belt and silk stockings thoughtfully provided by this minor Negress whore."

Will had to laugh at this one. It was the perfect scenario of a Washington sex scandal.

Ferguson let his guard down at Will's laughter and joined in.

"Damn it, Channing, why do they always have to keel over in some bimbo's undies? It would save the taxpayers of this Glorious State a fucking bundle in hush money if elected officials would croak at home in bed with their devoted wives."

"That would defy the laws of probability," Will volunteered. "A man has to sleep at home with his wife occasionally if there's going to be any chance of him dying there."

"As far as the voting public is concerned," Ferguson interjected, "Gillespie will have died peacefully at home in the bed next to his loving wife Theodosia—in his pajamas. Now my only problem is settling who I'll appoint to fill Gillespie's seat in the House for the remainder of the term."

Will couldn't resist the opportunity to get a jab in at Ferguson.

"Don't you mean who your wife, the governor, will appoint to fill his seat?"

Ferguson took Will's comment with good humor.

"Um. Just a slip of the old tongue. What I meant is who I would recommend to serve out Gillespie's term should my wife, the governor, ask my humble opinion on the matter."

"And what is your opinion on the matter?"

"I'll lay it out straight, Channing. Five years ago when you broke your back, I was sorry for you as a man. Nobody likes to see a guy wind up in a wheelchair, but I was just as glad to have you out of state politics. You know damn well I don't like independent-minded sons of bitches like you holding office. My life is much easier when politicians play ball *my* way on my team. That's no secret. Hell, the whole damn country knows that. As long as you were in office, being the damned renegade Democrat you are, you were strictly a burr under my saddle."

Will relished the "governor's" begrudging admiration.

"So what's changed, Ferguson? I haven't?"

"Washington's changed, that's what, Channing. That's why I'm sitting here with you right now. There's a goody-goody cripple in the White House, and it's not going to hurt the interests of the State of Texas if the governor appoints another goody-goody cripple to sit in the House of Representatives."

"So I'm a goody-goody cripple, eh?" Will found the description highly flattering, considering its source.

"Face facts, Channing. We've got an Eastern liberal-Demo president, and his Congress is pumping millions of taxpayer dollars into social programs around the country. If I put a little FDR in the House, it's not going to hurt Texas one bit. And you, with your liberal Democrat ways and your Eastern Ivy League education and your wheelchair—hell, how could I go wrong?"

Ferguson chewed his cigar stub, looking immensely pleased with himself.

"I won't vote your way, Ferguson. You know that."

"Sure. You'll vote what your sincere, honest politician's heart tells you. And if you want to tell the president about some great legislative program, your liberal heart has dictated to you, the president will listen, one cripple to another. And the result will be a helluva lot of federal dollars pouring into Texas."

"Are you offering me the appointment?"

"Are you turning it down?"

"Ferguson, I'm a cripple, not a fool!"

Will broke out into a long chain of laughter.

"So what's so funny, Channing?" Ferguson asked in response to Will's outburst.

"Just the damned irony of it all. I could have worked twenty years to get to Washington, like my father did. Now, just because I'm in a wheelchair, Washington is being handed to me on a platter."

Ferguson puffed cynically. "God works in mysterious ways."

Chapter Six

BART BRADLEY WAS ALONE AT HIS USUAL CORNER TABLE at The Back Door, listening appreciatively to the new musical arrangements Mike and the Streamlines were playing. This new sound was good, very good, he thought. Big, full-bodied sound, smooth as satin, dominated by a chorus of saxophones, clarinets, and muted trumpets. He'd taken something of a gamble when he told Mike Morales he wanted to be the first El Paso club to feature big-band, Benny Goodman-style music. It had been only two months since Goodman's opening at the Palomar in Los Angeles had crowned the bandleader as "The King of Swing," and the slick Goodman sound was heard constantly on the radio. Bart had sensed that this was going to be the hot new dance sound, but he had no way of knowing if local club-goers would take to it like radio listeners had.

For two solid months Morales had listened to the radio, bought every big-band-sound record he could get his hands on; he'd done his own arrangements in the style, then spent long days rehearsing the new musicians hired to double the band size.

Bart saw with satisfaction that the effort and expense had been worth it; at midnight the large, circular dance floor of The Back Door was crowded with elegantly dressed customers—by far the best crowd the club had seen in almost two years. The repeal of Prohibition had hurt the club's business considerably: since December of 1933, the revelers who had flocked to The Back Door to dance and drink could now choose from half a dozen similar clubs, all with legal drinking, all closer to the center of town. There had been many nights in the last year when there had been barely two dozen customers on a Saturday night. Now following a barrage of publicity about The Streamlines, The Back Door seemed to have recaptured the *crème de la crème* of local club society.

The band eased from the last strains of "Moon Over Miami" into "Stairway to the Stars." Not a single couple left the dance floor. The new formula worked—for the time being. Within a month or two all the other clubs would follow suit, and it would be the same old dog-eat-dog struggle.

Maybe it was time to chuck it all, he thought. The Back Door had seen its day, become a local legend of sorts. But things were different now. There were other clubs—that was part of it. But Bart was bored, tired of the routine, glamorous routine that it might seem. It was time for a change.

Bart glanced at his watch. Twelve-forty. She was late.

Funny, Bart said to himself, that he should still count the minutes until she arrived, that he should still feel a rush of anxiety, of anticipation when he knew he was going to see her. Why should he feel that way at all, knowing that, as usual when he saw her, she was with Will.

She had called earlier from the Channings', to ask if he could hold a table for them, for a party of eight or ten. He had frankly been surprised; she and Will had been frequenters of The Back

Door in its infant years, but since Will's accident, they had been only once. Tonight on the phone he'd warmed to hear their reason for coming: the mayor, a few of Channing's cronies, the C.O. at Bliss, possibly even the governor and her husband were coming along. Of course, Anna had seen a chance to give the club a boost. It certainly wouldn't hurt The Back Door's reputation any to have the governor stopping by when she was in town.

Bart spotted them across the club at the maître d's desk: Anna, with a pair he recognized to be the Fergusons, the mayor and his wife behind them, talking to some others.

She smiled and waved her fingers lightly at him when she saw him approach, an easy, familiar gesture, full of love and warmth. She had greeted him so many times over the years with just that little wave. It was a secret signal to him, a gesture of affirmation.

Bart loved those infrequent occasions when he saw Anna in evening clothes. Her beauty, which at home was too often masked in the practical clothes of farm work, emerged when she was dressed. The effect was like putting a handsome rock crystal under a black light, to reveal the hidden fluorescence. Tonight her inner light glowed with a special radiance. Her hair was pulled up off her neck and swept up into a dark crown of waves. She wore a turquoise bodice, cut low to reveal her full, firm breasts; at the hips the gown erupted into a sea of swirling turquoise ostrich plumes. Though she was thirty-seven now, the maturity in her face—the sharpening of her bone structure, the few fine lines at the eyes—only made her face more noble. He noted with satisfaction that more than one man in the club was admiring the little farm girl from Casilla.

There was the usual flurry of introductions and greetings as Bart saw the party to his table.

"But what about Will?" he asked, thinking that Channing might need assistance getting up the steps.

"He apologizes—sends his best—but he was wrung out. It's been a long day for him—a good day, I must say—but he really needed to turn in."

As she spoke there was a curious flicker, almost of anticipation, in Anna's eyes.

Anna had not gone to the club with the intention of being alone with Bart: She had thought Will and the others would be with her the entire evening. But, after an hour and a half of drinking and dancing, her companions had excused themselves en masse—with apologies for being "party poopers." They insisted that Anna not leave early on their account. "You're having such a good time, honey," as Ma Ferguson said. After all, they had their own cars, so she could stay as long as she liked. It had all seemed so casual, so easy—nothing suspicious, nothing out of the ordinary.

After the others had gone, after a few more drinks, and after a few more sensuous turns on the dance floor, it had been so easy to slip quietly away to Bart's office at the back of the club. It was more of a private retreat than an office, a dark, restful room with a burgundy carpet and rich, burled paneling wrapped in undulating curves around the room; a mirrored mantel reflected a glowing fire, and a deep leather sofa provided plush comfort.

"It's been a long time since we've been alone together," Bart said as he poured them brandies, then warmed the snifters in his palms.

"Six years this month." Anna nestled back in the corner of the sofa.

"How do you feel being here after all this time? This isn't exactly the most innocent—or safe—situation here, you know."

Bart walked over and handed her a brandy. He had loosened his tie but kept on his dinner jacket. He thought it would seem too anxious, too overtly sexual to start shedding clothes at this point. In the same vein he sat on the floor near the couch instead of next to her. He studied the fire thoughtfully as he sipped his brandy.

"You must be very pleased about Will's appointment. It's been rough on him—losing his career after the accident, living in that chair. I'm glad to see him getting another chance."

Anna detected a note of bitterness in his voice.

"That accident cost us all a lot," she said. "It's been a hard six years."

"It's taken everything I had to keep my distance, Anna."

She remembered that conversation when Will was in the hospital, when she had told him she had to stay with Will, that she couldn't endure the strain of an affair with him while having to renew her commitment to her marriage.

"I thank you for that, Bart. There have been so many times since 1929 that I have wanted to run away from everything, give it all up: the pressures of the family, the farm, and—I've got to say it—of Will's infirmity. I feel so damned trapped sometimes!"

Bart smiled, a smile of sympathy and concern; she noticed that his face had lost the intense angularity of his youth. There was a mellowness, a gentleness about him now that she had not sensed before.

"Who wouldn't feel that way, Anna? It's the old rock-and-hard-place story. But we both know you well enough to know you never could have lived with yourself if you had left Will. You're too loyal, too honorable. Before the accident, maybe. Afterward—no!"

"There have been times when I was so close. . . ."

"Why didn't you?"

"I knew you wouldn't let me."

Bart laughed at that. He reached one hand out for hers.

"You're right! I would have sent you right back home."

Anna was quiet, watching the fire while she gathered her thoughts.

"I suppose I'm growing up," she finally began. "I'm beginning not to be so angry about how my life has turned out. I'm thirty-seven now, my children are teenaged and will be grown soon. Mina has a woman's body and wants nothing more than to look like Harlow; she loves her car and her clothes. Sandro's already talking seriously about going to Europe to study music for a year before he comes back to college. They're becoming their own people. The day isn't too far off when I could be a grandmother—picture that! Everything seems so settled now, for better or worse. I have financial security, in spite of the Depression. I have a home, a style of living beyond my wildest dreams. I have lovely, intelligent children; a kind, loving husband; friendship; respect—the list of good things in Anna Cutter's life is endless."

A silence followed. They both knew what it was that Anna's life lacked, what both their lives lacked. It was difficult, after all these years, to say it.

The flames sent waves of deep, golden light into the room; the logs crackled; the rich, satisfying aroma of the brandy floated up into their nostrils. A warmth, an unspoken closeness enveloped them, pulled them back together. The gulf that fate had forced between them was closed; the unspoken had to be said.

It was Bart who turned to her, his hand still in hers.

"I love you, Anna."

He went up to her, his arms around her, her body against his. Six years—years of loneliness, of pain—vanished in that one movement he made toward her. His lips against hers were as familiar, as needed as they had been years before. The natural, instinctive meshing of their bodies, as powerful a force as it had ever been, was made even more so by their long separation.

When finally they pulled apart, they studied one another, their eyes reestablishing the familiarity long denied them.

Finally Anna spoke.

"What are we going to do?"

It might have been mistaken as a trivial question, had Anna's voice not been filled with a deep, genuine insecurity.

Bart, still sitting on the floor, leaned back against the couch, his head in her lap.

"I don't know," he said. Then he corrected himself. "I don't know what we *will* do. I can only think about the choices we have. What we *can* do."

Anna thought of the stumbling blocks, the false turns, the dead ends in her path. It seemed so often that there was no such thing as choice. Could she ever really take her life by the reins, lead it where she wanted it to go? She shared her thoughts with Bart and found, to her surprise, that he disagreed with her.

"You've made plenty of choices—you've exercised plenty of control. When your father left, you made the choice to stick it out at the farm. When you thought I'd died in Mexico, you chose to make the best kind of life you could with Will. When Will broke his back, you made a choice to follow your conscience and stick by him. I think you're confusing making choices with having control. That we'll never have—complete control. How do you think it's been for me, knowing how close I came to having you, 'free and clear,' you might say? How do you think I've felt seeing my son, my only link with immortality, grow up as another man's child?"

"You could have married, had a family."

"No—never." Bart's answer was firm, sure.

"Why?"

"I have loyalties too."

Anna felt a sudden wave of pity for Bart. He was so much—perhaps more—of a victim than any of them. She and Will had a life together, some kind of fulfillment. How selfish she had been to relegate Bart to outer darkness these last years, just to protect herself! She had cast him in the role of family friend, godfather to her children—safe, comfortable roles—anything but lover.

She went down to him, sought his embrace. Their bodies flowed, melted together with the same unquestioned ease they always had. This time no words interrupted their embrace; they went on until the moment passed, and they lay together, warm and naked in front of the fire.

Later, as they nestled comfortably together, Bart broke the silence.

"Anna," he whispered as he nuzzled her ear. "I want at least a part of your life. I'm not asking you to leave Will, to throw over everything for me. I just want to stake a claim in a small corner."

"Are you asking me to be your mistress once again?"

"Yes."

"I don't know, Bart. . . . I don't know if I can now."

Several hours later, as she left the near-empty club and hurried out to her car, Anna was too full of thoughts of Bart and the hours they had just spent together to notice a lone drunk sitting at a far corner table. But the drunk saw her, and when he did, his blue eyes hardened with deep, disguised anger, for he realized what his sister had been doing in Bart's office.

Chapter Seven

J. J. STEADIED HIMSELF AGAINST THE FENDER OF HIS truck. Shit, he said to himself, it's dark already. Just as well he get out of that bar, before he lost his damn ass.

Behind him, through the open door of the *cantina,* blared the tinny sound from the Victrola.

"Allá en el rancho grande . . ."

It had been that pretty little Mexican whore that had done it. She'd been hanging over him at the card table all afternoon, with her big brown breasts pressing against his back. She kept getting him to buy them beers. It was all a setup, he knew it. Just to get him drunk so those Mexican scumbags he was playing poker with could cheat him blind.

J. J.'s head spun into a white vortex that whirled down through his neck and chest to his stomach. His vomit spewed onto the ground and splashed onto his boots and the truck tire. When the retchings had passed, he wiped his face, then got into the truck and sped off along the dusty, rutted road that led from the adobe village of Caseta to the bridge that crossed the Rio Grande to the American side.

They're all no good, these Mexicans. A no-good sorry lot. A lazy, lying, cheating group of sons of bitches. They'll rob a man blind, prostitute their sisters, anything to avoid an honest day's work. Bastards ought to be locked up, every damn one of them. Or told to keep ten feet away from any white man. Those damn clip joints—every damn last one of them ought to be shut down.

That's it, J. J. said to himself as he sped along the dark river road toward Cutter-Channing Farms. Make these no-good bastards illegal. Close 'em up. Hell, his brother-in-law was going to be in Congress now. He'd do something about the goddamn Mexicans that were running the valley. Keep 'em all across the river where they can cheat and hire each other. Give the American side back to the Americans. There were too many decent white men out of work to let Mexicans get all the jobs.

J. J. reached under the seat and pulled out his flask. He took a deep swill of whiskey, felt it sear his throat and stomach. As he turned on the road toward the farm and Casilla he had an idea; he kept driving past the turnoff to Casa Grande, toward the low cluster of buildings that marked Hank's pride and joy, the Experimental Farm.

Might as well start by cleaning his own house, he thought. If the Mexicans had to be kicked back into place across the river, it might as well start with that gimpy pervert who was corrupting his brother. He'd send that queer bastard stumping back to Chihuahua. It was bad enough that his sister was sleeping with a goddamn greaser; now his brother was fooling around with one too.

J. J. flipped open the glove compartment and took out the .38 that lay among the jumbled papers. He felt the reassuring metallic weight as he slipped it into his jacket pocket.

There was a single light on at the back of the small adobe house that stood beside the acres of greenhouses. J. J. opened the door into the neat, sparsely furnished front room that served as Hank Cutter's office. Through the open doorway that led to the apartment at the back where Hank and Pablo lived came a stream of light and the aroma of beans and frying *taco* meat.

Pablo's young cousin was at the stove, stirring a skillet of fragrantly spiced meat. She was startled by the unexpected sound of footsteps but smiled when she recognized Señor Hank's brother from the big house.

"Perdóname, señor," she said, smiling self-consciously. She pulled back a stray wisp of black hair and straightened her simple cotton dress. There was nothing she could do about her bare feet.

"Dónde están?"

"Where are they? In bed?" J. J. strode brusquely past her and lifted the curtain that hung across the doorway to the bedroom. It was dark and empty.

"Not here, *señor*," she answered. She still smiled shyly; she had not yet caught the visitor's hostility. *"Fueron a Casilla. Para dos o tres horas."*

So the bastards were gone, probably up to some queer nonsense. He might just wait; he had nothing better to do. He went to the small electric icebox that stood in the corner, took out a cold beer, and settled into one of the wood chairs next to the table that stood in the middle of the room.

The young girl continued her cooking, her back to J. J. Her long black hair hung down her back; it stopped just at the place where her buttocks swelled out against the thin cloth of her dress.

"Cómo se llama? What's your name?" J. J. asked in his booze-slurred Spanish.

"Celia." The girl smiled shyly over her shoulder. She wasn't used to being alone with strange men.

"Celia, huh?" J. J. turned the name across his tongue appreciatively. She was one of those cute little Mexican tarts, the kind he liked. Young, before they got fat and saggy. She reminded him of that little tease of a whore back at the *cantina* in Caseta. This Celia that Pablo had brought across the river probably wasn't more than fourteen. Maybe younger. Slimmer, prettier than that whore across the river. Probably just as big a whore, though. They all were, he thought, these Mexican tramps. They start when they're ten or eleven. Sure, he'd seen plenty of them, selling it on the streets of Juarez. Hardly old enough to have breasts. He'd had lots of them for a couple of dollars in the alleyways and in the cheaper houses in the back streets. Young sluts with their smooth brown skin and no hair.

J. J. stroked himself casually through his trousers as he watched Celia at the stove. Maybe he'd stick around all right, knock off a piece before Hank and Pablo came back. This little bitch is probably hot to have a real man around the house.

Celia turned to get something from the table and saw J. J. grope himself. She flushed and turned away, thinking she wasn't meant to see. With one arm J. J. reached out and pulled her toward him; his other arm slid under her dress, his palm against her naked thigh.

"Come here, *señorita,*" he said, his speech slurred. "Let me take a look at that hot *taco* of yours."

Celia's surprise turned in an instant to fear and anger. She hadn't understood his English, but his meaning was clear. She stood back against the stove, trembly, wary, like a frightened doe. J. J. stood slowly, confidently, and approached her. His hands reached out and cupped her breasts.

"Don't pull away from me, Celia. I know you like it as much as the rest. Don't you want to try a little *chorro gringo?"*

His hands closed on her breasts, squeezed hard; then they moved lower, slipped under her dress.

Her back was against the stove, and J. J. pressed close against her. His drunken breath streamed across her face. His fingers probed hard, through her panties, and a stab of pain shot into her groin.

Though he was much bigger, she threw herself against him as he pinned her against the stove. The force of her weight, though ordinarily no match for him, caught him off-guard. He staggered to one side, lost his balance for a moment, and fell against the handle of the skillet. The skillet tipped and crashed to the floor, splattering hot grease across J. J.'s arm and onto the floor.

Even though numbed by alcohol, J. J. screamed out at the searing pain as the skin along the length of his forearm blistered and peeled off the underlying flesh.

As her attacker recoiled from the pain Celia broke and bolted for the door, but she was not fast enough. A brutal arm pulled her back, threw her crashing against the table. Then, a fist slamming against her face, and another and another. The brightly lit kitchen swirled into a vortex of red and purple; her stunned brain was only half aware of the rough hands that threw her back onto the table, that tore at her clothes, her flesh. She felt the crushing weight of his body, knew what he was going to do. Dazed, she waited helplessly for the pain she knew that was going to be down there when he entered her. She remembered, as if in her dream, the words of her mother.

"Celia, *querida,* it is always painful the first time. It is a woman's lot to suffer this."

But the pain never came; the man's weight was off her; he had done nothing.

"Bitch!" she heard him spit. "Bitch. Get up. Get up off that table."

Before she could react she was jerked off the table by her arm and thrown into a heap on the floor. Through her swollen eye-

lids she saw him looming over her. His limp manhood hung
from his open trousers.

"Come over here, *puta!* You know what to do. You've seen
your brother do this plenty of times."

She recoiled when she realized what he wanted her to do; she
tried to crawl away, under the table.

"Get over here, you little whore!" His boot slammed into her
leg, her belly. A wave of pain exploded into a scream.

"Shut up. Shut up, you little bitch!"

The blows came, again and again. Everything collapsed into a
dark sea of pain; pain that welled up into cresting waves, driven
by the wind of her own screams. Then Celia heard the storm
broken by a thunderclap. As she faded into unconsciousness she
knew it had been the sound of a gun.

"Are you sure, *muchacho?* Are you sure?"

Paco Sonora studied the angry faces of the grown men as
they riveted their dark eyes on him. The harsh light of the
kerosene lamp threw strong shadows. To Paco they looked like
dark angels. Avenging angels.

He drew himself up, feeling a grown man himself now. Never
mind that he had been stealing melons from the glass houses at
the big farm.

"*Seguro, Papacito.* It was *el señor* Cutter. Not the one who
lives at the glass farm. The other one. *El rubio.* The blond one."

Paco's father exchanged a knowing glance with one of his
companions. *El rubio.* Of course, it was J. J. They remembered,
when they were boys less than Paco's age, how the blond Cutter
son had tormented them, teased them. Called them "brown
niggers." *Caca.* Shit.

"He's an evil one, that *hombre malo. Bastardo.*"

The dozen men that crowded into the dark room broke into a
low, angry rumble.

"*Hola!*" A voice near the window whispered a warning. "*El
Jerife.*" He looked out carefully through the muslin curtain as
the sheriff's black Plymouth moved slowly along the deserted
lane toward the rail line and the main street of Casilla. The
sheriff and deputies, with Pablo, had already come by the Sonora house to ask questions about the murder. The men gathered there had known to say, "*Nada, señor, nada,*" when Sheriff

Hargis had asked. Only Pablo had looked suspicious at the men's professed ignorance, but he had said nothing to the sheriff.

When the sheriff's car had passed a safe distance, they sent Paco out after it. He returned five minutes later and confirmed that the sheriff and his deputies had turned onto the highway and driven fast toward Tornillo.

"Bueno!" Paco's father called out. *"Vámanos a la Casa Grande."*

A deadly pall had descended over Casa Portillo since Pablo and the deputies had gone into Casilla to try to find some lead on Celia's murderer. The maids, weeping at the news, had retreated into their rooms downstairs, with windows and doors locked, to say rosaries and light candles. Anna had sent Sandro and Mina to their rooms—an unpopular decision, since they had any normal adolescent's curiosity about the tragic events. But Anna felt it was enough that they knew young Celia had been murdered at Uncle Hank's house. She didn't want them to be on hand as the details of the sexual nature of the killing were discussed. She had called Will at his parents', where he had stayed for the weekend to get his father's advice on the first draft of his acceptance speech. He was going to come home immediately, of course, but he had warned her that it might be several hours before he could leave the city, since he'd given his driver the early evening off, and it might take some time before he got back to the Channings' to pick up Will.

Hank stayed with Anna, for which she was grateful. She knew, too, that her youngest brother, though private about his emotions, was devastated by Celia's murder. She had shuddered as her dark-haired brother, looking a decade younger than his near thirty years, described the scene.

"She was still alive when we got there, though she never woke up. The blood was pouring out, red, sticky, everywhere. Clothes torn . . . cuts and bruises. Her poor swollen face . . ."

She and Hank had decided to tell Ruth. She had been very bad the last week. Unable to get out of bed without suffering agonizing pain in her bowels, she had lain quietly, managing to drink only a few liquids. Morphine dulled the pain, left her on a serene, distant horizon. Ruth had understood clearly through her drugged haze what had happened. Her first reaction had been shock, then sorrow for the dead girl. She understood, too, how Hank and Pablo must have felt; she also advised her children to cooperate fully with the sheriff's office.

"This happened on our farm—in our home," she warned. "We have a responsibility to do whatever we can."

To that end she refused to take her next pill of morphine, even though it meant enduring greater pain, so she would be more alert to talk to the sheriff.

"So much evil, so much suffering," she whispered through her white, drawn lips as she sat the long vigil, waiting for the unknown to be discovered. "I wonder why it has to be this way, why our journey through this life is such a painful, difficult path."

She grasped her son's and daughter's warm hands in her thin cold ones.

"Why," she continued, "some lives end so quickly. Others—go on so long."

Hank and Anna offered up hollow words of consolation, as children are wont to do when confronted with a dying parent. They reminded her how well she'd been doing the last few months; they pointed out how much the morphine helped with the pain.

"Irrelevant, children. All of it irrelevant. I'm dying—it's as simple as all that. The one thing that unites us all, death. No matter how we get there—cancer, murder, a quiet old age—the destruction is always the same. In a few weeks my hopes and dreams will be as meaningless as the hopes and dreams of that young girl whose life was snuffed out this afternoon."

"Mother, don't torture yourself with all these morbid thoughts." Anna felt helpless, inadequate to comfort her mother.

"I'm not being morbid, dearest. Just realistic."

Ruth must have seen in their eyes that they didn't fully understand her point. She closed her eyes for a moment, gathering her strength, collecting her thoughts.

"Children," she began quietly, "have you ever wondered what happened to your father?"

Hank and Anna exchanged a quick, unsure glance. After some hesitation Anna answered.

"I—we—have never talked about him much, and never with you because I guess we thought the subject was too painful. But, of course, we have."

Ruth nodded in agreement.

"I was always grateful for your consideration. You never pried, never talked too much about him. I know now it shouldn't have been that way, not that you children did anything wrong—far from it. But I was spoiled, terribly spoiled, you might say, by being allowed to live in my dream world. I was never forced to face the truth. The truth that when he left, your father was gone forever."

"But you still loved him," Hank reminded.

"I always said that. I always told myself that. But I know now that it wasn't true. I was in love with a dream. And I learned that in the hardest, most painful way possible. You see, I have seen your father, just once, since he left in 1912. I saw him, talked to him, right here in Casa Grande."

Ruth paused while Hank and Anna silently absorbed the stunning news.

"It was only this spring when he showed up at the house unannounced. I didn't even know him, he was so changed. He was nothing more than a broken-down old derelict—a dying shell of a man. He wanted nothing more from me than a bit of money to go somewhere to die with a roof over his head and a bottle in his hand."

Anna found her mother's description of her derelict father curiously undisturbing, as if underneath it all she had always known this would be the end to her father's story. But how painful it must have been for Ruth to see him like that!

"I should have told you he was here," Ruth added. "It was unfair of me to deprive you of one last chance to see your own father. But I wanted to spare you—and myself."

"I'm glad you did it that way, Mama," Hank added. "Better to remember him the way he was once. I'm just sorry you had to see him that way."

"No, son," she disagreed, "it was best I did. Now the scales have finally fallen from my eyes. I can die knowing the truth.

My only regret is that I wasn't forced to see the truth years before—before it was too late. Before Alonzo was gone."

"What truth?" Anna asked. "That the man you loved, your husband, had changed beyond recognition?"

"No, the truth that I had stopped loving your father years ago when he left me. My love for Jonah Cutter died that spring when he left us after the flood. Died, leaving me only with the pain, the anger. I always told myself I still loved him after he was gone, but that was just an excuse—an excuse it's taken me years to realize I was making. I manufactured the dream of Jonah's return, the dream of my undying love for him, as an excuse for not loving again. So long as I pretended—to the world, to myself—that he was coming back to me, I never had to give my heart to another man. I never risked being hurt again. But oh, children, what a price I've paid for protecting myself like that, for I destroyed my second chance at happiness. What a fool your old mother was! What a fool!

"That would be the one lesson I hope my children would learn from me—that we only get to write the story once. If we want to make sure the story ends beautifully, we've got to do all we can to make it a happy story. That was my great mistake—I let one unhappy chapter become the whole book."

"But, Mama," Anna protested, "there's so much that's out of our control. We don't have choices."

"True. I couldn't control that your father left, I couldn't control that Alonzo died or that I have cancer. But in between those givens there is so much I could have done, so many choices I could have made. And my book might have had a happy ending."

Ruth took her son's hand, patted it gently.

"Hank, there has been a good deal about your life that I have had difficulty understanding and accepting. That's been a problem of mine—not yours. In spite of that, I recognize that you, of all the Cutters, are writing your happy ending. You've been more honest with yourself than the rest of us. You've made difficult choices but choices that have given you a real life, a meaningful life, based on what you like, on what you want. You haven't been seduced by the illusion of happiness, based on how things look on the outside. Your life isn't a lie all gussied up in the trappings of a big house and expensive clothes and new cars.

Far from it—and I expect there's more happiness in your little house and garden than there has ever been in Casa Grande.

"Since I'm not far from death and can afford the luxury of truth, I have to say that my other son is as much a failure as you are a success. Once again, I told myself lies about J. J., as I did about his father. I pretended for years that he was a better man than he was, that he would grow up, settle down, become some scrubbed-up mother's fantasy of a son. I had such high hopes, such grand illusions. It's hard for a mother, blinded by love and instinct, to see that one of her children is as big a failure as any cotton crop can be a failure. J. J. is never going to become a man, just as surely as Jonah Cutter is never going to walk through that door again.

"Anna, it's difficult for me to know what to say to you. We all have our private sorrows in this family—you as much as any of us. I know—I think Hank knows—the trap you are in, that you have been in for so many years. I admire your loyalty, your sense of honor, your sense of duty. But what a price you must have paid, what you must have suffered. As I understand so well, there are some losses that no material success can make up for. Perhaps someday you will write your happy ending."

Ruth was tired; the effort of talking had drained her, and she asked Hank and Anna to leave her to rest. She also wanted them to go out with her words fresh in their minds. It had taken her so many years to open herself to them, and she wanted them to get the most from it.

When they got outside Ruth's room, Anna excused herself to make a call to the city. Her mother's speech, especially after last night at the club, made her want to hear Bart's voice, even for a moment.

"Will?" Hank asked.

"No." She was matter-of-fact, and her candidness provoked a twinkle in her brother's eyes.

"I didn't think so. Fine, I'll go downstairs and give you some privacy."

Before she could leave Hank for her room they heard the front door downstairs and footsteps in the court. J. J.'s figure appeared below, bounding up the stairs.

"Hey, little brother," he called out when he saw them in the upper hall. "What brings you to the home place on a Saturday night?"

He came over to them, a stiff, insolent smile on his face. His clothes were rumpled, a stubbled growth on his face. His clothes reeked of stale alcohol and tobacco. Anna knew he hadn't been home since she'd seen him Friday night at the club. She just wished he would bother to find a place to freshen himself before coming home from one of his drinking and gambling bouts. It was even more offensive now—an intrusion on the time she and Hank had spent with Ruth.

"We were in with Mama for a while. She was feeling pretty good and kind of talkative." Anna was glad that J. J. had not been there. It would have stifled Ruth.

"Yeah? You two trying to get the will changed?"

Hank flashed in anger, but Anna spoke before he could.

"You're a snot, J. J. Keep your mouth shut!"

J. J. made a mock apologetic face, tinged with a leer.

"Hey, can't you two take a joke? Or did I hit the nail on the head? What's a guy supposed to think? It takes more than a free meal to get Hank to set foot in this place."

"Watch it, J. J. . . . ."

Anna sensed an anger surging up in Hank. She knew him well enough to know that once he was finally provoked to lash out . . . The thought worried her so.

"Look, J. J., I don't give a damn about your smart-aleck remarks or that you smell like every cheap *cantina* this side of Mexico City. We've had some big problems here today. Pablo's cousin Celia was attacked while Pablo and Hank were gone. She's dead."

J. J.'s eyes widened imperceptibly at the news.

"They know who did it?"

"The sheriff's department is asking around."

"One of those hobos that jump freights around here." J. J. shrugged his shoulders indifferently. "I guess we'll foot the bill for the funeral, huh?"

"You bastard!" Hank's suppressed anger erupted at his brother's callous remark.

"Listen, little brother, I had enough of you and that Mexican fruitcake you hang around with. For all I know, it was one of you perverts who messed up that Mexican girl."

Hank lunged at his brother, a cry of rage in his defense as Hank threw himself at his brother. Anna braced herself for the fight but was startled when J. J. screamed in pain and twisted away from Hank's assault.

J. J. stood a few feet back from them, doubled over with pain. His face twisted into an agonized grimace, and he clutched his right arm protectively. Hank stood poised, sucking his breath in great gulps, ready for his next assault.

It took Anna a few seconds to realize that Hank had not hurt J. J., that there was something wrong with his arm. She motioned for Hank to stay back.

"What's wrong with your arm?"

She approached J. J. where he crouched in pain.

"Nothing. Nothing," he gasped through clenched teeth.

She knew he was lying. She reached out quickly and pulled his loosened shirtsleeve up. J. J. gasped as the cloth pulled away from his arm. From wrist to elbow the arm was skinless, oozing pink flesh.

Anna recoiled, confused by the unexpected injury.

"I fell. This morning." J. J. tried to pull the sleeve down again.

From behind her came Hank's voice in a quiet rage.

"It's a burn. Grease burned you, didn't it? Look, there's grease on his pants too. You got burned when you raped Celia, didn't you? Hot grease from the stove. It was all over the floor. I saw it myself."

J. J. recovered himself, uncoiled from his writhing position. His pained grimace contorted itself into a twisted mask of cynical anger.

"You're crazy, Hank. You probably did it, you and that *maricón*. You're just trying to blame me for it."

Anna edged back toward the wall, sought the wainscoting for support. She stared at J. J., saw the truth in his face.

"You did it, didn't you?" Hank gasped. "You came back tonight, but we weren't there. She was alone and you molested her. When she fought back, you killed her."

J. J. regained himself. He stood up to his full height, the same indifferent leer on his face that had been there before.

"She shouldn't have fought me."

"Oh, my God!" Anna heard her disbelieving voice cry out and dissolve into sobs.

Hank grabbed her, pulled her away from the wall.

"Come downstairs, Anna. We got to call the sheriff."

"The hell you will," J. J. said, spitting venom. "The fucking hell you will. The girl's dead, it's too late to help her. You're not going to rat on your own brother, your own flesh and blood. We're going to leave things just the way they are. It'll all be forgotten in a few days."

No, Anna told herself. *This is not happening, I'm not hearing these words. A dream, it's a dream!*

"You are no flesh and blood of mine!"

The voice that came from Ruth's doorway was tiny, almost a whisper, but there was a deadly conviction in it.

She stood in her nightgown, her wasted body against the door frame for support. The small .22 glinted in her upraised hand.

"Get out, J. J.," she commanded in the same frail voice. "You are no longer one of us. Get out."

J. J.'s manner turned slimy, seductive. "Mama, you ought to be in bed. You're too sick to bother with this. It's just a matter between the three of us."

"You are no longer my son, J. J. You ceased to be that when you murdered that girl. You are a vile creature. An abomination."

J. J. made a step toward her. She fired a shot above his head. Her thin arm recoiled from the force of the firing, and the court echoed with the report of the gun and the sound of shattered glass falling from the dome to the marble floor below.

"I will be dead long before I can be put in jail," Ruth said calmly. "I have nothing to lose by shooting you."

"You would shoot your own son?"

"You are not my son—now!"

J. J. seemed to swell into a rage. He became a bloated, evil creature.

"Bastards, all of you. The filthy Mexicans have ruined you. That's all you care about, all three of you. Goddamned Mexican cock. That's what you all love!"

Hank started to lunge again, but Anna pulled him back.

"For God's sake, J. J., just get out of here," she pleaded. "Run away, do what you want—just get away from us!"

J. J. drew himself up even more. He looked smug, proud.

"Okay, big sister. I'll go. I'll let you alone with your house and your farm and your money and your crippled husband. It's all yours, little Miss Cutter. Except for one thing, one thing you can't have—thanks to me."

They stood in electric silence. He surveyed them one by one, a gloating, sadistic pride in his eyes.

"Bradley," he said. "That's the one thing I kept you from getting. I kept you from marrying that no-good spic. Who do you think tipped off the Villistas that one of their least favorite enemies was traveling alone in Mexico? Who do you think was responsible for your Mexican boyfriend spending a few years in prison? You have me to thank for that. And I'd gladly do it again. Anytime, sister!"

J. J. turned and strode down the stairs, leaving them in stunned silence.

J. J. was halfway across the lawn to where he'd left his truck parked in the drive when he saw them. Though it was dark, he sensed it was a large group; he could smell their anger. Instinct told him to hurry to his truck, to slip away before they got to the house.

He trotted to the truck, slipped in, and turned the key in the ignition. The sound of the engine alerted the approaching mob, and they streamed around the vehicle. By the time the engine had kicked over J. J. looked out on a sea of angry faces. Before he could make a move hands opened the door, pulled him out and onto the ground.

There was no shouting, no angry roar from them. They were at Casa Grande for vengeance, not attention.

J. J. tried to scramble to his feet, but before he could, a rake swung out of the darkness and slashed across his head. The sharp tines gashed his scalp to the bone, and the pain thundered in his head. Another rake slammed down on his back, and a hoe sliced into his belly. The wounds were deep but not fatal.

It was many minutes before their brutal work was finished.

Will dropped the telephone receiver back in its cradle. His shoulders slumped forward, and he rested his forehead on his palms in a gesture of exhaustion and defeat. After a long time, while he marshaled his remaining strength, he maneuvered his

chair away from the desk and moved it out of the library and
into the brighter, open spaces of the stair court. Anna was at
the front door with two of the maids, helping them hang the
purple-sashed wreaths on the door. The three women were
dressed in mourning: the old women in traditional black cotton
dresses to the floor, and Anna in a black wool suit and cloche
hat.

Will thought she had borne up under the strain of the last
two weeks terribly well. First, J. J.'s grim, shame-laden funeral,
now Ruth's death only ten days later. At least Ruth's funeral
would be imbued with love and sorrow, not anger and tragedy.

When Anna saw him wheeling himself toward her, she left
the maids to their task and met him halfway in the open expanse of marble floor. Her face was marked with concern, for
she knew what he had gone in the library to do an hour before.

"How did it go? I've been worried."

"As well as I could expect," Will answered. "Ferguson
seemed to be really disappointed. I guess he liked my politics
better than he let on. Of course, there was nothing he could do.
As always politics is a game of practicality, not sentiment. As
he put it, 'I just managed to keep one scandal out of the papers
with Gillespie. I can't turn around and have my wife appoint a
man to Congress whose family is already scandalized in every
paper in the state.' "

Anna was not surprised at what Will told her about his conversation with the governor's husband. They had known all
along, underneath it all, that Will could never be appointed so
close on the heels of what the papers called "The Cutter-Channing Tragedy." It had been an irrational hope that the one
bright ray in this black time might be Will's renewed political
career. That bright ray had been extinguished on the grounds of
Casa Grande, on the night of J. J.'s death.

Anna took her husband's hand in reassurance.

"I wish I could put in words how I feel. . . ."

"There's nothing to say, really, Anna. I've just got to live
with it."

Will gasped, stifled a sob. Anna knelt down beside him, her
arms around him. His chest heaved as he fought back the tears.
For the first time in his life Will came close to breaking, to
letting go in a flood of rage his anger at the blows fate had dealt

him. It had taken every ounce of strength in him to fight back from the terrible blow of the plane accident; one thing that had helped him overcome that tragedy was the hope, the dream of a renewed political career. Now that dream was shattered forever. At that moment, with Anna's arms around him, he wanted to spew out his anger, his rage. But he could not, for her sake. She had suffered so much, lost so much, with her mother, her brother. He could not bring himself to burden his beloved Anna with his agony. Once again he would have to be strong for her.

"Will, Will," she whispered. "It will be all right. I'm here."

"I know, Anna," he said, sobbing. "You are here, and I thank God for that. It will be all right."

Part V

THE YEARS

OF PRIDE

1938–1945

Chapter One

CONSTANZA VARESE NARROWED HER EYES CAREFULLY AS she looked across the crowd jammed into the garden room of Elsie de Wolfe's Villa Trianon. She intended the lowering of her shadowed, long lids over her famous gray-green eyes to look regal and seductive, which it did; what she did not intend was for anyone to know that she was squinting because her near-sighted eyes could not focus on her hostess and a cluster of guests at the far side of the gaily striped pavilion, near the piano.

Constanza was not a conventionally beautiful woman. *Striking* was the word most often used to describe her appearance. She stood almost six feet tall with a full, rounded figure that, had she not dieted carefully, might have blossomed into the Rubenesque. Her face was broad and smooth; her undistinguished nose and mouth were compensated for by her pale, translucent skin and her astonishing, large green eyes. Eyes, as the joke went, "that with one glance could make any man reconsider fidelity to wife and family—and which often had."

The feature by which Constanza was most easily recognized at Parisian balls or in the shops of the Place Vendôme was her thick crown of deep, golden red hair, which she typically wore pinned in a mountain of curls pulled up to reveal her lovely neck and shoulders, of which she was exceptionally proud.

Paris has always been home to women like Constanza, though in her time she was the best known of her ilk. Very little was known of her past and her origins. No one knew if she had ever been married, though she had a series of lovers for as long as anyone could remember. In earlier years—for Constanza had been in Paris for a very long time—her lovers had been men of wealth and position, though in recent years her tastes had turned to younger artistic types. Constanza's wealth was as well kept a secret as her age. No one knew where her money came

DENNIS SANDERS

from, though it was suspected that she had profited from her older, wealthy lovers. But she had her apartment on the Avenue Foch, her personal maid, winters in Cap d'Antibes, and a wardrobe so vast that one wag joked, "Constanza's closets could clothe the French army—if they were willing to fight in negligees and ball gowns."

Though Constanza's bearing was elegant and regal, she was by no means formal. Though she could, and often had, deported herself in a salon full of nobility and heads of state, she was known as a woman who knew how to have fun. She was as welcome among the costumed students at the Quatre Arts Ball on the Left Bank as she was at the Palais Royale. Her repertoire of off-color jokes was endless, and her slightly cynical wit made her a great favorite among the sleek fashionables at Elsa Maxwell's or Elsie de Wolfe's; she could amuse Noel Coward at luncheon with her marvelously told stories or converse intelligently with Gertrude Stein about modern art and literature.

Constanza in particular enjoyed Elsie de Wolfe's to-dos, even though it meant trooping the ten miles out to Versailles to Elsie's Villa Trianon, which she shared with her "lady" friends. De Wolfe had established her reputation as a decorator, based on her exquisite taste and skillfully put-together decor; her reputation as a hostess was based on the same set of skills. Elsie expertly mixed period French and modern in her rooms and made it work; her parties worked in the same way. At Elsie's the tired, if glamorous, old faces were always leavened with a generous sprinkling of unknowns and newcomers on the Paris social scene.

Constanza stopped a waiter long enough to commandeer another glass of champagne. Lady Mendl always served good champagne, usually a Dom Pérignon '28 or '29 and chilled to more than the traditional degree, just the way Constanza liked it. She spotted Countess Rossakoff behind the waiter and, knowing that the countess was always up on who's who and who's new in town, asked about the group their hostess was shepherding through the party.

"Oh, Connie, you *are* so predatory," Countess Rossakoff chirped with delight on being asked to impart some of her painstakingly gathered gossip.

"Well, they are a *handsome* group," Constanza replied, evading the countess's implications.

"Elsie's boys always are." Rossakoff screwed her prunelike face into an even prunier configuration.

"Pity she doesn't do anything with them."

"Oh, *mon Dieu,* never! Lady Mendl is a confirmed Sapphic. How she manages to find all these delicious young gods I'll never understand. Though from what I understand, most of them are Ganymedes."

Constanza squinted again, trying to focus on the group in discussion.

"This group doesn't look especially gay to me," she observed. "At least not all of them. Who are they?"

"Musicians. This season Elsie's adopted musicians. Last year it was sculptors. Before that, scenic and costume designers. Cecil Beaton, that crowd. These boys are from the conservatory —students of Boulanger. Milhaud and that crew. But I'm *dying* of curiosity—which one have you set your cap for? Surely you're not going to have affairs with *all* the males at the Paris Conservatory."

Constanza started to tell the countess to mind her own business, but curiosity got the better of her. Rossakoff could tell her what she needed to know: she wanted to be fully armed before she assaulted her target.

"The one second from Elsie's left. Tall, slender. Dark hair. Doesn't look very comfortable—probably shy."

"Ah, that one! I might have guessed. You do have impeccable taste. He's American—a Texan, of all things. And wealthy, so Elsie tells me. Oil or cows or something. Doesn't look like a *cowboy* to me—rather too refined and aristocratic."

"What does he do?" Constanza felt a twinge. There was something exotic, sensual about an artistic type from the Wild West. She suspected a sensitive wildness.

"Do? Why, I wouldn't know. I haven't slept with him."

Constanza shot a look of mock *hauteur* at the countess's good-natured teasing.

"Nor, I suspect, will you ever, *chérie.*"

The countess looked crestfallen.

"No, it's true. Not even footmen and stable boys want this wretched old body anymore. My days of glorious affairs are long past. I can no longer experience great love, I can only report it."

The hyenalike old woman brightened and clutched Constanza's arm with a conspiratorial claw.

"So, I accept my fate. And I will tell you *everything* I know about him, with the promise that you must tell me everything about the affair you are surely going to have with him—knowing you."

"You question my motives."

"No, darling, I understand them. Since I am *hors de combat,* I will share what I know, which is not much. He's a pianist, studying with Cortot, and I think theory with Boulanger. He has a flat somewhere in Montparnasse with the fellow next to him—that divinely willowy Englishman. I'm sure there's no hanky-panky between them, since that Englishman is screwing Genevieve Lefcourt three afternoons a week.

"As for the American, he's as of yet unconquered, at least by any woman I know. We had a few words at one of Elsie's "dos" in the city. He speaks French but with a *divinely* American accent. He's really quite sweet and rather bashful, though I suspect he's a terror when aroused."

"We'll see," Constanza let a bemused smile play across her lips.

"So you're going to be George Sand to his Chopin."

"Actually I had in mind to be Steinway Grand to his Paderewski. I see him improvising rhapsodic fantasies on my keyboard."

"A most thrilling idea," the countess said wickedly. "But do be careful when it comes to the fortissimo climax, *ma chérie!* At your age you're liable to break a string."

"Bitch!"

Constanza left the countess to bury her barbs elsewhere and sailed through the crowd to where the diminutive Lady Mendl was holding court with her protégés. She bypassed Elsie without a glance and went straight to the handsome American, who seemed a bit startled by the tall redhead's approach.

"I am Constanza Varese," she proclaimed, "and I will be simply heartbroken if you do not sit down this instant and play for me.

Mina sped along the deserted ribbon of the river road. The car's headlights cut into the darkness, illuminated the rutted dirt road and the pale trunks of the cottonwoods that lined it. Beyond the range of the car lights was a black void. She watched for the road that cut off to the right, leading to the Mirkovsky farm. She drove another thousand feet, then slowed, looking for the scarred tree trunk to her left that marked the hidden path that cut off from the road to a grassy, tree-canopied arbor next to the river. As she slowed and turned, her headlights played across the shape of the hulking black Cadillac parked among the trees.

Mina was surprised by the involuntary shudder that flittered down her spine. The Caddy had looked ominous, hearselike, waiting in the shadows. Strange that a car she'd seen dozens of nights in the same place should spook her. It was her nerves, she reminded herself. She'd been on edge all day. All those endless hours of conversation at Sunday dinner. Grandpa Jack and Granny Edna down from the city, her parents, sitting in that mausoleum of a dining room over roast goose and talking about Nazis and Fascists and British appeasement policies and whether or not there was going to be a European war. It had been bad enough hearing all these years about the Depression and the dust bowl and the New Deal and everybody being broke, even people with money. Now all she heard about was military aggression and oppressed Jews and rabid Nazis. It seemed like everyone was standing around waiting for lightning to strike or the earth to open and swallow them up. All they could do in the meantime was talk, talk, talk about their impending doom. No one seemed to know how to have a good time anymore. It was all a bore, these Sunday dinners, and she felt so left out.

Thank God she had Johnny. At least when she was with him, there was some fun, some glamour in life, not all of that high-minded, down-at-the-mouth squareness she got at home.

As Mina pulled up alongside the limousine, a black door swung open to admit her. She killed her own lights and engine and pulled her red fox cape close around her bare shoulders, not so much to keep off the January chill but because she looked smashing in it. She slipped out of her car and into the dark, cushioned warmth of Johnny's car. Even as she slid into the backseat next to him he pulled her against him and kissed her deeply, without a word. Mina gave in, let his lips and tongue have their way with her. She loved his warmth and fragrance; his skin always radiated heat against her, and there was a heady aroma of cologne and tobacco and brilliantine that surrounded Johnny. It was a rich male smell, and it excited her.

When they finally separated, Johnny fixed Mina a Manhattan from the small bar that folded out from the back of the seat. Mina stretched back in the plush moleskin luxury of the upholstery. The bourbon and vermouth burned her throat, but she could feel the effect of the alcohol almost immediately.

"I told you that you should of gone to the track with me today," Johnny remarked when she told him about her family Sunday. "Helluva lot more fun than all those political snobs your folks hang around with. We had a great time today. Lost a bundle."

"Johnny!"

Mina always had an involuntary reaction when she heard Johnny had lost at gambling. It seemed like such a waste. Yet Johnny always had an endless supply of it—thick rolls in his suit pockets. Mina admitted that there was something sexy about watching Johnny's hairy, manicured hands peeling four or five hundred-dollar bills off a roll and slipping it through the betting window. She felt sexy, even powerful being seen with a man who spent money like that. And she secretly loved being seen in public with Johnny, in the clubs and private casinos in Juarez—at La Cucaracha or The Kentucky Club or La Noche Grande, in which Johnny was a partner. Everyone in that world knew Johnny Rodriguez and his friends; they looked at him— and the woman on his arm—with admiring eyes.

"You sound like somebody's mother," Johnny shot back after her exclamations about his track losses. "And you're eighteen and gorgeous—too young to be anybody's mother."

He nuzzled her neck, then ran his hand along her thigh.

"That's why I always carry rubbers."

A flash of anger shot through Mina, but she held it back. Johnny was so irritating. Sometimes he would say something sharp and critical, like telling her not to "mother" him, or something vulgar, like the remark about prophylactics; at the same time he would be gentle and attentive. She never knew quite how to react, and it put her on edge.

"Come on, Johnny. Don't be in such a rush. It's only been three days since you saw me. At least let me relax a minute."

Mina moved her leg away from his hand, though she let him continue nuzzling her.

"Oh, I get the picture. Then let's really relax."

Johnny flicked on a small light over the bar tray. Sitting on the tray next to the liquor was a small round mirror, not much larger than the mirrored top of one of Mina's compacts. On the tray was a slender silver tube about three inches long, and four inch-long lines of cocaine, which Johnny had carefully laid out with a small penknife that lay next to the tray.

Mina leaned forward, took the tube, and held one end at her nostril and the other near one of the lines of white powder. She inhaled deeply through her nose and felt the pungent cocaine burn its way into her nasal passages. She repeated the operation once more with the other nostril, then handed the tube to Johnny, who snorted the remainder of the cocaine on the mirror.

By the time Johnny had finished and turned to kiss her, Mina was wondering how she could have been in such a bad mood before. A sense of optimism, of enthusiasm, suffused her. She was so silly to let her parents, her friends, anything, bother her. And wasn't it great that such a tiny bit of coke could make all her troubles seem so insignificant?

Johnny pulled her close. His hands stroked her breasts, her buttocks. She pushed against him, a deep need surging up in her.

"That's more like it, kid," he whispered. "That's my little Mina."

She felt him swelling against her through his trousers. Her hands clutched the massive, familiar bulge. Only three days, she thought, and she was already anxious for him. She opened his zipper and plunged her hand into the tangle of shirttails and flesh.

Johnny's hot, wet breath streamed out of his nostrils and across his face. His swollen tongue and lips roughly explored her own, then he pulled away.

"Before we get too far, I've got a nice little treat for you."

Mina didn't speak but waited for him to explain.

Johnny reached for the jacket that lay crumpled in the seat next to him. He fumbled in the pockets, then extracted a small leather case.

In the dim light Mina thought for a moment that it was a jewel case—that he was giving her a gift.

"Just look at this, baby. This will really put you on cloud nine."

Johnny opened the case.

Inside the case, against a rich velvet lining, lay a hypodermic syringe. Its chrome and glass glinted ominously in the light.

"Johnny," Mina whispered. "I don't know . . ."

"Don't worry, baby. Johnny knows what he's doing."

Every Wednesday, as she had for five years, Anna went to El Paso for the day. Her Wednesdays "off the farm" were part business and part pleasure. While in the city she would call on the bankers and accountants who handled affairs for Cutter-Channing Enterprises or meet with the cotton agents and purchasing officers who were so anxious to do business with the Channing farms—especially now that the political tensions in Europe had sent cotton prices on yet another prewar escalation.

Anna usually stopped for luncheon with Edna and Jack, though in the last years her visits had become less of a pleasure and more of a daughter-in-law's duty. The magnificent white-columned house on "The Avenue" was still as beautifully maintained as it had been in the golden years when Anna had first seen it, but the jewel was in a tarnished setting now: so many homes near the Channings' had suffered from the Depression and were ill-kept or closed or turned into rooming houses and homes for the elderly.

Inside was faded glory. The chandeliers still gleamed; the parquet was polished to mirror the *boiserie;* the gilt frames and damask still displayed their richness to the eye. But all the life had gone out of the house—the glamour, the spirit, the sense of fun and good times and creative ferment. Senator Jack was still as handsome a man as ever, tall and straight, with his full head of silver hair, but his mind had faded slowly into a dim, childlike thing. He wandered around the hollow rooms with his male nurse in tow, constantly looking for things he had lost years ago, asking why everyone was late, worrying that the maids were poisoning his food. And there were those times when he turned violent, threatening the maids, calling out vile words.

The doctors had said there was no hope for Jack—a clear case of senile dementia—and they had urged time and again for him to be put in a home. Anna and Will were torn about the idea, but Edna was adamant: Jack was staying with her in their home, so long as they could afford their live-in staff. Will and Anna wanted them to sell the house and move to Casilla, but Edna dismissed it with a curt "We have so little left, at least let us keep our home."

It was difficult to argue with Edna's position; they could certainly afford to have nurses and cooks on hand, yet in the back of their minds there was the idea that Jack, in one of his madder moments, might slip away from his nurses and attack Edna. Anna understood Edna's determination, though, because Jack Channing was the one activity left to Edna. In the last years her arthritis had gotten much worse; her tall, bony frame had become twisted and warped, and for over two years now she had joined her son in confinement to a wheelchair. She was in constant pain. Anna had watched many times as her knobbed, twisted hands clutched the arms of the chair, kneaded the wood until the knuckles turned white, as a distraction from the pain. The days of the grand parties and the banquets and Sunday salons filled with the rich and talented and beautiful of the city were gone. All of Edna's ferocious energy was boiled down, concentrated in her crippled body, and her only outlet was her devotion to Jack.

Anna was always depressed when she left the house. She always remembered the early days when Senator and Mrs. Channing had led such charmed lives. They had everything, and how she had admired and envied them! She never would have imagined them fading into such a sad twilight, and it hurt her to see them this way. Anna also knew that deep down she was frightened by Will's parents' fate; every time she saw them she found herself imagining what her life would be like in twenty years.

Because she knew the luncheons on Montana Avenue would be depressing, Anna reserved hours afterward for pleasurable diversions, shopping at the department stores near the Plaza

Theater, a stroll through the plaza to watch the two fat alligators who lived in the fountain basking in the sun. Or perhaps catch a new film in the rococo fantasy of the Plaza Theater—so charming with its auditorium designed to imitate the courtyard of an Italian villa, complete with vines climbing over walls and a ceiling full of twinkling stars. Anna enjoyed seeing films by herself; she enjoyed the luxury of being alone, being caught up in the oversize fantasy on the screen. And she enjoyed not having to talk to anyone about the film afterward. There were so many films in color these days—really magnificent, though the vividness sometimes made her eyes tired. Still it was quite an innovation and very realistic—certainly an improvement from the days when she and her mother and the boys had sat in the converted garage behind Wasserman's, watching Gloria Swanson and Francis X. Bushman while Ola rhapsodized on an out-of-tune piano in the corner.

Anna had been at the Plaza Theater a month before, when she and Will and a group from Casilla: Kate and Max, the Wilkinsons, Dr. Henderson, and May, had come up to see *Gone With the Wind.* She and Will had read the book the year before, and she had to admit that the movie was every bit as good. Today she saw *The Women,* in black and white, and obviously taken from a stage play. But the movie was interesting because its cast was all female with Clare Boothe Luce's wonderfully clever and bitchy dialogue. The film was really very funny—Anna was laughing as much as anyone, especially at Roz Russell's antics—but it was all about relationship problems—about divorce, love, about men and women having affairs behind each other's backs. It felt good to be able to laugh about such things.

After she left the theater, instead of going back to the parked car, Anna walked up the steep slope of Mesa Street to where the mansions of Sunset Heights overlooked the city. Halfway up the hill she turned on a side street, then into the alleyway that cut between two streets of Victorian houses. When she came to the back gate of the corner house, she turned in, climbed the steps to the wooden back porch, then took a key from her purse and let herself into Bart's house.

Even after five years of Wednesday afternoons Anna still noticed the antique mustiness of the house: it smelled of another century. Though her visits to the house were as regular and familiar as her meetings at the bank or her lunches with Edna or her movies at the Plaza, Anna still hurried up the dark, carpeted stairway; she still stopped to look in the mahogany-framed pier glass to reassure herself that she looked good; she still felt a surge of arousal as she opened the tall, dark door to Bart's room, knowing that he would be waiting for her inside.

Bart was already naked, standing by the corner table that held an ice bucket and an assortment of liquor bottles. He had heard her on the stairs and was already dropping ice cubes into a tumbler.

They were both used to their Wednesday afternoons. There was a familiar, intimate warmth to their greeting. Bart continued mixing drinks while Anna put her arms around him and kissed his chest. They exchanged a few words about how the day had gone, what the news was since they had talked last.

The years had changed Bart physically. His face still had the hawklike strength of his youth, but a few deep creases and lines added depth and maturity. His head of hair was still full but now with as much silver as black. His shoulders were still broad and straight, his arms firm and thick. But there was a fullness, a manly softness about him, a slight thickening at the waist and thighs that was as attractive to Anna as his leanest, hardest years. In her mind his body had changed over the years from the taut, poised panther, lurking in the jungle foliage, to the full-blown, mature lion, walking with unchallenged confidence among his pride.

As always their casual, inconsequential conversation blended into their lovemaking. Within minutes their drinks would be sitting half full on the table by the bed; Anna's clothes would be tossed across the damask chair in the corner, and the intertwinings of their pale naked bodies would be reflected in the beveled glass of the wardrobe across the room.

Their lovemaking—much like Bart's body—had ripened and matured. There was a spaciousness, an openness that had replaced the hot intensity of the early years. They had the leisure and the knowledge of each other's most intimate desires, to explore, to vary, to create. They would sometimes share an afternoon of little more than foreplay interspersed with laughter and relaxation; at other times they would generate an intense, almost otherworldly coming together in which arousal built into endless waves of orgasms.

This afternoon, when their lovemaking stopped, Bart, nestled against Anna's body, fell into a quiet slumber. Anna tried to nap, as she often did with Bart, but couldn't. The warm breeze that fluttered through the curtains would ordinarily have lulled her into a dreamy, cozy sleep, but today her mind was distracted by flickering, insistent thoughts. She found herself feeling irritated, frustrated, because she was going to have to get up in an hour, get dressed, repair her hair and makeup, and drive back to Casilla. It was no different from her usual Wednesday routine, but today the thought of it irritated her.

When she and Bart had first started their assignations in the city, the stolen hours had been golden, savory. She had not minded leaving him to return home, because it was so welcome just to be with Bart for those few hours. In the last year there had been an edge of discontent in their meetings, especially since Sandro had gone to Europe, since Mina was spending so much time away from home, since Ruth and Alonzo were gone. Even J. J.'s volatile presence was missed, and Hank and Pablo still lived their hermitlike existence at the Experimental Farm. The afternoons with Bart had once been fit into a hectic, full life. Now, with Casa Grande so much quieter, the Wednesdays at the house on Mesa Street were not enough. How wonderful it would have been if she and Bart could have gone for a drive together or gone to the Paso Del Norte for cocktails and dinner in the hotel's vast marble dining room. But the reddening sunlight through the west window was like an alarm clock, signaling that her stolen time was over; she had to get dressed and go back to reality.

"You're feeling lonely," she told herself. "Odd, Anna Cutter, but you're lying in your lover's arms and you're feeling lonely."

When Bart awoke, he sensed her mood and asked what was the matter. She tried to pass it off as nothing, but he insisted that she "fess up."

"I know this is going to make me sound like I'm a spoiled little girl," she confessed, avoiding the issue of loneliness, "but I don't want to go home. Isn't that silly? I don't want to go home, and I'm feeling angry about it because I know I have to."

"You don't have to, you know. No one is holding a gun to your head to get you out the door. Least of all me."

It was a curious remark, almost insensitive.

"I know I'm not being forced to go. But I am, by my conscience, by my loyalties. More than anything in the world I'd like to forget everything in the valley. Just pack it in, run away with you."

"We've tried that, darling. It didn't work out, and now it never can."

Bart pulled her close beside him, cradled her in his arm.

"Anna, I've worked like a damned Trojan to make myself as content as possible with our situation. God knows it's taken every bit of strength and self-control I've got. I thought you had come to accept things too. Accept that if all we can have is a few hours a week, we'll just have to make the best of it. We're not kids anymore. We don't have the options of youth. All we can do is behave like grown-ups—we're getting on to grandparent age, hard as that is to believe."

"Is having a secret affair behaving like grown-ups?"

"It's behaving like human beings."

"Sometimes I hate myself for doing it. I hate the dishonesty of it. And even after all this time it's still hard for me to face Will when I walk in the house. I feel so guilty, like I've misbehaved badly."

When Bart spoke, there was a flat, distant tone in his voice. "Do you want to stop?"

Anna pulled herself even closer against him.

"My God, no. Never. You are the one thing in my life that brings me any kind of fulfillment now. Everything else seems so hollow, so meaningless. Even the farm, something I thought would always make me happy, has just become a machine for making more money."

"What about Will? Is that a problem?"

"Will is still the kindest, most loving man anywhere. He's generous with his heart and his mind. That's one reason I feel so bad about everything. If I could hate him, if he were insignificant or pitiful . . . But he's good and noble, and he doesn't deserve what's happened to him. It's just that I feel so helpless when I see him. So inadequate. And it's worse, having to sneak around like I do."

"Aren't you being a little hard on yourself? You didn't put Will in a wheelchair, and you can't get him out of one, no matter how much you love him or how damned devoted you are. Don't you see, you're just feeling nasty because you're sneaking around, getting from me what you can't get from Will? Take it easy, Anna. After all, you're not the first woman who ever had a lover on the side. There have been a few million in history ahead of you."

Bart's words were unexpectedly stinging. She felt a confused anger, a need to defend herself without quite knowing what for.

"I do. I do recognize how guilty I feel—"

Bart interrupted her. His own voice had taken on a sharp edge.

"Let's face the facts—at least the facts as I see them. Like I said, we're too old not to think like grown-ups. To be honest, Anna, I think you do love both of us very much. Sure, you may say that the love you feel for Will is different than the love you feel for me. That sort of crap. But you still love us both. That's okay. I've made my peace with it, a compromise all around. Will gets the home, the family, the shared life. I get the passion, the sex, the intimacy. You get both—at the price of shame and guilt. So let's just accept the givens in the situation and make the best of it so we can enjoy what Lady Luck has deigned to offer us."

There was something goading, hurtful, about the truth. She felt prodded to the edge of tears.

"Oh, God, darling," she said, choking, "I just wish it could all be different. Simple. If we could just wipe the slate clean, start over."

"We can't," Bart whispered. His voice had gone tender again. "God knows I've wished it were possible."

He paused to light a cigarette, puffed deeply, and exhaled a long swirl of blue smoke, which curled and mingled with the motes that danced in the sunlight.

"Anna, do you realize how many years I've carried around a burden of anger, of real hatred for the world, since I came back from Mexico and had to accept that you would stay married to Will? That anger is as real now as it was thirty years ago. It's been my burden in life."

"It could have been . . . should have been so different."

Anna thought for a moment of J. J.'s betrayal, and the pain surged up through her in a nauseous wave.

"I've often—hell, constantly—thought what it might have been like if I hadn't been trapped in Mexico, if I'd come back in time."

"It would have been so wonderful. . . ."

"I wonder sometimes about that. We know each other now, as adults, as two human beings who have gone through life the way we have. But I try to think back, to remember who I was in those days. I think I was a very different Bart than I am today. Anna, I honestly think that it wouldn't have been what we thought it would be. In those days I really was a bit of a scoundrel."

"That was part of what I loved so much."

"Yeah, but would I have made you happy? After all, I was spoiled, conceited, arrogant. Used to getting anything and everything I wanted. Including women. I probably would have broken your heart. In those days Bart Bradley didn't deny himself anything. That's the irony of what happened to us—you were the first thing I'd ever wanted badly that I couldn't have."

He leaned down and kissed her forehead gently.

"You see, that's been the lesson in life I've had to learn. That I couldn't always have my way. If I hadn't been deprived of having you totally, I'm sure I wouldn't have grown up very much. And I probably wouldn't be a very nice character—I'm still spoiled enough as it is. Can you imagine if I'd had the biggest prize of all handed to me on a silver platter instead of it going to another man?"

It was a sobering thought, that the life she had dreamed she could have had with Bart might have turned out very different than she imagined. More sobering, still, was being reminded that their only choice was to accept what little they had, to make the best of it. Life with few options seemed bleak, gray. She also realized that she too seldom thought about the burden Bart had carried with him; he was a strong man and not one to complain.

"I am being too self-centered, aren't I?" she asked him. "Too caught up in my own problems. I forget that when I go back to Will and my children and the business and all of those things that fill my life, you're left leading a pretty solitary life."

"I like that in some ways," he answered flatly. "Or at least I'm used to it. But the rest of my life, the part outside of our relationship, has been bothering me lately. I've been feeling restless, dissatisfied. Thought about it a lot, too, and I know now what's the matter. I'm feeling middle-aged and useless. All the years I was running the club, even though I was kind of a social maverick, I was doing something I liked, something I believed in. It was nothing profound, just the pleasure of watching people having a good time, thanks to a place and atmosphere I'd provided. Now I'm restless to get back into something I can care about, something that can keep my brain busy when I'm not with you."

Anna wondered if Bart had found an answer, but before she could ask, he made an abrupt change of direction.

"You're still planning on going to Paris this winter to spend the last semester with Sandro, aren't you?"

"We're undecided. Everything was set, but now that the war has started, it's risky. Sandro has his heart set on staying until July—says he wants to see one last Bastille Day before he comes back to settle into life as a cotton farmer. It's just that Will's concerned that the Germans will move into France. Even though we're neutral, it could still be risky for Americans abroad. And it's impossible for Will and me both to stay the full six months. He wants to go for six weeks and have me stay on with Sandro. Now we don't know—it all may fall through."

Bart paused to light another cigarette. Anna studied his face. He looked moody, concerned.

"Something's come up, Anna. Out of the blue. The kind of thing I've been waiting for, to get me involved in something besides living off my investments."

He was pacing himself, building to something.

"I got a call two weeks ago. From General Messing. He's the one at Fort Bliss that I was at West Point with. He'd just gotten back from Washington from a round of meetings with the Chiefs of Staff and the State Department. In some quarters, at least, no one's taking chances that we're going to be neutral forever. The State Department is looking for civilian advisers—preferably men with several languages and a military background. The State Department is going to place a number of civilians in Europe, in some capacity for the embassies, as advisers and intelligence analysts. Messing said that on his recommendation the State Department would offer me a post."

Anna felt a sharp twinge. She was torn between the good news and the thought that Bart might go away. She forced herself to be honest.

"I don't know how I could stand not having you here."

"That's just it. Messing said I could have my choice of cities. London, Madrid, Lisbon—or Paris." His eyes brightened. "Don't you see? The post is only a year—July until July, the time when you'll be in Paris. I'd have time with Sandro, then after Will comes back to the States, we'd have four, five months together."

It was as if a cloud had moved from in front of the sun; a warm, radiant prospect opened for Anna, a prospect of time—weeks and weeks—with Bart, away from the reality and restrictions of Casilla. How many years she had hoped for such an opportunity, yet it had never come—until now. She could accept anything, a lifetime of Wednesday assignations, if she could only have a few months alone with Bart.

Then her natural caution took over.

"I don't know. We'd have to be so careful. I couldn't stand it if Will suspected we'd set things up. . . ."

Bart chuckled unexpectedly.

"Too late for that. He already knows a lot!"

Anna started to panic, but Bart reassured her.

"Not about that, you sexy goose. About the State Department offer. Messing did a bit of checking around before he talked to me. He knew that our families have been close for years, so he called Will, for a sort of recommendation as to my qualifications, character, et cetera."

"He should have called me," Anna interjected. "I'm the expert on your qualifications."

"Don't be a smart aleck. I don't know what Will said; must have been positive, since Messing didn't drop the issue. But Messing also must have told Will quite a bit about the post, because Will called me this week and said he hoped I would take the job and ask for the Paris assignment so I could 'keep an eye on his wife and son.' "

Anna didn't know how to feel; jubilation, hope, fear, uncertainty danced around in her. It seemed impossible that she

might have this particular dream come true; she wanted desperately to have it, to leave for France that very instant. Yet another part of her reminded her that she had been disappointed
and thwarted so much in the past, it could so easily happen
again.

The sun through the windows was now faded to an orange
ember. It was late, and there were still the miles to drive to
Casilla. That was all she could do now—go home, go about her
business. Life as usual. The dream of time with Bart might
come true; it might not. Until it did, she could only hope.

Chapter Two

OUTSIDE THE WINDOW OF ANNA'S ROOM THE TRAFFIC ON
the Avenue Montaigne was chaos. Autos had jammed the street
since early morning, and a cacophony of honking, gear-grind-
ing, and shouting filled the air. It was too warm to leave the
windows closed, yet the noise that poured in through the open
casement grated on Anna's nerves.

She paced through the suite, from the mantel past the love
seat, over to the window, then through the bedroom and into
the bath. She checked every closet, every drawer for what must
have been the twentieth time, but all her possessions had long
since been packed into the valises and steamer trunks that stood
near the door.

Eleven-fifteen and still no sign of Bart or Sandro. She rang
the concierge and asked yet again if by chance one or more
messieurs was waiting for her in the lobby: the concierge betrayed no hint of impatience when she insisted again that he
ring her the instant anyone asked for her at the desk. She then
had the switchboard ring Bart's room again, only to hear the
long, frustrating chain of buzzes from the unanswered room
phone.

From outside came a particularly loud shouting. She went to the window and saw two plump, agitated old Parisian men engaged in a heated argument about who was to blame for the locked bumpers of their cars. Ordinarily such a street argument would have seemed quaintly Gallic to Anna, but now the heated tempers betrayed a dread and anxiety. Above the chaos of the streets the rooftops of Paris were as beautiful, as magically seductive as ever; it seemed impossible that this exquisite creation of man might be destroyed by man—that Paris and all it stood for might be wiped from the face of the earth.

Anna was seized by feelings of dread and fear that Sandro and Bart might not come back. Perhaps the Nazis were already in Paris and Bart and Sandro already captured. Yesterday, when Bart had told her to prepare to leave, the idea of Paris being captured had been surreal, incomprehensible. Now it seemed all too real—and all too inescapable.

The last seven months had been magnificent, a dream come true, from the moment she had stepped off the Pan Am clipper at Marseilles to find Bart and Sandro waiting for her on the runway. There had been uneasy moments before the trip, even as letters from Bart and Sandro had arrived in profusion in Casilla, detailing their adventures "palling around" in Paris, and urging her and Will to come as soon as possible after Christmas. Then Will's spinal problems had gotten worse. The damaged, eroded discs caused severe pain in his upper back, making it almost impossible for him to sleep comfortably. Some nights he even resorted to Veronal to mask the pain. Finally the specialists in El Paso had put Will on a special hydrotherapy program—three hours every morning in a whirlpool bath installed in the sun room, with a physical therapist in attendance to supervise exercise designed to strengthen the muscles. The therapy helped a great deal, but the doctors insisted that Will continue the daily treatments for at least a year.

Traveling was out of the question for Will, and it seemed unwise for Anna to go to France alone, with England being bombed and most of Europe east of France in the clutches of Germany. She and Will had even discussed making Sandro come home early, before the spring semester of 1940 was finished, though they had finally decided that with Bart in Paris and the American embassy only a phone call away, Sandro could be called to safety if the situation became critical and the Germans invaded France.

Anna fought to hide her disappointment, but Will had sensed it, anyway. One evening, just before Christmas, he said unexpectedly over dinner, "I've been thinking about France. And how much you've had your heart set on it. Why don't you go?"

Anna pointed out the risk and uncertainty, to which Will commented, "If we think it's safe enough for Sandro, it's safe enough for you. Besides, since you can fly across now, you're only twenty-four hours from New York. And Bart's there, to keep an eye on both of you."

And Bart's there. She pictured herself in Paris with him.

"Who knows, darlin'," Will added. "Paris, all of Europe, may never be the same. Maybe you'd better see it while you can. So go for a few months. Lord knows after all these years you've earned a leave of absence from the farm."

"I don't like the idea of leaving you. . . ."

"Don't be silly, Anna." Will had grinned. "I'm not going anywhere . . . and I'd be happy to know you were having a good time with Sandro."

So it was settled, and she had made travel arrangements to New York by train, then twenty-six hours by plane to Marseilles, then with Sandro and Bart on the Blue Train to Paris, her first time there since her honeymoon with Will in 1920.

Anna had taken a suite at the Plaza Athénée, on the same floor as Bart's room. It was all very open, very above board. As their "unofficial chaperon" it was perfectly logical for Bart to stay close by. When Sandro came alone or with friends to see his mother at the hotel, Bart was on hand, like the close friend and neighbor he was. The three toured Paris together—dinner at Tour d'Argent, Sundays at the Louvre or in the Bois de Boulogne. There were student recitals at the conservatory where Sandro and the other students performed under the more or less approving eye of their teachers. There were the elegant salons in the sixteenth arrondissement, cultured, sophisticated "open houses" held by the wealthier and more cultured side of Parisian life that always cultivated the new crop of artists and students that flocked to the City of Light. And there were more unbuttoned, bohemian evenings at the drafty, cluttered flat Sandro shared with his English fellow student Nigel Eccles, evenings with an assortment of variously eccentric and unusual friends communing over a common interest in culture and wine and cheese, all provided in ample quantities. Sometimes these student salons were attended by Nigel and Sandro's teacher Cortot; Jean Cocteau was there once with a beautiful redhead named Constanza, whom Sandro said had been a good friend and had introduced him to much of Parisian life.

Sandro always played for his guests, and Anna in particular always enjoyed his impromptu recitals. There was a definite difference in his music making since he had come to Paris. The long hours of practice showed in far greater technical proficiency, and there was a poetry there that she had never sensed before. Cortot himself described it as "fire tempered by intelligence."

Anna often sat next to Bart while their son played, relishing the thought that, finally, in this special way, they could be a family together. Bart understood her thoughts as well. Often, as the fellow guests applauded Sandro, Bart would exchange a look with her, in acknowledgment of their proud secret.

During their days—so many of them were the gray, wet days of the Parisian winter—she and Bart were often alone while Sandro practiced and attended classes. They explored the city, the Ile St. Louis, Montmartre, the Left Bank, even the humble *cafés* and *charcuteries* of the working-class districts of the eastern part of the city. There was one memorable afternoon when they made love, hidden among the mausoleums and statuary of the cemetery of Père Lachaise.

The nights were theirs, too, after Sandro and his friends had gone back to the flat in the Rue de Varennes and left she and Bart at the hotel. Bart would light a fire, call down for champagne or cognac, depending on their mood, and they would make love in the flickering golden light. Afterward they would throw open the tall French windows that opened onto the little wrought-iron balcony and look out over the dark rooftops of the slumbering city. Perhaps most wonderful of all was the luxury of sleeping together—so long denied them. Their bodies, in the spacious linen-sheeted bed, would intertwine and move together through the night, until the distant church bells and pale eastern light awakened them at dawn.

Then in May—a glorious blossom-laden May—the death

knell to her dream sounded. The German Blitzkrieg swept Belgium and the Netherlands into German domination, and the French army crumbled, leaving France itself open for invasion. First Dunkirk, then the fall of Amiens and Arras.

Even though the northeast was under German control, France did not believe that she could fall. Surely the Americans would now give up their neutrality. Surely in a matter of days Roosevelt and the Congress would send their troops to France to repel the Nazis. The City of Light still basked in her own beauty, her own importance, her own inviolability. Hitler could never march down the Champs Elysées. Until the Americans came to save them, all Paris could do was eat and drink, to love, to enjoy, as she always had.

Anna had been caught up in the mood of disbelief too; the world did not exist beyond the confines of the city. It was so much easier to cling to each lovely June day, in the firm belief that some miracle would keep the Germans from Paris. It was an understandable belief, for the closer the Germans came, the closer Bart and Anna came to being forced back to the reality of America, of Casilla, of the rest of their lives.

Finally, on June thirteenth, Bart had come back to the hotel, looking tired and disturbed. For a week now he had spent long hours at the embassy, in emergency meetings.

She knew instinctively what he was going to say. France was doomed, and their time together there was ended.

The harsh ring of the bell startled her from her memories. It was the concierge announcing that Bart was downstairs.

In moments Bart came in without knocking. He was slightly breathless and must have run up the stairs.

From the alarmed question in her eyes he knew her concern.

"No, he's not with me. But he's all right. I'm sorry this all took so long. There was no way to phone. The lines were jammed. You must be in a state."

He pulled her to him and kissed her deeply. She could feel his heart pounding against her breasts. He lingered for a moment on her lips, then pulled away reluctantly.

"There's no time," he whispered.

"But where's Sandro? I can only guess what the Gare St.

Lazare is going to be like today. And all of his luggage to be gotten through this traffic as well as mine."

Bart went to the bar and poured himself a whiskey.

"I'm afraid, darling, you're about to make your first sacrifice to the war. The whole damned city is like the Avenue Montaigne, or worse. Forget the trains, forget your luggage. At this point it's all we can do to get you and Sandro out of here. The Germans are twenty miles from the city, and every second counts.

"Everything's set up—that's what took so long. I've arranged for an embassy limousine, with diplomatic escort, to take you and Sandro directly to Bordeaux. I have a man who will try to get your luggage out later, though there won't be any guarantees. The limo leaves at one from Port d'Orléans. I'm afraid you'll have to walk the three miles to get there, but it's the fastest way, given the traffic. Sandro's already on his way there."

"Bordeaux? I don't understand."

"Le Havre is still free but too far north for comfort. I don't doubt the Nazis will be there by tomorrow morning, and even if not, the Channel's too dangerous. I've gotten you on a freighter sailing out of Bordeaux on the fourteenth; the officials in Bordeaux have already been notified that you're coming—and to give you VIP treatment. You won't have any trouble getting through."

Anna suddenly felt weak, exhausted from the strain of the last days. Now the reality, the finality of their flight from Paris drained her of her last drop of energy.

She went to where Bart stood by the bar and leaned her forehead wearily against his shoulder.

"I think I need a quick shot of that too. One for the road, so to speak."

Bart poured two fingers of whiskey and handed her the glass. The liquid burned her throat, but the warmth was a welcome distraction.

"In spite of all the arrangements being made," she said, sighing, "I'm still glad I'm not making this trip alone. I'll feel so much safer with you along."

Bart gulped the last of his drink. His eyes focused on the window.

"Anna, you don't understand. I'm not going with you."

She didn't believe him, didn't want to. But the words had been clear and sharp, like a crystal dagger.

"No! You can't mean you're staying here. Not with the Nazis taking over. It's foolish—suicidal."

"Anna!" He tried to calm her. "I'm not staying in Paris, I'm going south—into Spain."

Anger welled up in her—blind anger at the thought that Bart was going to be pulled from her once again.

"But is this some kind of lark, Bart? This is no time to gallivant through Europe. If it's necessary for me to leave my luggage and flee, it's necessary for you too!"

"You don't understand, darling. I'm staying to work with Intelligence—joint American and British. They don't expect me to stay in France now—too risky—but Spain, later England. Depending on how the war goes."

"It's not safe here. You can't take that chance!"

"I'm not sure it's safe anywhere now."

Bart's voice had a calm finality about it that sent a shudder down Anna's spine.

"I can't bear the thought of anything happening to you. . . ."

Bart pulled her close.

"Now, darling, my heroic days are over. I'm too old to be the cloak-and-dagger type. I'm just going to be a bureaucrat—doing translations, reading a lot of secret reports written by the real spies. Maybe a bit of hanging around criminals and hoods to pick up a bit of information about the black market. Nothing too glamorous."

Anna could find nothing to say. The fear she had had for her own life had changed into something much deeper and more painful—the fear of life without Bart.

Though she struggled not to, she began to cry. She crushed her tearstained face against his neck, then her lips moved across his flesh. His comforting arms pulled tighter around her.

"Please, Bart," she whispered. "There's time—a few minutes. Please, just once more, before I have to leave."

His lips found hers; they searched, tongues probing, breath intermingled.

Silently they lowered themselves to the floor, their bodies in a feverish tangle. There, against the music of the frightened city, they made love.

"*Chéri,* you are not the first man to ask me to go away with him. *Vraiment,* Sandro, you are only one of many. But no man has ever succeeded in persuading me to go to his farm or his ranch or his castle in the highlands or his cottage in the lowlands."

Constanza lay back in the chaise in her *petit salon;* her golden-red hair cascaded down to her shoulders, framing her round, pale face. Her small mouth turned up a bit at the corners as she spoke, giving her an expression of wry amusement that might have been misunderstood as flippant, but her deep green eyes were filled with warmth and tenderness.

"But this is different, Constanza. I want to marry you!" Sandro sat on the floor next to her, his hair and clothes disheveled from their recent, hurried lovemaking. His face, still flushed with sex, was intense with emotion; his dark eyes betrayed anger and love.

"Trying to make an honest woman of me, my dearest?" Constanza lay back even farther, making no attempt to keep her satin dressing gown pulled around her. Her magnificent heavy breasts, her full hips and thighs, were casually exposed, a pink alabaster Odalisque.

"Don't be cruel!" Sandro's anger surged to the surface. "Are you deliberately trying to break my heart?"

"No, no! Never that!" She pulled him close to her again, cradled his head against her breasts; her flame-nailed fingers stroked his dark, damp hair lovingly.

"Sandro, my darling, you must understand your Constanza. I am lighthearted, *amusante,* gay—but never cruel, even when I make little jokes. But you see, my little Texas *pianiste,* you are trying to make me something I am not. Constanza can never be a wife or mother. She can only be a mistress, a lover. That is all she desires in life—it is her calling, her career. No man—not even the most tender, the most wonderful, the most desirable as you—can take her away from her chosen way of life."

"This would be different, Constanza. I know, I understand you—I love you."

"I am afraid, Sandro, that now your glorious youthfulness is showing. I do not mean to hurt you, *chéri*, but all of the men who have asked me to marry them have believed to the depths of their souls that they would be different. That their love could make a happy marriage. *C'est dommage*, Sandro, but love, though it is the noblest, the greatest of human emotions, cannot change the object of the love. *L'amour* does not conquer all. Even your love, Sandro, cannot change me."

Sandro balked at her words. She was so calm, so firm about it. Surely, given what they had shared over the last year, she would have a greater conflict in rejecting the offer of a shared life. Perhaps it was all just a brave front, to cover her real feelings. He ventured a thought.

"You're not just concerned about our ages and all that, are you?"

Constanza tossed her head back and emitted her silvery, musical laugh. Somehow the laugher was so filled with warmth that Sandro didn't find it offensive.

"Oh, my sweet darling, it is that and so much more too. True, I am old enough to be . . ."

She hesitated, censored herself through long habit.

". . . to know better than to marry one of my young lovers. You see, Sandro, our affair for you was like going to school. *L'école d'amour*. A valuable part of any young man's education. I am like a very good, very valued professor at a fine, respected school. No one would deny that you needed to learn what I have taught you, but to marry me would be like spending the rest of your life in school. Though the thought may cause you much sadness, it is time for you to take your diploma, to leave your alma mater—no matter how much you love her, how much you will miss her."

Sandro bit his lip, clenched his eyes, manfully fighting to control his tears.

"I feel like such a damned child," he said with a gasp. "I'm sorry if I embarrassed you."

Constanza stroked his head gently.

"You were a child when I met you, Sandro. But now you are a man—a beautiful man. And never, never could you embarrass me. You have made me feel young and beautiful and desirable. A happy woman."

Sandro stood beside her, his hand still clasping hers. "I have to go. We have to meet the car at one."

He began reluctantly to button his shirt. His eyes focused on the familiar details of the peach and gilt *boiserie* that had witnessed so many hours of their lovemaking. He had never imagined that he would be leaving the salon today without Constanza.

"I still want you to come with me, Connie. Not as my wife— but as a friend. You can't stay in Paris now. It's too dangerous. Bart has arranged papers and passage for you too. I told him you were coming, though I didn't tell him I was going to ask you to marry me. He just thinks you're a friend. But you can't stay here—America's much safer. You don't even have to come to Texas with me. If you want to, go to New York, Boston. If you need money, I can arrange that."

"You see—you *are* a man! No child would make that offer to the woman who has just rejected him."

"So you'll come?"

"No."

Sandro started to speak, but she interrupted him.

"Darling, this is my home, my life! I will run away from nothing. Pooh! The damned Nazis don't bother me. I have always known how to take care of myself. Constanza will still be in this lounge on the Avenue Foch long after the Germans have run back across the Rhine."

"I hope to God you're right."

Sandro was dressed, and there was nothing more to do but leave. Constanza stood and pressed against him, her warm, naked flesh against his clothing. They kissed intently, with a passionate lewdness that made Sandro want to take her again, heedless of what might be passing in the world outside.

Finally she pulled away.

"Thank you," he whispered.

When she spoke, her voice was unsteady and betrayed her emotions.

"Sandro, when you come back to Paris—and you will—you will come to see me, won't you?"

"Of course, I promise."

Finally he slipped out the door and into the uncertainty of the besieged city.

Chapter Three

IN THE YEAR AND A HALF SINCE ANNA AND SANDRO HAD
sailed back from France, the Channings, like many Americans,
had clung to the vain hope that they would escape the dark
cloud of war that was obscuring the world. At every dinner
table, every business meeting, every social event, there were
arguments, pro and con, polite and angry, about whether
America *would* get into the war, whether America *should* get
into the war. The plight of Britain and of the overrun nations
was dreadful, and it seemed impossible for Europe to remain
free from the Fascist monster if America did not join. Yet there
was the fear of what that meant to every American family.
Anna and Will knew they had a son who might be sacrificed;
Anna also knew that the longer the war lasted, the bigger it
became and the longer it would take for Bart to come home.
Lurking behind that was the terror that he might not come
home at all.

Bart wrote them regularly from Europe, for a while from
Spain, then from Algeria, Spain again, then England. His letters
were chatty, casual, good-natured, but lacked any real information on what he was doing. Anna also noticed that the letters
often bore several different postmarks, and all seemed to have
been opened and resealed by a censor, she assumed. She
thought of Bart constantly, but it was unsettling for her not to
be able to picture him in any one setting, as if the dark cloud
over Europe had swallowed him.

Life in Casilla had been quiet but busy during 1940 and 1941.
As it had in 1914, the distant war caused the Channing coffers
to swell. Military demand for cotton and for copper spurred
Will and Anna to maximize their output. Rising prices swelled
the flood, and the lean years of 1930 through 1933 seemed far

away indeed. Sandro had enrolled at the College of Mines. He spent weekdays in the student dormitory on campus and came to Casilla on weekends, when the house was livened with his music and with the company of newly made friends from the college.

Mina had finally enrolled at the college as well, though the move was halfhearted. She seemed to be doing it for lack of anything better to do, and her grades reflected it. Mina also stayed away from home many weekends, usually with the excuse that she was behind in her work and had to "cram." However, at the first of the month there would be bills from stores for clothing, bought on the days when Mina was supposed to have been locked in her room with her books. And on more than one occasion she called up her father to ask if he could possibly send her some extra gas coupons. She was obviously driving a lot around town. What worried her parents the most was that Mina was totally silent about who her friends were. When Mina had been at home, they had at least seen her with some of the local boys she dated—young men Mina rather summarily dismissed as "hicks." Anna recognized that Mina, like many teenage girls, aspired to more sophisticated company than boys her own age. Anna saw nothing wrong with that per se; she just worried that Mina did not have mature enough judgment to choose her companions carefully.

She and Will had talked often on the problem, but as Will had said, "There isn't much we can do, can we, short of following her twenty-four hours a day? Mina's always been secretive and stubborn; our keeping after her would only make her more so. All we can hope for is that we raised her right and that she'll have enough sense to take care of herself, to catch herself if she makes too big a mistake."

Anna agreed with Will in principle: they couldn't follow Mina the rest of her life. But there was a nagging concern with Mina, a concern she didn't have with Sandro. When her son had gone off to Europe, Anna had assumed that he would be human, that he would do things that she didn't approve of as a mother. But she had always trusted him, trusted his judgment. With Mina it was different. Anna worried that she didn't know her daughter well enough. There was no doubt that there was a distance, a barrier between them that didn't exist between Anna and Sandro. Anna was willing to accept that. It was just that Mina seemed so often to be angry, surly, anxious to pull away from her family.

Anna tried to attribute Mina's attitude to the fact that she was spoiled, which she was, and to her youth, which always needs to assert independence, even in a rebellious manner. But there was always that deep uneasiness that something was wrong with Mina's life. Anna could accept that Mina was determined to pull away from life at Casa Grande, to expose herself to a bigger canvas; she had accepted the same need in Sandro when he had asked to go to Europe. What was hardest of all in Mina's case was the sharpness with which she severed her apron strings; sometimes even the most casual inquiry provoked a curt "Everything is swell" to a blunt "Mama, you know I'm old enough to take care of my own business, and I'd like it if we just don't talk about it until doomsday."

Kate Mirkovsky had been with Anna one day when Mina had made just that remark. After Mina had left, Kate told her friend that she thought she was letting her daughter behave like a spoiled brat.

"As long as you and Will are footing the bill for the car and the school and the fancy getup, it's a damn sight your business what Mina is doing," Kate had warned with her usual candor. "Not to mention that you and Will have invested nigh on to twenty years of love and attention in the girl."

Anna had explained to Kate, rather defensively, that she didn't want to be one of those parents who gave money—or love—with strings attached.

"That's a smart attitude," Kate agreed, "provided it doesn't backfire on you. A body's got to watch his investments, and a kid's as big an investment as any piece of real estate."

Once the news of Pearl Harbor and what Roosevelt called "a day that will live in infamy" screamed across the American consciousness, everyone began preparing in his mind what the war would mean. The Christmas of 1941 was no different from most Christmases in the valley: clear, mild weather; many parties and celebrations; lovely decorated trees brought down from the Sacramento Mountains. But in the back of all minds was the thought that future Christmases might be very different. In addition to her worry about Bart, Anna had now to think of Sandro, since it was probable that he, like most of the valley's youth, would be drafted into the service within a matter of months.

In February Sandro received a notice to report for his physical; by late March he was packing to report for basic training at Ft. Hood, outside San Antonio. The news of the Japanese capture of Guam and the Philippines and of the German sweep across Latvia, Estonia, and into Russia brought home the dreaded reality that American soldiers would soon be in combat. The Channings knew that there was no guarantee that Sandro would not be among them; they recognized the reality that someone's sons had to be in the front lines, but like all parents, they secretly hoped their son would see safe, domestic duty somewhere in the States.

With American patriotism surging in response to the declarations of war, it was only appropriate to give the valley's sons a patriotic sendoff to the service. Sandro was only one of many; almost every military-aged male was either drafted or joined a branch of the service: Wilkersons, Pettuses, Rodriguezes, Calderons, Andersons, Vandermans, Gonzalezes. Max Mirkovsky, who was one of the first to try to enlist, was, to his dismay, one of the few his age who was not going, a victim of one bad ear and flat feet.

Will and Anna, with deference to the days of Ruth's charity affairs, organized a war-bond dance at Casa Grande with the departing sons in attendance with families and friends.

It was a bright, happy affair, full of music, bright decorations, and the contrast of evening clothes with stiff new uniforms. The casual observer might have called the ball "rousing," but on closer look, he would have seen the glints of fear and uncertainty that lurked in everyone's eyes, both those who were departing and those who were remaining behind.

Almost two years passed before Sandro was shipped overseas. As the statistics of American casualties soared into the tens, then hundreds of thousands, especially in the brutal Pacific theater, the Channings were thankful that their son was safely peeling potatoes at a base in Kansas. Still there was the uncertainty of not knowing when or to where he would be called.

There were occasional leaves for visits home; she and Will managed one trip to Kansas themselves. But Sandro's weekly letters, filled with the same kind of homely detail and half spoken loneliness that all soldiers' letters contain, reminded them that divisions were being shipped out weekly, often on short notice, often to destinations unknown.

Then, in January of 1944 came the letter telling them that he had been put on notice to go east, to Fort Dix, New Jersey, with overseas assignment, location unspecified. For Will and Anna it was like having a dread disease positively diagnosed, when before it had only been suspected. The uncertainty, the fear, descended over them like a dark thundercloud. Anna also had a gnawing fear about Bart as well; his letters had trickled off to nothing in the last year. Now the void of Europe was about to swallow up her son as well.

The night that Sandro was scheduled to leave for Europe, Will and Anna had dinner alone upstairs in the little sitting room that connected their bedrooms. Now they were alone in Casa Grande, the house was vastly too big; the downstairs rooms in particular cried out for the days when Sandro's music echoed through the halls, to the counterpoint of Mina's roller skates; when Jack and Edna sat in the library in animated conversation with Ruth and Alonzo; when Kate, Max, Will, and Bart played poker in the drawing room. In those days Casa Grande had been a large, beautiful home, the reward of many years of hard work for the family. Now it stood as a vacant monument to their wealth and their diminishing numbers.

Will and Anna hardly talked during supper. Foremost in their minds was that Sandro, at that moment, was on a train headed east, and both understood that the other was not inclined to talk about it too much; it had been a long day, as well, with a trip to the city to meet with executives from the smelting and refining company to discuss military contracts for copper ore. Will in particular looked tired and drawn; Anna had noticed the dark circles under his eyes and the occasional weary, massaging gestures he made on his forehead. When he had finished eating, he asked Anna if she would mind if he went directly to bed; he reached for the house phone to ring for one of the maids to help him into bed.

Anna spoke in an impulse.

"Don't bother them now, they're probably ready for bed themselves. I'll help you."

"That's too much trouble," Will protested. "You're not even finished eating."

Over the years Anna had grown out of the habit of helping Will into bed, something she had done religiously during the first years after his accident. It seemed in recent years that their schedules didn't coincide. Either he or she would go up to bed earlier than the other, and there was always a maid ready to help Will out of his chair and into bed. In the last decade, since Will's troubled sleep had necessitated him taking his own room so as not to disturb Anna with his long hours of wakefulness, their hours together had been reduced almost totally to daytime and early evening. Their nights were spent alone.

Tonight, without having thought it out, Anna felt a need to see Will into bed; the sense of loneliness that had stalked her these last years seemed now poised behind her, like a cat about to strike. The need to reach out to Will, to move closer to him, so long overlooked, now asserted itself again.

She pushed the chair into his room with the special low bed and furniture. Will undressed himself as far as he could, until he sat naked from the waist up in his chair.

His body was still firm and youthful, the skin pale and hairless, the body of a man of thirty-five. Will's arms, from years of exaggerated use in lifting his crippled body from the chair, had grown even larger and more muscular than they had been in his youth. Will lifted himself on the arms of the chair so Anna could pull down his trousers. In contrast to his trunk and arms, his legs were desiccated and useless, pitiful remnants of the finely formed limbs they had once been.

With a joint effort they maneuvered Will onto his bed; with crablike propulsion of his arms Will moved himself into position as Anna pulled the covers around him.

"Thank you, darling, I—"

She interrupted him. Her words came out haltingly: "Will, I'd like to be with you tonight. If you don't mind."

He smiled. "Of course not. I'm feeling lonely too. I understand. I'm just afraid I'll keep you up all night if my back starts bothering me."

"N-no, that isn't what I mean," she stuttered. "I want to *be* with you, to make love."

She felt embarrassed even as she said it. Will paused, taking in what she had said.

"But I can't . . . You know I can't." There was a note of pain in his voice.

Anna sat down on the bed next to him and stroked his cheek gently.

"After the accident there were those times . . . when we managed. Even though there were some things that were . . . impossible."

"But is that enough?"

"For me, of course," she answered. "I'm just sorry that it has to be so one-sided."

Will pulled her close to him, held her against his chest.

"Oh, darling, I'll do anything I can to please you. I still love you so . . . need you."

"Please, Will," she murmured. "Now. Let's not talk."

Will reached for the light cord, but Anna stopped him. "No . . . with the lights on. I want to be able to see you."

"It would be better if it's dark."

Anna felt a sudden rush of excitement, of longing.

"No, Will. Not in the dark. I want to be able to see you, to see us. The way we are."

He pulled himself up and onto her, his body strong and vigorous.

Chapter Four

IN MARCH OF 1945, WILL AND ANNA HOSTED A GALA war-bond benefit at Casa Grande. The Channings had organized a number of bond benefits during the war years at Casilla and in El Paso, and they were proud of the more than five million dollars they had helped raise for the war effort. The affair they planned in March was a special occasion, since all indications were that it would be their last. Since D-Day the previous June, and General Patton's landing in Southern France that August, Americans had come to believe that the tide of war had fully turned in their favor. With the RAF bombing of Berlin in January and the devastation of Tokyo on March seventh, the Axis's spine seemed finally to be broken. On the day before the benefit, as if to confirm for once and for all that the Allies were on the threshold of victory, Iwo Jima was retaken and the United States Army reached the Rhine at Dusseldorf.

For the Channings the tide of victory was dark and cold: Sandro had been listed as missing in action in France since the Battle of the Bulge, in December. The prospect of victory hung under a pall of uncertainty.

Casa Grande had been a veritable beehive since early in the morning of the benefit. The committee was expecting nearly a thousand guests, at twenty-five dollars a head, and to insure that the partygoing patriots got their money's worth, the benefit organizers had gathered a small army of volunteers to get things ready. One group of men hammered together a bandstand in the stair court; women armed with ladders and hammer and tacks hung streamers and paper lanterns; the caterers from the city set up long tables for food and drinks.

Anna had started her day at dawn with coffee and a checklist; she had continued nonstop until early evening. At this point in her life it was easy to understand why Ruth had thrown herself headlong into her charity work: these benefits, especially, were an incomparable distraction from her thoughts. It was a welcome relief to go three, four hours without thinking about Sandro. She had suffered so many nightmares in recent weeks, nightmares of his dead, decaying body in some slime-filled bomb crater in the combat zone. At least, occasionally her waking hours could be cleared of such terrible visions.

Since the day before the benefit, however, there had been another concern—Mina. Anna realized now that their decision, two years ago, to let Mina have her own apartment in the city had been a serious mistake. At the time, in 1942, after Sandro had been inducted, the tension at home between Mina and her

parents had been intolerable, with arguments alternating with
days of cold-shoulder silence. And there were the weekends
when Mina was supposed to have left the dormitory at the
college and come to Casilla but didn't show up at all—not even
a phone call to ease her parents' anxiety. Then there had been
the failure-level grades and finally the embarrassing phone call
from the dean of women, asking them why Mina had not been
coming to classes at all.

There had been a terrible scene when they confronted Mina;
she had not been on campus in three weeks. She rather per-
versely told them that she had "just been staying with friends"
and refused to reveal any more. This stubborn, childish position
angered her parents even more, and they threatened to take her
out of school altogether. In a sudden shift in style Mina had
broken down, cried: she was lonely; she was embarrassed because she was constantly compared with her studious brother;
she felt that other students resented her family and their money
and position.

Her litany of reasons had gone on for considerable length, in
the same vein, with reasons all plausible enough for her parents.
She had pleaded with them to give her another chance, one
more chance to do better. Perhaps if she could live alone, she
said, have a little place to herself, take a few courses instead of a
full class load, things might go better for her.

In the end they had agreed. Anna remembered now how
tearfully persuasive her daughter had been, and Mina had come
away with everything she had asked for. Now, in retrospect,
Anna recalled a vague feeling of having been manipulated,
hoodwinked.

Once Mina was set up in a cheerful little garage apartment in
a quiet newer area of bungalows on the east side of El Paso, she
shunned her parents almost totally. It sometimes seemed that
she only called to ask for an increase in her already generous
allowance. Anna and Will had talked about Mina's continued
lack of consideration, but they always opted for the route of
patience and tolerance.

All that had changed the night before, when they had received a phone call from Mina's angry landlady, who launched
into a furious litany of grievances about their daughter's abuses
as a tenant. Will and Anna had sat in stunned silence on the

phones as they heard complaints of Mina's "low-life friends,"
the all-night parties, the broken windows and furniture, the
whiskey bottles tossed out onto the lawn. That night, for the
second time in as many weeks, the landlady had called the
police to quiet her unruly tenant. After placating the woman
they had gotten Mina on the phone. To their surprise, instead of
being angry and defensive, Mina had sounded calm, relaxed,
even cheerful.

"I'm sorry we made too much noise," she apologized quietly.
"We didn't mean to. Sure, if you really want to talk to me, I'll
come down tomorrow, in the morning, before your party."

Anna had been on the extension when Will spoke with Mina.
After she had clicked off Anna said to Will, "Something's not
right. She seemed too easygoing, too casual. I don't trust it."

Will frowned, thoughtful.

"I think she was drunk" was all he said.

Anna looked at her husband as he sat in his chair. His face
was tense and drawn, his eyes sad and troubled. He lifted his
hands to the sides of his head and massaged his temples slowly.
She knew he was having another of his headaches; he had
fought them for weeks now. The cause was easy enough to
deduce, for they had started just after the news had come from
France that Sandro was missing in action.

"I'll get you a couple of aspirin," Anna said quietly as she
went and stood behind Will's chair and massaged his tight
scalp.

"That might be a good idea. I've got to be at my best for the
party tomorrow. It's hard to sleep sometimes, with one of these
throbbers."

Anna had wanted to talk about Mina, to try to sort out some
of her confusion and anger over her daughter's behavior. But
she couldn't force the conversation now, not with the way Will
was feeling. He had so much on his mind, so many worries.
They both did. Sometimes she did not know whether it was a
blessing or a curse to have to go on about their daily lives, the
familiar routine. At times it was the best distraction in the
world from worries about Sandro and Mina; at other times it
seemed ludicrous to have to deal with the trivia of farm and
home life when her son might be dead, her daughter an alcoholic.

Like all parents with a son away at war, Will and Anna had lived with the unspoken fear that death or injury would overtake their boy when others were spared. It was easy enough to paint pictures of heroes returning safe from battle, but the happy images only masked the darker scenes of death and unutterable loss. The picture of Sandro safely returned from the war had been destroyed in February when the telegram had come from Washington informing them that their son was missing in action. The dreadful news was not unlike that which had come to them now: their daughter, whom they fervently hoped was safe and happy in her apartment in the city, was leading as dark and troubled a life as they could imagine. It was a painful thing for Anna and Will, to realize that their children, whom they loved and treasured so much, had grown up to face the cruel realities of life. There was pain, suffering, even for them, no matter how much their parents wanted them to have golden, perfect lives. The only comfort in these dark, troubled months was the bond between Anna and Will, a love, a sharing that had grown, ripened. The heartache, the tragedy that surrounded them had only brought them closer together.

Anna left Will for a moment and went to the small guest lavatory off the stair hall, where she knew there was a bottle of aspirin. As she went back toward the library, vial in hand, one of the maids stopped her and handed her a crisp yellow envelope with the explanation that it had just been delivered at the service entrance. Even as the envelope touched her hand Anna knew it was a telegram from Washington with word about Sandro. Her belly wrenched and her hands went cold at the thought of what it contained.

She hurried into the library where Will sat. He saw in a moment, from the alarm in her eyes, that something was terribly wrong.

"What is it?" he asked, his hand reaching out for hers.

She stretched out her arm to him, the yellow envelope trembling in her fingers.

"I couldn't . . . I can't open it. Please, Will . . . help me."

Will reached for the letter with a hand that was trembling scarcely less than hers. Then he took a letter opener from the table next to him and placed the point against the sealed flap. He said nothing, but his eyes spoke for him.

With the faintest hiss the blade sliced through the envelope's edge.

It was after dark that day when Mina finally arrived at Casa Grande. Max Mirkovsky and his mother had just arrived and were unloading the truckload of block ice they had driven down from the ice house at Fabens when Mina's roadster pulled up by the back entrance to the house. The top was down, and Max immediately recognized the head of marceled platinum hair as Mina's. When he climbed out, he saw that she was dressed for evening: a red satin slip of a dress, pumps, a fur cape casually thrown across her bare shoulders.

"Kate, Max, you darlings!" she called out when she saw them. "Still laboring at this hour? What dull boys you'll all be!"

Mina hurried toward them, clearly unsteady on her feet. She threw her arms around them in turn, kissed them enthusiastically on both cheeks. Kate and Max exchanged a knowing look as they smelled the alcohol that oozed from her.

"You're dolled up fit to kill, Mina," Max complimented. "All set to make a big hit at the party tonight?"

"Silly! I've had this on all day—a big hit at the dog track. I could give a shit what I wear to these old-fogey affairs."

Max suppressed a flare of anger at her childishness, but Kate made no such effort.

"Looks to me, young lady, like you started your party real early."

"No earlier than usual, *Kate*," Mina shot back with a spiteful edge. As she spoke Max studied her face. Her eyes were puffy and bloodshot, and her skin was flushed and blotched. It was hardly the clear, untroubled face of a happy twenty-five-year-old; there was something haggard and unhealthy about it. The beauty that had been apparent when she got out of the car had evaporated on close inspection. What was even more troubling was her falsely cheerful manner, only thinly masking anger.

Mina started for the back steps, her gait unsteady. Max followed her, took her elbow as she made her way through the door.

Anna was in the dining room, making some last-minute adjustments to the flower arrangements on the table, when she saw Max and Mina come in from the butler's pantry. She had been fighting her anger at Mina all afternoon, but it was redoubled when she saw that Max was having to steer Mina on a straight course. She had been shocked and hurt enough to hear about Mina's drinking binges in the city; it was an even bigger shock to think that Mina had been driving in her condition.

"Sorry I'm late, darling," Mina slurred in her artificial, cheery voice. She saw from the look on her mother's face that the cheerfulness had no effect on her; Anna glared at her, her anger clearly showing. Mina averted her eyes, and a look of embarrassment crossed her face when she realized how apparent her condition was.

Anna tried to soft-pedal the situation.

"I think you should go upstairs and take a nap," she said quietly. "And then your father wants to talk to you, alone, before the guests start arriving. We have been waiting all day for you to get here. We've had news about Sandro."

Mina's flicker of embarrassment changed to sullen contempt.

"Don't bother me with bad news. If he's dead, I don't want to know about it. This is supposed to be a party, right? So I don't want to spend the whole damned evening talking about a dead soldier, even if he is my brother."

Her words were an unexpected slap.

"You don't mean that!" her mother cried. "You're drunk!"

"Tough shit."

"Mina!" Max hissed. "Watch your manners. There's company in the house."

"Screw that! This is supposed to be a party, not a frigging DAR meeting. Is Eleanor Roosevelt here or something?"

Mina pulled her arm away from Max with a jerk and wove out toward the hall.

Bitch! Anna thought. *My own daughter is behaving like a drunken little bitch! The heartlessness, to talk about Sandro like that.*

She glanced around the dining room at the other women, the caterers, the maids. They had heard the exchange; their eyes darted away furtively when they saw her looking at them. Max stood in front of her, his giant frame stooped in defeat, in hurt.

"What's wrong, Anna? What's happening to her?" Max sounded like a confused little boy. Her look told him that she didn't know.

They hurried out after Mina, hoping to get her upstairs and into her bed. If she slept for a while, surely she'd be better.

The marbled expanse of the stair court was drenched in festoons of colored streamers, paper lanterns, and balloons, and the stars and stripes was hung across the windows on the broad landing. The red-jacketed dance band was warming up for the first set of dance numbers, and Will, in his dinner clothes, was already near the front door, chatting with a group of early arrivals. He didn't see Mina as she came from the dining room and went toward the bottle-laden bar to the right of the stairway, which was already serving. Anna was glad of that. She and Max caught up with her at the bar.

"Mina, please—let's go upstairs for a few minutes," Anna called out softly, trying not to be overheard, to spare them any further embarrassment.

Mina ignored her mother and ordered a neat Scotch from the bartender.

"Mina!" Anna's impatience showed through her whisper.

Mina whirled and faced her mother. Her drink sloshed out onto her mother's dress and the floor. Her face was tight with anger.

"Will you leave me alone!"

Anna recoiled as Mina's half-shouted words echoed through the room. There was a devastating lull in the sound of other conversation, that pin-drop instinct that humans have when an unpleasant scene is about to be enacted in their midst.

"What do you want from me, anyway? You dragged me all the way down to this shindig, and now you're trying to hustle my ass off to my room, trying to get rid of me. What's the matter—ashamed of me?"

Anna stiffened at the confrontation. Mina's lovely young face was blotched from drink, distorted from anger; one strap of her dress had fallen off her shoulder, and her platinum hair had fallen down in her face. She had changed from beauty to slattern.

"Yes, Mina. I am ashamed of you. For behaving like this."

Mina shrugged, swallowed her drink. Her arm trembled as she raised the glass.

"Since when do you give a shit about Wilhelmina Channing?

I thought all you cared about was your goddamned money and your goddamned farm!"

Max crushed his fingers into Anna's arm, to control his anger. The hall had fallen into stony silence, broken only by the faint squeak of the wheels of Will's chair as he rolled himself toward them.

Finally Max could not contain himself.

"You little bitch! You got a lot of nerve talking to your mother like that! It's time someone took you down a peg or two, you little brat!"

"Stop acting like a brother," Mina shot back. "I got one of those. Besides, I don't need a big stupid hick telling me what to do."

She threw her head back, gloating in rebellion.

"So fuck you all!"

The blow came swiftly, Anna's palm flat across Mina's face. Anna knew she had struck her hard—she could feel the collision of flesh and bone reverberating the length of her arm.

Mina recoiled, sucked in her breath in shock. Her hand touched the cheek that bore the scarlet imprint of her mother's hand. Then the shock in Mina's eyes faded to a sullen defiance. She said nothing but turned and went up toward her room, stumbling now and again on the stairs.

Anna watched her daughter's painful, clumsy progress, then turned to face Will and the room of waiting guests.

The streamlined form of Mina's cream-colored Studebaker convertible sped through the illogical tangle of pedestrians and peddlers' carts and decrepit vehicles on Juarez Avenue. "Damned Mexicans can't drive!" she swore under her breath. She always hated the mile-long stretch of the avenue between the International Bridge and the major crossroad of Avenue of the Sixteenth of September; the traffic was always a mess, and the American GIs and Mexican men who hung out on the sidewalks outside the bars and nightclubs along the seedy neon-lighted strip always cat-called and whistled at the platinum-blond woman driving alone through Juarez.

Mina raced the motor in neutral as she waited for the light to change. A group of soldiers wove drunkenly across the street, leering at her through the windshield.

"Hey, Harlow, baby. How much? Bet that car costs a bundle to keep running!"

"I'd like to get her in the rumble seat. Yowee!"

Mina stared icily straight ahead, cursing herself for not putting the top up before she crossed the bridge.

Finally the light changed, and she squealed her tires as she sped to the left and down Sixteenth of September Avenue.

Johnny had told her to be there by seven, and it was almost half past already. The bastard was always so hard on her when she was late, told her he didn't wait for any broad; if she wanted to run with him, she'd have to learn to treat him with respect.

Respect! What a load of crap. Johnny was a vain, selfish low-life drug runner. A real no-good type. He hated her too—he hated all women. He just used them. She knew that—he didn't even pretend to hide the fact. He always said, "There's only one thing I want from a woman, and it ain't companionship. If I want companionship, I'll get a dog."

He made her furious when he said things like that; sometimes she would yell at him, spewing out her anger. Then he would grab her and kiss her hard and call her baby doll. When he was tender with her like that, her anger went away. Mina didn't always like it when the anger subsided. She wanted to stay angry at Johnny, to hate him enough to stop seeing him.

But she always had a good time with Johnny when they were coked up. When they were high, she felt optimistic, happy.

As she drove into the dark side streets Mina thought of the empty vial in her purse. Tonight she really needed to lighten up a bit; thank God Johnny had gotten a shipment in today. She had intended to make the vial of powder last all week, but she'd run out last night. The coke seemed to go so much faster with the injections. And she had deliberately used more a few times; it had been one of those tedious, irritating weeks with her landlady complaining about the noise, her parents calling to reprimand her, punishing her by insisting that she make an appearance at this damned war-bond cotillion they were hosting.

She hadn't meant to make a scene at the house—she didn't really like making a spectacle of herself or embarrassing her parents. But they made her so angry when they hounded her about having too much to drink or being too saucy with them. If her mother had just left her alone, let her have a few drinks, show her face to the locals, and go back home, it would have been all right. Now there would be hell to pay for her behavior. And the gossips would have a field day with Anna Cutter slapping her daughter at the war-bond dance. It was just as well that she had snuck out the back stairs and driven off to see Johnny. No reason to stay and face them all.

Mina slowed the car before the iron gates while the attendant pushed them open; she drove into the dark courtyard that fronted the shuttered stucco house and parked next to Johnny's Cadillac. There were other cars she didn't recognize—probably some of Johnny's set from the clubs.

Inside, the stucco tile-roofed *hacienda* was a sleek, modern fantasia of gleaming chrome and glass, a total contrast to the traditional exterior. The surfaces of the rooms—the terrazzo floors, the satin moiré upholstery, the burled veneers, the etched glass, bespoke not only the last word in style but vast quantities of visible money; there was nothing in Johnny's glittering, streamlined palace that did not shout very loudly, "I was *very* expensive." Had the house belonged to anyone else, Mina would have found it terribly chic and glamorous; because it was Johnny's, the place seemed vulgar.

Johnny was in the living room with two other men. Johnny wore a smoking jacket, though the other two were in dinner jackets. To her surprise Johnny didn't say anything about her lateness; he just kissed her, then mixed her a double Manhattan as he introduced his friends. The names slipped by her—all of Johnny's friends tended to blend into a sameness, a generalized dark and indifferent type.

Johnny kept up his usual cocky patter as he fixed her a drink. Mina could tell that he and the others were already flying; their faces had that kind of smirky glaze that coke brought on. She was feeling edgy herself and wished the others weren't there so she could ask him right out for the vial of coke. It was a cheap, helpless enough feeling to ask for the stuff from Johnny, anyway. It made her feel so dependent on him; asking in front of those two lounge lizards would have been even worse.

As it turned out she didn't have to ask. After he had handed her her cocktail Johnny reached in his pocket and pulled out a glass vial of clear liquid. He held it up between them, between thumb and forefinger, as a jeweler holds a diamond for inspection.

"Here's what you've been waiting for, baby doll. We've already had our first round. You got your needle with you?"

Mina nodded yes. She suddenly felt a smart of humiliation as her shooting coke was discussed so casually in front of the other two.

"I'll go in the bedroom," she mumbled.

"It's all right, baby. You don't have to leave the room. We're all big boys, right, fellas?"

A grunt of agreement came from behind her.

"No I'd rather—well, I have to powder my nose too."

Mina stumbled through her excuse. She had to get out of the room with the others. They gave her a jittery, clammy feeling. It would be all right once she had gotten high. Then she could relax, enjoy herself. She always could, afterward.

Without another word she took the vial from Johnny and turned toward the stair hall. As she walked away she felt Johnny's hand slide across her buttock, then slip lower, pressing into the crevice.

"Don't take too fucking long. You got a party to go to later, remember."

Mina tried to shut out the words. She hated Johnny when he was crude like that. But for now all she wanted to do was get upstairs.

Mina released the belt from around her upper left arm. Already the delicious warmth had spread through her body. Now she felt happy, relaxed. How silly for her to have been so tense earlier. No reason for all that. Life really was a lot of fun, wasn't it?

She stood up from the toilet seat, savoring the delicious giddiness as the drugged blood rushed to her head. The mirrored walls of Johnny's bath reflected her to infinity. A million blond heads, a million red-satin sheaths, ten million red-enameled nails. She leaned forward across the marble, gold-fixtured lavatory and held her face near the mirror.

Red lips, red dress, red nails. A good color for her. She must remember red. She studied her reflection. Yes, I am beautiful, am I not? And sexy too. There's a difference. But I must remember red.

Out of the corner of her eye she noticed the crook of her elbow. Her thin, pale arm, with a single red drop of blood poised at the point of the needle's puncture.

Even that is red too—blood-red. Must be careful, though. The marks are starting to show. Long sleeves, of course, that's the answer. No one could see them.

Mina looked in the mirror again, made a pouty, glamorous face. *Yes,* she thought to herself, *I'm beautiful.*

Johnny was in the bedroom when Mina came out; his smoking jacket was off, and the starched sleeve of his dress shirt was rolled up above the elbow. The end of the belt looped around his thick, hairy bicep was held taut by his teeth, and with his right hand he held the syringe at the crook of his elbow. His thumb slowly pushed the plunger down, emptying the fluid into his vein.

"Thought I'd have another round, baby. I'm in the mood to really let loose tonight."

Mina watched as Johnny finished and withdrew the syringe. He closed his eyes and sucked in his breath as the ecstatic rush coursed through him.

"Be careful, Johnny. You'll shoot too much."

Johnny pulled out of the first rush.

"Aw, don't be such a fucking prude, Mina! You're not my mama. When you know as much about this stuff as I do, you can tell me to be careful."

He started toward her, unbuttoning his shirt.

"I'm fine, baby, just fine. In fact, I'm in the mood to show you just how fine I am. You know how horny I get when I'm on a rush."

He reached down and groped himself, showing her beneath his trousers the bloated shape that hung thickly down his leg.

Mina stood immobilized as he touched her. His hands stroked her roughly through the thin fabric of her dress. His tongue, thick and wet, probed her mouth, her throat. His nostrils flared and snorted like an aroused stallion.

Mina usually melted at his touch, but this time—she didn't understand why—she stiffened. Johnny sensed it.

"What's the matter, baby?" His tone was sarcastic. "Don't

tell me you're not in the mood? Don't try to pull that bullshit with me, tell me you've got a headache or something. We both know you come to Johnny for a lot more than coke. 'Cause Johnny's got more than enough of everything to give you."

His hand went into her dress. Thumb and forefingers closed hard around her nipple.

She started to pull away.

"Johnny—not right now, please. In a few minutes."

"Come on, sweetie, don't keep Johnny waiting." His sarcasm melted into thick, anxious lewdness. "You know I don't like to work for it. I don't have to. 'Sides, you look real fucking attractive tonight. Mike and Tony thought so too. They're gonna come up and give me some help tonight. We decided it's time you tried a few things you haven't done before."

Mina was shocked into rage at his words. She tried to push away from him, but he grabbed the neckline of her dress and shoved her back toward the bed with a sharp rip of fabric that left her lying back, exposed. Her fear and the effect of the drug paralyzed her. She lay stunned as he opened his trousers.

"You spoiled rich bitches are all alike." He leered down at her as he displayed himself to her. "You like to be forced. Well, you've come to the right place."

The other two appeared next to Johnny, leering down at her as they stripped off their clothes.

Chapter Five

FROM HER LOUNGE ON THE EAST TERRACE OF OAK SUMmit Farm, Mina looked out across the long expanse of lawn that sloped down from the rambling Gothic-style stone estate to the tree-lined banks of the Penoscowee River, which flowed through the valley below. The early weeks of May had been mild and sunny, and the hills that folded up protectively around

Oak Summit were in the full flush of their brightest spring
green. Several flocks of small birds—Mina had never before
spent time in a place where there were so many varieties—
hopped and fluttered around the freshly mowed lawn, reaping
the benefits of what the gardeners' blades had stirred up. Their
greedy search was interrupted only by an early-morning croquet game at the foot of the lawn near the river, and by the
occasional stroller in robe and slippers, who struck out from
the terrace for one of the secluded paths that wandered through
the woods surrounding the open grounds of the estate. Across
the valley, toward the Berkshire foothills, the sun hung in a
sparkling-clear sky. It promised to be another lovely spring day.

Mina kicked off the fringed wool lap robe to get the sun on
her body and legs, but as soon as she had, the damp, still-cool
morning air on her bare legs made her think better of the idea
and pull the robe up again.

"Texas, it ain't," she joked to herself. Early May at home and
the days would already be intensely hot. She would have been
deeply tanned from her early-morning hours of swimming and
lounging beside the pool.

How she wanted to get some color! When she pulled down
the blanket, her bare calves had been a sickly, yellowish white—
so ugly, so unhealthy-looking. At least when she had looked in
the mirror that morning, her face showed some traces of a
healthy, tanned color from her hours on the terrace. That was
encouraging. And for the last week or so, when she was shower-
ing and caught a glimpse of herself in the long mirror on her
bathroom door, her body looked less devastated, less shame-
fully ugly, than it had a month before. She shuddered as she
recalled her first look in the mirror after those nightmarish first
days of withdrawal. The reflection showed a thin, broken creature, old beyond her years. The twenty-five pounds she had lost
in a week of night sweats and violent vomiting had left ribs
showing through the skin and shiny, irregular stretch marks
around her hips and breasts. Her eyes had faded to a lusterless,
vacant blue, sunken in deep, purplish-gray sockets. The skin on
her face was yellowish and dry, like an old woman's and laced
with broken veins and small bruises from the strain of retching.

In the last weeks her weight had slowly come back almost to
normal, and the most severe ravages of withdrawal had begun

to ebb from her face. Mina knew she still looked terrible—the body was going to take its own time—but she at least didn't look so dreadfully sick that she couldn't even indulge in vanity.

Reconciled that the suntan she wanted to acquire would have to wait until later in the mild eastern spring, Mina reached to the little folding table that the attendant had brought earlier and poured herself a second cup of coffee. She watched with satisfaction as the spout hovered over the cup with only a trace of unsteadiness. She remembered her first morning coffee on the terrace, just after her release from full medical care. The embarrassment, the helplessness, she'd felt when she had tried to pour herself coffee only to find her hand shaking so badly that she poured into the cup, the saucer, and onto the linen and the muffins. Then the final humiliation of the silver pot crashing down and shattering the cup. When the attendant had gotten to her, her hands were still shaking uncontrollably, and she was in tears.

"There's some progress," she complimented herself. "At least I may be able to eat in public again someday." Encouraged, she reached for the pack of Pall Malls on the table, from a treasured carton sent by a sympathetic, chain-smoking Kate, and for the gold- and black-enameled Cartier lighter that had been a gift from Grandma Ruth some years ago when she had finally reconciled herself to Mina's smoking.

Her daily ration was five cigarettes, since the doctors thought more "might cause nervousness," and the first smoke of the day was a little test she gave herself, tougher than pouring coffee, to see how much her steadiness and coordination had improved. She placed a cigarette carefully in her lips, concentrating to hold it steady. Then a slow, careful arc to bring the lighter up, a flick of the wheel with her thumb, and the flame touched perfectly at the tip of the cigarette with only the slightest quaver. Mina held it there longer than she had to, just to show off to herself.

Her arm trembled without warning and knocked the cigarette into her lap.

"Damn it," she cursed under her breath. She picked the cigarette up from the blanket and brushed the bits of ember and ash onto the flagstones.

"You do that just like Bette Davis, kid!"

Mina was startled by a big, booming voice behind her, every syllable proclaiming that a Texan spoke. She whirled around, then gasped in shock at the sight of Max, in an out-of-character three-piece tweed suit, beaming down at her with a package in one arm and his Stetson in the other.

Mina instinctively brought her hand to her face to shield it from Max's gaze. Her face was warm and flushed from surprise and embarrassment.

"Max! But what the . . . I . . ."

"Surprised, hey?" He grinned, looking very pleased with himself, like a kid watching his mother open the Christmas present he's gotten her.

"I know I probably shoulda wrote a letter or sent a wire, knowing how women are about being dropped in on. But I figured, hell, as long as I was up this way, might as well drop in."

Max kept up a chatter to give Mina a chance to recover herself. As he spoke he pulled up an iron garden chair close beside Mina's lounge. He eased his giant figure into the inadequate-looking seat and leaned forward, elbows on his knees. His sunburned, grinning face was close to hers.

"It's real pretty up here," he rambled on nervously. "All these trees and flower gardens, bet Pablo and Hank would have a field day. And lots of those white frame houses and churches. And New York City! Whew! That's something else altogether!"

Mina still only half believed that Max's earnest, familiar face was next to her, smiling and talking in his old shy but enthusiastic way. Since she had awakened from the horrible nightmare of withdrawal, Casilla seemed to be another life, very long ago. Cutter-Channing Farms might easily have been on another planet, and the girl called Mina Channing was someone other than the sobered, dried-up woman who answered to the same name at Oak Summit Farm. Even the long letters from Mother and Father, as full as they were with news, well-wishing, and love, were more like letters found in someone else's drawer and read surreptitiously. Mina had spent hours on the terrace, walking in the gardens, in the hydrotherapy rooms, in the crafts lounge, trying in vain to find an opening in the cloudy veil that obscured her from her past and her family.

Even the staff, the other patients at Oak Summit, people who were sharing the same difficulties and who were helping her, were distant from her. She had begun to despair of ever feeling anything besides the dry hollowness that was her life every waking hour.

"It's so good to see you, Max," she finally managed, wondering if her voice sounded as tired to him as it did to her. "You're my first visitor, you know. I wasn't planning on anyone till week after next, when Mama and Dad come up. I wish I'd known. I'm sure a mess this morning."

She instinctively reached up and touched the snood she had put on to hold back her limp, unwashed hair.

"You look fine."

Max took her hand as she took it away from her head and held it gently. His own large hand was warm and rough from hard labor. She had once looked with distaste at the hands of the peons and Uncle Hank and Max. They seemed so crude, with the calluses and scars and broken nails. Now Max's hand was reassuring, like the smell of damp earth.

Mina smiled self-consciously.

"We both know I look terrible—like death."

"Don't say that."

"It's true, Max. There's no point in flattering me. I was almost dead, and it shows. Just look at my face! Is this what a healthy, red-blooded nineteen-year-old girl is supposed to look like?"

"Don't be embarrassed, Mina." Max squeezed her hand. "Sure you're thin and so pale that it looks like you've been playing in the Caliche quarry. But your eyes are clear, and they ain't looked that way since, well . . ."

"Since I started on the drugs and booze." She found it easy to get the words out. Dr. Brody would approve. "Talk about it, Mina," he'd said. "Face up to your problems. Your family and friends are on your side, if you'll just be honest about your addiction and your unhappiness."

Max averted his eyes for an instant, and his cheeks colored.

"If you don't want to talk about all that . . . well, it's all right. I understand."

"Doctor's orders. No pretending, no hiding. Everyone knows why Mina Channing is spending her spring in Connecticut—at a very exclusive finishing school. For wealthy young drug addicts."

"Don't be hard on yourself, Mina. Everyone at home cares about you a bunch. About the troubles you've had. We've been worried for damn sure, worried sick. But I—we—knew you was a brave kid with a lot of gumption in her. That's why, when your folks told me you was doing real well, I wanted to come see for myself."

Mina felt her throat getting tight. Max's sincerity and concern were so touching.

"Oh, Max, this is such a sweet thing for you to do." She leaned her head back on the cushion and closed her eyes wearily. "It's been hell. You can imagine . . ."

"And lonely?" he asked.

She nodded. "Yes, now that the worst is over. The days are long and quiet, and I've got a lot of time to think."

"Maybe that's what you needed."

She was struck by his perceptiveness. She looked at him and smiled.

"You're such a dear man to come see me. But I hope you didn't have to come too far out of your way."

Max chortled.

"Only about two thousand miles."

She didn't understand. Then it struck her what he'd done.

"I'm flabbergasted, Max! I mean, it's wonderful that you came all the way up here to see me. But I don't understand *why!*"

"Don't you?" Max looked uneasy. "Then I'd better have out with it. Cigarette?"

He offered her the pack from the table, then took one himself. When he gave her a light, she noticed that his hand shook as much as hers had.

"I've known you since you was a kid, Mina. I remember when you was born. I was 'bout thirteen then. Your granny called my mama and told her to come over to be with Anna while she was in labor. I was curious as hell and wanted to go along. But a big hailstorm came up and scared the bejesus out of the horses. Mama made me stay at the farm to keep them quieted down. I'll never forget—when she got back, she was cussin' mad because the hail had dented the hell out of the new

Ford while she was driving over to your mama's farm. I recall lots of things about your life you probably don't—your first birthday party when you put your cute little fist right through the cake. And the time you cut your foot wide-open on a tin can lid in the yard behind the old house, and I was sure you were going to get blood poisoning or lockjaw and die."

"I remember that," Mina recalled with a smile. "I think I just bled a lot and demanded ice cream in bed."

"And I saw you grow up. Learn how to ride. You was such a pretty, cocky young thing. Proud of your horsemanship, proud you mastered both English and Western saddles. And I was proud of you—you were smart and clever. You dressed better than any of the other girls in Casilla, even the ones with money too, and you carried yourself well. When anybody laid eyes on Miss Mina Channing, they knew they'd laid eyes on someone real special."

"That was a long time ago, Max. I can't even remember what it was like to feel . . . special. And to be honest, I never noticed that you were paying that much attention to me. Were you really?"

Max made a good-natured face at her.

"Don't get too big for your britches, missy. Keeping an eye on you wasn't a full-time occupation. Just sometimes. And don't forget we're kind of from different sides of the track. Sure, our folks go way back, got started together when the farms were just river bottom and mesquite. But the Cutters and Channings have gone on to big things—big money. Mama and I are still simple folks, and I like it that way. We work damned hard, but we keep a lot of complications out of our lives too. Now you and me, that's where we're real different. I'd rather shovel manure and weed cotton than drive a big convertible around to all-night parties and spend all of the next day in bed with a big head and my stomach on the floor."

Max stared down at the terrace. His fingertips tapped together nervously.

"Dear Max, you are such a sweetheart—such a kind man. I guess in the last few years, when I've been such a foolish girl, I really did take you for granted. I forgot what a good, considerate friend you were. I was too busy being reckless."

"That's what got to me, Mina. Knowing what a fine girl you

are, knowing the kind of woman your folks raised you to be. It hurt like hell, seeing you get in with that wild crowd, drunk half the time, speeding around in that damned little Studebaker, a couple of fancy Johnnies hanging on to you. Letting everything go down the drain—your schooling, riding, your family."

The desperation of the last years came back like a flash flood. She covered her eyes with her palms to try to hold back the tears.

"Oh, God, Max, I'm so ashamed of myself. So damned ashamed. What a silly, spoiled bitch I am! I hate myself for the way I've behaved. How could anyone want to come to see me after what I've done?"

"I'm not a real smart guy, Mina, though I think maybe I'm smart enough to know that you're a great gal underneath all your bullshit and phony fanciness."

"How can you say I'm 'great'? You've seen me so drugged I couldn't stand up. You've seen me call my family every ugly name in the book!"

Max stood up abruptly, his frame towering over her. Something like anger, but not quite, flooded through him. His chest heaved, and his fists clenched while the knuckles showed white.

"I can say that because I know just how great you are—and because, God damn it, I love you!"

There was a stony silence after his words, interrupted only by the occasional distant click of croquet balls and the chatter of birds.

"I don't know what to say, Max," she finally managed in a soft, dry voice. "I'm very confused right now. Nothing makes much sense to me right now—least of all you telling me you love me, out of the blue."

Max took her hand again, and she didn't resist.

"But this ain't out of the blue. I've always been hanging around. It's just that you never noticed. I've been feeling this way for a long time."

"I find that so touching—so kind." Mina thought hard for a moment. What did she feel? Surprised? Embarrassed? Flattered? She remembered many declarations of love, which were usually declarations of intent to have sex. But there was something that touched a deep vein in her, that released a trickle of warmth and well-being, when Max said he loved her, coming as it did, when she felt so thoroughly empty and worthless and undesirable.

"Are you sure you're not just feeling sympathy for me," she continued, "seeing me in such a rotten mess?"

Max felt a quick rush of anger at her questioning of his motivation.

"I got to tell you something about me, Mina. Something important, and I want you to listen real hard. I ain't such a good-looking SOB, and I for sure ain't very bright or clever like all those slick dudes you were hanging around with. I ain't fancy, neither. I like stew and a few beers on Saturday. I like to ride around in my pickup, and I don't like to read 'cause I'm not very good at it. Most folks would say I'm a hick, but that's okay with me. 'Cause I got one thing most people ain't got. I'm honest. Damned honest. Honest with other people and honest with myself. So when I say I love you, you can damn well know it's gospel, 'cause I'm not telling myself any lies about what I feel.

"You probably think I'm a crazy cuss for hauling myself up here when I should be back home seeing to thinning out the cotton. So you should know coming up to Connecticut was damned important to me! I don't expect you to feel any particular way about me just now. Hell, I wasn't planning on saying all this right out. I was kinda thinking to get it out gradual."

"Like getting a colt broken to the bit?" Mina couldn't resist the comparison.

"Kinda." Max winked. It was good to see Mina smile. The pain and hollowness eased from her face.

"Do you want me to fall in love with you, Max?"

He blushed again, a deeper red than before.

"I just want you to give me a chance. Get to know me a bit. Think some about what I have to offer a woman. Think some, too, about what you really want. Like I said before, Mina, I've known you a long time, and I know the kind of woman you really are. You got yourself in hot water 'cause you didn't have anything to care about or to work for. You come from a hard-working breed, Mina. It's in your blood. It's just that by the time you came along there was so much money, so much being done by everyone else, you felt just plain useless. Hell, if I felt useless, I'd go out and get high all the time, too, just to forget how goddamned useless I felt."

Mina studied Max's face, his blue eyes looking out rather sheepishly from under sun-bleached brows. Big, easygoing Max, someone she had regarded much as a friendly, affectionate farm dog. Now he was sitting next to her, professing his love for her. Probing to the core of her unhappiness. Of course, he was right! That had all come out in the hours of painful conversation with Dr. Brody. Beautiful, rich, useless Wilhelmina, who had nothing to do but ride expensive horses and buy expensive clothes. Everyone else had something *important* to do: Will, his politics; Anna, the farms; Hank, his nurseries; Sandro, his music. But Mina was just an expensive bit of extra baggage in the Cutter-Channing family. What difference did it make if the baggage was filled with alcohol and cocaine? Could it be that Max really did understand? The thought gave her some glimmer of hope.

"To be honest, Max, I don't know who I am now. I loathe what I was, but I can't say yet what I'll be from now on. The future is an idea I can't quite grasp yet. Since I've been here life has been measured in seconds. It's hard to imagine what months and years are like. What my life will be like."

"Can I stick around for a while?" he asked. "Not to put any pressure on you, now. Don't think that one bit. Just to have some company. I suspect these Yankees aren't over-warm and friendly, are they? And I'd kind of like to be around, now that you're getting your life started up again."

"I'd like that, Max—very much." Mina couldn't help but be amused at the irony: Max, of all people, coming to Connecticut to play spiritual nursemaid.

"But what about the farm? Can your mama handle everything?"

Max looked conspiratorial, then broke into a wide smile.

"That's *all* taken care of. Your Uncle Hank and Pablo are going to watch my place for a while. It's all set."

"How much does my family know about this?"

"Most everything. Your mom and dad and I had a long talk a coupla weeks back. About how I was feeling. Since they knew you wasn't supposed to have company till next week when they came up, they phoned special to your doctors here to see if he'd let me come."

"Sounds like a conspiracy to me." Mina didn't know whether to be angry or not.

"Well, they did say they hoped they'd see me when they get here."

"Will they?"

"I'm checked in at that visitors' lodge they got here. Swell room too. Got a fireplace and a pretty view of the hills over there."

"I give up!" Mina protested in mock despair. "My life is still out of control."

"We'll see about that, honey, won't we?"

Max stayed for the week and spent every free hour of Mina's day with her. They ate together, breakfast and lunch on the terrace, weather permitting, dinner in the small, tastefully furnished dining hall. Max was amazed at how unhospital-like Oak Summit was. Except for the rule allowing guests to enter the public rooms in robe and slippers, the place seemed more like a fine, small resort hotel or a private estate than a drug and alcohol rehabilitation center. Even doctors and nurses rarely wore uniforms, to give their "guests" a greater sense of normalcy. It was fascinating to watch the other guests. To his surprise Mina was not the youngest, though most were middle-aged, some quite elderly. All showed in varying degrees the ravages of their past problems: the dulled eyes; puffed, dissipated faces; unsteady hands. But within a week, as he observed and chatted with most guests every day, he saw change and improvement, and no more so than in Mina.

For her part it was the most natural thing in the world to have Max with her. The sense of vast loneliness that had haunted her ebbed away with his arrival. She felt perfectly comfortable holding his hand, touching him, having his arm around her as they walked through the gardens or sat by the fire in the lounge. They talked for hours about silly, funny things and about difficult and painful ones too.

When Will and Anna arrived at Oak Summit the following weekend, Mina and Max were standing on the steps of the stone portico to greet them. All morning as well as the night before

on the train, being driven to the hospital in the car that Oak
Summit had sent to Penoscowee to pick up the Channings,
Anna had been restless and anxious. She hadn't seen Mina since
those painful, nightmarish days in March; now she found herself afraid to face her daughter—afraid of disappointment if
Mina hadn't changed; afraid of seeing what her daughter might
have become; afraid of finding Mina changed but still a
stranger.

In the flurry of activity after the car had pulled up in front of
the stone portico at Oak Summit where Mina and Max stood
waiting, arm in arm, Anna and Mina had faced one another.
Their eyes locked and held one another for long seconds as each
woman looked for questions, for answers, in the other's gaze.
Mina's gaze seemed to her mother to be guarded, hesitant, but
steady. There was no shame in it.

Finally they moved toward one another, a few hesitant steps,
then a quick rush to embrace. As she felt her daughter's arms
around her, as she held her close in her own, it was as if troubled years melted away. Half-spoken words were obscured by
tears. No matter. Anna knew her girl had come home to her.

Will and Anna stayed the week. By their second day they felt
comfortable with Mina and her surroundings. It was clear that
Mina was still physically weak and emotionally fragile, but
there was an inner air of strength about her that had never been
there before. Will had described it as "serenity," and Anna had
to agree. They noticed, too, how easy Mina found it to discuss
her problems, the drugs, her therapy, even the horror of the
brutal rape. She seemed to have no secrets. It was also clear to
them that she was as attentive, as intimate, with Max as he was
with her.

When Max asked them if he could go to Connecticut alone to
see Mina, he'd made no bones about how he felt about her and
what he hoped to accomplish by seeing Mina at Oak Summit.

Max had done them the courtesy of asking their permission,
though at the time, Max's bullish determination made it clear
that he would probably go even without their good graces. They
had said yes, not from any high hopes that Max's feelings for
Mina would sweep her off her feet, but from the conviction that
at this low ebb in her life, Mina would feel better about herself

if shown that someone of Max's honest, forthright values could care enough for Mina Cutter to travel across a continent to see her.

After their first days at Oak Summit, what Will and Anna saw of the young couple's behavior was altogether different than what they'd expected.

"I'm getting old," Will joked one night after Mina and Max had gone to their rooms and he and Anna sat up late in front of an ember fire in the darkened empty lounge. "It's been a long time since I was their age. But, hell, it sure seems to me that they're in love. They sure *look* that way."

Anna agreed. But given what Mina had been through—not just the last months, but the last years—it didn't seem possible that she could fall in love with Max; Anna could only imagine how wrung-out, how drained, Mina was. Still, there was the evidence of the way they looked at each other, the shy but comfortable way they held hands, walked together, sat quietly together hour after hour.

"Max does seem to be a miracle worker," she told Will.

Will smiled back at her, that easy, boyish smile that the decades had not altered one iota. The yellow-gold warmth of the flickering firelight obscured the lines of age in his face and turned his silver hair back to the golden blond of his youth. He had pushed his body forward in the chair, head slightly back, elbows resting gently on the chair arms, as if propped comfortably in an easy chair. It was as if Will Channing, junior partner of Channing, Allen, & Channing, had come to visit Miss Anna Cutter once again and was stretched in front of the wood stove at The Old Farm, regaling the young lady farmer with tales of the world.

"I don't think Max is that much of a miracle worker, darling," Will volunteered with an impish, sly grin. "Just an example of what a combination of love and determination, liberally applied, can do."

"Do you really think it works?"

Even as she said it Anna realized she had let Will's double meaning slip by her.

"Work?" Will made a mock incredulous face. "We're living proof!"

Chapter Six

BEFORE ANNA AND WILL HAD LEFT OAK SUMMIT WITH Mina and Max for the train back to Texas, Dr. Brody had met privately with the Channings in his cluttered book-lined office.

During the last week Mina had spoken often of Dr. Brody, quoted him, praised him for what he'd done for her. Anna had found Brody gentle and well mannered; he listened intently to what one said but kept his own reactions closely guarded. It was difficult to believe that such a reserved, rumpled little man could see their strong-willed Mina safely through the hurricane of her withdrawal.

"Mina's doing well—very well, all things considered," Dr. Brody said as he offered Anna and Will a glass of Scotch from the locked bar behind his desk. "I feel comfortable in discharging her this week, though I do have a few observations to pass along to you."

"We're pleased . . . no, that's hardly the word," Will volunteered, "we're *amazed* is more like it, and grateful. She's *changed, recovered.*"

"I suppose all parents in our position say this," Anna added, "but I don't know how we can repay you."

Brody winked naughtily. "Our fees here are quite stiff and sufficient enough. So let's worry more about what's going to happen to your daughter now. The first thing to remember is that though Mina *seems* changed, she isn't. One doesn't become a new person in five or six weeks. I don't mean to worry you, but it's important to keep in mind that though Mina has gotten away from her cocaine and alcohol, she hasn't gotten away from her problems. She may be sober—in all senses now—but only now can she really start getting at her problems. This is going to become even more apparent when she gets back home and tries to start functioning in her old life among the people she knows. After all, one reason why Oak Summit works is because it is a totally artificial environment."

Brody gestured over his shoulder.

"There aren't too many locked liquor cabinets in the real world, so to speak. Once she's home, Mina has to go it on her own."

"To be honest, Dr. Brody," Anna confessed, "I don't know exactly how to behave toward her. I want her to know I want to help, but I don't want her to think I'm being a watchdog or a policeman or anything. . . ."

Will picked up her thoughts.

"You see, we're worried about doing too much or too little."

Brody was thoughtful for a moment.

"The most important thing for you to do is to learn that Mina's problems are Mina's problems. Don't make the mistake that most parents do—don't take the responsibility for your daughter's problems. That will only make you feel more guilty and add to the problems. You can be concerned, loving, supportive, but you can't solve Mina's problems for her."

"But there must have been so many things we did wrong, so many ways we contributed to her . . . breakdown."

Anna sought the comfort of Will's hand. Her own was clammy from nerves.

"Don't be too hard on yourself, Mrs. Channing. It is impossible to judge in retrospect what would have happened, 'if only.' You see, I know your little girl pretty well by now, even though I saw her for the first time five weeks ago. I've gotten to know her because in those five weeks we've spent a lot of time, many long hours, talking. She talked openly, honestly with me, and I listened carefully. That's why after only five weeks I can understand a good deal about her.

"My recommendation to you both, when you get back to Texas, is to start with honest, open, straight talking."

Anna found Dr. Brody's words comforting but vaguely disturbing.

"I don't know," she murmured. "It seems to me that we've always been very honest with our children."

Except for one thing, she added to herself. Except for Bart. That was her one secret.

"I get his point, darling—at least *I think I do.*" Will interjected with a note of enthusiasm. "Of course, Doctor, you aren't talking about telling lies to our kids or that kind of thing. What you do mean is talking about our own feelings and problems—opening up about things."

"Exactly!" Brody seemed elated, positively illuminated by Will's comment.

"It's the hardest thing in the world for us *Homo sapiens* to do. We've tried to hide our feelings, to keep up a brave front. Unfortunately it leads to enormous gaps in our understanding of one another. I can give you a perfect illustration. I see sitting here in my office two human beings—man and wife. I'm smart enough to know that you've both had your share of problems and then some. The wheelchair is ample evidence of that. And I know enough about your life to know the struggles you had with your farm as a young girl, Mrs. Channing. Yet what most people see when they look at you is not the history of your problems but the history of your success."

Brody studied them for a moment, his eyes piercing.

"What they see is two powerful, strong individuals. Individuals who have acquired wealth, success, social prominence. Individuals who give every appearance of having triumphed over every problem life has thrown in their path. To be honest, if I met Mr. and Mrs. Will Channing at a cocktail party, I might find them intimidating myself. Just imagine how a sensitive, insecure young girl finds them. No one, not even your closest family members, can see the fears, the angers, the sorrows, that you carry around with you inside your head. They can only see the impressive facade you present to the world, and that leads to a lot of misunderstandings."

Brody knew his words had hit home. Both Will and Anna sat wordless, staring at him, their faces a mixture of shock and revelation. It was the reaction he had hoped for, and he felt more confident than before that things would go well for Mina when she left Oak Summit Farm.

"It's too soon, Max! I can't think about that—about *anything* now."

Mina heard the fear, the anger in her voice. She pulled away from Max. Her arms hurt from the pressure of his fingers around them; her lips felt puffed, almost numb from the long, hot pressure of his. She half turned, but Max held her firm. She looked away for a moment, then, though she didn't mean to, found herself looking up into his face. She had never seen Max look this way before. A purple-clouded storm had swept across the usually sunny landscape.

"I'm not going to play cat-and-mouse with you, Mina. I'm not going to hold anything back from you."

The pressure of the strong fingers tightened around her arms.

"I love you, Mina, and I want to marry you. That's my intention. I don't care a damn bit if I have to wait till hell freezes over for it to happen. But I'm not going to keep any secrets from you as to what I want."

"Are you trying to make an honest woman of me?" Mina was intentionally bitter, cynical.

"God damn it, Mina, don't put yourself down so."

Max felt a sudden shock of rage, but it passed into tenderness. He pulled her against him, held her frail body gently against his own heaving chest. She didn't resist.

"I'm not trying to do anything but share my life with you," he whispered. "I'm trying to make you my wife."

Mina said nothing, but Max heard the faint sound of her crying muffled against his chest.

"As for the other," he continued sweetly, "I have . . . well, I'm not a virgin, either. It don't matter to me."

Through her pain, her confusion, a bubble of laughter welled up. Dear, sweet Max, so honest, so sincere, trying so hard to make her feel good, feel clean, feel worthwhile.

In her mind she saw herself in Johnny's bedroom. The three of them on top of her; their lips, their hands, restless, grasping on her bared breasts and thighs; their trousers open, the warmth of their brutal flesh.

She tried to picture Max, gently bumbling through some awkward adolescent encounter. He would probably not experience in a lifetime what she had known in the last few years.

The irony of it all was heartwarming.

"Thank you for telling me, Max," she teased gently as she wiped her eyes with her palms. "It doesn't matter to me, either."

He kissed her again, long and hard. There was nothing gentle or bumbling about the kiss.

"Mina, darling, I'm sorry to pressure you like this." He took on an embarrassed, apologetic tone. "I don't mean to, it ain't fair. I just get so damned anxious for you to know how I feel and—"

She put her finger to his lips to stop him. His eyes were troubled; it was clear to her that he was suffering. She suddenly felt that she was the strong one, that she was in control, that he needed her for protection. It was a strange, magnificent sensation, wanting to envelop and shelter this warm, tender giant of a man.

"Not now," she cautioned. "Let's talk about it later."

When the Channings arrived back at Casilla from their week in Connecticut, there were two important letters waiting for them among the fat packets of mail that had been sorted and stacked on Anna's desk in the farm office. One was from Sandro, written from the hospital in France, telling his parents that he expected to be released from the doctor's care almost any day. He would be temporarily assigned to a unit in Paris while awaiting papers and a troop ship sailing for America. A month, at most six weeks, and he would be home.

" 'It's hard to imagine being back in Casilla again,' " Will read from the letter, with a thinly disguised quaver in his voice. " 'I mean, *really* being back, since I've often been there in my mind these last couple of years. The crop must be knee-high already, and by the time I'm home, it'll be up to my waist or better. And I never thought I'd look forward to one of our hot-as-blazes summers, but I am. I guess Casilla hasn't changed much—I'm sure you two are as perfect as ever and not a day older. But I've changed—the world's changed. I'm kind of looking forward to being back where things are the way they used to be.' "

The second letter, postmarked in New York, was from Bart. Though Bart's letters were always addressed to her and Will and were full of news and comments for both of them, Anna was always on edge when his letters came, afraid that this time there would be some slip of the pen, that in a careless moment Bart might write a word, a phrase that was too personal, too revealing. It was a double bind, though, since what she wanted more than anything was to read an outpouring of Bart's true feelings.

She had to content herself with reading between the lines. Bart wrote of the German defeat, the retreat across the Rhine, and the liberation of France. Then he described at length his impressions of Paris, becoming once again the City of Light after the darkness of the Occupation. In his narrative he mentioned a number of places—the Tuileries, Café Pont Neuf, the little iron-gated fountain court on a narrow stone street in the Quartier Latin, the long, columned gallery of the Plaza Athénée. Each place mentioned had a reference to liberated Paris; in the fountain court Bart saw French children with sticks bayoneting a flour sack meant to be Hitler; at the Plaza Athénée, which had been taken over by the American Air Transport Command, the gallery was filled with file cabinets and bulletin boards and a military bureaucracy managing troop and supply airlifts. They were typical of the postwar scenes any American might have described in a letter to home, but each place was also where Bart and Anna had been during their last time together in Paris. It was Bart's little message to her.

Bart was also on his way home—the letter had been written in New York—and he expected to be in Casilla in about a month, after a few weeks of meetings in Washington.

It was ironic that the war had separated Bart and Sandro, only to bring them close together in France; Anna regretted that she had had no way of knowing what Bart's movements would be or that he would even be in France at all. She couldn't help but think how good it would have been for Sandro to have Bart visit him during his recovery. It had been agony for her and Will, knowing so little about Sandro's condition from the other side of the world. It would have been comforting to know that Bart was at his bedside, but that was the way life was. Opportunities were missed, gone forever; the pieces of the puzzle didn't always fall neatly into place.

At least now a few pieces were falling into place: her son was coming home safe from the war; her daughter had fought her drug addiction. Her lover was coming back too. Her longing for him, which had been buried deep inside these last years, now intensified, grew, fought its way to the surface. As Will read

Bart's long letter to them, Anna sat in her chair in the library across from Will. She watched her husband's still-handsome face as his blue eyes concentrated through his reading glasses.

There was no doubt that she and Will had grown closer in the last year, since the night Sandro had been shipped out to Europe. They now slept together every night. Even though Will's insomnia occasionally kept her awake, they both had commented on how much less troubled Will's sleep had become. The physical closeness of sleeping together had also led to a gentle, undefined sort of sexuality between them, based on hugging and caressing. Will's body would always be dead from the waist down, and Anna regretted that she could never fully satisfy him when he had learned to so fully satisfy her.

Now that Bart was coming back, she wondered how she would feel about being with him. Their months in Paris were still in her thoughts every day, but in four years those memories had assumed a distant, almost mythical status. She and Bart would never have another Paris, she knew that. They would have to be content with their Wednesdays in the city. Anna was sometimes troubled by the thought that even the Wednesdays might not be the same once Bart was back, since things had changed so much between her and Will.

One resolution Anna and Will had made on the return trip to Texas was to take Dr. Brody's advice seriously. During the train ride, and back at Casa Grande, they spent many hours talking together and singly with Mina. It was a painful and revealing process and one that required a good deal of courage on all their parts. Will and Anna had to be careful not to probe too deeply, not to advise Mina too much but listen to her instead; for Mina was still smarting from the shame she felt her life had been for the last few years. Still, over a period of weeks, by dribs and drabs, their true feelings leaked through the once impenetrable barrier that had stood between them.

When they had first gotten back to Casilla, Will and Anna had been uneasy, not knowing quite what to do with Mina. Max had understandably monopolized her time on the train, but now he was back at his farming and only around some evenings; with most of the summer ahead there was no question of school —the college summer session was already under way—and

Anna told Will she was frankly concerned that with too much time on her hands Mina might be tempted to fall in with her old crowd and her old ways.

"I think Brody gave us the best advice, Anna," Will cautioned. "We've got to let her take responsibility for making her life go right."

Anna agreed—she understood the principle behind Brody's advice—but she also knew she had that deep, motherly instinct to guard her children, to guide them along the safest paths. It was painful for her to override that instinct.

Fortunately Mina did her part. Brody seemed to have planted healthy seeds in Mina's mind as well. The first week home she came down to breakfast looking pale, but more energetic than she had in months.

"I went out to the greenhouses yesterday and spent a few hours with Uncle Hank," she announced offhandedly during the meal. "I asked him if he thought I could do it, and if you didn't mind, if I could help him and Pablo out there. You know —transplanting seedlings and tagging and wrapping plants. I don't know the first thing about horticulture, but it would be good for me to learn, don't you think?"

Her parents endorsed the idea wholeheartedly with a cautionary "Only if you and your Uncle Hank want to do it," in order to let Mina know that they expected her to make her own decisions.

Mina started work for Hank and Pablo that day. Anna was at first concerned that her daughter, who had never shown any interest in any kind of work at all, with the exception of horesback riding, would soon grow bored with long hours of physical activity. By the end of the first week Anna was concerned that Mina was working *too* hard. She would be in the greenhouses before breakfast, then back out all day, and back at the house barely in time to change for supper. After all, Mina's weight was still down, her body still visibly weakened from the drugs. Yet she seemed to be thriving on the long workday, and her conversation at supper was full of talk about what she'd done and learned that day. Max, who came for supper or for visits after supper, looked to be as pleased with Mina's new-found interest as her parents were.

One afternoon during the second week, Anna drove out to

the greenhouse to see Mina. She was working alone in one of the damp, hot glass enclosures filled with long rows of wooden tables covered with plants in various stages of growth. Mina was busily unloading a plot of geranium cuttings onto one of the pebble-covered tabletops.

"I just came out to see how things were going," Anna said as she overtook Mina halfway down the long rows. "I hope I'm not interrupting?"

"Of course not." Mina paused to wipe her perspiring forehead on the sleeve of her shirt. Her hair was tied up in a kerchief; her cotton culottes and denim apron, as well as her hands and face, were soil-streaked. "You don't mind walking along with me as I set these out? I've still got another ten trays to do, and I still haven't even started on the rows in the other greenhouse yet."

Mina held out one of the newly rooted geranium cuttings in its paper box for her mother to examine.

"Doesn't look much different from any other geranium. But it's one of the new varieties Hank and Pab developed in the last couple of years. I still don't see how they do all that hybridization stuff. Hocus-pocus to me. I can see the results, though. This variety has deep red blooms—'full-bodied' color, as Hank would say. He said the color is so red-blooded and all-American that he wants to give it a patriotic name when he puts it on the market next year. I suggested 'Iwo Jima' to commemorate all the American blood shed there."

Mina made a face.

"Hank thought that was macabre. He wants to call it the Harry Truman. Not exactly elegant, but I guess it gets the point across."

Anna replaced the young plant beside the hundreds of siblings that covered the table.

"You're really enjoying this, aren't you?"

Mina looked at her mother and with absolute candor in her face said, "It beats the hell out of drugs and hooch."

Mina's directness was unexpected and a bit brutal. Anna still found it difficult to talk about the harsher side of Mina's problems.

"I've shocked you, Mama. Sorry. Didn't mean to." Mina

went back to her methodical transfer of cuttings from tray to table.

"I'm still uncomfortable with all this, I suppose."

"That's okay. Me too. But I can't pretend that it never happened, and not so long ago."

Before Anna could think of what to reply, Mina continued her conversation.

"Max has asked me to marry him."

"I'm not surprised," Anna replied. "He's made his intentions pretty clear for some time now. I figured if he hadn't already, he would very soon. Your dad and I haven't pried. We knew you'd tell us what you wanted us to know."

To Anna it seemed too good to be true. Max was such a fine, strong young man; he had the kind of solid, rocklike strength that she felt Mina needed. But deep down Anna didn't quite trust that Mina's life could sort itself out so easily, that her daughter could change so totally, so fast. Sometimes the pieces of the puzzle fell into place too easily and made one wonder if, a little while later, one couldn't work at the puzzle and see that the pieces that had fit so easily had been put in the wrong place after all. Anna hated herself for that element of mistrust, but it was still there.

"I don't know how I feel about managing that," Mina continued. "I'm not sure what any of my emotions are anymore. I'm not my old self, but I don't think I'm my new self yet, either. I couldn't forgive myself if I married Max, only to find out that the old me is still there somewhere. That's why I won't pretend I was never an addict. I have to keep reminding myself of what I was at one time."

"Do you love Max?"

Mina paused in her task. She turned once again and fixed her eyes on her mother's.

"When Max asked me, back in Connecticut, I wasn't sure. It didn't seem possible that such a nice man could really love me and want to marry me. Now that I've had more time with him, I know I do love Max."

"Then why are you so afraid?"

"Because I don't love myself! I loathe Mina Channing. She's a drug addict, a boozer, a slut. Yet she has one glimmer of decency and conscience in her, and that conscience won't let her marry Max Mirkovsky. He deserves better!"

Anna grabbed her daughter and pulled her close. Mina's chest heaved with emotion, and she seemed on the edge of tears.

"Don't talk like that, Mina. It isn't true." Anna held Mina like she was a small girl again, who had been awakened in the middle of the night, terrified by a bad dream. "You know none of us think of you that way. And certainly Max doesn't, or he wouldn't have asked you to marry him. So you see, darling, you're the only one who thinks so little of Wilhelmina Channing."

Mina looked up at her mother. Her eyes, full of anger and tears, were the same clear blue as Will's.

"How can I help it, Mama? Oh, I know what Dr. Brody said, about how everyone hates himself deep down, how we all are harder on ourselves than anyone else is. But I can't forget how I've behaved, what I've fallen to. I know it, the whole damn world knows it!"

"Mina, you have to realize that no one hates you because you have problems. Of course, it's easy to understand how low you feel about your past, how embarrassed and ashamed you are about it. But you're no different than any other man or woman on the face of the earth. You've had problems—serious problems—and shortcomings—serious shortcomings. What's most important is that you've faced up to them, matured, grown. Anyone who matters is going to feel sympathy and concern for your problems; anyone who matters is going to love you and respect you for having pulled yourself out of one of those dark pits that our lives throw us into."

As the two woman embraced Anna remembered how many dark pits had swallowed her during her life. Somehow she had always managed to claw her way back up to the light.

Anna caressed her daughter's thick honey-colored hair and remembered how she had held Will's child close when she was a baby with hair the color of pale wheat. She felt as much of a caring mother now as then, though she had the bittersweet knowledge that, though a mother's caress could smooth away the hurts of a daughter of two, they were helpless against the hurts of her daughter now.

"We all are awfully hard on ourselves, aren't we, Mina? I

can't really tell you how much blame I've heaped on myself, torturing myself because I was such a failure as a mother. I suppose in many ways I feel I am somehow the cause of your problems."

"How can you say that? You always were so perfect. You and Papa both. Dr. Brody helped me to realize that's part of my problem. You see, you and Papa never did anything wrong. You were good-looking and well liked. You were educated and successful and charming. You had everything and were everything. Whatever you set out to do, you did—better than anybody else. I guess when I was little I thought that was great—having a mother and father that were so great. But as I got a little older I started to feel so damned worthless and useless. I couldn't do anything except sit around the pool or drive fast cars or wear expensive clothes. You and Papa and Sandro were accomplished and important. I was just Wilhelmina Channing, spoiled, rich little bitch. It was even worse after I got started on booze and cocaine. Even though I was doing it and kidded myself that I *liked* doing it, I really knew it was wrong.

"I would come home from one of my nights out, hung over and drug-dazed and only half remembering what stranger I'd been intimate with that night. Just before I would fall asleep— pass out is a better term—there would be one moment of lucidity through the haze. I would always think of you and Papa. Think of your love. Of the devotion, the honesty, the downright purity of what you've shared all these years. For that lucid moment I would feel jealous of what a noble kind of love you and Papa share, and I would feel the horror of my own filthiness and the horror of knowing that I would never share with a man what you and Papa share."

It was as if an unseen hand had taken an ice pick and plunged it into Anna's heart. The pick punctured the thick membrane of hypocrisy and secrecy that wrapped around Anna's heart, and in an instant she understood fully her daughter's deep self-hatred, because it was the image of her own.

Chapter Seven

BART STRUGGLED THROUGH THE TANGLE OF KHAKI-UNI-formed GIs who went to retrieve their duffel bags from the overhead racks of the railcar. He had purposely gotten up from his seat early and taken his single suitcase down, knowing that there would be a stampede as soon as the train slowed and moved alongside the El Paso station. No sooner had he taken down his bag and started for the forward door than the home-coming soldiers, who had filled every seat in the car but one, had taken his lead and flooded into the narrow aisle.

"I give up," Bart muttered as he was bumped from the rear by one anxious soldier, then narrowly escaped a clout in the head by an out-of-control duffel bag, more or less in the hands of a short, stocky private in front of him.

"Jeez, mister. Take it easy." The kid grinned up at him with-out a hint of anger in his pug-nosed face. "Hell, can't blame us if we wanna get our asses off this goddamn train and into a bar. If you'd been where we'd been, you'd be goddamn glad to get your butt back in one piece too."

"You got a point there, soldier. Guess it's good to be home." Bart put his case on an empty seat and leaned against the back of the chair, resigned to a wait while the traffic ahead cleared up.

"Well, I ain't home just yet—that's Alabama. Just like this war ain't over just yet. But I'm close enough to home, and the war's close enough to over to make me get out and celebrate. You got any kids in the service?"

It was a logical question; in the last five years Bart had gotten used to servicemen mistaking him for a civilian. He'd always found it charming, how they would regale him with war stories and say how lucky he was to be "old enough" to be out of things.

"Yes, a son."

What the hell, Bart thought. It's safe enough here, no one would know. He felt an unexpected swell of pride at being able to say that his son was in the service.

"Army?"

"Corporal, Seventeenth Division."

The GI whistled appreciatively through his teeth. "They got hit hard. The Bulge. I had a buddy in Basic in Wichita who wound up with the Seventeenth. He's gone. Yours okay?"

"He's fine. A leg wound but nothing permanent."

"Yeah, I'm lucky, too, sort of." The soldier winked. "All I got was the clap."

As the train slowed and jerked into the shadow of the station an outcry of enthusiastic, good-natured obscenity went up from the soldiers.

"Hot damn! El Asshole, Texas, home of Fort Fucking Bliss!"

"I'll be shit-faced before sunset."

"Watch your privates, private. Those two-bit whores'll bite 'em off, chew 'em up, and spit 'em out."

"Yew wan' my seester, meester?"

"Hell, I want the closest damn thing Juarez has to Rita Hayworth. Even if I got to hock my socks."

"You better damn hock 'em first, 'fore some hooker steals 'em."

"Fuck Hitler."

"He's dead, you Okie butthole. That's what we did, remember."

"So Fuck Hirohito."

"Yeah. I hear those Japs like it up the backside."

"Yeah. Japs and leathernecks."

As the car began clearing and Bart moved along the aisle, he remembered his return from the First War, the Great War, the War to End All Wars. The doughboys of 1918 had carried with them the same reckless sense of freedom as these GIs did. Their dead buddies were gone forever, buried in that blessed forgetfulness that descends on soldiers after combat. Tonight these youths would get drunk, get laid if they weren't too drunk, then start the rest of their lives with a hangover. The reality of the war, never forgotten, would bury itself somewhere deep inside them while they went home to find what was waiting for them.

When he had come home from the First War, Anna had been foremost in his mind; she was the chalice that awaited him at the end of his crusade.

What a naive fool he had been, to think that life went according to plan. That life lived up to one's expectations. These soldiers all had their chalices waiting for them at the end of their crusades. Like Bart had been, they were naive enough to think that the prize would be theirs; in a quarter of a century they, like Bart now, would still be wending home from crusades, the chalice still kept from them.

As Bart neared the door a familiar-looking face appeared on the platform between the cars. He looked closer. The resemblance was there, all right, though the face was older and leaner, the body taller and bigger. Then the soldier turned to step aside to let someone pass. Bart saw him full-face.

"Sandro!"

Sandro looked into the car, startled to hear his name. In a second he focused on Bart, the surprise of recognition lighting his face.

Bart managed his way onto the platform, and the men embraced spontaneously, jostled by the steady stream of men spilling out of the car and down the metal steps to the station platform.

Bart clambered down beside the train, followed by Sandro, with a cane in his right hand, more gingerly negotiating the steps. He winced as his leg flexed.

"How's it doing?" Bart asked as he took Sandro's elbow and helped boost him down.

"Not too bad, actually. Fair amount of muscle damage in the thigh. That's what's sore and stiff. Six months, they said, and there may be no limp at all, once the muscle grows back."

"I'm glad it wasn't worse."

Sandro smiled the same timid, but genuine, smile that reminded him so much of Anna.

They followed the khaki throng across the open-air platform toward the hulk of the neo-Spanish terminal building. All around them were the scenes of reunions with lovers and loved ones; Bart remembered 1918, when he came back from Europe, when Anna had been with Will and her family, when they had only had a quick, brother-and-sisterly embrace. She and Will would be here together again, and their embrace would have to be just as careful, just as safe.

"I don't see your folks. They must be inside."

"They don't know I'm here yet. They think I'm coming in tomorrow. We docked at Norfolk, then got shipped out to New Orleans. I was supposed to have a day layover there before picking up the *Sunset* for home. They had a couple of AWOLs, I guess, and the CO bumped me forward since I was a gimp. I decided to show up at the farm—kind of a surprise."

"I'm sort of sneaking in too. There was a letter from Anna when I got into New York last month, full of news about you, about the wedding. It was the first I'd heard that you'd been shot. My mail was pretty erratic when I was in Europe—some of it lost, a lot of it censored. I was in France, you know, when you were in the hospital."

"No shit? Didn't you know where I was?"

"Not until I read your mother's letter in New York. Then when I heard you were recuperating at Beaunais . . . I could have come up, I was in Paris and Versailles most of May."

"Versailles? Mama wrote me that you were in England. That's why it was so frustrating when we were shipped over. We didn't even know where we were going. When we landed at Southampton, it was the first time we knew it would be England. And there was no leave, no way of asking around for you."

"I wouldn't have been there. From forty-two on I moved around quite a bit. Portugal, North Africa after Rommel collapsed, Italy after the surrender."

"Were you a spy?"

"Not that glamorous, soldier! Mainly hanging around a lot of black marketeers, pretending to be one myself, and picking up what information I could from the shadier side of the war business. Criminals have a way of transcending politics, you know. They can find out what's going on around a line faster than the best espionage men in the Defense Department."

"Too bad you couldn't have known where I was, even if you couldn't tell me where you were. I mean, that way you could have seen me at the hospital. I was even in Versailles the week before I left. I had a day furlough."

There was a strained tone in Sandro's voice. Bart put a reassuring arm around his son. He had to remember that Sandro was still very young, that he had just been through the black numbness of battle and the lonely terror of a close brush with death. Young soldiers put up a brave front, but it is nothing but a brave front.

"I wish I'd known, too, Sandro. At least we made it—separately—back together here. But what the hell were you doing down in Versailles? Strange place to go fresh out of the hospital on your only one-day leave?"

"I had some friends down there. Americans, from before the war. I used to go to Paris there when I was studying with Nadia. There was someone I was looking for, who I hadn't heard from since thirty-nine. I went to Versailles, thinking Elsie might know where she was. But Elsie and her friends had gone back to America."

There was still that strained tone in his voice.

"You must mean Elsie de Wolfe," Bart said. "I know the villa —I was there a few times myself, years ago. I was there last month, too, to a few parties the British officers had. They'd taken the place over after the Germans surrendered.

"It's odd, Sandro, that we've been passing so close by each other but not connecting, missing each other by a few seconds or a few feet. I may have been at de Wolfe's when you went by. Who knows? I was in Versailles a lot that month. I may have been upstairs using Elsie's latrine when you were downstairs, asking the Brits about Elsie. And now we run into each other, by a hair's breadth, between the cars of a train. If you hadn't turned when you did, I could have let it pass as one of the hundreds of GIs who look a little like you. . . . There's always such a fine, fragile line in our lives, between things going one way or another. If we'd missed here today, I would have seen you in a few days at the wedding. But there are times when the slightest chance that keeps people apart can make a big difference."

Sandro thought of Constanza, during their last meeting at the apartment on the Avenue Foch. She had been so close to coming with him; if he'd had only another few minutes he could have convinced her to leave Paris. If only.

The doors of the terminal took them into a frantic sea of soldiers and civilians, bobbing about and looking for familiar faces and bags and footlockers. The din from the crowd echoing in the cavernous waiting room made conversation difficult.

Sandro and Bart made their way through the crowd and to the baggage window, where a jostling crowd of soldiers stood in several snaking lines as olive-drab duffel bags were heaved one by one across the claim counter. Sandro's plans for the next few hours were open. His discharge was still being processed, and for a week he would still have to report to the medical officer at Fort Bliss; he'd been told he had a two-day pass on his arrival in El Paso, but he had to call the officer in charge to confirm. If all was in order, he was planning to catch a six-o'clock train for the hour's ride to Casilla.

"Mama wrote me that she and Dad were having a supper tonight," Sandro said as he handed his bag across a low counter. Bart took it for him, and they walked toward the exit. Just family—Mina and Max, Kate, Hank and Pablo. The big bash is tomorrow, my official hail-the-conquering-hero party. Knowing Mama, she's invited half the county. You'll come down with me, won't you?"

"Of course. I wouldn't miss one of Anna's parties. Hell, I can even pretend it's my welcome-home bash too. You know us loners—we have to get our family feelings vicariously, since there's no one to welcome us with open arms."

Bart meant it as a joke, and Sandro took it that way. But as he said it Bart knew it was no joke at all. It had always been painful watching from the sidelines as Anna and Will raised Sandro. Bart could watch; he could even participate in the benign, caring "Uncle Bart" role he'd taken on himself. But the real hurt came from never having Sandro call him Dad; he could never stand in the doorway at Casa Grande with his arm around Anna as they watched their son coming home from school, from the fields, from the war. That was Will's privilege. Bart thought Will was probably a better father to Sandro than he could have been. Certainly Will's life was more settled, less maverick. Then, too, Bart's life might have been different if he could have been Sandro's acknowledged father. Damn it all!

Why couldn't he just say to Sandro, "You're my son! I sired you, I love you. I'm proud watching you become a man"?

They stepped out again into the bright midafternoon sun, their eyes squinting against the glare from the tireless landscape of the desert city.

"Whew!" Sandro whistled in mock amazement. "I'd forgotten what July is like. It must be a hundred. First thing when I get home after I kiss Mama and the folks is strip naked and jump in the pool."

"Sounds great. Wish I could join you."

"You're coming down tonight, aren't you? To dinner?"

"I'm not invited. Remember, no one knows I'm in town yet."

"Aw, come one. You know everybody's going to be itchy to see you. I mean, you're *family* too. Come on."

"I'm *sort* of family, Sandro." Bart played with the irony of the situation. "But I don't want to get a reputation as one of those kissing cousins who shows up uninvited for dinner. Besides, Corporal Channing, I've been away a few years myself. I've got to stop by Mesa Street and see if the house is still in one piece, then to Casa Portillo tomorrow to start digging out from under five years of unopened mail. And, to be honest, I've got to spend the night trying to decide if I should take boot-black to my hair before anyone else sees it. I'm not getting any younger."

Sandro's squinted face studied Bart's in mock seriousness. Bart wondered what he really saw there.

"You are getting kind of gray, old-timer. Distinguished is the polite term, no? Tell 'em it's premature from all the pressures of wartime espionage."

"Fuck off, soldier." Bart playfully grabbed Sandro by the neck. "Or learn to respect your elders."

"Ow, *sir!* The least you can do, if you're not going home with me, is buy me a drink. There's gotta be some saloon down here by the station. I still got to get HQ on the phone and see if leave is legal. It may take hours to get through—I might as well drink while I'm calling."

Bart suggested they walk a few blocks from the station toward the cluster of taller brick and concrete buildings that ringed the plaza and the heart of downtown. The stretch between the station and rail yards was an older part of town; the frame or stucco buildings that lined the somber, narrow streets near the depot were survivors of another generation, when the streets were unpaved and horses and buggies were tethered to porch posts along them instead of cars nosed against parking meters.

As they neared the first corner an olive-drab bus passed by. A whistle attracted their attention to an arm waving at them. Bart recognized the soldier from the train, just before he'd seen Sandro. Bart knew he must have drawn a logical conclusion seeing Bart walking beside a limping young soldier with a cane, and he was just as glad the soldier had seen them from the bus instead of in the station, when he might have blurted out what Bart had told him.

They turned onto a narrow side street. Though the sun was still high, a score of lighted neon signs proclaimed the hard-drinking bars and cheap transient hotels that cluster like barnacles near every city's rail station.

"Not exactly Montana Avenue," Bart said as he switched Sandro's bag to his other shoulder to relieve the pressure. "Not as bad as most of Juarez, either. But there's an old saloon down here I used to come to when I was your age. Run-down now, I guess. But in the old days—before my time—it was pretty damned elegant. Stained-glass transoms, brass chandeliers. Had one of the fanciest carved mahogany bars I've ever seen. Used to be a big hangout for local politicos, a lot of bigwigs from the Villa and Carranza days. Probably nothing but old winos these days."

To Sandro's surprise Bart paused at a new-looking facade of glass brick and stainless steel; neon suspended in the two large windows that framed the door proclaimed that Lone Star and Pearl beers were on tap inside.

Through the doors Sandro saw that the bar's attempt at *moderne* updating had ended beyond the sidewalk. The bar inside was dark and cavernous. He saw an expanse of white-tiled floors, with intricate green-and-red geometrics worked into the mosaic; the surface was buckled and cracked, and missing patches were filled in carelessly with concrete. To the right the bar, a long expanse of baroque enthusiasm, dominated the room. Its beveled mirrors were obscured by a newly spouted jungle of calendars, posters of bullfights and Uncle Sam, decals, and beer signs. The brass of the gas chandeliers was tarnished to a deep brown, and many of the cut-glass globes were missing or jaggedly broken.

There were more customers than Sandro would have expected for a midweek afternoon. Half a dozen men, some Mexican, some Anglo, sat at the bar, some engaged in talk with the beefy, bald-headed bartender. A few more groups sat at some of the dozen or so cheap chrome tables and chairs that were scattered irregularly around the expanse of tiled floor.

In the back Sandro saw a cluster of GIs standing by a gleaming red, white, and blue jukebox. As he and Bart sat at a table near the window Lena Horne's voice echoed incongruously through the saloon.

". . . stormy weather, since my man and I ain't together . . ."

"Not exactly an up tune for your homecoming? Draft?"

Sandro nodded, and Bart signaled their order to the bartender.

"Pop isn't my first love, for sure," Sandro answered. "But this kind of stuff is great. At least they didn't play 'Mairzy Doats' or 'Bei Mir Bist du Schon.' Those were about the only two records at the rec room at the hospital. They got played hours on end, day and night. That music is deadly enough to kill germs—or patients. God spare me from ever hearing Kay Kaiser or the Andrews Sisters again!"

"No Chopin in this man's army, heh?"

"Only when I played. There was an old spinet in the rec room too. Out of tune to beat the band, and more than a few keys missing. It was a challenge finding pieces to play that didn't have too many of the missing notes in them."

The bartender deposited two foaming mugs in front of them. Bart dropped forty cents on the table, but the man pushed the coins back toward him.

"*Amigo,* forget it, on the house!" he said in accented English. "You didn't send this boy over with that leg."

Bart was thankful the remark slipped by Sandro, and he just thanked the bartender.

"So what now, Sandro? School? Music? Settling into a career as heir to Cutter-Channing Farms?"

"The farm, of course. I may try to go to College of Mines

part-time. But I know Mama's going to be depending on me more and more now. I have to keep reminding myself that she's forty-seven now—"

"I have to keep reminding myself too," Bart interrupted.

"All the maids and foremen and field hands in the world can't make up for the fact that she's got the full burden of running the farm."

Bart was struck by Sandro's matter-of-fact tone. It seemed too rehearsed, too pat, and it didn't ring true.

"Of course," Sandro added almost inaudibly behind his beer mug, "now that Max is going to be in the family, that changes things."

"Does it? Your folks are not going to turn control of the farms over to Max or you?"

"No-ooo . . ."

Sandro drew the word out, as if he were reconsidering finishing it.

"But let's face it," he continued. "Max is, well, a born farmer, if you know what I mean."

"I think I do. He's a 'born farmer,' as you call it, because he *likes* to farm. And you don't."

"Touché."

Sandro grinned sheepishly, his face red. The two men held each other's eyes for a moment, recognizing a moment of honesty between them.

Sandro continued. "Look, Bart. I know what I have to do. I know what my responsibilities are. My family's important; they've worked hard to give me what advantages I have. The least I can do is take over the business. I know I'm capable of doing it, and I care enough about farming to make a go of it."

"I admire your lack of selfishness. But what about your responsibility to yourself?"

"I don't understand what you mean." Sandro retreated again behind his beer mug; he held it to his mouth and sipped slowly.

"I think you do. Remember, I've watched you grow up. I've seen that you've always had a mind of your own. Gone your own way, even if your way was very different from everyone else's."

Sandro put down his beer. A sly smile crossed his face.

"I guess I got that from you," he said flatly.

In a second the tables had been turned. Bart found his eyes grazing the gloomy corners of the bar, the shadows of the tin ceiling. *Don't lose your cool, Bradley,* a voice urged him. *Remember your intelligence training. Hold their eye, don't waver. Let them do the explaining.*

He focused his gaze back across the table.

"Oh?" He managed to sound only mildly surprised at Sandro's words.

"Sure. I never told you this before. Never had any reason to. But you've always been . . . let me put it another way. It's not easy growing up in the middle of a cotton farm in the middle of the desert—even growing up rich—if you're different than everybody else within a day's ride. Before the war, everybody I knew wanted to play football and get drunk across the border and to marry the farm girl with the biggest tits and settle down and grow cotton. I wanted to read books and play the piano and drink wine at home at dinner like we always have. And dammit, I'm not sure I want to marry any farm girl and grow cotton. But I always thought I was weird for being so different. I couldn't help the things I liked, but I was ashamed of liking them."

Sandro stared hard at the table, his fingers toying nervously with the ring.

"I even thought there was something wrong with me. That I was queer."

"Sandro, don't—"

"Relax. I found out differently."

He looked at Bart again, his gray eyes echoing Bart's own. There was depth in Sandro's youthful face, a maturity before its time that took Bart back to the early years with Anna, when she hardly had been a child, but with a woman's depth and determination.

"From the time I was a kid you were the only man I knew who was different. You didn't do the kinds of things every other joker did. You weren't a farmer. You didn't have a wife and kids. You had a nightclub and some fancy set of wheels. You had unusual friends and good-looking women around you. You traveled around the world and gave parties everybody talked about, even if they weren't there. You rode well and shot well—things a lot of men can do—but you talked about Shakespeare

and Rubens and Mozart too. I remember thinking how swell
you were—how much I wanted to grow up to be like you."

Sandro smiled self-consciously.

"Shit, Bart, I'm talking like you were Babe Ruth or something."

"Compliments accepted. But a lot of men can clear a six-foot
fence, English saddle, and talk about Shakespeare over beer
later. That's not much to set your sights on."

Sandro pondered, trying to pull out his thoughts.

"I guess in your world that's true. But in mine, at least when
I was a kid, you really *were* different. And you liked being
different—I could tell. It kind of oozed out of you. I liked that;
that was how I wanted to be. You made me feel better, even
good, about not being like everybody else. Whenever I saw you,
I didn't feel so bad about myself. I wasn't lonely."

Bart studied his son. Sandro's face was etched with the unquestioned pain of young manhood. He was still years away
from irony and bitterness.

"There's a price to be paid for being different, Sandro."

The youth's eyes questioned him.

"Loneliness."

Bart thought of the years wasted, irretrievably part of the
past. His son was grown; he, himself, was facing those slow,
declining years of old age. It was all too inevitable, too much
out of one's control. Bart wanted to run out of the dark, hot
bar, out into the glaring July sun. He wanted to run down the
half deserted street, faster and faster, until he had run back into
his youth, when all of the mistakes, the follies, the misfortunes
of life lay before and not behind him.

Sandro's eyes wandered around the shadowy recesses of the
room. Bart could tell he had slipped very far away; Sandro's
deep gray eyes were unfocused and distant, his face clouded by
a faint but visibly painful melancholy.

"It's obvious you're not thinking about farming. But I've
been around long enough to know you're thinking about some
woman. If you don't mind talking about it."

"There's not a hell of a lot to say. I met her in 1938 in Paris.
She was . . . older. Beautiful, kind. Glamorous, at least to a
hick like me."

"And she taught you everything you'll ever need to know

about women." Bart smiled wickedly, in appreciation of the
universality of some kinds of human experience.

Sandro was at first put off by Bart's comment, then he understood the other man's intent and shot back with, "And then
some. Her name was Constanza. She was really quite a beautiful and cultured woman. And I was madly in love with her. Of
course, at the end of a year, things took their natural course.
She made it quite clear that I was one of a long series of
younger lovers she'd had. I was heartbroken. She was tolerant;
after all, she'd played that scene before. So I was shoved out of
her nest on Avenue Foch, to lick my wounds alone and make
my way in the world."

"Surely you're not still in love with her?" Bart questioned.

"That was years ago. But the look you just had on your face
wasn't exactly that of a young man fondly recalling his first
encounter with an older woman."

"A lot happened. The war started—just a few days after our
little 'heartbreak.' I tried to get her to come back to America
with me. Not to marry and settle down. Just to get away from
the war. The Germans were already marching in Paris."

"So she was the 'friend' I arranged papers for?"

Sandro paused, as if he didn't want to continue.

Bart encouraged him with a look.

Sandro continued with his eyes fixed on the table.

"We lost touch. As you know, I came home and wasn't back
in France until this year. After the German surrender, when I
was out of the hospital, I tried to find her. That's why I went to
Versailles—to see if Constanza might be at Elsie's or if someone
there knew where she was."

"And?"

"It was hard enough finding anyone from thirty-nine. Most
were abroad or holed up down south somewhere. I had no luck
until just before I was shipped back to the States. By chance,
one day in the Jardin des Plantes I ran into the woman who had
been Constanza's maid. For some reason, God knows why, she
and I recognized each other. Guess I was looking for any face
associated with Constanza. I asked . . . I heard . . ."

Suddenly Sandro was having difficulty talking. His eyes
misted, his voice choked.

"She had taken up with a German officer during the occupation. That was . . . so like her. She loved men, she loved parties, laughing, good times. Politics didn't mean much to her, but surviving did. If loving a Nazi lieutenant would help her get through life, she'd fall in love and show him as good a time as any young American student. But this time it didn't do any good. In forty-four she was taken away to the camps. They came one night, a bunch of Germans, and took her to the Gare du Nord and put her in a cattle car. No explanation, no nothing. Can you imagine, my Constanza, always so beautiful, so elegant, jammed into a cattle car?

"Until the maid told me, I never realized Constanza was Jewish. She was one of those women with a vague history and a vague birthdate.

"The maid never saw her again. Like everyone else on the cattle cars, she just disappeared."

Bart asked if Sandro had any word of her. After all, there had been many camp survivors. Thousands were even now just beginning to find their way home.

"I did find out. The maid had seen a Jewish man, a jeweler, who knew Constanza. They'd been taken to Bergen-Belsen together. She endured . . . everything that the prisoners endured there."

"Is she . . ."

"Last winter this jeweler heard from survivors from the women's barracks—that Constanza had been shot. Executed by a firing squad for leading an uprising among the other women. Can you imagine, Bart, this spoiled, elegant creature of drawing rooms and boudoirs, leading a revolt against Nazi monsters? They said that when they tied her to the post, with the whole camp and the other Germans watching, to make an example of her, her—her head was shaved and she only weighed eighty pounds. She stood there and looked the goddamned Nazis in the eye and told them to go fuck themselves."

There was a long silence. The dime in the jukebox had run out while Sandro was talking; the only sounds in the bar were the occasional clinks and rattles of the bartender's activities and the subdued sounds of the handful of conversations among the group in the bar. Bart broke the silence.

"I'm proud of you, Sandro. That must sound strange, after what you've just told me. What happened to Constanza must be very painful for you; it's obvious you loved her very much. That's why I'm so proud of you. I respect a man who is sensitive and caring and who is man enough to admit it. I also respect a man who can genuinely and deeply love a woman. In my book that's the true measure of a man."

Sandro took in Bart's words, carefully turned them over in his mind. In the abstract he agreed with what Bart said, but when he heard them applied to himself, they seemed like exaggerated praise: Sandro had never thought much about what his love for Constanza said about him; he only knew he had loved her deeply, without question.

Sandro thought it was interesting that Bart had said that in the first place; the drift of their entire conversation had been unexpectedly serious and personal. He would have expected, after so long a time without seeing one another, that he and Bart would have had a more extroverted, war-story and family-reunion kind of talk. Sandro didn't mind; there was something very warm and touching about Bart's honesty. Sandro had always sensed that Bart was a man of depth, of intense seriousness, but his style was closed; he didn't share his secrets with the world.

"I thought of you a lot while I was overseas," Sandro began, not sure whether he would be able to get out what he wanted to say. "It's kind of crazy, who and what you think about in combat situations. I kept thinking about you, remembering times we'd spent together before the war. Whenever I thought about those times, I thought about my mother too. That was kind of odd, until I remembered certain things about my feelings about Constanza—how I looked at her, how I talked around her, even in a room full of people. I kept thinking about us, then I'd go back to Casilla and those memories of you . . . and mother."

So it was going to come out after all! Bart suppressed his flush of panic, held his outwardly calm front.

"You're in love with her, aren't you?"

"You're her son. What do you expect me to say?"

Sandro was suddenly embarrassed.

"I've put you on the spot. I'm sorry. Let's drop it. Forget I said anything at all."

It would all be over in a few seconds, Bart reminded himself. Twenty-four years of pretending; the pain of exposure might not be as bad as he thought. At least Sandro already knew; there were no surprises for the boy. It was just a matter of getting the words out.

"Yes. I do love her. I have for years."

Sandro smiled, his face suffused with a childlike, pleased warmth.

"I'm glad to hear that, though I can't say why. All those years of unrequited love can't have been easy for you. Seeing her with Dad, watching them have a life and a family together. That's the heart of that loneliness you talked about, isn't it?"

Bart nodded.

"I guess there's some comfort in knowing she doesn't suspect a bit. It would have made things tough on both of you—as friends, I mean—if she'd known how you felt about her when she's so totally wrapped up in Dad."

Bart's anxiety bubbled up into laughter at this unexpected news. So Sandro had only figured out half the story. Well, there was some comfort and safety, at that. "But how do you feel about it?"

Sandro, still smiling, leaned back and said, "Like I said, for some reason I can't explain, I like the idea. It's swell that we talked about it, too—just a little secret between the boys, right?"

"We'll shake on it."

Their hands clasped across the table. The gesture had started out half jokingly, but they both recognized a new bond between them. Bart, for his part, was glad that Sandro knew the part of the truth that meant the most: how he felt about Anna. For Sandro's sake, perhaps the rest was best left unknown.

Sandro excused himself from the table to ask the bartender if there was a public phone in the bar. As he leaned over the bar, waiting for the bartender to distract himself from the intense conversation he was carrying on with two old alcoholic types perched on stools at the far end, Sandro studied the magnificent, if neglected and abused, woodwork. Bart had been right; in its day the place must have been a showplace of Victorian opulence; above the bar hung rows of grime-covered sepia-toned photographs of varying sizes. Some were formal studio portraits—serious-looking men with the short hair and luxuriant mustaches popular at the turn of the century; there were other, more candid photos—some of groups of half a dozen men on horseback, others seated self-consciously at tables indoors, their faces whitened by the photographer's sulfur flash. Sandro thought some of the photos might have been taken inside this very bar, from a few visible details of the floors and dark woodwork. There were also several large group photos of twenty or more men lined up in rows, some in suits, some in loose-fitting white Mexican-style *camisos*. In the group photos, and in others as well, many of the men conspicuously carried weapons, rifles, shoulder holsters with pistols, and *carabinero* belts bristling with rows of bullets.

"Admiring our little rogues' gallery, Corporal?" The bartender, glass and towel in hand, strolled toward Sandro with an upward jerk of his head toward the group photos.

"Yes, sir. Looks like they're from the Mexican Revolution days."

"Yep. Believe it or not, this old rat hole was a big hangout for a bunch of big shots in those days. Villa and Carranza met here late in 1910 and thereabouts. Villa's wife lived just a few blocks from here on Oregon Street for a long time. That's Pancho and Carranza in that picture up at the left there. Taken almost where you fellas are sitting."

Bart had noticed Sandro's interest in the photos and slipped in beside him at the bar; he was soon engaged in animated conversation with Sandro and the barman about the days when the saloon had been witness to history.

"I was here quite a bit in 1914 and '15," Bart told the appreciative bartender, who immediately gave them another round on the house. "Before Villa ruptured with the U.S. government."

"So you must have known some of these guys." Sandro looked as he had when still a boy, when he would ask Bart to share some of his endless repertoire of adventures.

"Hell, yes. Most I don't recognize at all—Villa and Carranza, of course. I remember Pershing sending couriers down here when we were arranging meetings between Villa's bunch and our government."

"I remember those days." The bartender helped himself to a beer. "I lived up t'Albuquerque. My uncle owned this place—left it to me awhile back. He and my pa were Anglos, my mom

Mexican, lots of family in Chihuahua. The whole family was feuding over what sides to take when Villa told Uncle Sam to screw off. So you were with Old Black Jack Pershing, huh?"

"Second aide. We were in Chihuahua together and later in Europe during the first war."

The bartender scowled appreciatively.

"Military *honcho*, eh?"

"Hola! Gringos!"

They were interrupted by an unexpected voice from the group of three Mexican men who were drinking quietly to their left. The one who called out was in the middle of the three. He leaned forward drunkenly on his elbows; his gray hair was stringy and disheveled; his puffy face and dull, bloodshot eyes revealed a hopeless drunk. He stared at Bart with eyes that seemed to focus with difficulty; his alcoholic smile revealed a mouth only half full of yellowed, broken teeth. His two drinking buddies seemed only mildly interested in what he might have to say to Bart and Sandro.

He said nothing, just held them for a moment in his unfocused gaze, then turned and swilled heartily from his whiskey glass.

Bart resumed his chat with the bartender when the drunk's voice echoed out again in the bar, loud enough to be heard over the jukebox.

"Gringo! Gringo cabrón!"

Bart rolled his eyes at the bartender. It was a nuisance being interrupted by an old drunk.

"Qué pasa, viejo?" Bart asked. "What's up, old-timer?"

The drunk, his head wobbling from the booze, made a face that indicated disgust.

"Don't pay attention to the old fart," the bartender advised indulgently. "He's a pain in the ass sometimes—likes to shoot his mouth off."

Bart smiled placatingly at the old man, then turned to start up his own conversation again but was interrupted once more.

"Hey, you, tall one," the drunk called out in Spanish. "I heard you. You came to Mexico with the pig *gringo* cavalry. You tried to get Villa, hey, but they showed you bastards who was boss."

He launched into a long string of curses, damning Bart, General Pershing, the U.S. Cavalry, and Woodrow Wilson.

When the invective had died down, Bart spoke to him in Spanish.

"Take it easy, old-timer. That was a long time ago."

"And he hasn't been sober since," the bartender joked. The bartender strolled down to where the men sat and, pulling himself up to full size, leaned forward toward the drunk.

"All right, Quintero, cool down. I don't give a damn how much you drink, but I won't have you bothering my other customers."

Quintero scowled at the bartender and, with a sweep of his hand, knocked his glass and one of his companion's off the bar. Whiskey splattered the bartender's apron, followed by the sound of ice and glass shattering on the floor.

"Okay, you two. Get this bum out of here. You can come back if you want to, but don't bring him. Business ain't that bad."

The two others, who had seemed mildly amused by Quintero's outburst, were now clearly irritated that his behavior had cut short their drinking session. They climbed unsteadily off their own stools, then helped the even drunker Quintero down from his, all the while scolding him in Spanish for getting them kicked out of the bar.

The trio moved unsteadily away from the bar, toward the door. When they passed Bart and Sandro, Quintero pulled away from the other two and weaved a few steps until he was next to Bart. Bart turned to face the old man, who barely came up to Bart's shoulder. His face was contorted in drunken anger.

"Take it easy, *viejo*," Bart said. "Don't worry too much about the old days. They're long gone."

"*Cabrón!* You killed my mother! You *gringo* piece of shit."

Bart suppressed a grin at the drunken nonsense. He reached out a friendly arm to pat the old man on the shoulder.

"You know I did nothing of the kind. Relax, buddy, and go sleep it off."

Quintero staggered back to avoid Bart's touch. His hand slipped inside his tattered jacket, then pulled out again with a dark flash of steel.

Sandro saw it first. A jolt of terror shot through him.

"God, he's got a gun!" he half whispered, his voice choked.

Bart drew back coolly. Instinct told him to move slowly, to avoid quick gestures. He held his hands out to the sides, palms out, in a nonthreatening, exposed gesture.

"Quintero, you old fool," the bartender spat. "Put that goddamned thing away and stop showing off. It's probably not even loaded."

One of Quintero's companions touched his arm gingerly, to get him to put the gun down. Quintero jerked away angrily.

"Bastard American *caballeros* shoot my *mamacita!*"

By now the rest of the customers sat in stunned silence and watched the stalemate at the bar, not sure if it was a drunken joke or not. Bart, Sandro, and the bartender eyed Quintero, not sure of what move to make, but his puffy, dulled eyes gave them no clues.

The only sounds in the bar came from the jukebox.

"Bei mir bist du schon . . ."

Finally Bart broke the standoff.

"Okay, Quintero, I understand you, why you hate the American soldiers. Why don't we just sit down and—"

Without warning the pistol rang out with a deafening burst.

Sandro felt Bart thrown back against him, the bigger man's weight sending them both to the floor. There was a scream, a cry; perhaps it was Bart, perhaps someone else. Shouting and noise, too, as Quintero was wrestled to the floor.

Sandro's arms were pinned under Bart; he pulled them free, still cradling the wounded man against him. His freed hands were warm and bloody, the terrible, familiar, warm red of the battlefield. He cradled Bart's head against him and watched, helpless, as Bart's pierced heart pumped its lifeblood out onto the cold tile floor.

As Bart's eyes glazed over and faded, the dying man's bloodfilled throat tried to speak. The lips moved soundlessly, but death came too soon for him to call out her name.

Chapter Eight

ANNA LAY AWAKE BUT MOTIONLESS IN THE DARKNESS OF her bedroom, listening to the faint night sounds coming through the windows to mingle with the distant echo of voices from downstairs.

The Veronal had taken effect. She was calmer now, almost tranquil. It was as if she were floating in her bed, not lying on it; her limbs were heavy, her breathing smooth and regular. The crying had stopped.

Bart is dead.

The words echoed again and again in her brain, trying to drill their bleak, simple message into her understanding. One part of her—the part of her that had collapsed on the cold marble of the courtyard floor when Sandro had called from the city—had already comprehended what had happened. Another part of her refused to believe: the words were impossible, nonsensical, meaningless. Bart might be away from her, as he had been so many times in the past. But dead—never.

Anna turned her head. In the dim moonlight that filtered through the draperies she saw the faint outline of the sedative bottle on the night table next to the bed. The part of her that had already accepted the fact of Bart's death reminded her of how quickly, how comfortably, she could join him. She reached out and touched her fingertips to the vial.

Perhaps it was only her imagination, perhaps it was real, but Anna smelled in the summer air the dark, moldy smell of wet river mud. She closed her eyes and was transported back to the little adobe house of her youth. It was just after the flood, and the house smelled of the river; she was once again a little girl, frightened and hurt because someone she loved, someone she needed, was gone.

No, she told herself. Not then, not now. No giving up, no giving in. Always before, when the dark pit that lurks in the shadows of every life had swallowed her up, she had fought her way out again, back to the light at the top. This time the pit was deeper and darker than ever before, but there still had to be a way out somehow.

From downstairs the voices echoed softly, like a veiled melody. The voices of her son, her daughter, her husband, her friends. The reasons to go on, the means to go on. She was not alone now; she never had been.

Anna pulled herself up and sat on the bed until she had a better sense of her groggy limbs. Then she carefully launched herself toward the dressing room. A few minutes later, after she had made herself as presentable as possible, she slipped into the soft light of the upstairs gallery. As she did she spoke to Bart. It was almost a prayer.

"Be with me now," she whispered. "This time will be the hardest of all."

She paused at the broad landing where the great fanlight windows looked out toward the western mountains, a ghostly landscape of blue and gray under a newly risen moon.

How cruel life could be! She and Bart could have shared such a life together, but fate had constantly channeled and diverted them, like the manipulated and controlled waters of the Rio Grande. How doubly cruel that after she had spent so many years learning to accept what little happiness she and Bart could share together in secret, even that should be taken from her. How much she wanted something to hate, for heaping so much that was unfair on her.

As if it were a sign, a figure on horseback appeared dimly on the distant deserted road from Casilla. From her window Anna watched as the dark figure galloped across the landscape and disappeared in the midnight shadows by the river. It was Bart, she knew it. It was him, passing one final time through her life. For that was what Bart had always been, a horseman passing through her life, her heart.

She turned away from the dark landscape and went down the last broad flight of stairs toward the dining room. The warmth of candlelight flowed out of the half opened doors, along with the warmth of familiar, loved voices.

Mina and Max were married at Casa Grande two weeks after Bart's death. Over three hundred guests attended the noontime ceremony in the flower-laden court. Many guests were there out of friendship, though others were there out of curiosity, for it was no secret what had happened to Mina Channing a mere five months before. As the wedding march was played by the orchestra, Mina appeared on the first landing of the stairway, framed by the triptych of fanlight windows. She stood for a moment on the landing, a lovely young figure in a sea of cream satin and *point-de-venise* lace. Even through the veil it was clear to the guests that Mina's face was tanned, healthy-looking, and full of that special radiance that only happy brides have. She proceeded down the last broad flight of stairs, her train cascading behind her, then joined her father at the foot of the stairs and, in a gesture that would not long be forgotten in the valley, pushed his wheelchair down the red-carpeted aisle to the garlanded arbor where Max stood with the minister and Sandro, the best man.

After the ceremony the entire house was given over to the reception. A dance band held forth in the ballroom, and tables set up in the drawing room and dining room groaned with food and liquor. Max and Mina slipped away from the throng at four, to catch their train for Los Angeles. By eight the party had died down, and Anna was able to slip upstairs for a much-needed rest.

Shortly after ten Will rang up on the house phone and asked Anna to come downstairs. She dressed quickly and walked out onto the balcony outside her room. The house was quiet, the hall below glowing warmly from the candles Maricita had placed on the great carved tables standing along the walls; the hall seemed to have blossomed overnight with Hank's magnificent roses.

The library door was open, throwing a shaft of light across the dark, shining tile floor. She could hear faint voices and knew that Sandro and Will were still talking together.

As she reached the half landing on the great stairway and turned to walk down the wide flight that spilled onto the expanse of the court, Anna realized that the house had never looked so beautiful. Strange, how this big, drafty, impractical

house—so often gloomy and for these last four years so empty
—should suddenly, in a day, be transformed into a home, full of
warmth and light and life.

Anna walked toward the library door, but when Sandro saw
her, he stood and came out into the hall, closing the door behind him. His limp startled her; she still reacted as if it were
some hurt he had recently contracted. He kissed her lightly on
the cheek, then pressed his own cheek against hers, putting his
arms around her, hugging her for a moment. How like him:
gentle, affectionate.

"I asked Papa to ring you to come down."

"Did you catch up on all you had to talk about?"

"And then some."

Anna smoothed his hair, ran her hands quickly across his
forehead in a concerned, motherly way, looking for any ravages
of the past years that might have crept into his face. Sandro
looked rested, whole, unmarked from the war. But he looked
somber, too, though he had always had a serious air about him.
Perhaps Anna had just forgotten what an intense man her son
was.

"Can we go somewhere and sit awhile?" he asked, taking her
by the arm. "The music room?"

"It's your favorite, isn't it?"

They walked across the dark expanse of the hall to where the
double glass doors of the music room stood open.

"I'll bet you even had the piano tuned."

She laughed. "Of course, don't I always?"

"Old Joey Smith died, oh, it must have been late in forty-
two," Anna said. "There's a new fellow who drives down from
the city every few months now, or should I say his wife drives
him down. He's blind too. Seems to know what he's doing.
Hope he's as good as Smith was."

"Strange, isn't it," Sandro remarked, "how blind men have
such fine hearing, though I guess it's just a matter of one sense
compensating for another."

Sandro groped for the wall switch in the darkened room, and
the room was suddenly flooded with light from the chandelier.
The piano stood, as ever, angled away from the window, the
great curve of the top sweeping through the air like a black

wing. To Anna it seemed less like a coffin tonight than it had these last four years.

"I used to think about Smith sometimes, when I was in France. You know, something I never expected about—well, 'combat situations,' as they call them—is the boredom. Hour after hour of quiet, but it's quiet with tension. You sit there with all your buddies around. But you can't really relax and talk, so your mind wanders. I think most of the guys thought about anything that was far away from war. You know, home cooking, clean beds, hot showers, girls at home. I did that mostly, myself. But I'd seen so many poor guys shot up, broken arms, eyes bandaged, amputees. Sometimes my thoughts would wander, and I would sit there, waiting for something to happen. And I'd start thinking about what it would be like to have a certain injury. A missing arm, a crippled leg, blind, scarred. I'd try to imagine what it would be like to be one of those ways. I guess Papa's accident made me think a lot about these things too. So I'd sit there and make a list in my head, listing my priorities for war wounds. 'Let's see, would I rather be blind than lose an arm? Or blind in one eye and lose one finger? Or both legs instead of the arm?' That sort of thing."

"God, Sandro. . . ."

"Sorry, Mama. It's not all that bad. I shouldn't have even mentioned it. The piano tuner got me thinking, and Papa and I were talking some about . . . well, the years since the accident."

"Will has been so anxious about you. He isn't the type to open up about what's on his mind. But I know it was with him every day, that horrible fear that you would be killed or seriously hurt. I don't think he could have stood up under the strain. It's taken all his strength, these sixteen years, to deal with being in that chair. And if you had wound up the same way, well, I think it would have been more than he—"

Sandro interrupted her sharply. "You underestimate him, Mama. He's the kind of man who can deal with whatever life throws in his path. That's just what we spent two hours talking about. I saw a lot of heroes and would-be heroes in the war. I know a brave man when I see one."

While Sandro spoke he fixed Anna with his eyes, looking at her directly, intently from the chair opposite her. She realized how much he had changed. Perhaps it was the war; perhaps it was just the difference of four years. He had become a man since she had seen him last. He wore his new status well, and Anna felt a sudden rush of pride in her son.

"Yes, Sandro, Will is very . . . special. I wish you could have seen how he worried when he heard you had been wounded, saying, 'What will we do, Annie, if something has happened to keep him from playing again?' "

Sandro smiled faintly. "Papa really is swell. How many farmers would worry so much that their only son might not be able to play the piano again? Most old bastards would only have said, 'My God, what if he can't drive a tractor!' "

They laughed, but Anna couldn't help but notice a dark look of deep pain pass in his eyes. The war was still with him.

How much Sandro looked like Bart! That had become even more apparent with his return. That slight hardness, that new leanness in his face, the way he moved, laughed, smoked his cigarette: there was so much of Bart in him. Sometimes she thought for a moment that she was looking at Bart, the way he had been . . . many years ago.

Anna spoke quietly to Sandro.

"I hope that you feel you can always open up to me about . . . the war. I know now you probably want to think about it as little as you can. But if you ever need to get it off your chest, to talk about it . . ."

"I won't. It's funny, but I noticed how all the guys I was with over there, all we could talk about, once we shipped back to the States, was the good times. Whenever we'd B.S. about 'the war,' it was always how drunk we were one night or how the mess sergeant fell in one of the latrine trenches. The crazy stuff. But never what we were really living through over there. I'll bet it was the same with guys in the first war. Did you ever hear them talking about killing anyone or dodging bullets, unless something funny happened when they were dodging the bullets?"

Anna felt a sudden surge of emotion. She pictured her son, in that hell she couldn't even picture clearly, and other sons, all too young (was anyone ever *not* too young?), and here they were, sitting in the music room, quietly talking. That carnage and suffering and destruction seemed so far away, so unreal. Her son was sitting next to her, holding her hand. There were many other sons who were rotting in the ground. She was thankful that her son was here, but God, what price so many had paid!

"Is it that bad, that horrible, that you can't talk about it, the reality of it?"

Sandro was quiet for a moment. Then he changed abruptly. "Want me to play for you?"

She remembered that the fighting was still going on.

Sandro walked hurriedly to the piano. He stood in front of the keyboard, rolled a couple of chords, as if he were just passing by. Then he sat down, positioning himself carefully, lowering the bench a bit, moving back an inch or two.

He put his hands on the keys, holding them in playing position for a moment, then dropped them back to his lap and turned to where his mother was sitting across the room.

"It's been four years since I sat here. And so many times during that four years I really thought that I would never play for you, in this room, again. It's good to be home."

He launched immediately into playing, an impassioned Scriabin étude, full of the fire and mercurial brilliance he had always captured so well in his playing.

Yes, Anna thought to herself as the waves of sound filled the room that had known his playing for so many years and had been silent for so long, it's good to have him home. Especially now that she needed so much to have some part of Bart, some remnant of his life, near her. Two great voids had been left in her life during the war years. One void, that great, painful void, would be with her for the rest of her life. But at least with Sandro's homecoming the other void was filled.

It had been a happy day at Casa Grande, the house suddenly overflowing with love and happiness and well-being. But there was a poignant sadness mingled with the joy, for those who would have loved so much, who deserved so much to be there. Anna had never thought much about the afterlife; her life was so much involved in matters of this world and of the living. But now she liked to think that the spirits of those missing from their happy household—Bart, Ruth, Don Alonzo—were close and part of the happiness that had finally come to the Cutter family. How much she had longed during the wedding celebration as she mingled with the festive crowd in the great hall; how much she had longed to turn and see her mother, stately and elegant, slowly descending the staircase as she so loved to do during her beloved "entertainments"; how she longed to turn and find Don Alonzo surrounded by guests, regaling them, charming them with one of his stories of the old days; and, most of all, how much she wanted to turn and see Bart striding in through the doorway as he had done at so many parties over the years— walking fast, always arriving late, searching her out across the room as he talked with the guests.

But she would never glimpse him across the room, never catch him watching her through the crowd, never see the ironic, bemused smile play across his face as he made friendly small talk with her and other guests while making love to her with his eyes.

Yes, one void would never be filled.

The music built toward the final, great climax, a veritable torrent of crashing chords and brilliant octaves, a tumultuous passion of sound. For a moment a wave of pain, of inutterable loss swept over Anna, but she struggled against it; she fought it back. She knew she must always fight it.

Fighting! Her life had been just that, a constant struggle. It was as if her life were a river, she constantly battling against the current, caught in rapids and whirlpools. She had wanted so much to find a rock, an island, a branch, anything that would give her security, a solid footing, a feeling of peace and solidity. But every time that rock, that branch came near, it was slippery, untenable, and she would lose hold, or a strong current would carry her back into the torrent.

The only solid ground in these endless, difficult years had been Will and his love for her, his understanding of her moods and her needs, his patience and guidance. For so many years she had been torn by her complex, conflicting emotions about Will and their situation. Then the war and all its changes had brought her and Will even closer together in those long, quiet months of waiting and worrying. She and Will would spend long summer evenings taking a "walk," as he jokingly called it, she pushing him in his chair through the grounds. As they passed through the almost magical beauty Hank had created around Casa Grande, they would talk about their lives, about the past, good things and bad. Will would always make her laugh, remind her of a funny experience or a happy moment. And she would always remember that summer so many years ago when Will had made her feel good about herself, had made her get over the hurt of first losing Bart. And they had been married.

Though it had taken her many years to realize it, Anna now knew that she and Will had a good life together. From making the best of a situation they had grown close, grown to need one another and to help one another. And in the years to come—if only she could forget, keep the past from haunting her—they would have a solid, happy autumn of their lives together. But there were times since Bart's death when, lying alone in the vast darkness of her room, she would long to feel Bart next to her, around her, in her. Then she would be restless for days, sharp, irritable, always thinking of him, sick with the loss of him. Somehow Will always knew that she was tortured by private demons. He never pressed her to talk about her mood; he merely let her be alone with her thoughts until the pain subsided and Anna was herself again. And when these painful days were over, she would always feel a gnawing, haunting guilt for her betrayal of Will Channing.

The music soared to its final chord, followed by a sudden charged silence in the room. Neither Anna nor Sandro spoke for a few moments, then she said quietly, "Thank you."

Then Will's voice came from the hall.

"Bravo. You're playing finer than ever."

"A bit rusty in places."

Will wheeled himself into the music room. He was looking pleased.

"That's just a matter of practice. But you have more to say, more depth in your playing than before. Don't you agree, Anna?"

"Of course. Your music has always moved me, but that was, well, something very special."

"Your mother's looking a bit withdrawn. Have you told her yet?"

"No."

Anna looked anxiously at the two men. "Told me what?"

"Do you mind if I stay?" Will asked.

"I'd rather." Sandro was quiet for a bit, looking down ner-

vously at the keyboard. "You see, Mama, it's not just my playing that's changed. It's the way I feel about it. When I was
overseas, during all those months of combat, wanting nothing
more than to get away, I thought constantly about Casilla,
about the farms, about you and Papa. How much I wanted to
be back here with you, knowing that if I lived, I would have this
waiting for me: family, comfort, security, a good, solid life. But
being over there, surrounded constantly by death, by suffering,
also made me think about what is really important in life, what
I really want and need."

He paused for a moment and looked over to see Will smiling
and nodding encouragement.

"I know that I've got to be true to my nature, to do what
gives me happiness. Even if it means sacrificing a lot. Even
sacrificing everything. And for me, that means music. I want a
career; I want to make it my life. It's been hard for me to tell
you, knowing how much it meant to you to have me coming
home, coming back into the family, to the farm, to the 'great
Cutter-Channing tradition.' But doing that would be the greatest mistake of my life."

There was a long silence after Sandro's speech. He watched
his mother, eyes averted, her hand, with the slightest tremble,
raised thoughtfully, protectively, to her lips.

So this was Bart's legacy to their son! Sandro was to go his
own way, to be his own man, as much as his father had been.
He, too, was to be a horseman passing through her life, riding
to whatever dreams and destinies were given him.

She stood and walked to her son, who sat at the keyboard.
She gently took his head between her hands and kissed him on
the forehead. Then she said quietly, "I wish you happiness and
success."

Anna turned and walked out into the hall, toward the library.
Sandro and Will looked silently at one another, knowing full
well the shock Anna was bearing at this moment.

Then Will asked Sandro to play for him, and he did, for
hours filling the house with a wash of sound and beauty.

It was in the early hours of the morning that Will came to the
door of the library, finding Anna with a book of poems, reading
aloud but softly to herself.

"May I interrupt, darling?"

"Please." She closed her book.

"Are you all right?"

She smiled. "No worry. I'm fine. My thoughts all sorted out. I suppose I've always known, underneath, that we would lose him to a higher calling of sorts. And I really do understand. I've learned a lot about acceptance of fate over the years. And I have you to thank for that—for teaching me the quality of acceptance."

"Why, thank you, my dear. I'm flattered."

Anna gave a quick laugh. "Oh, Will, always so modest. And are you pleased?"

"And proud. He's gifted in a way that mere farm folks like us aren't. He's always had a special, powerful quality about him, like a magnet, drawing people to him, drawing love to him. But then, breeding tells, and he's from fine stock."

Anna felt a sudden jolt but tried not to register shock on her face. Will's words—they could be taken so many ways, including the full knowledge of it all.

Then Will spoke again, and she knew.

"I'm proud to call him my son."

Anna fought back the tears, the sob that welled up in her throat like a hard fist.

How extraordinary her life was! And how extraordinary the love she had known, had shared, had been given—and was still being given. Her heart had been broken, but it had never turned to stone.

In that moment of subtle, unspoken understanding Anna felt supremely happy.

When Will spoke again, it was in a lighter tone.

"It's getting late, darling, but I don't think either of us is going to be able to fall asleep, tonight of all nights. What do you say to a long stroll through the garden?"

"Charming idea!"

"Then up and at 'em."

She took Will out through the French doors into the terrace. It was a cool morning, the house slumbering in the moonless, predawn sky. They went in silence out through the dewy, fragrant garden, each alone with their thoughts. Anna thought about her life, about tonight, and finally, seeing the house—her home—ghostly white in the darkness, seeing the fields stretching endlessly in dark rows, she felt very good about her life. Very good indeed.

For a moment she remembered that morning so long ago when, sitting in a pony cart, she rode away from her childhood to her destiny. She saw for a moment that bloody dawn sky and remembered how ominous it was—and how beautiful.

She and Will moved through the garden to the very edge, where only fields stretched out before them. They looked out over what they had made there in the valley and what had made them: the vast fields of cotton, growing, living, producing. Life.

And as they stood there feeling the dew rising from the fields, they heard the birds singing their morning songs. And another dawn came, cool and gray.

Dan Lavette was the son of an Italian fisherman. What made him think he could become the patriarch of a dynasty? Find out in **THE**

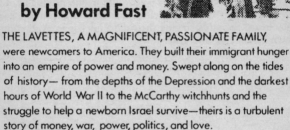

IMMIGRANTS
SAGA
by Howard Fast

THE LAVETTES, A MAGNIFICENT, PASSIONATE FAMILY, were newcomers to America. They built their immigrant hunger into an empire of power and money. Swept along on the tides of history— from the depths of the Depression and the darkest hours of World War II to the McCarthy witchhunts and the struggle to help a newborn Israel survive—theirs is a turbulent story of money, war, power, politics, and love.

THE IMMIGRANTS SAGA stunningly portrays the members of this extraordinary American family—the immigrant founders and passionate inheritors—and the fierce struggles they overcame to fulfill their magnificent destinies.

☐ THE IMMIGRANTS 14175-3-68 $4.50
☐ SECOND GENERATION...................17915-7-41   4.50
☐ THE ESTABLISHMENT.......................12393-3-50   4.50

DELL BOOKS   B941A
P.O. BOX 1000, PINE BROOK, N.J. 07058-1000

Please send me the books I have checked above. I am enclosing $ _____ (please add 75c per copy to cover postage and handling). Send check or money order—no cash or C.O.D.'s. Please allow up to 8 weeks for shipment.

Name _____

Address _____

City _____ State Zip _____